The Fallen Ideal

Ash Sharma

ISBN: 979-8-365-69760-7

PREFACE

I feel that it's important to consider the context under which I wrote The Fallen Ideal.

By way of background, I conceived the idea almost ten years ago and in that time many things have changed; in the world, in those that I know and of course, unsurprisingly, myself.

I went from an individual in his twenties to an individual in his thirties. I studied, worked and travelled. I was fortunate enough to have made close friends, have great experiences and also less fortunate in that there were moments of sadness and despair. Equally, these are all the constituents of a life that has begun to be lived and I'm grateful because they've allowed me to observe and understand the world from a unique perspective.

When I contrast this perspective to the one I possessed at the age of twenty, I can't help but feel that my younger self may have been missing something (I suspect I'll make a similar excuse at the age of forty).

This point is pertinent because I believe that the ideas I consider in The Fallen Ideal were still in their infancy. And so, I wonder whether I might've written the same book had I started yesterday.

That being said, I still felt a responsibility to complete The Fallen Ideal, even if it might not entirely reflect my current philosophical view of the world. Nevertheless, having reread the story, I recognise that it still strikes at ideas which are at the core of my belief system.

Not least because the concept of an idealist and what it means in the twenty first century is one which I regularly consider. The title also plays upon an ironic and recurring sentiment in my own personal life which is rather difficult to ignore.

To anyone who reads this story, I hope that you enjoy it and gain an understanding of the ideas that a young twenty-something was slowly and carefully coming to terms with. And to everyone who shaped my view of the world as it currently stands - thank you.

ACKNOWLEDGMENTS

I have many people to thank for helping me complete this story.

My sincerest thanks goes to Katie Glasner, Amandeep Ghag, Omer Ghani and Sukhraj Randhawa for reading my early drafts. The value I gained from all of your feedback was immeasurable and turned my story into something which I could really be proud of.

A notable thank you goes to my close family and my friends from school. Your continual guidance on a personal level has kept me balanced more times than I care to count.

To my flatmates over the years, my apologies for being anti-social. In the process of building this story I was probably not the most entertaining person to live with so thank you for putting up with me. In any event, hopefully this book acts as proof that I was actually in my bedroom writing something.

I'd also be remiss if I didn't give a thank you to all of the people I worked with at FTI Consulting over the years as well as those at P&G. The mere fact that so many of you were willing to entertain me at the pub while I described the ideas underpinning my story and also my often grandiose vision of how to construct stories was always very welcomed. You were all extremely supportive and a consistent reminder that there were certainly more important things in life than just work.

Finally, thank you to anyone who continues to be an idealist. In a world which continues to propagate suffering, despite being few in number, your contributions may be the most important of all.

CHAPTER 1

Purpose. It was a quality which was visible whenever he walked. As if he was always driven towards a destination, even if he had nowhere to be. Yet the cost of it didn't matter because everything he believed was eternal and despite better judgement, he always felt invincible.

Nevertheless, at this moment, it was the way that Jack Morse carried himself as he tore down the street in the fading sun. The edge of his trainers smacked the face of dry concrete with each step and the only other sound was the ruffling of trimly cut jeans and a casual navy blazer hugging a half ironed blue shirt and a pair of slim shoulders.

Jack hit the corner of the road. He stopped and removed a thin cigarette from his pocket. Taking a lighter from inside his jacket he clasped the cigarette between his fingers and set it alight. As he stared up into the London sky he inhaled for a second. A dark grey flume of smoke emerged from his lips, lingering in the air until it fell away from his line of sight.

He slipped the lighter back into his pocket and watched as a handful of clouds engulfed the sky. Short, messy, brown hair and the faintest touch of stubble masked a youthful face that was still smooth and soft. The only exception were his eyes. They were light brown but shrewd, hardened by knowledge and an awareness of lives neither lived nor seen. Jack took another draw and continued down the street.

After a few steps someone cut across him. He must've emerged from a side alley although Jack couldn't be sure. He politely tried to step past him but the man turned to face him and blocked his path.

Jack was reasonably tall but this man was taller. He was dishevelled, his face tantamount to a pile of gravel, and his body nothing more than a series of colossal boulders clumped together. He had nails which were long, yellow and chipped in certain places while his eyes drooped over a severely crooked nose. He wore a dark green coat, torn and worn out and scuffed brown shoes, the soles of which were almost certain to fall off by the end of tomorrow.

"Ya' got the time son," he mumbled.

The voice was gruff and his breath stank of dried vodka.

"Sorry," Jack said quickly. "I'm already late. I've got somewhere to get to."

Jack pressed ahead but the man dropped to one side, refusing to let him pass. He may as well have been a barrier at a train station.

"C'mon. Whatcha' being like that for? I'm waiting for a bus and I need to know the time otherwise I might miss out. Help me out yeah?"

Jack looked at him sternly, craning his neck upwards. "I don't have it. Sorry. I need to go."

He tried to walk off but the man remained where he was. He gave the appearance of being still but he seemed to grow in size, the way shadows unexpectedly grew as the sun traversed the sky. Jack looked up and noticed that he was moving slightly closer, second by second as the silence waned. The beer stains on his coat flooded the air around him and the dirt from his skin fell to the floor like leaves from a tree.

Jack felt the distance between them slowly vanish and within moments, before he knew it, he was wedged between the wall of a nearby building and the man who, only a minute ago, had appeared from nowhere.

"Just the time son. I'm not asking ya' for anything else."

His eyes scanned Jack's body, the blood across his pupils racing with enthusiasm.

The man slowly raised his hand and placed it around Jack's arm. Not far below it, the cigarette continued to burn, a sliver of ash beginning to build on the tip.

Jack felt the back of his trainers rub against the wall behind him as the man's grip began to tighten.

"See here. Ya' get it now?"

Jack instantly lifted his hand and grabbed the free arm of the dishevelled man. Jack violently tugged on it, dragging him forwards so their faces were almost touching. There wasn't a scar or fissure on his skin that Jack couldn't see.

He stared into the man's devilish eyes. "No...I don't."

The man breathed heavily, his clutch noticeably stronger now. The hot air from his misshapen nostrils almost roasted Jack's hair.

Jack's pulse hadn't changed. If anything, it was slower than before. There was an inexplicable and peaceful fluidity that cycled through him. With each pass, he became calmer, immune to the pressure building around his wrist and still careful so as to avoid dropping the cigarette tightly clasped across his fingers.

Jack could feel the man shaking. Though it wasn't the shivering of a man who was scared. It was the rattling of a man who was preparing. Preparing for what, Jack would never know.

A young woman had just exited a nearby building and was ferociously racing towards them.

The dishevelled man, without thinking, released Jack's arm and scurried off in the other direction, shrinking his head between his shoulders like a large insect in retreat.

Jack watched as the man disappeared down the street, methodically tapping the ash that had accumulated on his cigarette. Noticing some dirt on the sleeve of his blazer, he casually wiped it off and felt a small stinging feeling around his wrist.

After several seconds the woman was stood in front of him.

"What was all that about?" she exclaimed.

"It was nothing," Jack dismissed. He positioned himself so that he wasn't against the wall anymore.

"Didn't look like nothing."

"Trust me - don't worry about it."

The woman engulfed a flume of air and instantly flinched at the horrid smell of grit and decadence. She watched as Jack breathed in and out, his face noticeably calm and his body more so, almost at odds with their environment.

"You sure?"

"Yes!"

"Alright…just asking."

Jack glanced behind him once more and saw an empty street, sprinkled with parked cars and overcome by silence.

"Hang on, I gotta' ask." He turned back to the woman. "Were you like…spying on me or something?"

"Ummm…sort of. Stafford sent me out here. He told me not to let you up for your interview."

"Really?"

"Yep. He said to first go find out if you're worthy…"

"*Worthy?*"

Jack couldn't help but smile whenever he spoke to Katrina. The quirky sense of being, the random surges of hostility mixed with a subtle touch of innocence often made him wonder whether this was the time to which she truly belonged.

"Stafford wants to know?" Jack queried. "…Or *you* want to know."

The brown in Katrina's hair caught the light of the sun as it began its descent and sat atop her shoulders, floating from side to side. Her slender physique remained stationary, gently breathing in and out.

"If I deem you worthy," Katrina said, arching her shoulders back and ignoring Jack's question, "you can go in and do your interview."

"You already know me. You don't think that's enough to deem my *worthiness*?"

"Nope. Sorry."

Katrina could feel a sense of delight emanating through her body as Jack struggled to understand what he was being subjected to.

"Still smoking I see," Katrina said, scrutinising the cigarette in Jack's hand.

"It's my last, believe it or not."

He turned and took another puff, his expression glistening with sadness.

"Don't look so glum. You'll be smoking again before you know it."

Jack smirked. "That's not what *last* really means."

"Well…you say that. You held on to that one even as some gargoyle was about to tear your arm off."

"Don't be ridiculous," Jack said, rotating his wrist. A small ounce of pain shot up through his forearm. "He was just asking for the time."

Katrina's eyes momentarily departed from Jack's and gazed down the street. The man was long gone by this point.

"He would've done something else if I didn't turn up when I did. That cigarette in your hand may really have been your last; burnt out and lying on the ground."

"I don't think so."

"How?" Katrina's tone had turned more forceful. "He probably would've torn you apart. How can you be so sure that's not what would've happened?"

"It doesn't quite feel like my time," Jack quipped. "Don't think the world would've allowed it."

"*The world*? That's amusing."

"Maybe the world looks out for the ones who are better."

"Really? *You*. Right here, right now – smoking your last cigarette; waiting for an interview. You – the man that nothing can beat. Not destiny, not fate, not even the will of the cosmos huh?"

"Look, say what you want but I've got no problem fighting the good fight ...not least in the realm that became so damn bad."

Katrina did little to hide her scepticism. "Those are noble intentions for someone who knows so little."

"Maybe. But then there aren't a lot of people like me left are there?"

"Oh yeah? And where exactly did they all go?"

"Probably got lost somewhere...trying to do the right thing. The last of the free men."

Katrina could sense the seriousness in Jack's voice and yet she was unwilling to desist.

"There's a reason they're lost Jack. But I suppose we all are in some way. *Even you*."

"Maybe...but we'll see."

Jack tapped some of the ash off his cigarette and thought for a moment.

"Now," he continued. "Can I go to my interview? Or do I need to empty my pockets for any spare cigarettes?"

He started smiling, and then Katrina remembered why she was so fond of Jack.

"Jack, believe it or not, I may just give you the benefit of the doubt…"

"That's quite a nice compromise," he chuckled.

Katrina turned around and gestured her hand towards the building she'd arrived from.

"You have my permission to see him now. I deem you worthy, Jack Morse."

She spoke with such a degree of majesty that the sarcasm in her voice was almost non-existent.

Jack laughed. "Well, isn't that an honour."

Katrina continued to smile, all the while wondering what kind of individual might be so undeterred by fear or consequence or possess so much faith in their own will.

Jack took the concluding breath of his cigarette and then threw it into a nearby bin.

"See you round."

"Always a pleasure Jack."

Katrina watched Jack walk away and it was there that a subtle realisation began to dawn upon her. That the type of idealism which plagued Jack Morse was unlike any other that she had seen. She'd never encountered it before and she would probably never encounter it again.

But as Jack took those steps towards the building, he himself began to wonder, whether those things that he had believed in for so long were nothing more than a few fading ideals.

CHAPTER 2

"Where on earth are you taking me?"

Edward Stafford was mumbling as he stumbled through the grim darkness of the wide office corridor. Currently, he was being led by another, past his own office and towards a different room.

His eyes were strained as he attempted to look out in front of him, cyclically casting his hand out in front of him and waving it side to side as if he were swatting flies. Each of the bulbs peppered along the ceiling of the corridor normally illuminated it in brightness although at present he could only see one which was switched on and projected a dim gloom over the faded blue paint on the walls.

Even the soft pat of the carpet felt different through the shade. Steps in the murk rather than nylon and polyester made the journey all the more uncomfortable.

"Katrina?" Stafford said. There was a moment of silence. "I'm asking you a question Miss Miller."

Katrina spun around. Her cheeks were glowing, tearing through the dark cascade of the corridor.

"It's just a little further. We'll cut through the Square

and then you'll see."

"I think I've spent enough time there this week," Stafford remarked. "And see what?"

Katrina continued towards the end of the corridor, her long brown hair flicking in suit. Her lack of concern for Stafford's ever growing paranoia was increasingly more evident.

She led Stafford to an arched doorway, the door itself sealed shut.

It was 11.30pm and Stafford still had no idea what was going on. He scratched his head, the strands of black and white hair slipping between his fingers while his bones creaked as they curled up and down.

Shifting his eyes left and right, trying to gauge a sense of his circumstances, the lack of clarity became ever prominent. He suddenly regretted wearing a jumper and neatly ironed shirt wherever he went, items that did little to quell the growing heat and anxiety cradling him as he tried to discern Katrina's current objective. Age had provided little wisdom for such an encounter.

Almost an hour earlier Katrina had called him.

"Professor, where are you?" She rushed her words, mixed between fast pace and equally aggressive curiosity.

Six months had passed since he hired Jack although sometimes it felt like years. The late night calls and complex discussions were so frequent by this point that time played a different game, both in Stafford's mind and in his ability to gauge reality.

"Home," Stafford replied, rubbing his eyes. He was preparing for bed not before being startled by the chaotic rattling of his phone. The vibration against his wooden bedside table reverberated through his room until he answered it.

"I think you should get down here," Katrina said. The seriousness in her voice rocketed through the phone. "I've been taking a look at the projections we issued to the buyer. I think we've got a small problem."

Stafford raced down to the Field as soon as he heard. The Field in this instance was not a literal field, but the fifth floor of a building. One that housed a small research team consisting solely of Stafford and Jack Morse. They were also accompanied by an equally small investment and operational team, of which Katrina was one.

Her team was the business mind which tempered Stafford and Jack's mathematical theorising.

When Stafford arrived Katrina was stood in his office, stubbornly refusing to provide him with any details. She merely suggested they head to the Square. "I think that's where I left my calculations…maybe?"

"What do you mean, *maybe*? You sounded quite sure on the phone?"

Before Stafford could get a reply, Katrina bolted and headed for the Square.

The shape of the Square was exactly as its name suggested. It was large and open plan, where both teams frequently congregated to deal with countless business and logistical issues. Although Jack and Stafford had their own offices, they regularly found themselves sat around a table in the Square, vehemently arguing with Katrina over some precarious or minute detail surrounding their business proposals.

There were two entrances to the Square, each on either side of the room and both leading to separate elevators. Both were also adjacent to large stone columns, the purpose of which Stafford never quite understood.

At present he was stood in front of one of these entrances, unable to see what lay beyond the door and into the Field. The door, rarely shut anymore, sparkled with an emerald tint. Given he never looked at it head on, he wasn't sure if it was actually green or just had a natural sparkle coated across it but either way it dazzled whatever vision he had left.

He stared at the door and then turned his gaze to Katrina. Her eyes reminded him of the emerald on the door, constantly drawing his curiosity. An innocence was trapped inside of them and they echoed a subtle of touch of beauty, impossible to forget but paired with a wit sharp enough to constantly keep him on his toes.

In the shadow, only her striped white blouse stood out, tucked into what was probably a black skirt.

"This is where you open the door Ed."

"*Ed?*" No one had ever called him Ed before. "You going to tell me what I'm expecting to see?"

"Wouldn't be interesting if I told you the answer," Katrina replied, a sound of mischief in her voice. "And last I heard, you're in the business of interesting."

Stafford sighed with disappointment. He grabbed the handle of the door and yanked it downwards. Stafford leaned forwards, the stiffness of the hinges slowly beginning to give way. He gave a final push and the door swung open.

What he saw was something completely unexpected.

The entire doorway, and all that lay beyond, was covered by thick black smoke. Wraithlike, the taste of embers.

Stafford inched forwards. It didn't feel like fire, and yet he walked as if it was; with great caution while at the same time desperate to see whether such a mystery might finally unravel itself.

Stafford thought of Katrina. *Did she plan this?*

He craned his neck around only to observe a slender silhouette drift through the smoky doorway. Two arm-like shapes jolted forwards and pushed him, catching him off guard and hurtling him into the Square.

"You're taking too long," Katrina shouted.

Stafford struggled to maintain his balance, almost falling over if not for the ghostly outline of a chair which broke his fall.

All the sociopaths start off innocent don't they…

As he turned his sight upwards and lifted himself off the chair he began to make out more figures in the shadows. Before he could gather his bearings, a whirlwind of noise sailed towards him.

"Surprise!"

A collection of voices was shouting into his face and his ears suddenly felt like they had been slammed by a mallet.

The walls of the Square materialised into existence. He could see decorations littered across the ceiling, and a handful of shiny overinflated balloons scattered across the floor. A buzzing noise cut through the room and the blades of a nearby fan spun like undersized jet engines, swirling up nearby smoke and sweeping away the room's obscurity.

Now that he could make out the room in its entirety, he felt more confused than when he had arrived. Peering through the final remnants of smoke he saw someone walk towards him, swinging both of their arms like they were paddling through the air.

"*Jack!*" Stafford said, his expression completely startled.

Jack Morse stepped through the smoke, his messy brown hair floating through the clouds. Around six feet tall and a fairly slim build, he was noticeably taller than Stafford when stood beside him.

"It wasn't a bad surprise was it? Maybe a bit on the theatrical side though."

Katrina popped her head through the doorway. "Don't make it out like you had nothing to do with this. What idiot uses smoke bombs in an office building?"

Stafford's head was spinning. "Hang on. Before we get to any of this nonsense – what the hell is going on?"

Jack and Katrina glanced at one another. "Where to begin," Jack said, scratching his chin.

"It's a surprise party genius," another voice said. Her voice was still hidden amidst the final remnants of smoke but Stafford knew who it was.

The thin spire like figure emerged from her own dark smoky shell as Stafford heard the faint sound of heels sinking into old, rough carpet. Even at this hour she dressed as if she had just returned from a business meeting, clad in a trim navy jacket and skirt. Her face was long, blonde hair whisking down past her shoulders and behind a pair of worn out eyes and few wrinkles to show for her countless years of hard work.

Elizabeth Jones lightly tapped Stafford on the shoulder. "It's a reason to celebrate. Congratulations on a job well done I suppose."

The words were polished, each pronounced gracefully and just as it was intended. Newscasters would've taken notes if they could.

"We could have celebrated someway else," Stafford said.

"Hardly," Katrina scoffed. "It wouldn't be a surprise if we didn't surprise you."

Stafford shook his head in dismay. "Of all the ways…"

And then Stafford recalled precisely why people might go to so much trouble to surprise him.

CHAPTER 3

Upon recollection, this negotiation often stuck out in his mind. The others may not have remembered it but as far he was aware, it was one of many important steps in a long journey that sought to rectify wrongs and finally restore balance.

In a small dreary hotel room, somewhere on the outskirts of Lebanon, four men sat in the faint glow of two tableside lamps. Despite their dull intensity, the heat from the bulbs poured into an already sultry room. The walls looked flimsy, ready to collapse at the slightest display of force and projected a dank smell that engulfed the air.

Three men, all Arabs, sat opposite a relatively dishevelled Englishman behind a long, sturdy table. The Englishman's eyes were worn, and his body aging by the second. He saw scars that he didn't remember and felt aches that he had given up trying to fix.

The air tasted sticky, making the Englishman's throat dryer than normal. He pursed his lips while small beads of sweat started to materialise at the base of his forehead. He took a small gulp and proceeded to begin.

"Let me just start by saying, I'm glad you all took the

time to meet me this evening. I appreciate you're all busy men so I don't take it lightly."

The man in the centre expressed warmth, his demeanour welcoming but equally inquisitive.

"Not a problem my friend." He spoke faintly but his accent was what any foreigner might consider traditionally Middle-Eastern although the quality of his English was impressive by anyone's standards.

"Look," he continued. "I'll be honest…me and my partners are curious. We're curious about what you have to say."

"Tarik, I want to show you something."

The Englishmen had a small bag by his feet. He leant over and removed a small grey file which he placed on the table. He slid it across the table and directly into Tarik's hand.

Tarik opened it and started flicking through the pieces of paper inside. There were a few photographs, some professional looking reports and numerous maps with annotations scribbled across them consisting mostly of rough comments and calculations.

The men next to Tarik took turns analysing the documents and the Englishman watched as puzzled looks passed cyclically between them.

One of the men was staring at the maps he had been handed and then slammed them on the table.

"Where did you get this?" he demanded.

"Mansoor," Tarik said sharply. "Calm down. Our friend has only provided us with information. What it shows is not his doing."

"Correct," the Englishman said. "But if I was going to answer your question…I'd tell you that I stole it."

Mansoor glared at the Englishman with suspicion and his disquieted expression hardly went unnoticed.

"A thief?" the other Arab man said.

"…for justice," the Englishman said smiling.

"Hm. I suppose that's respectable."

"You're too easily impressed Faris," Mansoor spat. "This bastard obviously wants something. We don't even know him. And I know plenty of bastards already – don't need one more."

Faris appeared indifferent to Mansoor's comment and the Englishman got the impression he was being especially kind, which he found peculiar given the severity of the situation. He had been expecting Mansoor-esque reactions across the table.

"So what does this all mean?" Tarik enquired.

"It's not a well-kept secret that together, the three of you have financed and now control several armed factions and militias across the Syrian region. Peacekeepers was one word I had been told. Another was warmongers. But thankfully I'm not in the business of rumours. I'm in the business of evidence."

The Englishman's eyes scanned over the documents he had just passed over.

The three men leant back with caution. Any role in political or military affairs would be met with harsh judgement by their enemies; domestic and foreign. For every additional individual that was aware of their activities, the dangers which surrounded their engagement increased tenfold. Whatever secret they thought they were keeping didn't appear that way anymore.

"The thing is," he continued, "is that some people don't like peace in any capacity. And they don't like competition either. Let me be straight with you gentlemen. The men in those photographs. The weapons and vehicles. They're there right now. They're moving. I have it on good authority, and those reports will confirm, that they intend to stop the peace – the one that you all so desperately seek."

"Why?" Tarik asked.

"Because they want to. They're better equipped. Far better funded. They'll find all of your factions. Massacre them one by one; without hesitation. It's only a matter of time. They all have a stake in this like everyone else and it's their intention to see their solution through to the end."

"So what?" Mansoor fired. "You're just here to warn us?"

"Don't be ridiculous," the Englishman replied. "I'm here to provide a solution."

"Go on…" Tarik pressed.

"Their commander's a powerful man. But he's new to this region. He doesn't have a presence. He also doesn't have the same sort of power that these pictures suggest. Without his instructions, the people in these photographs are blind and they are *not* a threat. Your enemies aren't self-sufficient…*not yet*."

Tarik took another look through some of the photographs. He tried to make out some of the people standing in the foreground. The faces were blurred but their intentions were vivid and unmistakeable.

A small group of men massed around a burning car in the centre of a local village. They stood, chests pumped outwards, holding up their assault rifles in the air with glee, as if the recipients of awards and honours to come. In the background, women and children fled the streets. Others staggered, leaning against the buildings, wounded, whilst others carried the dead.

Tarik could see them all moving through the violence. At any point the young man in the centre would swing around and open fire at random. The probability that anyone in that photo were still alive at the time of this conversation was so minute that Tarik almost thought it pointless to try and even make out their faces.

"So what do you propose?" Tarik enquired, shifting the photo in the direction of Mansoor.

"Their commander has set up a small base not too far

from where these photos were taken. It's there he keeps the arms and vehicles that he distributes to the local men under his employ as they gain his trust."

"How do they gain his trust?" Mansoor asked.

"By doing as he says."

"Any aircraft?"

"Helicopters. Several Hinds that we're aware of. There could be more. I'm unsure."

The Englishman was starting to become irritated by the heat in the room. The beads of sweat slipped from his forehead and trickled down his face. He wiped them away and rubbed his hand against his trousers.

"Regardless of the equipment," he continued, "his men are few."

Mansoor leant forward. "Who'd be that foolish?"

"Someone who wants to stay hidden. That's why no one knows of his existence and I suspect he'd probably prefer to keep it that way."

"So how did *you* find him?" Tarik said.

"Let's just say that I have an *active* interest when it comes to the whereabouts of their commander," the Englishman replied.

The three of them said nothing in return. For the first time they finally understood a little more about the man who sat opposite them.

The Englishman smiled. "I propose we attack the base that this commander is situated at. We launch the assault at nightfall and vanquish his insurgency before it starts. Then…you're free to carry on with the peace."

"What of the commander?" Faris said.

"The only condition of this arrangement, is that once the battle is over, you keep the commander alive. You bring him to me and I'll kill him myself."

"So it's revenge you're after," Tarik said.

The Englishman looked at him carefully. It was a look fuelled by hate, one so genuine and honest that it instantly caught the attention of Tarik and his associates. Few might ever find a better motivation for war.

Mansoor shook his head. "Tarik, this man isn't here to help us. No matter how real his intentions. You just need to take one look. He's clearly got his own agenda."

"Yes, but…"

"But nothing." Mansoor cut Tarik off. "The second his interests misalign with us he'll betray us. He gives us some intelligence and we should be willing to fight his war? We don't need an outsider telling us what to do. We can handle this…commander ourselves."

The Englishman cleared his throat. "How long do you think you can keep this up? Your war against the state."

"As long as we have the money," Faris muttered.

"And yet even that's in short supply."

Mansoor shuffled in his seat slightly.

"I'll co-finance this effort," the Englishman said. "And once this is all over, I'll continue to do so. Plus, anything we find at the base; aircraft, weapons…it's yours."

"You want none of it?" Mansoor said.

"No. If I get what I want, then I'll have no need."

Let me ask you something," Faris said. "Why have you picked us? If you have enough money to finance a war effort, why haven't you bought a PMC of your own and launched an assault on this commander yourself?"

"The last commander I trusted to lead a war on my behalf betrayed me and my allies. This time I intend to place my trust in someone who has something to gain from our victory."

Faris nodded.

"Where will you be when this assault takes place?" Mansoor said.

"I'll be there on the ground," the Englishman said. "I intend to bring the commander to justice myself if I have to."

"If that's what it takes," Mansoor said. A small hint of

approval glossed over his face.

"*Justice*," Tarik remarked. "What an interesting word."

"What do you mean?"

"My friend, I trust that you will help us. I have no qualms with that. I just want you to realise that whatever noble intentions you think you have, are just an illusion. There's nothing noble about what you want."

The Englishman exhaled. "I plan to end the life of someone who very much deserves it. Tell me how wrong that is?"

"There are so many men that *deserve it*. It just so happens you're picking one that has also wronged you. That's the reason you're here. Not because you seek peace. You seek for yourself. Don't pretend as if we believe in the same thing. Your belief comes from something…"

"Comes from what?"

"Something else. Something different."

The Englishman sat silently.

"Just be open to the possibility that no matter what you do or what you sacrifice, you still might not get it."

The Englishman nodded. "I know what I'm doing. And I know the consequences."

"I know you do. I also know that you won't let me down."

The Englishman observed the three of them in earnest.

"So, then…does that mean we have a deal?"

Tarik glanced at his two associates who seemed to be nodding in agreement.

"It seems we do my friend."

The Englishman stood up and shook hands with each of them.

Sooner or later he would find the justice which he so desperately desired.

CHAPTER 4

"So have you given it some thought?"

Elizabeth's body had sloped forwards without her even realising. Opposite, Stafford sat in a deep state of pontification, mulling over his current predicament. He kept his arms folded and his head tilted down, as if he was concerned that any eye contact might hinder his decision making.

Realising Stafford was hardly done thinking, Elizabeth sat up straight, her overarching height quickly noticeable.

"A team of four you say," Stafford said, finally raising his eyes.

She nodded. "Katrina and Max leading the logistical side and me as an oversight. You build the tool with assistance from Max as necessary."

Stafford seemed to be grumbling under his breath but Elizabeth couldn't be sure.

"The mathematics behind algorithmic trading is a little advanced Elizabeth and I've met Max. Lovely gentleman, sure. But he's an ops man. Doesn't have the technical experience." He shrugged his shoulders. "I'm sorry, but I just don't think he's up to the challenge."

She exhaled. "Look, this doesn't have to be state of the art. Only solid enough. That's all my money needs to do and then I can source the funding and investment on a much bigger scale once we really get something going. Max is more than capable of getting you there."

"I want Jack."

"Christ. I told you that recruiting Jack at this stage is *not* necessary. Bring him on when we get funding."

They were both sitting around a glass table in Elizabeth's office, far away from the Field and in a much more glamorous part of London, while their reflections unassumingly peered back at them.

"It *is* necessary. He has the skills to build this. The boy is a remarkable mathematician. It was clear even from the days I taught him. I've worked with him before too – seen first-hand what he's capable of. Max doesn't compare and your insistence to keep Jack off the team will put this entire venture in jeopardy."

Elizabeth was younger than Stafford. Not much younger, but still old enough to have seen her fair share of business deals land into difficult waters. Her company, financed all by herself, specialised in early stage investments, often helping individuals such as Stafford lift their ideas off the ground by whatever means necessary; capital investment, operational expertise or even in just an advisory capacity.

"You want more equity?" Elizabeth asked.

"It's not about equity. It's about doing what's right for the company."

"I've worked with Katrina and Max. I know they're capable. But I don't know this Jack character. I don't know if it's worth it."

"It doesn't matter if you don't know Jack," Stafford said, his tone expressing some agitation. "I know him. So trust my judgement on this."

Elizabeth tapped her fingers against the glass. The

sound caught Stafford off guard, who was expecting an immediate response to his statement.

"You're one the sharpest people I know Edward. But you are not a businessman. And you don't understand human beings. They're not fixed quantities. They don't live on the blackboard."

Stafford glanced at his reflection. He noticed his collar was sticking out from over his jumper in a slightly awkward fashion and then considered at what point Elizabeth might've noticed too.

"When it comes to maths I trust your judgement unequivocally. But sometimes you think with your heart. When you're running a business you need less of that – not more. Bringing someone like Jack on board might present that problem."

"How do you even know what Jack is like? You've never even met him."

"Because you like people who are like you. I know what you're like. And so by comparison, I know what Jack is like."

Stafford squinted his eyes, almost in disapproval of Elizabeth's logic.

"Sometimes it's better to think about the wider picture. It's not all profit and loss."

"What you think is the wider picture, is very, very narrow. You don't see what I see. Keep thinking about your version of the 'wider picture' and it's not going to end well. The last thing I need is for any risk I've already got on the table to be doubled."

"Jack won't be involved in decision making. He's here to help me build the product. You don't need to be worried."

Despite Stafford's words, there was an anxiety beginning to blossom in her mind, like flowers on the first days of spring.

"I wouldn't be doing my job if I didn't worry about

these things. I like to think I'm a good judge of character, that's all."

"And I'm not?"

"No," she replied bluntly. "There's some foolishness in you Edward. I don't mind it. But I'm here to make sure it doesn't get us into trouble."

"Well it won't. I see people in more perspectives than just one."

Elizabeth shook her head. "There are lots of perspectives. You're just not picking the right ones."

Stafford glanced back at the table, purposely trying to avoid eye contact.

"Look I'm sorry. I'm not trying to be harsh or hurtful. I respect you a lot Edward. But I only want to make sure that everything runs as smoothly as possible. That's all."

"It will."

He combed his hands through his hair, neatly drifting it to one side.

"Whether you like him or not," he continued and reengaging eye contact, "I need someone who can do this. Max, unfortunately, cannot. Unless you have a young, sharp mathematician sitting around in your deal team I suggest you rethink your position."

Elizabeth pondered for a few seconds, her anxiety slowly beginning to bloom. With it came uncertainty and at that moment all she could picture was the continual rolling of a die. Each time it rolled, her heart beat faster and sank further. She felt as if she was in a game of Russian roulette with herself; destined to fail.

"Fine. He's in."

"Like that?"

"Your argument is stronger than mine. So I concede."

"So you don't think I'm foolish?"

"I think…" She paused. "Max can't build this product. Jack can. And that's enough."

Stafford's agitation returned. "Anything else?"

"I think that's it. I think we're fine here Edward. Call Jack, set up a meeting. Get him on board."

Stafford stood up. He adjusted his collar, his being suddenly turning whole again.

"Thanks Elizabeth," he said warmly.

"Anytime Edward."

He left Elizabeth's office and despite initially feeling like a winner, something in the back of his mind told him he hadn't really won.

.

CHAPTER 5

Up until now Elizabeth had been the beating heart of the company. She had injected the initial capital; pumped the money that kept it alive and functioning. But that couldn't last forever. Securing an outside investment was the only thing that would allow their venture to thrive.

Unfortunately, most people she spoke to had little appetite for taking a stake in a company that used obscure and untested forms of maths to trade financial markets. One by one, Elizabeth extinguished the contacts in her rolodex. Remarks such as '*next time Liz*' or '*doesn't quite fit my portfolio*' became commonplace just as much as the pleasant apologies that often followed.

As the number of rejections steadily increased, she eventually received an unsolicited call. Someone heard that she and her mathematician partner were seeking an investment for an algorithmic trading company and that they were interested in providing funding.

Within twenty four hours Elizabeth was sat around a table with the man in question. Alongside her was Stafford, and upon Stafford's insistence, Jack.

"He needs to be here," Stafford implored. He had been

in his office when he received Elizabeth's call. "If this Reinhart character asks a technical question I need someone like Jack there ready to answer it."

"He won't ask a technical question," Elizabeth said. "But again, if you really think it's necessary then fine." Elizabeth had learnt not to argue with Stafford over such trivialities. She knew it wasn't worth it anymore.

The next day, Joseph Reinhart, accompanied by a timid young man enshrouded in files and documents, was sat opposite the three of them.

Reinhart was smartly dressed and had a shrewd and fierce look on his face. Age was certainly catching up with him; wrinkles weaved in and out the sides of his face like rivers joining into the sea. He wore a baggy, grey two-piece suit, more out of comfort than anything. His tie was silver, meticulously knotted against the backdrop of a white shirt. His hair was reminiscent of an ash cloud, shining grey and clumped together, parted to one side and matched by a thinly trimmed beard.

The young man passed Reinhart a sheet of paper decorated with tables and bullet points. He pulled it close to his face and his eyes shrunk into tiny beads as he scanned it up and down. After a few seconds he placed it down on the table.

"So...what am I looking at here? I was told this opportunity might be of interest."

Elizabeth was, rather assumingly, expecting an accent of some kind but Reinhart spoke with a command of the English language that rivalled her own. He spoke differently, emphasising certain words at random, and without ever looking at him, could suggest privilege and good fortune.

"Yes, definitely." Elizabeth said. "And look, I really do appreciate you meeting with us."

Before she could continue Reinhart cut in. "Let's try to get the point as quickly as we can please."

Jack and Stafford edged closer to the table although Elizabeth didn't seem to move from where she was. She promptly continued:

"Edward Stafford and his associate Jack Morse have built a complex trading tool, based off some mathematical ideas the two of them recently developed. The technical specifics are set out in the documents I provided to your assistant. The ideas themselves are unrivalled, and with enough capital to trade with, I believe the returns for everyone involved will be stellar. As time goes on we're also planning to spin out a lab specialising in artificial intelligence which might be used to set up additional businesses."

Reinhart's eyes swung between Elizabeth, Jack and Stafford.

"I have a pool of investors who are willing to put up funds totalling over £100 million to invest," she said. "Given projected returns on the money we get plus fees, and assuming the funds start growing over time, I'm currently valuing this venture and the technology at around £30 million which, all things considered, is pretty conservative."

"Ok. I'll take you. I'll foot you £6.75 million. At 45%."

Elizabeth's face dropped. "You have to be joking," she snapped.

"I wish I were," he said, shaking his head. "But that's what I think its worth."

Reinhart's associate was scribbling furiously, documenting every word of their exchange and much to Elizabeth's annoyance.

Stafford tried to rationalise Reinhart's figures but in every case he failed. He could make no sense of them. "You'd be the majority shareholder...right away," he said. "And value us at just £15 million - half of what we were considering."

Reinhart was looking elsewhere, smiling and seemingly uninterested in what Stafford was saying.

Jack had not said anything up to this point. He was under the impression that the meeting was going to be straightforward and that Elizabeth would soar through the negotiation. He glanced in her direction, noting the irreconcilable solitude on her face.

He took a small breath. "The tech we've built is far superior to anything else on the market. It's worth a lot more than £15 million."

Elizabeth's eyes latched on to him, like a magnet. They felt like bright, hot lights that might cast themselves over a prisoner attempting to escape captivity. Despite the heat, he continued nonetheless.

"You either offer us more, or take a smaller cut. You know we can't agree to this."

"You know this from what?" Reinhart said. "Your many years in corporate finance?"

"No." Jack appreciated Reinhart's condescension as much as his offer. "I know because it's obvious."

"He's right," Stafford added. "We built this thing with two people. With operational help from Elizabeth. Imagine what happens with a full team. Imagine the possibilities. It dwarfs £15 million."

"Yes. And when that becomes a reality I'll take you at a better valuation."

"But you'd have 45% of it already," Jack said. "The upside's gone at that point."

Reinhart lifted his eyebrows, the small grey hairs scratching against his forehead. "Well that's how it needs to be. Sorry Jack."

"Where else are you going to find this technology?" Jack fired.

"That's not the question. The question is where else will I find this return? And there are plenty of other investments which will yield it. All of which don't have this sort of risk."

"But –"

"Don't pretend like you're in this business Jack. If I may say so, you're a little out of your depth…"

"So you'd be willing to throw it away," Stafford said. "The sheer possibility of this company…just to screw us over."

"Yes. Take it or leave it professor."

Stafford and Jack were against the wall and Reinhart was refusing to move. They struggled to understand what the purpose of the meeting was. Why bother with such a ridiculous offer; one which was never going to be accepted.

Was he purposely wasting our time?

"Come on," Jack said. "Be reasonable. 30%."

"No."

Jack poured his hands through his hair. "What would you want, to even considering this valuation at 30%?" *start*

"Nothing. I've told you my terms. Either accept them, or don't."

Jack saw his own confused expression on Stafford's face.

"Look what if," Jack said, but before he could continue Elizabeth stood up.

"Thank you for your time Joseph. I think we're going to decline."

Reinhart was slouched in his chair, staring blankly at Elizabeth. His associate halted writing, placed his pen down with great care and precision, and rather dramatically, settled both of his hands on the table.

"Elizabeth, maybe we can still salvage something," Stafford said. "Let's keep going. We've come this far."

"No," Elizabeth said. She flicked her head to the side, trying to be as dismissive as she possibly could without saying anything else.

Jack and Stafford both came to their feet. Reinhart was still drooping in his chair, eyeing the two of them with anticipation.

"Thank you Elizabeth. It was interesting hearing what you had to say."

"I said very little if I'm honest."

She turned around and made her way towards the exit. Her speed and posture were impeccable and the sound of her heels knocking against the floor reminded everyone of an old fashioned metronome which ticked faster than it should have.

Stafford followed her although Jack remained where he was.

"Off you go Jack," Reinhart muttered. "Deal's done."

His words rang with a raspy undercurrent, attempting to express a mark of authority over him.

Jack ignored him and left for the exit, wondering what Reinhart could have possibly gained from all this.

The three of them were silent until they got into a taxi back to the Field.

They all sat down but before either Jack or Stafford could say anything Elizabeth fired off.

"The two of you don't have a fucking clue sometimes."

"What are you talking about?" Stafford said.

The taxi pulled off the side of the street and accelerated aggressively down the road, pushing everyone back into their seats.

"He gave us a shit deal. As soon as it sounded like he was only there to mess around you should've stopped and ended the negotiation. The two of you made us look naïve and weak – just for even *considering* that ridiculous offer."

"Yeah, but…" Jack tried to raise a point but Elizabeth cut him off.

"Yeah but nothing. You need to learn that not

everyone is here to be amicable. This isn't a theoretical problem. It isn't something you can rationalise. Human beings don't work that way. They're complex. People like Reinhart are complex. Understand?"

"I just thought we could get him to agree," Jack said.

"Well, that was the last thing on his mind."

Jack looked out the window and saw buildings blurring past him. He attempted to determine how fast they were travelling but the feeling of loss was disturbing his sense of speed and direction.

"He might've slipped...we don't know."

"Idiot!" Elizabeth's voice resembled the way a headmistress might scold a small child. "You never learn."

"*I never learn?* You ever learn how to talk with a bit of respect?"

"*Respect?!* What *respect* do I owe you exactly? Last time I checked, you had to earn your respect."

"I was right next to Stafford, building the very product you're trying to sell. We wouldn't even be in this position if it wasn't for me. You're saying that doesn't count for anything?"

"It doesn't count for a seat and voice at a table you're not ready to sit at. Solve the equations, write the code, build the product – naturally, I'm very grateful. What I'm not grateful for is you playing hero in a conversation with a type of man you know nothing about."

"If I can build the product, I can gauge a guy like Reinhart."

The taxi suddenly halted at a red light and everyone jolted forwards. They all felt the seatbelts sear across their chests.

"Oh Jack," Elizabeth remarked. "Jack, Jack, Jack. You absolutely cannot."

And why the hell not, Jack thought.

He kept his thoughts to himself. Stafford never

enjoyed hostile arguments between friends and Jack cared enough not to drag this one out any more than was required.

Later that day, as the evening drew to a close, the three of them were sat in the Square trying to devise a new plan of action.

Jack and Stafford were sat scribbling down equations, both doing their best to forget their performance from earlier that day.

Elizabeth was sprawled out on the floor scanning through her phone. She was attempting to find any associate she hadn't already contacted; any individual she may have forgotten or overlooked. Darkness was creeping into the Square and the brightness of her screen was straining her eyes.

Before her eyes gave way her phone started to ring. The number wasn't saved nor was it one she recognised.

She answered it. "Good evening. Elizabeth Jones speaking."

"Good evening Miss Jones. My name is Frederick Harris. I'm calling on behalf of Nalbanthian Investments. Have you got a moment to talk?"

"Ah…yeah, sure. Um…how can I help you?"

"Well, I'll just get straight to the point. I've been told by several people you're currently in the market for an investor."

"Um…" Elizabeth stuttered. "Yes. Yes we are."

Jack and Stafford both swung their heads in her direction.

"Algorithmic trading – is that correct?"

"Correct. Off the proprietary technology we built here."

They both rushed over while Elizabeth got up to her feet.

"Impressive. That's just the sort of thing we've been looking for. There's so few opportunities in that areas these days so it's certainly peaked our interest. Interestingly though, we heard that Joseph Reinhart had met with you."

"Yes. Although nothing really emerged from that. The deal he presented wasn't one we were willing to accept."

Frederick started to laugh. "That doesn't surprise me. From what I know of him he likes to play hardball. I just wanted to check you hadn't taken anything from him since we'd much rather prefer keeping him out of any agreement. It'd be a lot easier that way."

"Nope. Not a thing."

"Good. Truth is, he probably would've been back."

"Really?" Elizabeth was stunned. That was the last thing she expected.

"Definitely. From what I hear this idea is very cutting edge although a little risky too. He probably wanted to make an investment but was trying to be...adversarial. I suspect he's kicking himself now. I know him fairly well – a bit of a wacko if you ask me, but someone who's been interested in this field for a long time. Just went about it the wrong way I think. I hear he's been in some hot water the past few years too, liabilities-wise if you know what I mean, so I imagine he was counting on this. God only knows why he took the approach he did. Then again, I've heard enough stories about Joseph to give me nightmares."

"*Nightmares?*"

A little dramatic, Elizabeth thought.

"Yeah, believe it or not. People say he's all over the place when it comes to ideas and plans. Does the stupidest things at a whim. Don't think you needed that if I'm honest."

"No. Probably not."

"Precisely. Now look, I'm definitely not like Reinhart. Take me seriously when I tell you that I'd like to meet sometime this week. I'm almost certainly going to make you an offer. But I'd like to meet you and Stafford formally before we're ready to seal the deal."

"Yes, absolutely. How does Friday sound?"

"Sounds fine to me. I'll also be bringing the head of our fund; Mark Nalbanthian. He normally has oversight for all of these investments. He was the one who suggested I get in touch. He's very interested in what you have to offer."

"Yes please, bring him along. We're happy to get into the specifics of things if you like. That's no trouble at all. I'll send you through the preliminary information so you can take a closer look at the business and a formal invite too."

"Great. Thank you Elizabeth. See you then."

Elizabeth hung up the phone. She clasped it tightly in her hand and stared at it closely, unsure whether the call was real or if it took place in some pocket of her imagination.

Jack and Stafford were staring at her with anticipation.

"So…" Jack said.

A large smile crept on her face. "I think we're finally getting funded."

And so, on Thursday night, the team decided to surprise Stafford and celebrate the first stage of closure in their venture. As the smoke finally cleared, Stafford mused about the next stage; who would assist them, what would be their new, great challenge and whether there were other surprises that lay ahead.

CHAPTER 6

"So you're telling me," Stafford said, taking a sip of his drink, "that you generated all this smoke using…"

"Smoke bombs," Jack said nervously.

Stafford looked mystified. When Jack mentioned it to him earlier he thought he was joking. He didn't realise the anxiety on his face was an indication of his honesty.

"In my defence, Katrina said that we should try and create an ominous effect when you came in."

Jack pretended not to notice Katrina's displeased expression.

"I was actually thinking of some balloons falling from the ground. Not the opening ceremony to a rock concert," Katrina said. She shook her head in dismay. "You can thank Jack for that little display."

"I'm still surprised you got Elizabeth to go along with such a ridiculous idea," Stafford said.

"She was…a little confused when I told her my plan," Jack said.

"Can't imagine why," Stafford remarked. "I suppose social niceties were never really your thing were they? How much effort did this whole debacle involve exactly?"

"Not as much as you think," Jack said. He spoke with an unusual trace of pride. "All we did was mix three parts salt peter and two parts sugar and mix it in a pan with some heat."

From the way it sounded, Stafford thought that Jack almost built them as a hobby.

"After that," Jack continued, "we poured it into some cardboard casings and stuck some paper fuses in. Then we let it harden. The rest…well, you know the rest."

Stafford's bemusement was coupled with an equal sense of intrigue; particularly around the fact that Jack and Katrina had gone to so much effort to surprise him. For the amount that they both disagreed and argued, he continued to be surprised by how well they worked together. Both were vastly different people; both viewed the world through opposing lenses; and both were ever willing to concede.

Others that operated under such dispositions would have torn each other to shreds by this point but with Jack and Katrina he noticed a rather peculiar phenomenon, which was that over time they had come to grow fond of one another, working together far more frequently, often out of choice and attaining results that neither he nor Elizabeth might have expected.

Katrina picked up a small cardboard sphere and began throwing it to herself. "We accidentally bought too many ingredients so we have something like ten spare bombs sitting on the table."

Jack laughed to himself, much to Katrina's indignation. He was the one who decided to buy the extra-large bags of ingredients in the case of some unlikely event where they may run out.

Katrina unexpectedly threw the bomb to Stafford who stumbled as he caught it. The texture of the cardboard was rough yet Stafford could still feel hardened liquid inside, almost like a clay mould. A small thin roll of paper protruded from the outside, acting as the makeshift fuse.

"This is pretty impressive," Stafford said, placing the bomb on the table next to him.

Jack removed his lighter from his pocket. The edges were blunt and worn out and as he gripped the surface his fingers could feel tiny chips and bumps that had accumulated through a decade of unawareness.

"You know, this is the first time I used this thing since I stopped smoking. Didn't realise it was helpful for lighting homemade weapons."

"Yeah, who'd have thought?" Stafford said.

"Oh yeah, I forgot you stopped altogether," Katrina said. The reminiscence to a time not long ago almost felt therapeutic. "Guess you stuck to your word."

"Surprised?" Jack said, his eyes widening.

Katrina looked away, trying to dodge the question. "Not at all," she muttered quietly.

The awkward smirk on her face was enough for Jack to know that she was probably expecting him to remove a pack of cigarettes from his pocket any day now. Surprising or outplaying anyone, although mostly Katrina in particular, brought him a good deal of satisfaction. In the case of Katrina, it gave him an excuse to suggest why he was probably smarter than she was; a conversation that would almost certainly end with screaming, shouting and the possibility of any projectile, large or small, chaotically hurtling towards his head.

Just as the conversation fell into a lull, Elizabeth walked into the room, Max Mortimer just behind her.

For the past hour, Elizabeth and Max had been on the phone, managing other engagements and issues. Elizabeth's portfolio spanned far and wide and Max was her primary operative, advising numerous businesses and fine tuning and sharpening anything out of place.

Slightly older than Jack and Katrina, both of whom studied together a few years prior, Max was a financier first and foremost, well versed in the mystic arts of debt, equity and deal making. His expertise ran parallel to Katrina who operated across a range of disciplines and business dimensions. Her well-roundedness often complemented the adept profit and investment acumen which Max brought to the table providing Elizabeth with an effective investment team.

While dealing with some of Elizabeth's other matters, Max showed up late and missed Stafford's grand entrance. Upon arriving he and Elizabeth almost instantly disappeared and took a series of phone calls in the other room.

Max glanced around the room, chuckling. "So Jack, you actually went ahead with those bombs then?"

"Yep."

Max rolled his eyes. "Classy. I'm devastated I missed out."

"Probably for the best. Would've hated to see you spend the evening trying to rub smoke coloured stains out of a three-piece suit."

"I detect a hint of sarcasm," Max said, furrowing his brow.

"In your presence I wouldn't dream of it," Jack said cheekily.

Max unbuttoned his suit jacket and sat down on a nearby chair. The ink coloured fabric of his jacket shined under the glow of the LED light hanging over his head. As he breathed in, his chest expanded like a balloon and pushed up against a light, crisp blue shirt. He had long hair which was roughly swept to one side over a thick square jaw and a youthful face. Planted behind the legs of the chair, were two elegant brown oxfords, the tips of which were dug into the carpet.

"Max, I hope you're all done with phone calls now," Stafford said. "I'd ideally like to celebrate with *everyone* that made this possible."

"Don't worry, I think I'm finally done for the day. And I appreciate it. It's been…challenging, but I'm glad I've been around for the ride. I'm hopeful about the future you know."

"Me too."

Max clasped his hands together and glanced to Katrina. "But I wish it was all good news," he said frowning.

"Yeah…" she mumbled.

Max attempted to catch Katrina's expression as she spoke but she awkwardly avoided eye contact.

"No need to be so evasive. You're off to do bigger and better things! There's nothing wrong with that."

Katrina shook her head. "Let's not get carried away."

"I'd say it's pretty impressive if you ask me. She offered you what again? VC partnership right?"

"Well…sort of, yeah."

"The bad old world of venture capital. I can't say I'm not jealous."

"Well you kind of do that right now don't you?"

Max shrugged his shoulders. "In some capacity, I suppose."

"Where exactly are you off to again?" Stafford asked scratching his head. "I keep forgetting."

"Nothing's finalised but an old friend of mine is starting up a venture capital firm. Obviously it's a risky endeavour but she realised she was lacking some contacts and decided to pull me in. I've always wanted to do my own thing and I've got the right experience so she's offered me partnership in the firm too."

"Yes, of course. I remember now." Stafford's expression turned glum. "It's a shame though. I'd be lying if I said we won't miss you around here."

Wherever Katrina looked, she recalled different memories about her time working here. Each recollection was vivid in its own way, appearing in her mind like a momentary flash. Some were stressful or frustrating but for the most part they were fun or consisted of Jack saying something ridiculous while she explained an operationally complex concept to him.

"Yeah. I'll definitely miss it here. But don't start the waterworks yet. My partner and I were actually planning to take a small starting investment from Elizabeth so I'll still be obliged to help out from time to time."

"Thank god," Stafford said. "I don't know how we'd manage without you."

"Well, like I said, nothing's finalised. The phone call was pretty casual. For all I know she probably didn't even mean it when she asked. We might be getting worried for nothing."

"Relax," Max said. "She'd be a fool not to have you."

"We'll see. It's been like a few weeks. I've got a feeling nothing is going to come of it."

"Either way," Elizabeth cut in, "we still get to keep you around. That's what really matters."

"You know Elizabeth, sometimes it feels like I don't even exist," Max said.

Elizabeth spotted a faint smile, partly endearing and also sarcastic, perched on his face.

"Yes, yes, yes. Of course. How could I forget you too Max. Securing the much needed trading capital for our investment. I, if not all of us, are indebted to you for your services."

"Well... if you say so."

Jack, almost displaced by the comment, immediately jumped in. "If we're handing out credit for securing capital then I think you're being slightly neglectful to a certain key individual."

Max's head swivelled around the room. "Oh yes, so key." He stood up and took an open beer bottle from the table. Compared to Jack, Max was shorter in stature although much stockier. He took a small sip and started smiling, as if bemused by his own thoughts. "More key than I was probably hoping."

When the stakes didn't matter, Max loved to inspire drama. To him it was all theatre. Real life would fall into an illusion the people on stage scrambled to find freedom. The play would go on and he'd desperately wait to see which of the actors might break free and see the story for what it was.

"*More key?*" Stafford enquired.

"Key is a funny word in this context. Mostly because it's ambiguous." Max sat back down and stared up at the ceiling, ruminating to himself. "You can be key in a good way and you can also be key in a bad way."

Elizabeth didn't enjoy the feeling of tightness that suddenly struck her body. It left an aftertaste of anxiety as she tried to reply.

"In what *way* do we mean exactly?"

"Don't be so dramatic," Jack leapt in. "We did exactly what we were supposed to do."

Max held his bottle of beer by the neck, spinning it in small circles and watching as the water on the surface slowly dripped down its exterior.

Unable to refocus his attention, he simply replied. "Sure. You're not wrong about that."

Elizabeth's anxiety still hadn't subsided. "I feel like I may have been speaking to myself. What exactly happened at this meeting?"

"He's fucking around," Jack said. "We got the deal done. We just needed to be a little smart when we were dealing with the investors."

"Really?"

Max placed his bottle on the floor and quickly looked up. "Yeah, yeah. I'm just messing about. It all went smoothly. And to his credit, I almost certainly couldn't have done it without Jack. As annoying as he may be, he definitely finds solutions where they're required. Trust me, no need to worry."

"Alright...if you say so."

Elizabeth sat in silence, twitching unnervingly while Max took another sip of his drink.

After a minute of discomfort Stafford decided to cut in.

"Jack," Stafford said. "Elizabeth was telling me earlier today that there's one more bit of information we need to show Frederick, either at the meeting or before."

"Which bit?" Jack asked, naturally welcoming the change in tone.

"Results of the back-testing. Should confirm how our algorithms have been doing with historical data."

Jack briefly pondered for a moment. "I think I've got all that on a USB at home. I can send it to you tomorrow morning."

"Excellent. Then I think we'll all be set."

It was then, in that fleeting moment of complacency, that in the corner of his eye Stafford saw it. His head craned upwards and in the direction of the door.

A tall, slender man in a thick black jacket stood in the doorway opposite the one which Stafford had entered from. The jacket covered the edges of navy, leather gloves and a loosely fitting crew neck sweater. Adjacent to the man was another, almost the same height and dressed in a similarly dark fashion. The first had a thick blonde beard covering his face while the other had a hint of stubble.

"I think it's time to finish up here," the bearded man said.

He spoke slowly and carefully enough to suggest that he carried himself with a degree of fastidiousness.

"I'm sorry – do I know you?" Stafford asked.

"No. You're not really supposed to."

He remained silent.

The man with the stubble scratched his cheek. "Get on with it. We need to leave."

"Fine. Stafford, get up – you're with us. Now."

"What the hell are you talking about?"

"Fuck sakes. Stand up. You're coming with us. Now. Don't make me say it again."

"Excuse me. I don't bloody well think so. I've no idea who the hell you are. I'm not going anywhere."

At that moment it was as if two different languages were being spoken; one side demanding a request that the other couldn't comprehend.

The man with the stubble pulled back the side of his jacket and drew a small pistol. The manner in which he removed it was so casual that he seemed not to have a care in the world. He pointed it in Stafford's direction. "Yes you are."

Everyone's hearts sunk instantly. It was as if an anchor had been dropped through their bodies. The situation had turned so unbelievably bizarre and no one could make sense of it. One moment everything was fine and then the next their reality was tearing at the seams.

"Why do you want him?" Elizabeth said. She spoke quietly, trying not to agitate either of the two men.

The bearded man shrugged his shoulders, his expression almost carefree. "Something about some investment. I don't know the specifics."

"So you have no idea why you're taking Stafford?" Jack said. He was still standing, although he remained very still.

"Listen mate, it's not our job to know. It's the job of this bloke." The bearded man removed a phone from his pocket. "He said to call him as soon as we arrived. He can tell you."

The bearded man pressed several keys into his phone and then stretched it outwards, facing up in his palm. The dial tone blared across the room.

The man with stubble stared at Katrina and then Max, both of whom tried to avoid eye contact. They looked at the walls, and then the floor, and then anywhere else, all the while trying to concentrate on the sound of the phone. They sat, their minds ticking away like clocks, until the tone stopped.

A cold voice began to speak. "You're there?"

"Yeah," the bearded man replied. "You're on speaker to the room. Professor's standing in front of me. You've got the stage."

"Good. Stafford listen carefully. There isn't going to be an introduction. Only some instructions. My associates have probably made this clear already but I'll repeat it for good measure – you're leaving with them...*tonight*."

Stafford was silent. He was still trying to come to terms with what he was hearing.

"Everyone else – you don't call the police. You don't tell anyone else. You don't do a thing. You sit tight and let life play out. Or else the consequences that emerge will not be something you enjoy."

"How would you even know?" Katrina said. She didn't realise but her voice was quivering. "How would you know...that we told someone?"

"I don't exercise power lightly. But I'd certainly learn it eventually...and then I'd do what I must to ensure what I set out to do."

No one could fathom exactly what the man meant, and yet his words were enough to stifle any dissention. They all froze, unable to reply. But despite all the fear he was feeling, Jack saw an opportunity.

"Why are you doing this?" Jack said. "What do you want with him?"

The man on the phone stopped. "Who is this?"

"Jack Morse," he said.

"Some kid in the office. Works for Stafford I think," the man with stubble said.

"Right. Well Jack, since you asked so kindly, I'm here for Stafford so that I can stop this investment of yours from happening. Unfortunately it's become something of a threat and it's made some people very unhappy. And so this venture you're all planning isn't going anywhere. I'm shutting it down. Understand?"

"What? No I don't. That doesn't make any sense. Why do you care if this deal goes through? It's a trading firm?"

"My actions are necessary. That's all you need to know."

"Are you joking? Why?" Jack could sense himself getting flustered.

"Listen to the sound of my voice…do I sound like I'm joking?"

His tone rung with an icy rasp, and as the sound resonated through Jack's mind, he seriously began considering the sort of person he might be conversing with.

"Right. Then if we're done –"

"No," Jack interrupted. His heart started racing. He knew he had to do something. He couldn't give up and leave Stafford to be taken. There was still a card he could play.

"You need Stafford don't you?" He waited. "So, the truth is, I don't think you'll do anything to him. Leave, take him, go ahead. I'm still going to call the police. Forcing us to stay quiet - it's an empty threat…we both know it."

The man on the other end sighed. "Is that right…Jack Morse?"

Jack didn't respond. His muscles stiffened, waiting for the man to continue.

"Men like you…they always think they're ready. Ready for some war. Make the call…I dare you. Just try, and then see. See what transpires."

"You won't harm him. You can't."

"*Really.* Such bold words Jack." He paused. "Take him…the financier, the man who works for Elizabeth."

Max's face flooded with terror. "What?"

The man with stubble swung his gun into Max's direction. "Looks like you'll be joining the party mate."

Jack almost fell to his knees. He felt his heart shatter to pieces. "Wait…why are you –"

"Do not underestimate my resolve," the man said. "You need only remember its potential."

"Look you don't have to take him," Katrina stuttered. "We won't call anyone…just calm down."

"I'm calmer than all of you. That's how I was able to make a decision which would end the heroics of man standing in a world that he doesn't understand…am I right Jack?"

Jack couldn't move.

"No second warning. Call anyone, contact anyone, and I will execute him without a second thought."

Fear ran through Max's veins, the magnitude of its current drowning out what little courage he had left. His mind couldn't process what was happening. He exchanged looks with Stafford who was equally as horrified.

"I'll take your silence as confirmation. Now…take them. Let's end this before it gets any more complicated."

The man with stubble flicked his head backwards. "You heard him."

Max and Stafford slowly walked forwards, their knees rattling. The entire scenario was surreal, a lucid nightmare unravelling as the seconds counted down. They walked across the room, falling behind the bearded man, the dark muzzle of a pistol trailing their path.

The man on the phone continued. "I'm going to leave you all with the encouragement to trust your instincts – and do the wise thing in a situation like this. Understood?"

Silence.

"*Understood?*"

"Yes" Elizabeth said bluntly. "Understood."

"Then this means goodbye."

The call disconnected. The bearded man placed the phone back into his pocket. He and his associate stepped backwards, their feet scraping against the floor. The bearded man held Stafford by the arm while the other gripped Max. They searched them for phones and other devices, briskly patting them down from head to toe and whatever they found, they threw it on the floor. Turning them both around, they stepped through the exit and headed downstairs.

Jack, Elizabeth and Katrina all stood still, unable to register anything. They were all thinking about the same thing. Stafford. Max. The man on the phone. His will. His capacity for violence. His resolve – one which, even now, after everything that had transpired, they would continue to underestimate.

CHAPTER 7

Merely a minute had passed but it sang like an eon.

But once the music stopped, Elizabeth tore her phone from her jacket pocket and ruthlessly began tapping.

Katrina went from a state of anxiety to utter bewilderment. "Wait, he literally just said."

"Doesn't matter," Elizabeth snapped. "This isn't over."

"Who are you calling?" Jack said.

"An old associate of mine. He's an investigator that I used a while back on another matter."

"Is he good?"

"He is." Elizabeth was still scrolling through her contacts. "But he's a bit of a rogue."

"In what sense?" Katrina said. She was trying to make eye contact with Elizabeth but her eyes were glued to her screen.

"In the sense that…he's an outsider. So no one will know he's looking for Stafford. It also means that he can be a bit…extreme sometimes."

"*Extreme*," Katrina said. She was liking this less and less.

Elizabeth found him. *Sebastian Sinclair*. She started dialling and put the phone on speaker.

After several rings someone answered.

"Yeah." He sounded tired. The exhaustion was evident from just that word alone. It expressed pain, a lack of will and no desire to engage in conversation. It was both articulate and jagged at the same time. The sort of incoherence that you found with a man of privilege that had fallen from his perch.

Elizabeth pressed on. "Sinclair, it's Elizabeth Jones. I'm sorry about calling you at this hour. I know it's been a while and I appreciate it's late but I need your help. I've got a job."

"What?"

"It's urgent."

"It's coming 2am," he mumbled. "Are you being serious?"

Elizabeth got the sense he wasn't paying attention and it was clear he feigned little interest in her problem.

"Yes, I'm being serious. Two of my colleagues were just kidnapped. They got taken by two men. Literally minutes ago. Took orders from some man on the phone who threatened to *kill* one of them if we called the police."

There was heavy breathing. "What the hell am *I* going to do?"

"I don't know," Elizabeth said. She was becoming more unnerved. "You do this for a living don't you? Investigating stuff like this. And you're not a police officer either. So you can help."

"No I can't. I've been out of this business for a while. These days, only thing I want is to try and get by."

"Don't be ridiculous! What does that even mean?"

Excess vigour and an obvious lack of empathy pushed the boundary of what Elizabeth was willing to say in order to accomplish the outcome she desired. She ignored the fact that her finger was twitching and that her mind was so quick to dispel any feeling of guilt for attempting to draw Sinclair into her problem.

"It means that I'm tired! It means that I want to be left in peace and that I want nothing to do with this. And it means I don't want to hear from you again."

"Please, I've got no one else I can turn to. You have to help me. Their lives are at risk!"

"Elizabeth, this sounds like way too much for me. I'm sorry. Just leave it will you."

"Don't be such a coward! I need your help."

Katrina rarely saw Elizabeth angry but Stafford and Max's kidnapping had knocked her off balance.

"You want to try and get by," she continued. "Find them. And there's £250k waiting for you when it's over."

Jack and Katrina weren't sure if they misheard but Elizabeth had a deeply serious look on her face. That was a lot of money, even for her standards.

Sinclair wasn't speaking but Elizabeth could hear his thoughts. She could hear him mulling it over, carefully considering whether it was worth it.

"You do this for me, and you're done. You don't need to take another phone call again."

Sinclair started coughing violently. Elizabeth waited, but it persisted. It sounded as if he were in genuine pain.

"Sinclair – are you ok?" she asked, her tone suddenly switching to that of concern.

"Yeah," he spluttered. "I'm fine."

"Ok."

"So let me get this straight - I find these two guys – 250?"

"250. You have me at my word."

"You must want them back pretty badly." He continued coughing.

"Yes. I do."

"Alright then. Send me your address and a brief summary of the issue so I can think it over." The coughing subsided. "I'll be there tomorrow morning. 9am."

"Thanks. I knew you were the right person to call."

He hung up and Elizabeth took a deep breath, the strain in her body slowly evaporating.

"Why?" Jack exclaimed. He walked towards Elizabeth, trying to make out the expression on her face. He couldn't tell if it was confidence, fear or complete apprehension.

"I told you why," Elizabeth replied. "We need them back."

"This guy is ridiculous," Jack said, still unable to fathom what she was thinking. "He didn't give a shit until you decided to pay him some stupid amount of money. Exactly the sort of person we need to help us. We probably could've done it ourselves."

Elizabeth's temper flared.

"Jack, calm down," Katrina said, trying to alleviate the tension.

"Excuse me," Elizabeth fired. "*Ourselves*. I saw your contribution, you fucking idiot. Trying to outsmart this guy, showcasing your bold intelligence. Didn't think he'd take Max did you. Didn't think he'd take collateral damage. Very impressive Jack. Fantastic work. We don't lose one person. We lose two."

"I was looking for a solution. I wasn't about to stand there and let Stafford get taken away. I thought if we could corner him he'd rethink his position."

"Oh, he definitely did! He only took Max because of *you*. What the hell were you thinking? What did you think was going to happen? He accepts defeat, ends the call and everyone goes home like nothing happened."

"He would've kept talking – we could've found out what he wanted and then present a counter. Swing him into an alternative."

"Did you hear him Jack…did you *really* hear him?"

Jack didn't understand the point Elizabeth was

making. "Yeah, I heard him."

"I don't think you did. Or else you would've known what came next."

Katrina stepped closer to Jack. "Jack, guys like this…they're hard to predict. But one thing is for certain – they don't stop. I don't think we really understand what we're dealing with."

"He's like any other person. He has wants and desires. I'm just trying to figure them out. We do that, we get leverage. There's nothing wrong with trying to win. I know I did the right thing – whether you disagree or not."

"I don't question your motives Jack. But I think someone like Sinclair…might be what we need. He has a touch we might be lacking."

"Ok. Fine. If he can help, then more power to him. I'd welcome it. But whatever happens, Sinclair or no Sinclair, I plan to get Stafford and Max back. I'll do whatever I have to."

Elizabeth and Katrina didn't doubt Jack's words. His conviction was undeniable. Even in the darkness, the intensity in his eyes was discernible. Although in that moment, they both wondered what force lay underneath his conviction. And whether it was truly enough.

"Let's meet back here in the morning," Elizabeth said. "I think a nights rest will help clear our heads. We meet Sinclair at nine, talk him through what happened, and then take it from there."

The three of them left the Field and no one said anything on the way downstairs. There was nothing more to say. No pleasant goodbyes. They all left for home, in pure wonder of what was to come, what may befall them and, in the darkest recesses of their minds, whether success was even a possibility.

CHAPTER 8

Jack was sat down in Stafford's office. He glanced out the window, the orange light of the sunset shining into the room. The décor was straightforward enough. White paint and messy shelves stacked with piles of paper as high as the ceiling permitted. Folders and plastic sleeves filled with loose documents were spread over the floor with no apparent logic. The room was flooded with books of all kind, from finance to physics to computer science, a few brand new but the majority mostly worn-out.

He saw several certificates and awards hung on the wall. One or two small trophies were planted on the corner of the table, slowly gathering dust alongside a handful of USB sticks without their caps.

The room felt tight and closed off and the objects inside seemed like they were stuck to one another.

Stafford was behind the table, directly facing Jack.

It was six months before he had been taken. It was the day Jack had been interviewed.

Within the hour that had already elapsed, Stafford spent much of it reacquainting himself with Jack. Occasionally he'd ask a technical mathematical question, curious about his approach or general thoughts, but in each instance Jack's answers were exactly what he would've hoped for. The answers of a man who clearly had a grasp of the issue at hand and would bring the desired skillset to the venture he was building.

"So...have I convinced you yet?" Jack asked.

Stafford's disposition during the interview suggested to Jack that this was nothing more than a formality. Jack had been taught by Stafford while he was at university and had also assisted him on another project a few years prior. During that period the two of them had built a strong rapport and possessed a strong understanding of how the other operated.

"More or less." Stafford flicked a small piece of lint from his jumper. It landed on the table, scraping past the base of one of his trophies and wiping away a pocket of dust. "But I already sort of knew the answer."

"If you did, then why the hell did you go and send Katrina outside to start quizzing me about god knows what?"

"I had no part in that," he chuckled. "She heard you were coming and decided to find out about you all on her own. I can't stop that girl. She does as she pleases. A good, and bad thing. Mostly good. But when it's bad, it's bad."

"Tell me about it." Jack's mind flashed back to his countless encounters over the years; encounters which made him laugh, smile, frustrated, angry and more often than not, confused.

"What did she ask you?"

"Nothing too complex. My purpose in life I guess."

"Sounds pretty complex to me."

"Maybe."

Stafford ruffled his hands through his hair. "After this little adventure is over, what do you think is going to happen?"

"Sell, make some money. Whatever you do when you wrap a business up."

"No, no, that's not what I meant. I'm talking specifics. What do you want to do?"

"Jesus, not you too," Jack grumbled.

"Listen, whatever you say now won't change my opinion. I just want to know, that's all."

Darkness was beginning to engulf the light of the sunset. Whatever shine the trophies on Stafford's desk had before was slowly disappearing, their outline gradually vanishing into nothing.

Jack stared into their metallic exterior. His reflection was nothing more than a large blur.

"As the years go on, I'd like to do more. More good, that is. I don't think there's enough of it right now."

"That's very respectable. But I don't think people really share your enthusiasm."

"Of course they don't," Jack said. His tone was flat, and whatever light heartedness was previously in his voice was all but gone. "But that's because they don't believe in it. They don't believe it's possible – to do it."

"Jack, if I'm honest, *I* don't believe it. It's a bit of a tough sell don't you think?"

"Well you should believe in *me*. Because I plan to do it."

"Easier said than done. The world sometimes imposes rules on us. Rules that we can't get around."

"Maybe. But if you want to do what I want to do, that shouldn't be a deterrent. Someone has to do something. I'm not saying I'll do it tomorrow. But when the opportunity arises, when the chance emerges for me to finally do something…you can bet that I will."

Stafford shuffled the papers on his desk to one side and leant forwards. His eyes latched on to Jack. There was initially some uneasiness to him, bubbling under the surface. It shook his heart, urging him to say something.

But then Stafford rationalised it away, sweeping it aside along with his better judgement. He smiled.

"Look, you can do whatever you want Jack. You're more than capable. The world needs people like you, and sometimes I wish I was as brave as you were when I was your age."

The expression on Jack's face lightened. "Thanks."

"Come back here Monday morning. Katrina will get you sorted with HR and I'll brief you on where I'm currently at. I've got a pretty solid idea of where I want to be in the next few months."

Six months later, as Jack headed back home from the Field, he realised that where they were right now was the last thing either of them would have ever expected.

CHAPTER 9

The morning came and Jack, Katrina and Elizabeth were already in the Square, pacing up and down in a flurry of different directions, trying not to collide with one another.

Katrina's black skirt fluttered back and forth, the top of which was covered by a thin, cotton blue cardigan and a cream coloured blouse. Elizabeth wore another impeccably fitted outfit that didn't seem to move even as she rushed from one side of the room to the other.

Seconds after the clock struck nine, Sebastian Sinclair entered the Square and saw everyone turn to the door. Tall and broad shouldered, he was wearing a charcoal suit which tightly enclosed a dark blue shirt. A subtle beard protected a distinguished expression; one that outlined the possibility of wisdom gained either through accumulated knowledge or accumulated hardship. His stance was wide and he kept both feet planted firmly on the ground.

"Sinclair," Elizabeth said, stretching her hand out. "Thank you so much for coming."

"No problem."

Sinclair shook her hand, and then introduced himself to Jack and Katrina. He craned his head from left to right.

"This is a nice setup isn't it? What do you do here?"

"Algorithmic trading," Katrina replied.

"*Algorithmic*. That sounds a little too advanced for me. How's that all work exactly?"

Katrina could instantly see that finance was not Sinclair's area of expertise. She carefully explained how the business intended to function and where each of them fit into the operation.

Before she could finish Sinclair stopped her.

"But there's two more right? The ones who were…"

"Yeah," Katrina said. She briefly hesitated. "Max handles the finance and operational stuff with me. Stafford's the one who designed the core idea."

"Got it."

Sinclair glanced around the Square. He attempted to read one of many blackboards filled with equations and calculations but gave up very quickly. The tables were littered with scraps of paper and financial projections. A small noticeboard, lodged between two blackboards, held up a blank calendar and underneath was a half-full water cooler along with a handful of paper cups affixed at the side.

"So tell me," he said, looking first at Elizabeth and then to everyone else. "Any of you. What exactly happened here? And try not to leave out any details. I want to know everything."

Together, the three of them recounted what happened. At various moments Sinclair stopped them, probing for details and specifics. Questions such as "*what did he sound like?*" and "*what was he wearing?*" were asked again and again albeit at no point were any of the answers written down, let alone any part of the narrative which was provided to him.

Sinclair stood still, his eyes aimed at the floor, viciously focussed on a small patch of the carpet and listening as carefully as he could. Even as he asked a question, he looked away, refusing to make eye contact with anyone.

Once they'd finished he raised his head, his sight falling on Jack.

"Do you know why they took him then?"

Jack still lacked a sense of clarity on the matter but he could gather that Sinclair's incisive gaze wasn't ready to accept silence as a response.

"I still don't know for sure but it's probably that someone didn't want this venture to kick off. They took Stafford specifically. And that was probably because he was the key player in all of this so they needed him out."

"And you're in the business of trading, investments – using computers and stuff?"

"It's a bit more complex than that, but sure."

"A lot of money to be made?"

An unusual grin lit up Sinclair's face like a Christmas tree.

"Yeah, if you do it right," Jack said, crossing his arms. "And lots of people do it. Our technology is good but there are loads of other people that could make the same money doing it differently. Thing is, you don't see any of them getting kidnapped."

"But this is all new isn't it?" Sinclair's grin was replaced by a thin glimmer of curiosity. "What you've built here. So it's different from what people have seen before."

Jack was wearing his navy blazer again, the buttons of which he began to fiddle with.

"True. It's just that a circumstance like this is unheard of."

He moved on to playing with the buttons of his shirt. Its dark grey colour resembled the colour of the smoke that erupted the previous night.

Sinclair's sight shifted focus.

"Elizabeth?"

Her eyes shone at him with a flat, penetrative stare and Sinclair realised she had already contemplated the question long before he'd asked it.

"Someone must have had something to lose if Stafford finished the project. We had a meeting today to finalise funding as well. Him being taken right before that isn't a coincidence. If you're looking in from the outside, the only thing you have to lose is —"

"Money," Sinclair jumped in. "But that's too obvious see. What about the more subtle. Who didn't like him?"

"He was a mathematician," Katrina said. "Not a four star general."

"It doesn't matter." Sinclair didn't appear to appreciate the sarcasm. "He can still piss people off. You're telling me there's no one."

"I really don't think so. He's too nice for his own good. He wouldn't know how to make an enemy even if he tried."

Sinclair was still sceptical. "He ever piss either of you off?" His attention was directed to Jack and Elizabeth.

Jack shook his head. "I've always liked working with him."

"Same applies to you I guess?" Sinclair said turning to Elizabeth.

"No. I'd be lying if I said our working relationship was a hundred percent smooth. He definitely knew how to get under my skin sometimes. His approach to things was a little… different to mine. But I only knew that because I worked so closely with him. Outside, he was a hard man to hate. And for those that were close to him – kidnapping would have been an excessive response no matter what he did."

"Well, that's not useful," Sinclair said. He flung his arms out in frustration. "You need to give me more!"

Katrina edged back with caution.

"We're telling you everything we know. Surely this all

just suggests that it's about money."

"That's too easy."

"So was my GCSE Science exam. Doesn't mean I asked for a new paper."

"You've got quite a sense of humour," Sinclair said bluntly.

"I was in stand-up before I moved into business."

Jack accidentally let out an unexpected snigger and Sinclair's scorn swept the room.

"But you see our problem," Elizabeth cut in. The tension eased off like a kettle that had just finished boiling. "It's not clear why he was taken. And so it means leads are a tricky thing to come by."

"Yeah, I do."

Katrina walked past one of the tables and began collecting piles of paper together. "So what did you do before you became an investigator, if you don't mind me asking?" There was a flair of curiosity to Katrina's question and it didn't sit well with Sinclair.

"Are you concerned that I'm not up to the challenge?"

"No. I just want to know a little more about your background. Wouldn't you?" She tried to gauge Sinclair's mood but it seemed highly static. He had hardly even flinched. "I don't know…where were you when we rang you yesterday night?"

"On my way to bed. Like anyone else I guess."

"You sounded pretty angry when we called you. And exhausted. Were you out?"

"Of course I was angry. I told you I'm not interested in this sort of work didn't I."

Katrina nodded. "That makes sense."

"And yeah. I had been out having a few pints at my local. *Grayson Arms*. Was almost home when you rang me so I wasn't really in the mood for chat – especially about another job."

Sinclair rubbed his fingers over his temples and began

to yawn. The bones in his jaw clicked and sounded like a rusty light switch.

Katrina placed the pile of papers she had amassed on to the edge of the table. "Yeah, we got the sense you were reluctant so I think we all appreciate you helping us out here. Without you, we probably wouldn't get very far."

"Don't start thanking me yet."

"Course not. You'll have to earn that." She tried again. "So before all this…what is it you got up to?"

Sinclair examined Katrina with great care and attention and it hadn't been the first time. It was here that she spotted something she couldn't quite put her finger on. The behaviour was offbeat, the reactions struck her as odd and there existed a distinct presence in his eyes that seemed independent of his body.

"I thought I was here to find Stafford. Why am I the one being asked questions?"

"The questions aren't exactly controversial. You're here helping us. It kind of makes sense to know."

"Well it doesn't."

"I *really* think it does."

"Fine," Sinclair snapped. "Former military. Since then, spent a few years as an investigator."

There was a short pause but before Katrina could respond Sinclair continued.

"Sufficient? I don't exactly appreciate the lack of trust. Especially when I'm here to help you with *your* problem."

"We know you are," Elizabeth said softly. "Just calm down. Katrina doesn't know you that well, and we're all just a little on edge right now. Clarity can sometimes help in moments like this."

"It doesn't matter." There was a hint of aggression in Sinclair's voice and his focus was centred on Katrina. "You want him back or not? I can walk right now…you can go get someone else."

Katrina didn't respond. She saw it in his eyes again.

"I didn't think so. I don't need someone questioning my character or my credibility. And trust me – when it comes to it – and it will definitely come to it - you're going to need someone like me."

"What do you mean?" Jack asked.

"From the sounds of it, these people, the ones who took your friends, don't sound very noble. And something tells me you'll need a person who can match it."

Jack shook his head. "I really don't think that's the kind of game we're looking to play here. We just need to get Stafford and Max back. Nothing more than that."

"You hired me to help you," Sinclair chuckled.

"I know. But whatever you're suggesting…it's probably not necessary. I think we can do without it."

Sinclair walked towards Jack. His stride was calm and his arms swung casually by his side, as if such a topic of conversation was one he'd frequented before. He raised the side of his jacket. Holstered in his waist was a small pistol.

"Jack you don't know it, but if you want Edward Stafford and Max Mortimer back, sooner or later, you might have to do something you don't like doing, to a kind of person you haven't met before."

There was an essence of disquiet in Jack now. "Look, calm down. I really don't think it's going to come to that."

"You just told me they threatened to kill Max if you said a word…"

"Yeah, but –"

"Whether it does or doesn't, either way, if it comes to it, I have no problem killing the men that stand between you and your friends. Because that's the sort of people we're dealing with. That's pretty clear to me. And it should be clear to you. That's what I'm being paid for right Liz?"

Jack looked at Elizabeth who shared his look of unease. Sinclair was stood in front of him, his face oddly composed.

"But do we really –"

"Yes Jack," Sinclair interjected. "We do."

CHAPTER 10

Jack and Katrina were sharply pacing down the street, the Field looming in the background. Glancing back momentarily, Jack could see its deep red brickwork towering over the street. In comparison, all of the other buildings seemed either too new or too glossy. Others were miniscule, hardly forming any kind of dent in the sky.

Jack turned his attention forwards and noticed that Katrina had already jumped several steps ahead. He picked up his speed just as Katrina swung her head around, having not realised how quickly she'd been walking.

She had suggested that everyone in the Square could use a short break and decided to pick up coffees, dragging Jack along for company. As far as anyone was aware that was the impression she had given.

They veered off the street and took a right on to a bustling street stocked with cafes and shops. Well-dressed professionals and suspect rogues alike sat outside, admiring the sunshine raining on to the street. Some sat with company whilst others were alone, minding their own business, all of whom were inevitably plagued by some internal conflict of their own.

Katrina skirted past a young couple that was walking too slowly for her liking. As Jack caught up she tapped him on the arm. "So what's your take on Sinclair?" she asked bluntly.

Jack was surprised. That wasn't the question he'd been expecting. "Why are you asking?"

"Why not? He's important to us. I'd like to get your thoughts."

"Well, I suppose he's a bit serious. Then again, maybe that's what we need."

"*A bit*," Katrina scoffed. "He's stupidly defensive. It was almost ridiculous."

"Most people in his line of work probably are. I'd be too."

"No you wouldn't."

Her pace was swift, forcing the two of them to continually dodge oncoming pedestrians as quickly as they could see them.

"Come on," she continued. "We still don't really know his background. It was such a non-answer! What did he say again, something like -"

"*Former military. Spent a few years as an investigator,*" Jack recalled. "I remember what he said. It's brief…I'll admit."

Katrina was tapping away at her phone. "I wonder…"
Sebastian Sinclair London.

"What are you doing?" Jack asked.

She typed the words into a search engine, inquisitiveness finally getting the better of her.

"Hang on…" Katrina clicked on the first link. Her eyes fell upon one result in particular. *Silent Solutions.*

The website was simple but well laid out, detailing the services of a small and local private investigations firm.

Jack peered over at Katrina's phone. "Silent

Solutions? Is that Sinclair's company?"

"Yeah. Jesus. Talk about bad PR. It sounds like he assassinates people for a living."

"Yeah," Jack chuckled half-heartedly.

The two of them leant against the wall and huddled around Katrina's phone.

As Jack moved in closer his arm brushed against the cardigan wrapped around Katrina's shoulder.

"Very soft."

"Yep." Katrina's eyes were still fixed on her phone. "You want it?"

"Not really my style."

"Sorry. Forgot you had a predilection for jackets."

"I'm glad you pay attention."

Jack tapped a link on Katrina's phone. "Go there."

"I'll admit, they do make you look pretty smart." She tapped the back button on her browser. "Already been there. Nothing interesting."

"Well, I also couldn't deprive you of those cardigans. They make you look so cute and delightful."

"Aww. Such a sweetheart."

"What can I say?" His eyes continued to scan the page. "Try that one," he said as he pointed to the bottom of her screen.

"Interesting," she muttered.

Katrina continued to dig around the website, flicking over glossy photographs of the London skyline and bullet points detailing the various services under offer; *asset tracing, internal corporate investigations, due diligence –* the list went on. She continued scrolling until she saw Sinclair's name tucked away at the bottom of one of the pages.

Sebastian Sinclair has countless years of experience in high risk jurisdictions and private investigations.

Former military and private service;

Notable experience includes working with Zero Bridge

as senior co-ordination officer in charge of the protection of the HRG Group while conducting oil related operations in West Africa.

Mr Sinclair has also led Zero Bridge teams in the Ukraine, Somalia and East Asia co-ordinating high security protection and military operations.

Jack flicked his head back against the wall. "I've heard that name before."

Jack started typing into his phone. *Zero Bridge.*

"What are you looking for?" Katrina enquired.

"*Hang on…*" Jack replied sarcastically.

Numerous search results opened up. The first was a sponsored link to the Zero Bridge website although that wasn't what was catching Jack's eye. He wasn't interested in the corporate jargon. It was something else. He knew he'd find it eventually. He scrolled down the page.

"*Zero Bridge soldiers forced to flee West African nation after allegations of torture come to light*"

Bingo.

News article after article jumped out of the screen, detailing some sort of crime or allegation in a far-flung pocket of the world. The name Zero Bridge was continually tied up in some capacity. Sometimes their involvement was passive and other times it was extensive, ranging from small time advisory work to large scale assaults. On occasion the article was filled with images of atrocities or dishevelled communities whilst on others it contained excerpts where Zero Bridge "*declined to comment*".

Katrina's eyes lit up. "Zero Bridge! Of course! I remember them."

"*Zero Bridge accused by Kremlin of executing Russian-backed troops in Crimea*"

"*Zero Bridge pays undisclosed sum to Chinese government to settle claims of gross misconduct and negligence*"

"These stories came up a lot some time back," Jack recalled. "Less so now I guess. But it's weird why Sinclair would mention something like Zero Bridge on his website. Especially given the amount of media attention it used to get. Attention that was mostly negative."

Katrina raised her head, pondering for a second. "His clients might not care. The sorts he probably crosses anyway. Probably works in his favour. I suppose they just need someone who can do the job."

"Yeah."

"And I'm curious," Katrina added. She dropped her voice. "To what extent was Sinclair involved with the allegations against Zero Bridge?"

"I've got no idea," Jack said. "But I'm begging you...please do not ask him. He's here to help us – we don't need this shit storm to blow away our chances of getting back Max and Stafford."

"I won't...but you saw it Jack – he was *senior co-ordination officer*!"

Jack struggled to match Katrina's degree of scepticism. Her ideas and theories continued to flood into the open, each more nuanced and detailed than the last. Such a brand of inquisitiveness must've been innate, he wondered. No one could learn how to posit so many wild accusations at once.

"Don't you think you're jumping a little too far?"

"Not really."

"I think you need to dial it back. The situation here is...precarious. We don't need to take any undue risks."

"*Undue risks*?"

Jack sensed Katrina's agitation and expected the worst. While others were more reserved, Katrina didn't see the need to hold back; especially with Jack.

"You're pretty blasé when it comes to risks aren't you Jack?" Katrina snapped. "I thought surely you of all people wouldn't mind?"

"What are you getting at?"

"Max told me what happened when you both met with those investors."

Jack's throat turned very dry. It stripped him of his willingness to reply or even provide some form of justification.

"Don't worry," she continued. "He told me in confidence. In the hope that I might finally realise how ridiculous you act sometimes. I said I'd keep it under consideration. Although, I guess the stupidity of your actions varies now doesn't it?"

"That was different," Jack finally replied. His voice was stiff. "There was good cause."

"Not how Max describes it."

"Nonsense. Max has the imagination to turn his daily commute into a Hollywood screenplay. I'd take his descriptions with a pinch of salt."

People often enjoyed dramatising their own lives whenever they recounted them to others. The addition of theatricality to the mundane was a staple for those who lived in the realms of the ordinary and secretly longed for excitement. Yet, it was the reverse which was far more uncommon. To reduce or diminish the trials and tribulations of the past; the dangers that had come and gone, was synonymous with a person who had truths to conceal.

Katrina thought back to Sinclair and the stories that hadn't been shared; the one's hidden from view; the ordinary lain atop the unfathomable.

"Jack. On a balance of probabilities, do you really believe Sinclair is clean? Off the back of those Zero Bridge stories alone?"

"Of course not. But we'll never know for certain. There's nothing concrete connecting him to those stories."

"If he's as senior as his website suggests, and he was

on the ground, he must've known what was going on. At least something. Almost certainly."

"But you can't prove it!" Jack retorted. "You know you can't. There's nothing substantial against him."

"Let's think about it in totality. He only accepted this job for the money. He wasn't going to before. Only when Elizabeth puts up a substantial sum on the table."

"Oh c'mon. Who wouldn't?"

"And...what he said to us before we left. This weird, almost deluded willingness to kill people...as if it were nothing. As if it were almost a certainty. You said it yourself Jack – is it really necessary?"

"Katrina, he's doing it to get Stafford back. It's a risk he's willing to take...for all of us."

"Him walking around with that gun doesn't exactly fill me with joy either."

"Yeah...guess a guy like him probably needs one."

Flurries of pedestrians continued to make their way past them. Katrina spotted certain individuals at a time, trying to ascertain what any of them might possibly think of the situation at hand. Would they agree with her; that there was far more to Sebastian Sinclair than they realised. Or was she being paranoid?

Jack placed his phone into his pocket. "Whether he's willing to do something or not, I don't think it'll come to that. We can trust him."

Katrina slammed her palms into her face. "How on earth do you know that?" Her hands had muffled her voice slightly. "You're not looking at this clearly. You never do. There is something amiss here. We need to be cautious around him. There's a side to him that we have yet to see. I'm telling you."

"I *think* you're being ridiculous. We just met him. And he wants to find Stafford. Just like us. Surely that should be enough? What the hell more do you want?"

Katrina dropped her hands by her side. "Ok Jack.

Whatever you say."

Jack looked at her suspiciously. "That's it? You're convinced?"

"No. But I don't think I can't convince you any further...so I think we're done here."

"Jesus," Jack snapped. "Don't talk to me like I'm a fucking child. What are you trying to say here?"

"You're being deceived," Katrina scowled. "Thinking this is all ok."

"How, exactly?"

Katrina rattled her fingers against the wall, all the while glaring at Jack. "What would you do if you saw him kill someone? Or better yet, if he told you to do it?"

"That's a stupid question," Jack said dismissively.

"Sinclair thought it was a fair possibility."

"It won't come to that. And even if he did ask me – I wouldn't." Jack paused. "It's hardly necessary."

"God you're so convinced of yourself aren't you?"

"What do you mean?"

"That you see through it all. That, compared to you, the rest of the world is merely a land of fools, liars and degenerates."

Jack stared out into the crowd. No one noticed as he watched some overtake others, a handful who slowed down to admire their surroundings and a particular few who made so little progress that he couldn't make out what direction they were going in.

"Sinclair isn't deceiving anyone. I'm sure of it."

The sunshine was pounding the street, blinding Jack and Katrina. They were both squinting, struggling to see the other's expression.

Katrina rubbed her eyes. "I hope you're right Jack. I really do."

She kicked back against the wall, launching herself back into the stream of pedestrians. Jack waited a few seconds, still unsure where Katrina stood on the matter.

Upon realising he couldn't figure it out he kicked off as well, falling into the bustle of confusion and dissonance.

CHAPTER 11

Max was patiently waiting for the second. Second Old Fashioned that was. Having anticipated the moment he'd finish the first, he had ordered the second accordingly.

Sugars, bitters and bourbon and a thin orange peel were all it took apparently. It seemed so straightforward that Max sometimes considered whether a job as a barman may have been more enjoyable than that of a financier. Then again, the satisfaction that came with closing a deal was something he'd likely struggle to live without.

He looked at his first glass. It was nearly finished. There was so little bourbon left that the orange peel was almost entirely exposed. He leaned in, but rather than stare from the top, he looked in through the side of the glass and at the peel. The barman had been reasonably elegant in his approach, ensuring that it spiralled at least twice before he plopped it into the glass. Through the glass Max saw a disjointed loop, stretching across the entire space and then shrinking as it wound itself upwards. Some sparkles of sugar still remained in the last remnants of the bourbon, huddling together as even they became aware that they were the final pocket of existence in a drink that Max could consume in mere seconds if he chose.

Comes with the territory, he often rationalised.

He finished the drink and pounded the glass on the table. The barman spun around, swiped the empty glass, and slammed a fresh drink on the table.

Max gave the barman a thumbs up and pulled the drink towards him.

Unbeknownst to Max, in less than three weeks, two men would arrive at the Square, for reasons which, at the time, he would be unaware of, and take him away into the dark.

Max glanced up at the clock above the barman. It was quarter to seven; Wednesday evening.

That kid better fucking turn up.

A few hours ago Jack was in the Square. He was sat by a small wooden table, swarmed by scraps of paper. Some had fallen on the floor while others precariously hung on to the edge of table.

Jack was trying to make sense of whatever remained on the table but realised there was little he could draw out. He started to daydream, but before his could mind wander far enough his phone went off. It was Max.

"Yeah," Jack answered.

"Jack. I've got a dinner tonight with some potential investors in the fund. I need you to attend."

"What?" Jack said, sounding startled. "Where did this come from? What if I have plans?"

"You're not that popular," Max replied. "Don't get ahead of yourself."

"Funny. Where is it?"

Jack scrambled to find a scrap of paper that wasn't occupied with mathematical symbols. He eventually found one and started noting down what Max was saying.

"The Dove," Max said. "You ever been there?"

"No. Never even heard of it"

"Not surprised. It's a small Italian outfit in South Kensington. Meet me inside the bar at 6.45. I'll brief you on the plan. Wear your nicest suit and don't be late."

"Sure."

Max hung up and Jack realised he'd probably need to make an effort to iron his shirt for the first time in years.

Jack strolled into the lobby. He had plucked an old slim three piece navy suit from his cupboard and paired it with a white shirt and spotted blue tie. The suit was cotton, thick and glowed in the lights of the chandeliers that encircled the venue.

The walls and floor were layered with a cyan coloured marble. A waiter was stood by a large wooden lectern, directing people into the restaurant. The smells of oregano and pesto from nearby dishes drifted into the lobby and immediately reminded Jack that he hadn't eaten for almost six hours.

Jack caught sight of the bar, opposite the entrance to the restaurant. He headed inside, past numerous black and white photos hung against the wall, mostly of previous visitors all of whom were celebrities, politicians or athletes and appeared to have particular penchant for Italian food. Most of them garnished enormous smiles on their faces as they sat with dishes of pasta and lasagnes in front of them.

As soon as Jack entered, the lighting dropped from bright and friendly to dark and gloomy. The air that filled his lungs was peppered with illusion, escape and sadness; leftovers from men long gone and buried.

Jack spotted Max, sat in front of the barman. He was also wearing a three piece of suit; plain, dark brown accompanied by a white shirt and burgundy tie. A pocket square of the same colour was wedged into his right breast pocket and coiffed out into the open.

Max turned around. "You made it." He turned to the barman. "Let's get one more."

"Is that an Old Fashioned?" Jack enquired.

"Yeah."

"Could I get a white wine instead?"

"No. Don't be silly. Drink one of these. You'll make a good start on finally getting your head straight."

"Is that how you coped with not reaching five foot ten."

Max took a sip of his drink. "You know Jack, your cocky arrogance really fucks me off sometimes. But from time to time, it does put a smile on my face."

"It's all I ever wanted," Jack said, gleaming.

Max was sat on a cushioned bar stool. Jack took a seat next to him and the barman placed another drink on the table. Jack swallowed a small amount of it and felt the bourbon burning his throat.

"You drink these all the time?" Jack wheezed.

"Occupational hazard in my realm," Max grumbled, staring into his glass again. "Suppose they don't really serve drinks with equations and algorithms now do they?"

"Not as far as I'm aware."

Max swung his head around the bar. There weren't many people around, even for a Wednesday evening.

"Let me break this down for you Jack. Elizabeth and I have been trying to pool together people who might be willing to invest funds into the venture; funds to manage that is. Getting people to invest in the company is a totally different story given its inherent risk nature. Anyway, we've had limited success given the whole thing is fresh and we don't have a track record but the three people I'm meeting today are our best bet to get things off the ground. They're some of the only people willing to take a punt on something brand new. Something that only we do. I've got the relationship with all three so Elizabeth told me to run with it. I've met with each of them separately a few times but there was a recurring theme."

Jack shook his glass, wondering if the ice in his glass might melt faster. "What's that?"

"They all want to meet the guy who's making the damn thing."

"Stafford?"

"No. They've met Stafford. They want to meet the nuts and bolts guy. They want to meet the guy who makes it all a reality. That's you."

"Seriously."

Max nodded. "They're not here to fuck around. They enjoy doing their homework – probably something you all have in common."

Jack took a bigger gulp of his drink.

"I was planning to meet them all tonight. But they contacted me earlier in the afternoon asking if you could come too. Finally give them the chance to meet the wizard's apprentice."

"So here I am…"

"Here you are…"

Max watched as the father of a small family shook hands with the waiter at the lectern who immediately ushered them all in. Max thought his son was arguably the smartest dressed eleven year old in London right this second.

"They're going to ask you some questions about the maths, the strategies," Max continued. "Just tell them the truth – the kind of stuff you tell us whenever we're not listening. They're not stupid so don't dumb it down but keep the explanations simple. Got it?"

"Yeah."

"Now as for the investors. We've got three coming tonight. There's Marina Sanchez, a Spanish real estate investor who's looking to diversify her business's holdings. Then we've got Ajay and Vijay Hothi. Brothers, and also both private equity magnates in their own right."

"I've heard of the Hothis," Jack said.

"I'm not surprised. They're both serial dealmakers. But their names have been floating in the news a little bit recently. One of their deals went south, in a pretty bad way."

"What happened?"

"Ajay and Vijay both used their funds to co-invest in a large Nigerian chemicals company. Turns out, the former, and now deceased, CEO was paying bribes to local businesses to win supplier contracts. Someone in the company leaked the story and then once the Nigerian government found out they decided to sue the company. The impending litigation and the costs associated with it are huge, not to mention the fact that the reputational damage and off-book accounting to cover up the bribes has diminished the value of their investment."

Even as just an observer, Jack struggled to place himself within the story. It all sounded so covert and theatrical that he wondered whether Max or the press had been taking liberties with the truth.

"I'm confused. I thought there's some process of checking before you make investments like this."

"You do. It's called due diligence. And in this case, it wasn't done that well."

"Whose job was it?"

"Ajay says it was Vijay's job. Vijay says it was Ajay's. That's almost certain to lead to litigation between the two of them."

"But someone must know what really went down," Jack said.

"Look, I'm not a judge or a lawyer, so I don't particularly care. What I do know is that the former CEO used to be a government minister in Nigeria. People suspect that's why the Nigerian government are taking such a hard line. Send a message to the world that they don't condone that sort of behaviour – especially from one of their own."

"Kind of makes sense."

"That brings me to my next point. Ajay and Vijay are not on good terms right now. They're here together only because they're both keen on the investment. But do not – and I fucking mean this – do not bring this matter up. If they bring it up – turn the topic to something else as quickly as you can otherwise things will turn real nasty real fast. I *do not* want this dinner taking a turn for the worse."

"Elizabeth and I are targeting about £50m of funding between the three of them," Max continued. "That's enough for us to start making some serious returns and gain some traction on the street and attract some even bigger players to the table in the coming months. It also means I probably need to close two out of the three. Any less and we don't hit that number and then things really start to fall apart."

Jack began to turn anxious. "Because less assets means less returns for the fund which means…lower valuation?"

"You got it son. And that opens a whole new wave of problems."

Max was trying to gauge whether Jack was fully aware of what he was saying. His eyes were floating elsewhere. He still seemed complacent with the matter, as if there were other thoughts rumbling through his mind; other ideas that needed to be culled.

"Jack?"

Jack's eyes quickly pulled back to Max.

"Pay fucking attention. Let me make it clear – one more time. Don't stray from the subject matters you're asked. Don't talk complex business or bring up *any* of the stuff I just mentioned. You'll start a fire that none of us are going to be able to put out. Got it?"

"Jesus, I get it. Listen, my only problem is this other investment that the Hothis are involved in. Shouldn't we at least offer a solution if they bring it up. They'll surely appreciate it."

"Shut the fuck up Jack," Max snapped. "What did I *just* say! I've been doing this for a very a long time. As soon as we turn to the topic of a bad deal, people get angry, things get tense and pretty soon everyone's going to get fucked off. Stick to what you know."

"I'm not fucking stupid," Jack retorted. "Last I remember, I work at this company. I don't need you tell me what I can and can't explain. I even recall that I was brought in because you weren't up to the job of building the very thing that's going to make us all so much money. So assume, for just a second, that when I'm asked something, I probably *do* know."

Max recalled that a disregard for his intelligence wasn't something that Jack openly welcomed. It was like a stain, a mark on Jack's ego and a scribble over the sensibilities that he believed made him a more versatile thinker. Nevertheless, Max didn't care. His obligations and loyalties were to Elizabeth. The feelings of Jack Morse weren't about to change that.

"Jack, you are valuable. Don't ever think otherwise. But you're also valuable to the extent you do as you're told. Do your job, and leave my job to me. This is not your average meeting. As far as meetings go, it's pretty fucking important. Underst-"

The waiter from the lobby had tapped Max on the shoulder before he could finish.

"Your guests have arrived sir."

As the waiter turned to leave Max noticed his glass was still full. In the midst of his conversation he'd apparently forgotten to drink it. Max picked it up and necked its contents within seconds. He slammed the glass on the table and rushed into the lobby.

Jack leapt off his stool and followed. His drink remained where it was.

CHAPTER 12

The elevator doors whooshed open on the fifth floor. Jack and Katrina stepped into the corridor, carrying two coffees each and a small trail of steam in pursuit. The remainder of their journey had been quiet. They only decided to speak when it came to deciding what coffee Sinclair might enjoy. Given his stern character they had agreed a black Americano was probably appropriate.

Walking towards the Field they could hear several voices. Edging closer they heard one that was unfamiliar.

They entered the Square and there stood a man; one who neither of them recognised. He was facing Sinclair but watched as Jack and Katrina entered. He had a younger face than Sinclair's; one sheltered by thick black hair, mostly flicked up and towards the side apart from several strands that rested against his forehead. His jaw was decorated with a hint of stubble and he carried a pair of piercing dark blue eyes that were filled with an emotion that was unplaced.

He was slim, dressed in a pure white shirt and a long, thin, black coat. He placed his hands into his coat pockets.

"More guests?"

His voice was deep and eloquent and from his perspective, questions hardly ever went unanswered.

Sinclair was peering at him suspiciously. "Do you mind telling us who you are?"

Jack quickly realised that the man hadn't been here very long. Glancing at Elizabeth and Sinclair he saw they had the same expression as him – a combination of bewilderment and confusion.

Jack and Katrina placed the coffees on the table, mindful not to take their eyes off the man before them.

"I'm someone that's looking for Edward Stafford. I understand he works here."

Jack's heart instantly sank.

Jesus. Again. What does he want with Stafford? Jack thought.

"He's not here at the moment," Elizabeth said. "We've got a meeting later so he's decided not to come in today. I'll probably catch him later this evening so I can tell him you popped by Mr..."

The man nodded. "That's unfortunate. It's important I meet him."

"Stafford's an important man," Sinclair said. "Most people often say that."

"So important that he's...well, potentially *missing*?"

Katrina took several steps back while Sinclair's hand edged towards his waist.

"Who are you?" Jack enquired.

"It's funny what you learn from your surroundings. The place, the people. I look around here and you know what I see." He stopped, momentarily catching the tension creeping into the air. "I see problematic circumstances."

He very carefully removed his hands from his pocket, his eyes fixed on Sinclair's. "It's ok. You don't need to shoot me. We're all allies here."

Sinclair's hand flinched. He didn't realise he'd telegraphed his moves so blatantly.

"Stafford's not here," he continued. "Neither is the other guy who works here – Max. And you all look like you've seen a ghost – just by the mere fact of me asking you about him."

"Look, we already told you –"

Sinclair started but the man cut him off.

"And you," he said flicking his head in Sinclair's direction. "You definitely don't work here. I didn't even need you to touch the pistol to figure that one out."

Everyone in the room could feel the walls closing in around them. There was nothing hostile about the individual and yet he displayed an undisclosed amount of authority over their surroundings. He spoke about events as if it were his prerogative to do so.

"I'm guessing you're not security so you must be here to help. Help with finding…Stafford and Max?"

Jack couldn't believe it. How could someone have deduced the problem merely from a brief analysis of one room and the people inside it?

"What do you want?" Jack asked.

"You ask some very direct questions son," the man chuckled. "Try to be just a little subtle in the future will you?"

He stopped to admire the light touch of embarrassment on Jack's face.

"I heard you're looking for an investment opportunity," he continued. "So I've come to enquire. There's nothing wrong with that is there?"

"Only if you're lying?" Jack retorted.

"*If*, being the dominant word in that sentence."

"Well how do we know? You could just as well be anyone."

"Let me correct that for you."

"How?"

"My name is Michael Carter."

Elizabeth picked up her coffee and took a tiny sip. A

jolt of caffeine pulsated through her veins. "Should I know that name?"

"You should now."

"Mr Carter, I'm the one in charge of investment opportunities. If you had a query you could've just called."

"I like building relationships in person."

Carter scanned the room. He could almost taste the opposition surging from each of them; opposed to his being, the mystery of his character and the potential dilemma of his origin.

Sinclair continued to scrutinise him, attempting to make some form of psychological deduction and yet he faltered in every capacity. Were he to concede, he might be led to accept the inevitable conclusion that Michael Carter was an enigma in every sense of the word. An incumbent truth in a situation that already lacked clarity.

"Carter, I'm afraid to tell you this, but the investment round for this opportunity is closed. We already have the funding we need."

"And now, interestingly, no one to build the product. I don't think your current investor will look too kindly on that. When do you meet with him?"

"This evening," she replied bleakly.

"If I were to find him…might you reconsider?"

"Reconsider what?"

"Cut me in. If I find him – bring me in on the deal. Think of me like an investor in distressed assets."

"*Distressed*. That's…funny."

"We don't need your help," Sinclair said, waving his hand outwards.

"Before I became an investor I was in military intelligence. I can help."

"I was military too."

"Then we should make quite a pair."

"That wasn't what I was getting at."

Jack scratched his head. "So you're saying you find him – and all you want is a stake in the company?"

"Consider it my reward. Nothing else. It's a fair trade."

Sinclair glanced at him with suspicion. "There are easier investments to make. Why this one?"

"It's valuable. And when I spot something of value that no one else is looking at I'll make a play for it. No matter the cost."

"Maybe it's not a bad idea," Jack said to Sinclair. "What have we got to lose?"

Sinclair shook his head. "Don't be stupid Jack. We have everything to lose. For once, just assess the problem properly. We don't know anything about him."

"You should know that I'll find him," Carter said. "There's nothing else to it."

"Position is filled," Sinclair said.

"Then where is he?"

Carter was peculiarly adept at aggravating Sinclair with so few words. A point hardly lost on everyone in the room; particularly Katrina who had remained noticeably silent for the duration of the discussion although intrigued nonetheless by Carter's existence. An individual with little to say and even less to justify his being was a circumstance that was materialising ever so frequently. Whether this particular circumstance was good or bad had yet to be determined.

"Enough." Elizabeth placed her coffee back on the table and crossed her arms. "Alright. We can agree terms after we find him. And that would depend on how helpful you are. But I've never reneged on a promise Mr Carter. You find him – and you'll get what you want. I have a deal to close tonight. Get him before then and we're in business."

In the corner of her eye, Elizabeth could see Katrina's mind racing away, her voice tucked away inside. Katrina spotted the focus placed upon her and took a sharp breath.

"Sounds fine to me," she said innocently. "The more the merrier."

"Ok," Elizabeth said.

She caught Sinclair's gaze. "Fine with you?"

Sinclair wiped his hands over his suit jacket several times, the touch of wool therapeutically brushing against his palms. "Fine. If that's how you feel, and as long as it doesn't interfere with *our* agreement."

Elizabeth nodded.

"But," he quickly added and pivoting his body to Carter. "If I sense distrust, if I get the feeling you're not being straight with anyone of us...I won't give any warning. I'm far too old for misunderstandings. I'll handle it. And no one is going to stop me."

"I wouldn't have it any other way," Carter said.

Sinclair's threat did little to disturb the solid and patient look on Carter's face. Nonetheless, he had to believe Carter understood the consequences that might follow if he were to break their unwritten agreement. It was the only leverage he had with a man he still didn't quite understand.

CHAPTER 13

After brief introductions, Carter was brought up to speed with what happened. Like Sinclair he listened carefully, although asking fewer questions. As the story progressed, he felt himself bombarded with numerous theories and possibilities, some vanishing as quickly as they appeared as more information came to light.

"So…" Elizabeth said. "Any questions?"

Carter composed himself. "It's slightly off topic but…how did you get involved?" His finger was loosely pointed at Sinclair.

"Elizabeth is an old contact of mine. She got in touch as soon as it was safe to do so."

"Right. And you answered the phone that late?"

"I had been out for drinks and was on my way home. Just chance I guess."

"Convenient. And you took the job there and then?"

"More or less."

Katrina's disgruntled expression was just visible enough so that Carter might notice.

Carter peered at Sinclair. "Fairly understanding of you. No persuasion involved at two in the morning?"

"Well, I don't work for free if that's what you're getting at. You asked for a stake in this company and I asked for cash."

"How much?" Carter asked.

Carter could see an invisible wall rising around Sinclair's persona. The question appeared to have bothered him.

"Two hundred and fifty thousand," Elizabeth said, ushering herself into Carter's line of reasoning. "I suggested the number; in order to get him to agree."

"Ok."

"Is that an issue," Sinclair said defensively.

"No. I just wanted to know your motivation. And money's a better motive than most things. It's also less risk."

Less risk until a bigger pay out comes in, Jack thought. *Carter must know that surely?*

"So what now," Katrina said, swiftly changing the topic. An exasperation in her voice stood out as she spoke. "We haven't really done a lot these past few hours."

"Has anyone checked the local news?" Jack enquired.

"Why would we do that?" Katrina said.

"The men who came here and dragged Max and Stafford into the street against their will – you don't think there could've been some sort of commotion last night? Anything? Someone may have saw something. You know what Max is like – he makes a fuss about anything."

Elizabeth nodded. "That's very true."

"Seems logical enough," Sinclair added.

Before Sinclair could look at his phone he noticed Jack was already tapping his screen. Sometime ago he wasn't so dissimilar, a man possessed by the phantom of curiosity although it was only logical that such traits were a product of youth and would eventually diminish over time.

Carter stood silently, his hands sheltered in his

pockets.

"Found anything?" Carter asked, lifting his hands out his pocket. He rubbed his hands against his stubble. There was an uncomfortable look on his face, as if he were trying to determine how much longer he had until he may need to rid himself of it.

Jack's eyes remained fixed on his screen. "…I think so."

Katrina paced over to Jack. She leaned over, her hair brushing across his face.

"Hey, watch it," he said, waving her hair out of his eyes.

"Wow. That's…"

"Yep." He handed her the phone. "I told you there'd be something. Don't think it's a coincidence either."

Katrina started reading. She lifted her head up. Behind an awkward smile sat a whisper of shock. "Oh god."

"Katrina, what is it?" Elizabeth asked.

"Go on," Jack said.

"This story…it's about two men who were murdered last night. Witnesses initially saw them escorting two other individuals. After that, the two men were found dead in the street, not far from here. Eight shots fired across the two of them. Mostly dressed in black, one with a thick beard. The paper is asking for anyone with details to come forward."

"Yeah, let's not do that," Jack muttered.

"No, this is very odd," Sinclair said. "If the people who took Max and Stafford are, in fact, dead, then they'd be free?"

"So where are they now?" Carter said.

"If they were genuinely free, they would've come back here, or at least told one of us if they felt unsafe," Jack said to Carter.

"Or…they had more assistance."

"We don't know if the man on the phone had more

involvement," Sinclair added. "It's more likely they've still got him – and there are more players we haven't seen yet."

Carter agreed. "Yeah, not having any cover on an operation like this is very risky. Could be quite a problem. And I get the impression that this man on the phone wasn't exactly a fool."

Elizabeth sat down on one of the plush chairs. Her coffee was within reaching distance. She grabbed it and took a large gulp. "I might be stating the obvious here but this is not the sort of place where people are shot in the street."

Jack's face lit up. "Is there a possibility the murders are also related to Stafford then?"

Sinclair laughed. "What – another crazed killer who has an interest in an algorithmic trading start-up? What are the odds?"

"The odds of *one* was pretty small and look how that turned out," Carter said. "At this point, I wouldn't be so quick to rule out two."

"So who then?" Jack said, staring out of the window.

No one in the field knew the answer. Everyone's silence was enough to confirm that.

The light of the sun glimmered against his eyes just as Katrina raised her head.

"I've got a friend who works around here," Katrina said abruptly. The sudden change in reasoning caught everyone off guard. She stood up and headed for the door. "They're only down the roads so I might go ask if they heard anything. Don't think it'll take too long though. I'll be back soon."

Before Jack could even call her name she had left, his eyes still reeling from the glare of the sun. As his sight returned he merely caught the ghost of a young woman's light brown hair.

CHAPTER 14

More information, not squabbling, was the key to figuring out what happened and why. Katrina knew there were facts missing; data which might unravel the knot in her mind. However, the information she sought wasn't about to come from a friend. In fact, no such friend ever existed. Her answers would come from the Grayson Arms.

Jack had done very little to convince her of Sinclair's intentions and all she needed was the right moment and cover story to pursue her suspicions. As soon as Sinclair mentioned the Grayson Arms she knew she'd need to go there. Something about him still didn't sit right with her. It was distrust but in a way that she'd never experienced. There was a dichotomy to his character that she couldn't reconcile. He spoke like a man convinced of himself but lying at the same time. Even now she still didn't know what to believe.

As the light breeze scuttled through her hair, there was a part of her that continually asked whether the journey was worthwhile or if her foolishness had finally gotten the better of her. She had no idea what to expect. It was entirely possible that Sinclair's story would check out. It was possible that her pursuit was a waste of time and that she had been stupid for ever considering it.

And yet, with each passing second, her commitment to her destination accelerated. Therein lay a curiosity she was unable to ignore and one that would either confirm Sinclair's trustworthiness or disavow Jack's misplaced faith in him. With hindsight she knew it would eventually become obvious; pure stupidity or pure genius.

Katrina wasn't unfamiliar with the Grayson Arms. She had been there before and knew exactly where it was. The fact that it was local to Sinclair suggested he probably didn't live very far from it either.

Within a few minutes Katrina found herself standing on the corner of a street and opposite her was a large, slightly run down pub. An archaic sign hung from the roof and blunt, foggy shapes vanished and reappeared through dirty windows surrounding the ground floor. A few wooden stools were planted outside and empty ashtrays had been perched across the windowsills.

She leaned forwards, trying her best to push the heavy doors in front of her. Before she could make any progress an elderly man on his way out swung the door open and let Katrina in.

"After you love."

"Thanks," Katrina beamed.

She walked inside and headed towards the counter. The pub was a little busy, the smell of lunchtime food drifting across the room and various members of staff scurrying like ants across the floor with plates of drinks and meals in hand. The light whiff of ale passed her nose as one of the waiters lost his balance and spilt too much over the floor. He scrubbed it up with the bottom of his shoes and continued to his table, unaware that she had noticed.

At the counter two men were pouring pints. One was an older gentleman while the other was younger, both dressed in neutral coloured shirts and jeans.

Katrina raised her hand and flagged one of them over.

"Hey, you alright," the younger man said. "What can I get you?"

"Um, I'm not really looking for a drink see."

"Yeah, sorry. I think you might've come to the wrong place then luv'."

"Tell you what," Katrina said. Her face glowed with an intense brightness. "I'll take a small gin and tonic if you can help me with one or two questions…if that's okay?"

The younger man scratched his head. Long strands of ginger hair fell past his ears and against the edges of a narrow face. Both his arms were thin and he seemed to be shepherding a misshapen beard that was obviously still in development.

"Alright. Why not?"

He plucked a glass from underneath the bar and dropped it in front of him. Behind him were several bottles of gin and a miniature fridge stacked with bottles of tonic water. He took one of each and mixed them together. He didn't seem to make any precise measurements and poured everything as he saw fit.

Katrina paid for the drink and took a sip. "Thank you very much."

"No problem."

He took a rough glance around the room to see if anyone may have needed anything. A small band of gentlemen were sat in the corner around a table filled with pint glasses. They were all staring up at a large television screen, watching highlights of a football match. Every so often they erupted in cheers and slammed their glasses on the table like a band of oddly dressed Vikings.

Others sat on their own, eating silently and reading a newspaper or were in groups, quietly chatting amongst themselves.

The young man's attention fell back on Katrina. He noticed the way her hair floated above her shoulders and he liked the way she smiled at him.

"So what do you wanna' know then?"

"I know this sounds really weird and I'm sorry in advance, but basically, this morning I had plans to meet a friend of mine and he never showed up. I haven't been able to contact him all day but we briefly spoke yesterday and he mentioned he was going to be here for drinks. Maybe late last night. Maybe with friends. I'm not really sure. But I wanted to know if he'd been by or if you'd seen him. And if he was all in one piece by the time he left."

The young man's older colleague crept by and overheard Katrina just as she was explaining herself. He wore thick glasses which he pushed up the bridge of his nose and his hair was thinning quicker than he'd like to tell himself.

"What's all this then? She looking for a friend?"

The younger man turned to his colleague and chuckled. "Yeah. But we probably need a bit more detail before we can tell her anything."

Katrina rested her hands on the wooden surface of the bar and the stick of stale wood lightly pressed against her fingertips.

"Well, he's about 6'2. Light beard. Kind of serious looking. Short-ish brown hair. Might've been wearing a suit?"

The men exchanged glances with one another.

"Was he alone?" the elder man asked.

"Not sure," Katrina said.

She could hear the foolishness in her own voice. She knew she was clutching at straws.

The elder man's face turned pensive. He turned to the young man. "Weird she comes asking questions about some guy after last night right?"

"What do you mean?" Katrina asked.

In a fit of enthusiasm, Katrina bumped her knee into the bar without realising and she wondered if anyone else had heard.

"Bit of trouble. We don't normally have that many problems mind you, but we had this one guy yesterday, wore a suit, probably same height as the guy you're talking about. Started with a few friends but after they went he was on his own for a few hours, ordering drinks non-stop."

Katrina leant forwards.

"Nothing wrong with it," he continued. "He paid for 'em all. Fine with us, yeah!" He gave a small chortle which sounded like a broken vacuum. "But not too long before closing he walked over for a final drink. He orders, and while he's waiting there's a few blokes next to him finishing up. We give him his drink and he just starts staring at them. They're havin' a laugh about something or another but he keeps looking at 'em right?"

"Yeah, yeah," the young man said. "Then he turns around, out of nowhere, and says '*what the fuck you lot laughing at.*'". His eyes widened. "Whole thing was so random."

"When did this happen?" Katrina probed.

The young man thought for a second. "Late. At least past 1.30am."

The elder man nodded. "The guys were obviously surprised, yeah. Things got heated, some of them tried calming things down, but this other guy just didn't give a shit. He was slurring his words and getting aggressive. Voice started getting angry, raspy, you know?"

"Yeah I can imagine."

A waitress walked over to the bar and took several of the drinks the men had poured up and placed them on her tray and walked off to a nearby table.

"We told them all to calm down," the young man said,

"but this guy in the suit just loses it. He squares up to the lot of them. Must've been asking for a beating. That's what we thought anyway. There were at least five of them. Guy would've had no chance."

"After that we tell them all to get out," he continued. "We don't need any of that. So they go. Now just as we're closing the door this guy in the suit grabs one of the other guys and throws him across the street."

The elderly man shook his head. "Comes out of the blue. The guy's friends go for him but this ain't like nothing I've seen. Swings left, right, knocks them all to the ground. And quick. Out of a fucking movie he was. Completely lost control."

"Oh god," Katrina gasped.

"He kept going but you could tell the guy was out of his senses. Stumbling around, screaming and shouting. Serious fucking issues."

"I don't know much about street fights but I would've thought they're always like that," Katrina said.

"Not like this…this guy was off…real off. Unstable's the word. Fucking unstable."

A sliver of discomfort fell on the younger man's face. "Before we could do anything he just stumbles off, the rest of them lying on the floor, completely wiped out…for no reason. I just don't get some people."

Katrina's heart was starting to race. "Yeah, it's an odd one isn't it."

Could it have been?

Shit. What if it was…does that mean he lied…

"You said this guy was your friend?" the elder man asked.

Katrina tore out of her train of thought. "No…I just…that's probably not even the same person you're talking about. Don't think my friend could pull off something like that."

"Okay…good. Well, stay safe. If they are the same,

trust me, you're better off not being friends with this kind of bloke."

Katrina smiled. "Will do. Thank you so much for your help."

Katrina prepared to leave but the young man pointed to Katrina's drink. "You not going to finish it? Hardly even touched it."

"Maybe next time. Thanks again."

Katrina turned and headed for the door. As she stepped outside she took in a deep breath, her body shuddering ever so slightly.

What do I do now?

Katrina walked back to the Field. Despite what she heard, she had no proof Sinclair was the person who had been involved in the incident at the Grayson Arms. All she knew was that there was a man who looked somewhat like him and had been involved in a fight shortly before they had rang him. There was also no evidence that Sinclair was involved in the various allegations against Zero Bridge. Everything remained speculation up until this point.

Maybe Jack was right. Maybe she should just trust Sinclair and let him do his job. None of this information was related to Stafford; it wasn't going to get him back. All she had done was fuel her own paranoia and led herself astray from the matter at hand.

And yet…what if I'm right?

The conviction inside of her was addictive; compounding on itself. It was an inability to be deterred despite the danger. She couldn't place where it came from and then it occurred to her that she had seen the same quality in Jack, time and again, over and over.

Upon arriving at the Field she stopped and removed her phone.

No harm I suppose…

She started typing.

Michael Carter. Investor.

No relevant results appeared.

A little weird.

Carter's actions weren't particularly suspicious but his sudden appearance certainly made him an oddity by nature and the lack of information on him only supported that theory.

Nevertheless, Katrina knew that whatever anomalies surrounded Carter, they were dwarfed by those that surrounded Sinclair, and if ultimate resolution was the objective, then Sinclair was a definitive threat.

CHAPTER 15

After Katrina left there was little progress.

Sinclair phoned several of his contacts to try and learn any additional information about the murders but no one seemed to know anything. There had been no leads, next to no evidence or witnesses and so there was very little to go on. With each passing conversation, Sinclair's tone became increasingly more terse and his casual wandering around the room slipped into hurried pacing.

During that time, Carter continually searched for facts and information that grounded his understanding of the problem. His curiosity led him to probe Jack and Elizabeth for information about their business and Stafford's role there. He bothered them about possible business associates and former academic colleagues. He questioned them about technology providers and suppliers. He was even willing to probe their landlord. And, at a certain point, Jack found himself explaining the calculus behind one of his deep learning models.

Nothing stood out to Carter but he was confident there was an obscure facet of knowledge that he may have been missing. He sensed there was one intermingled between the current universe of known facts yet despite his best efforts, he found nothing of value and simply watched as Sinclair's irritation dragged on.

When Katrina eventually returned her defeated expression, as far as anyone could tell, suggested she hadn't found anything useful.

"Anything of use?" Elizabeth asked.

"Nope. My friend knew next to nothing. Did you guys find anything else?"

"Not really," Jack said, glancing at Sinclair.

Sinclair was still scowling but began to explain the lack of information from his contacts.

As he continued, Carter noticed something in the corner of his eye. His eyes had been casually scanning the room but he spotted Katrina staring at him, almost as if she was trying to get his attention. He recognised an anxiety that asked not to be identified but preferred to be discussed elsewhere.

Sinclair finished his explanation and Katrina instantly cut in.

"Carter," she said cheerfully. "Did you find something useful?"

"No, can't say I did. I just tried to find out a little bit about Stafford and the business to see if it might spur some thought."

There was a sense of deliberation on Katrina's face before she replied.

"You know Stafford asked me to draft a deck summarising the company's operations the other day. It's over in his office if you want to take a quick look."

"Oh really," Carter replied. "Yeah, sure. That'd be helpful. Lead the way."

Katrina led Carter down the corridor to Stafford's office. They stepped inside and Carter couldn't help but spot the careful categorisation of certain books; firstly by subject matter, then alphabetically where necessary. Such meticulous detail served as a backdrop for a contrasting disarray of research papers scattered across the shelves and tables.

Carter stared at Katrina, noting the same imprint of anxiety that he glimpsed earlier. "So what is it you want to talk about...*really*?"

"It's about Sinclair," Katrina said, lowering her voice.

Carter raised his head slightly in a degree of curiosity. "What in particular?"

Something about Carter's fascination made Katrina uncomfortable although it would do little to deter her course of action. Her mind had already been made up.

"There's certain things about him. They don't..." Katrina began to fidget with the buttons on her cardigan. "They don't add up."

"Like what?"

Katrina's focus drifted to the window and then back to Carter.

"Just before me and Jack saw you for the first time, we had both looked into him. Just some searches in the public domain. Nothing too out of the ordinary."

"What made you do that?"

"He's off. Like...really off. None of us know anything about him. Not really. Elizabeth only called him because she was desperate but she has no idea who he is as a person. He's only taken the job for the money. He was even telling us earlier how he's willing to kill someone where necessary. It's not exactly the kind of stuff you casually bring up. He's...unstable. I can see it. At one point I asked him a few difficult questions and he suddenly snapped at me and got unbelievably defensive. I mean, seriously – who the hell are we dealing with here?"

Carter wanted to respond but Katrina rushed to continue before he could speak.

"Apparently he even worked for that PMC, Zero

Bridge – the one that was in the news sometime back. Remember? Conducted operations in all the places they were accused of war crimes or executions…"

"I know the one," Carter finally cut in. "Doesn't really say much though. A lot of PIs are former military. And Zero Bridge is not a small organisation. They hire from everywhere, so the probability of them hiring people like Sinclair is pretty high."

"That's not it," Katrina muttered. "There's more."

Carter leant forwards.

"I didn't go to visit a friend earlier."

"Then where did you go?"

"I went to the Grayson Arms. Sinclair said it was the pub he'd been at before we rang him."

"What! Why?"

"Just…I wanted to be sure he wasn't lying."

"Fucking hell," Carter said, shaking his head.

There's suspicious and then there's something else.

"Alright, fine…you find anything?"

Katrina paused for a few seconds. "I think he was lying about what he told us."

Carter's eyes widened. "You better be very sure before you make statements like that."

"I am sure," Katrina fired back.

"So you're saying he wasn't there?"

"No. He was."

"So what's the problem?"

"I spoke to the barmen there. They remember a guy in a suit, late last night round 1.30am. Had drank a lot and then suddenly got into a violent fight with a group of guys. Beat the crap out of all of them. They said it themselves…hadn't seen anything like it before, that he was unstable, that he was off…sound familiar?"

Katrina could see the increasing look of concern on Carter's face.

"You weren't there when he flipped at me either. It

was so unexpected. He gets aggressive when he's challenged. The more I think about it, the more worried I get."

"So what are you saying…he's lied about what he did last night? And that he's actually a lot more unstable than he lets on. You worried he might do worse?"

Katrina shook her head. "Look, I don't know. I just know that I was right to look into it because it's clear he's telling us stuff that isn't true and who knows what else he could be lying about."

"You told anyone else?"

"No…just you."

Carter looked perplexed. "Really. Not Jack."

Katrina shook her head again. "I didn't think he needed to know just yet."

"Why?" Carter probed. "I thought you were both pretty close. Well, that's the impression I got anyway."

"No…we are. It's just that…Jack's a smart guy – but he's way too trusting for his own good. The fact Sinclair is willing to help find Stafford is enough for him to discount all the evidence. I needed to tell someone who was independent…and could help if things get out of hand."

Katrina's gaze was penetrating Carter's, trying to draw out some sort of solution yet he remained unhinged.

"Leave this to me," Carter said. "There are a few things I need to look into first before I'm certain this is a problem."

"Like what?"

"Don't worry."

"So what do I do until then?"

"What you've been doing up until now," Carter said smirking. "Playing the person who's fine with everything."

Katrina's face turned sour.

"Well I'm not." Katrina analysed Carter for a moment.

"I looked into you too, you know…

"Really?"

"Yeah. Want to know what I found?"

"Enlighten me," Carter said, his voice turning satirical.

"Nothing" Katrina said blankly.

"I suppose I'm just not that interesting."

"I don't trust Sinclair right now but don't for a second think I believe your story. I know you're hiding something too. And the fact you do it so easily, so carelessly, worries me even more."

"You're very bright Miss Miller…and somewhat untrusting. I'd be careful keeping such a sensibility at the forefront of your mind."

"And why's that?"

"Believing you have no allies and that everyone is out to get you isn't a nice feeling to carry around with you. It's a weight on the soul. Trust me on that."

"Fine," Katrina said. "But that doesn't mean I should trust you just for the sake of having you on my side. If I've got a reason not to believe you, you better believe I'll take it."

"There's nothing wrong with that. But I'll say what I've said from the beginning. Like the rest of you…I'm just here to find Stafford. I'm here to make an investment. Our goals are aligned. You have my word."

"If our goals were really aligned, you'd be straight with me."

"I have a better understanding of how the world works. Right now, I'm as straight as you need me to be. All you need to know is I'm on your side – whether it's to find Stafford and Max, or deal with Sinclair. I want what you want Katrina."

"Alright. Whatever you say."

Katrina still looked agitated but Carter's willingness to accept the possibility her theory might be true was comforting to some degree.

"Let's go back outside," Carter said. "I don't want anyone getting too suspicious."

"Sure."

As they left Stafford's office Carter's phone started to buzz.

"You mind if I take this. Shouldn't be too long."

Katrina nodded and walked back towards the Square. Carter went into Stafford's office and closed the door.

"Jeff?"

"We got it."

Jeff's voice boomed down the phone. He spoke carefully, placing a great deal of consideration on how many words he might use and why. His American overtone sometimes felt alien but it was almost always direct. It reminded Carter of patriotism, freedom and stubbornness.

"You got my message then?" Carted asked.

"Yeah. We looked into him."

"And…"

"I think you can trust him. Does what he says. And pretty good at it too."

"I see."

"Where'd they find him exactly?"

"Contact of Elizabeth."

"I suppose she is well connected. Not surprising."

Carter exhaled heavily, the traces of fatigue showing up on his face for the first time all day.

"Jeff, this thing with Stafford…I didn't expect it to be as complex as it is. We're running out of time."

"I know, I know," Jeff said. "We just have to deal with it and make sure everything goes as planned. Does anyone suspect anything? Any idea why you're really here?"

"No. As far as anyone's aware, I'm an investor who's got a financial incentive to bring him back. There's nothing more for them to know."

He said it as if it were nothing. The deception felt

casual. It had been so long since he could ever tell the truth. Such days were nothing more than distant memories now.

"No, of course not. This chapter's coming to an end. For everyone."

Carter closed his eyes. "I don't think I've told you but I've been having this dream recently."

"A dream?"

"Yeah. Over and over and over. It hasn't stopped. Not for a while. It's always a bit different though. People standing in new places, the colour of the walls, the lighting, but it always ends the same. It comes to a close. I finally find him...then it goes black. But I can never remember anything. *How* it happened? *Where* it happened? *What* happened? I just remember the pain. The one that never seems to leave. Like it's here to stay."

In that moment of recollection, Jeff was unsure how to respond. Could he relate? In some ways, possibly. But his experience was different from Carter's. His mind existed in another realm when compared to anyone else and there was no one that could find it, draw reason from it or extend a branch back to the ordinary.

"Get a grip," Jeff said. "Keep your head centred on what's going in front of you. I was already anxious about this whole job from the start. Don't give me a reason to be right. Remember, this isn't about you. It's about Haddad. Right?"

"Yeah."

Carter stared out of the window and down on the street, fixated on the troves of people walking into the horizon, their lives so far and detached from his own.

Did you find anything else...anything?" Carter asked.

"Well, this is what I needed to tell you. There's more. We decided to take a look into his medical history too."

Jeff stopped speaking for a split second, just to let the words sink into Carter's mind.

"Medical history? What on earth made you do that?"

"Experience. If there was a secret, we imagined it'd be there. You also said you wanted more so we went looking for more."

"I guess that's true. Well…?"

Jeff paused.

"Apparently he's been seeing a shrink for the past few months. Says he drifts in and out of severe depression. Has sudden bursts of anger. You seen anything like that?"

"Not exactly. But the girl I'm working with suggested he's a bit unstable. She thinks he got into trouble at a local pub and violently attacked some of the other people there."

"That's not exactly comforting. Well, he's not on any meds. The shrink thinks he can handle it on his own."

"A bit careless."

Carter could hear typing on the other end of the phone.

"It says he's unsure if it's mental health related – to do with past military service. You think given the risk he might get a pill or two."

"Military. He went on about that a few times."

"Yeah. Ten years, and then a nice long stint with Zero Bridge."

"The girl dug that one up. I'll bet he's got a few stories to tell. What have you got on his service record?"

"Nothing. The file stops. I think the security is tight so the guys on my end need some more time."

"That's fine."

"So you think he's not a problem…for the ultimate investigation?"

"No. But still…"

"Still…," Jeff interrupted, "a medical file detailing deep undiagnosed psychological problems is probably worth looking into. The last thing we need is some kind of episode that we don't see coming."

"My thoughts exactly. We don't need a liability. Not

right now. Not when I'm this close."

Carter was slowly pacing, the phone pressed against his ear. He knew there was something missing.

"Jeff, do one more thing will you. Dig up anything you can on his family. I need a holistic picture of this guy before I'm satisfied."

"That could take some time too."

"Whatever it takes. Just call me when you've got everything."

"Sure. His file says one or two things about alcohol abuse as well. What's your take?"

Carter scratched his head. "The girl's story is sounding more and more likely." He paused. "Let's get everything we can. I don't want any loose ends. The stakes are too high."

"Don't worry about it. We'll find out soon enough. You just focus on you."

Carter stopped pacing, and took a sharp breath.

"If it's nothing then it's nothing and we carry on as normal," Carter said calmly. "But if it isn't...then I think I'll deal with Sebastian Sinclair in a very different way."

CHAPTER 16

Max had requested a small private dining area for the dinner he'd organised with his would-be investors. He was such a regular at the Dove and had spent so much money over the past decade that they were always willing to fulfil any of his requests.

Max had requested a small private dining area for the dinner he'd organised with his would-be investors. He was such a regular at the Dove and had spent so much money over the past decade that they were always willing to fulfil any of his requests.

The waiter had taken them to a spacious room above the restaurant. Scattered across the walls were more photographs of celebrities although there were also several paintings. One was of a group of farmers picking sweetcorn in the fields. Another was similar, except that instead of sweetcorn, the farmers were picking tomatoes.

The ambience of the room provided a sense of intimacy, one that was different from downstairs. The colour of the marble was dark blue rather than the cyan which was downstairs and the lighting was dimmer than the main restaurant.

A vast circular table covered by a sparkling white table cloth and an assortment of cutlery and glasses rested in the centre of the room. Five wooden chairs encircled the table while the smell of fresh bread and olive oil consumed the senses of everyone that walked in.

After the waiter, Max and Jack walked inside, followed by Marina Sanchez. When Jack was first introduced to her in the lobby, at five foot ten, long black hair and a slender physique, he was almost certain that he was meeting a super model rather than an investor in real estate. Marina was wearing a light blue shirt, tucked into a long grey pencil skirt and stood in sharp, pointed one-inch heels. Given the formality of her attire, Jack suspected she may have just left her office.

Ajay was wearing a smart grey jumper while Vijay was wearing a grey two-piece suit. Both men appeared almost identical; light brown skin, tall, very skinny and clean shaven. The only difference was that Ajay wore a thin pair of horn-rimmed glasses. Although they were apparently approaching the age of sixty, from afar anyone couldn't have imagined them to be older than fifty.

As everyone took a seat, Max shuffled between them both, making every effort to ensure that Ajay and Vijay were either not sat next to or opposite each other.

The waiter asked what type of wine people would like and everyone seemed to be content with white. Jack noticed that on this occasion, Max didn't appear to have any objections.

The dinner began with general formalities. Max asked how general day-to-day business was going, not expecting any answers which were out of the ordinary. Marina explained how she was spending more and more time in London, having fallen in love with the London property market. Ajay had apparently promoted a number of his subordinates in order to take on more responsibility for managing his portfolio while Vijay had recently tried leaving the office on time so that he could spend more time with his kids.

"My son's leaving for university next year," Marina added. "At this point, he's so intent on drinking with his friends I think spending time with him now is a moot point. Better you take the time now Vijay."

Although Marina's English was impeccable, Jack could still detect a hint of Spanish in the background.

While everyone spoke, Jack began cutting up slices of bread. Unsure how thick millionaires preferred their bread, he noticed his hand was trembling. Having successfully cut a decent number of slices he started to pass them around the table. Much to his relief, as everyone took a slice no one seemed to mind their thickness.

"So Jack," Ajay said as he dipped a piece of bread into some olive oil. "Tell me a bit about yourself. I spend so much of my day talking shop, sometimes it's nice to hear from someone else."

Jack sipped some of his wine. It was sweet, soft on the tongue, and unlike anything he'd drank before. He tried to guess the price but hazarded a guess that it would be high.

"Well, I was a mathematician back at university. That's how I met Stafford. He used to lecture me, and then supervised me during my Master's degree. After that I did a few consultancy type projects; mostly machine learning and data science type stuff. I even worked with Stafford on an old venture of his. And then a little later I got the call to come work with him again."

"I see," Ajay said. He softly chewed on his bread. "What about outside of work?"

Oh fuck, Max thought. *This kid is about as dull as a wooden spoon.*

The question caught Jack by surprise.

"I- I read a fair bit. I also like movies. Typical stuff I

guess. Nothing exciting."

"I love movies!" Marina exclaimed. "My board almost mutinied when I suggested we convert one of our portfolio holdings into a cinema."

"Always one for trouble aren't you?" Vijay chuckled.

"They're all so uncreative," Marina scoffed. "They lack vision and scale."

"I guess that's why you're here at this table and not them," Max said.

"Exactly! Bunch of amateurs."

Marina took a swig of her drink. Max could tell she was beginning lighten up. If he could get Ajay and Vijay slightly tipsy he knew he could swing the dinner in his favour.

"But please Jack, tell me," Marina continued. "How do these algorithms work? I'm not a maths person. I studied finance. But I'm very curious. How do you make us more money than the average algorithmic fund?"

Jack took everyone through the fundamentals of the technology first; machine learning, deep learning and reinforcement learning. He realised that if he explained those ideas first, anything that came afterwards would make much more sense. He then drifted into the different investment strategies him and Stafford had devised and how different algorithms in those areas could be used in novel ways to find new opportunities in the market. For the duration of time that Jack spoke, neither Marina, Ajay nor Vijay interrupted. They all seemed to be mesmerised by Jack's explanation. In a sense, Jack understood what Max meant when he said they were all very smart; the reason they didn't seem to ask any questions was because they understood exactly what he was saying. Had he made the slightest error in his logic, they invariably would have noticed and stopped him dead in his tracks.

"Have you done any back testing?" Vijay asked.

"Yep. From the work we've done so far, the returns

are running between 20 and 30%. I'm in the process of finalising a complete set of figures."

"We can send you all a copy of the results once Jack is done," Max added. "Just to quell any questions you might have."

"I'd really appreciate that guys," Vijay said. "Thank you."

A short while later the waiter entered the room and asked what everyone had selected as their starter. He was very polite as he spoke, ensuring his staff were topping up everyone's glasses whenever people made their requests; mostly a combination of bruschetta and a variety of salads.

After the waiter and his staff left, Marina took a gulp of her wine. "Ajay. It's definitely good to see you. I so rarely see you on the circuit these days since you've devolved responsibility."

"It's a young person's game Marina," Ajay replied. "I try and take a back seat now."

"It's a shame. There's none like you and Vijay, I always say it. Which reminds me! And tell me the truth…after everything that's happened, should I still be doing business in Africa?"

A cheeky grin fell on her face.

Fuck sakes, Max thought.

"Depends if you enjoy litigation," Ajay said. His tone was relatively relaxed "I'd tread lightly."

Vijay slouched back in his chair. His lanky body drooped over its edges. "You can always do business there Marina. Just make sure you've done your homework. The man who ran the Nigerian company Ajay and I bought paid bribes to private companies. There's a theory he even overcharged those companies for chemicals and sent some of the excess back to the executives he originally bribed just to sweeten the deal. Everything looked wonderful on paper until he died and people found out what happened. Now, as I'm sure you're all aware, we've been sued by the Nigerian government. We've even had to pay for a private internal investigations team to uncover what's going on – all so we can appease the UK and US governments who are accusing us all of not doing our jobs. Although, no one is expecting much from them so we kept it a two-person job just to keep costs low; costs that are soon to mount up due to other reasons."

Vijay picked up his glass and drank a considerable amount from it. "What I'm trying to say here my dear, is that life, and the government, gets a kick out of fucking you around."

"I can imagine," Marina said.

After a brief moment of silence Max quickly glanced at Ajay. He didn't appear to be making eye contact with Vijay.

Hopefully we can get off this topic.

"There must be a solution though," Jack said. "Surely."

Fuck sakes! One goddamn thing I told him!

"Oh really," Ajay said. He pushed his glasses up the bridge of his nose. "Any ideas?"

"I'm not an expert, but this wasn't your fault right. The CEO paid the bribes."

"Our army of solicitors and barristers who charge us thousands by the hour have already told us that," Ajay said mockingly. He was beginning to sound agitated. "But it was *our* company when some of the bribes were paid so people are assuming the liability sits with us. So...I'll ask you again Jack. Any ideas?"

Jack tried to think of something to say but Ajay quickly continued.

"You're a numbers man Jack. Not a lawyer. Not a financier. Not a politician. Numbers. You want some advice – don't give me false hope. I don't need it when I'm thinking about my investmen-"

"Give the boy a break Ajay," Vijay interrupted. "He only wants to help. Not like you did anything particularly useful when the shit hit the fan."

"Hey, come on guys," Max said. "I thought the plan was to not talk shop here."

Marina leant into the centre of the table. Her glossy black hair fluttered by her ears. "He's right. Everyone take a breather."

Ajay raised his hand, as if to motion that Marina should stop speaking.

"What do you mean I didn't do anything useful?"

Vijay let out a small guffaw. "Leaving your idiot foot soldiers to handle one of your largest external investments is one thing."

"Oh fuck off."

"You left a handful of inexperienced toddlers to manage your due diligence too."

"*My* due diligence? Where the fuck were you Vijay? Where the fuck was your team? While you were off taking your son to the movies, who had their finger on the pulse? Why couldn't a single one of your managers tell me how our man in Nigeria became so popular with businesses across every city in less than two years?"

"Look, I think we should maybe talk about something else," Jack said.

"No, no, no" Vijay rasped. "Stay out of this Jack. My brother needs to learn to watch his mouth. He apparently thinks his nephew sabotaged our deal rather than his own incompetence. How could anything ever be the fault of the great Ajay Hothi. Absolved of all responsibility by virtue of being *you*. Idiot."

Ajay stood up. "Thank you for the wine Max but I think I'll be passing."

"Shit, Ajay please," Max pleaded. "Just take five minutes and come back. Take some time to think this all over."

"I'll be heading to the bar and I don't intend on returning. Do not follow me, Mr Mortimer. *I mean it.*"

"Just think it over. This deal – "

"I've made up my mind Max. And once it's made, it's made. You of all people should know that." He gazed over to Jack and Marina. "See you both."

Ajay stormed out of the room. His stomps down the stairs resonated around the room.

Vijay removed his phone from his pocket and started tapping away. "Think I might order a taxi. My appetite has suddenly vanished."

"No, no, not you too," Max said. There were small beads of sweat running down his forehead. He could sense his body was flustered. "Just stay a few minutes and we'll talk it over."

Vijay got to his feet and buttoned his suit. "Sorry Max. This just isn't feeling right. No hard feelings. It's maybe just one of those deals that was never meant to be."

Vijay turned and left for the lobby.

It all felt so sudden. Within minutes it had all collapsed. Max saw everything slipping from his grasp and despite his awareness of what was happening, there was absolutely nothing he could do. There came a point where the entire conversation was a runaway train, its momentum unstoppable in the face of anything that anyone might say or suggest. It only took one inciting question to throw the situation into disarray. One innocent question, one topic, one idea that was warned against. And yet, for some peculiar, odd and absurd reason, it materialised.

Max turned to Jack, his eyes riddled with rage and fury. Why, after so much caution and so much counsel, would he have asked that which he was not supposed to ask?

CHAPTER 17

"I know we've been over this but I'm going to ask you guys again."

Sinclair was sat on one of the chairs, his head held in his hands. They could barely make out his voice.

"Does Stafford have any enemies?"

Jack, Katrina and Elizabeth all shook their heads in unison.

"No," Elizabeth sighed. "Why do you keep asking us this? You must have another theory, surely?"

"Because…" His voice bellowed inside of his hands. "There is no other reason. To go to this much trouble means you really want someone out of the picture. Somehow, and in some way, Stafford pissed off the wrong person."

Carter walked into the Square. Jack was throwing his empty coffee cup to himself. It landed in his hands just as Carter caught a glimpse of the conversation.

"I can't believe we're talking about this again" Katrina mumbled.

"If you have any bright ideas I'd love to hear them," Sinclair retorted.

"No. But I do quite enjoy hearing the same one over and over."

"Then what is it? Who else has a reason?"

Jack's eyes lit up. He squeezed the cup in his hand, the crinkling of plastic summoning everyone's attention. "There is someone…"

"Who?" Elizabeth asked suspiciously.

"Reinhart…"

Elizabeth's eyes widened. She quickly begun to put the pieces together. "Oh god…he could not have…"

Sinclair raised his head. "Who's Reinhart?"

"He's an investor," Jack replied. "We met him shortly before this all happened."

"How?"

"Initially, we were struggling to secure funding," Elizabeth said. "Then earlier this week we had a meeting with someone called Joseph Reinhart. His team called me out of the blue requesting a sit down. Unfortunately, it didn't go well. He offered us ridiculous terms that severely undervalued the company."

"How did you respond?"

"We turned him down."

"What was he like?"

"Unstable. Demanding. Unreasonable. Not the sort of person you go into the business with."

"But you did get funding in the end," Carter added.

"Yeah. I received a call from a placed called Nalbanthian Investments later that evening. They'd heard about our technology and were willing to get involved."

"I see. What was the name of the person you spoke to?"

"Frederick Harris. He was calling on behalf of Mark Nalbanthian – the person we're meeting with today."

"Ok."

"But this Reinhart guy," Sinclair said. "What else about him makes him a person of interest?"

"Well, I'm not quite convinced he's a person of interest," Elizabeth said.

"Why?" Jack asked.

"Who would go to the trouble? It just seems so ridiculous."

"You were there – you met him – the guy was not normal. And remind me…what did Frederick say to you on the phone yesterday? About Reinhart?"

"He suggested Reinhart had lost out. And that he probably wanted the investment but was playing hard ball."

"He called him something too right? What did he call him again?"

"Jack, I don't think it's relevant."

"Of course it's relevant. This is the only lead we have. I think Carter and Sinclair deserve to know."

"What did he say?" Sinclair asked.

Carter's eyes latched on to hers. She sensed his focus bearing down on her.

"He called him a wacko. Adversarial."

"There you go," Jack blurted out.

"The words of one man are hardly indicative of anything Jack. Don't be so rash."

"Well it sounded like Frederick had dealt with him before. He's a better judge of character than we are."

"Jack," Katrina said. There was a softness to her voice that immediately calmed everyone down. "We've never even met Frederick. So we're certainly not in a position to judge his conclusion of Reinhart."

"He's better than nothing," Jack said.

"You're not wrong there," she confessed. "But let's just approach this with a bit of care."

"I am. I'm just trying to iron out the fact that it's not impossible."

Sinclair nodded. "It's not. Whole thing sounds credible if you ask me. But let me make sure I've got this right. You think, this investor, Reinhart, lost out to this other investor, Nalbanthian, and so, he decided to take the problem into his own hands and take Stafford away…for what?"

Jack pored over the question the same way he'd approach any problem. His faculty for playing out potential scenarios was a staple of his persona. He sometimes felt distinct. Everyone on one side and himself on the other. Between them a gulf of insight.

"Maybe he thinks he can force Stafford to work for him. Or force the algorithms or technology out of him; using persuasion, maybe force. Taking Stafford reduces the downside of missing out. And getting the information creates an upside and a greater motive to take him."

Carter and Sinclair both looked as though they agreed.

"It seems likely," Carter said. "If he's got access to capital then hiring a team wouldn't be much of an issue. Especially if the potential pay out could be way more if he gets the information he needs."

"You must hear how ridiculous this sounds when you say it out loud," Elizabeth said.

"Yeah," Jack said amusingly. "But guess what – it doesn't make it any less plausible."

Elizabeth's fiery gaze was burning its way through Jack. There were times she could barely stand him. His cockiness, his unwillingness to listen, were all red flags mounted across the terrain of her judgement. They were indicative of man who would never change, whose ideas were planted into the ground and ready to last to the very end.

"No one's denying it's ridiculous," Sinclair said, attempting to cut the tension in the air. "But it's still likely. And we have nothing else right now."

Katrina could sense Elizabeth's frustration. She knew this line of reasoning was making her feel nervous, and that its sheer unpredictability was going to create a great deal of uncertainty.

"Even if it's all true," Katrina said, "Reinhart would still have Max. And so, we're still constrained to the same variables. We need a way of getting to Reinhart without putting Max in danger."

"That'll be difficult," Carter said. "But there's always leverage to be had."

"I like your optimism Mr Carter," Elizabeth remarked.

Carter smirked. He gazed out of the window, his thoughts masked by silence.

Katrina noted the contrast between him and Sinclair. How there was almost no circumstance where he found himself agitated. Every comment or remark slid off his psyche, whereas just next to him was another who would defend his views with such aggression that it was startling.

Before she could contrast them any further Carter's phone buzzed. The sound cut through the room, alerting everyone.

"Excuse me. I just need to take this."

He rushed outside, heading back the way he came and towards Stafford's office. He glanced down at the name on his screen.

J

Carter's footsteps echoed along the walls and sailed through the corridor as his shoes stomped against the floor. He came to the door of Stafford's office and answered his phone.

"Jeff," he whispered.

"I found it."

He stepped inside and shut the door.

"What?"

"Something you're not going to like."

CHAPTER 18

The aura of suspense which Jeff had built up wasn't so dissimilar from a horror story as Carter eagerly awaited his update.

"We got his service record like you asked," Jeff said. "But there's all sorts of stuff here Carter. Not like we were expecting."

"How so?"

"Stories about aggression, anger, alcohol abuse, substance abuse…it goes on. The list is crazy."

"What? I thought he served for ten years. There's no way he could continue his service for that long."

"Of course not. It all seemed to start around a certain point. And that's where it got interesting. We also have the files relating to his family…his wife in particular. She died quite some time ago. Stage four lung cancer. The whole thing was all very sudden. Happened while he was away on duty. He was completely out of contact - never even got to see her. It went from start to finish before he had any idea. After that his mental state took a pretty serious beating and he completely lost it."

Carter's feet were fixed to the ground, agonising over

each detail he heard in case he might miss something of importance.

"That's when the drinking started," Jeff continued. "And everything else along with it. Numerous cases of substance abuse during his time in the service. That's what led to all of this anger and violence. Over time it just became a part of his profile. There are countless stories of attacking fellow soldiers, civilians. Every professional he spoke to just fills their pages with question marks. No one can make any sense of the man."

"Why did it get so out of hand?"

"If I were to guess, probably because he loved his wife. Far as we can tell she was the only thing outside of the war he had, the only thing he cared about. He didn't have anything else. So when she went, it tore him apart. In some ways it doesn't surprise me."

"How is he keeping it under control? He's not like that all the time now is he?"

"Who knows? The file we found regularly refers to some kind of 'hero' syndrome as well. This desire to run in and save the day...'no matter the consequences or damage to anyone else.' That's how most of these altercations started. It was because he tried doing something stupid, or decided to be a hero. Don't think people took kindly to his rash thinking and it led to a lot of disputes – physical or otherwise."

Carter shook his head. "No. This isn't making any sense."

"As time went on, he started forgetting stuff. Huge cases of memory loss. Mainly the drugs and alcohol I think. You seen anything?"

"No. I've seen none of that. The only thing I can relate back to is what the girl mentioned – allegations of instability, a potential drunken brawl and that's all. But the rest...it's all stuff I haven't seen."

"What made her go and find that stuff out?"

"She thought he was aggressive, a loose cannon. She didn't trust him. Figuring out he was Zero Bridge didn't help either."

"Smart girl. Jesus, given what we know now, who the fuck knows what he did at Zero Bridge. Everyone knows the stories. I wonder whether he had something to do with what went on over there."

"It's starting to sound more likely."

"Fucking hell. Imagine what he might've done."

"Look, I don't want to think about that. All I know is that this guy is beginning to sound like a problem."

"I'm going to ask you a question and I need a very serious answer. Do you think he can be trusted?"

Carter was leaning against the window, continuously tapping his head backwards against the glass. Jeff could hear the light tap of Carter's head bouncing back and forth through the phone, ticking away as if it were a metronome.

He briefly closed his eyes only to reopen them almost immediately, one conclusion prevalent across his mind.

"No," Carter whispered coldly. "He's a liar. Unstable or not...he should've told us the truth. We have no idea what he's capable of. And worse than that...we have no idea what else he's lying about."

"Carter, I think you should also know. We ran his financial history as well. Sinclair is heavily in debt at the moment. I'm talking to the tune of millions. Mortgages, outstanding liabilities, legal expenses. Even the addiction he has...it's pushing him further and further into the red."

"Elizabeth told me he only took this job when she was willing to offer him £250k."

"Given what I'm seeing, that's still not enough to pull him out."

"Christ...do you think it's possible he could be..."

"Compromised?"

"Yeah. Or at the very least, susceptible."

"I don't know," Jeff muttered. "These are just the facts. I've read the file. I hear what you're telling me about him. He sounds like an unpredictable fuck. *Anything* is on the table right now."

"If someone has applied pressure, paid him off to make sure we don't get Stafford, we're in a serious fucking problem. We need Stafford back."

"Carter, that's a big leap. You honestly got to ask yourself if he's the sort of guy that might turn if given the option. Is the potential for becoming a liability actually there?"

Carter walked towards Stafford's desk. As he did so he noticed his reflection in the walled casing around one of Stafford's certificates. Stood there was a man who didn't know what to believe right now, a phone clutched in his hand, trying to gauge the potential for chaos.

"He's dangerous. He's desperate. He could still be lying. It could mean anything."

"Then we need to take a course of action. I can't afford to let this lie."

Carter pulled the phone away from his face and checked the time. It was just past noon.

"The clock's ticking. I'm going to need to confront him out in the open."

"Woah, woah. That's a bit extreme don't you think? Can't you take a calmer approach to this?"

"I don't have time for anything less. I need to know everything, and I need to know it now."

"Carter, you need to keep a low profile. For a lot of reasons. This isn't the way to do it."

"Doesn't matter. I know what's best here."

Carter could hear Jeff grumbling over the phone. "You do this, and you risk bringing a lot of attention, and a lot of questions out into the open. I'm not comfortable with it."

"Trust me – this is the optimal way to deal with it."

"Really? You're telling me with all your ideas and crazy plans, you can't think of another way to find out what Sinclair's agenda is?"

"No. Not with these constraints. We need Stafford back and I need to act now, or I risk failing. One way or another...I'm going to find out if Sinclair has deceived us."

"Ok. You're the man on the ground and maybe you know better than I do. Do whatever you have to. But remember why we're here and what's at stake. *Do not screw it up.*"

"Wouldn't for a second. Thanks."

Carter hung up the phone. He walked back to the Square, engulfed with a desire for answers.

As he stepped inside his eyes met Sinclair's. Whether he was a man of lies or honesty was the question which plagued him now.

To Sinclair, the look was brief and yet to Carter it felt as if it lasted an eternity. He knew nothing of what Carter knew; the realisation that there was a potential for deception, parading through the room in plain sight.

But now that Carter knew, now that Carter wasn't willing to accept anything less than the truth, it was his turn to fire.

He opened his mouth, pausing for just a second before he spoke.

"Sinclair, could I speak to you outside quickly?"

"Yeah, of course."

The two men walked towards Stafford's office in silence, neither expecting what would transpire in the subsequent conversation.

CHAPTER 19

Carter's immense coat hovered across the ground as he sped down the corridor and led the way to Stafford's office. He ignored the small details he had noted earlier; the poor gloss of blue paint, the dirt on the floor and the odd feeling of suffocation.

Stopping short of entering the office, he turned around. His shoes squeaked against the floor and their shine stood out against the dull colour of the carpet.

Both Carter and Sinclair were straddled between the office and the corridor. The sudden halt took Sinclair by surprise and he waited to see if Carter would say anything. After a time he grew tired of waiting.

"So what is it?" Sinclair asked.

He leant forwards, scornfully, the way someone might anticipate an unintended gift.

Carter took a sharp breath and the tip of his hair briefly floated above his forehead before falling back down.

"Last night, when you were at the Grayson Arms...remind me. When did you leave again?"

Sinclair's head filled with disbelief.

Is he being serious?

"This again…I think I've already–"

"You never told us what time you left. I just want to know. That's all."

"Really. Well, I don't see what that has to do with anything."

"I think you'd be quite surprised."

An unusual type of pressure slowly materialised against Sinclair and without realising he took a tiny step backwards.

"Ok. I left at 11. Satisfied?"

Carter kept his gaze fixed on Sinclair. "An uneventful night then. No altercations or problems?"

"I thought that was all?"

"What's another few minutes going to hurt?"

"What the hell are you trying to get at here?"

"Calm down. They're just questions."

Sinclair was beginning to dislike Carter's approach. He could sense something in the air which was far more sinister than just an ordinary line of questioning.

"These don't feel like questions. They're something else and I'd prefer you lessen your tone when you speak to me."

"I don't think you left at 11," Carter declared. "And I don't think your evening was as uneventful as you've made out."

"Are you calling me a liar?"

Any normal man might feel their body surge with tension or fear at such an accusation. Maybe they would say something out of turn to alleviate the strain in the conversation. But Carter didn't reply. As if he were critiquing a film, he merely studied Sinclair's reactions with a hawk-infused stare.

"Why the fuck do you think I'm lying?" Sinclair exclaimed.

"Last night at the Grayson Arms a man in a suit, around 1 or 1.30am violently assaulted a group of men, for no apparent reason other than he was possessed by some force of lunacy."

"So what?"

"You were there weren't you? And a man with your description gets into trouble, not long before you're called by Elizabeth – heading home."

"And you think that's me?"

"I think it's pretty damn possible, yeah.

"That sounds like a complete load of shit."

"I really don't think so. I think you're hiding something from me, from all of us."

"Who the fuck do you think you are throwing around these accusations. Like I need to answer you of all people. Fuck off."

Sinclair was raising his voice now.

"We don't even know who you are," he continued. "And you got the gall to ask me questions about who I am. Answer me a question why don't you. Where is this all coming from? Why the fuck have you suddenly decided to start asking me all this shit?"

Carter didn't move. He stretched out his fingers, grasping at the air, his nerves unhinged.

"The facts don't any make sense right now and what you've told us is not an accurate account of what happened. So I want to know why."

"How the hell would you even know that?"

Sinclair thought back momentarily, his body shuddering in the haze. He knew Carter had nothing; no evidence. Certain even.

But Carter was far from finished.

"Those final years in the service. You ever regret wasting them…the drugs, the alcohol, the addiction. You ever wonder whether you could've done better?"

Sinclair's eyes widened in horror.

How did he…

Carter continued. "Precisely how many civilians died

when you were around? How many of your men went to their deaths because you couldn't get a handle on what you were doing?"

"Fuck off! You have no idea what you're talking about."

Sinclair's voice roared through the corridor. So much so that Jack, Katrina and Elizabeth all came running towards them.

As they came upon the situation they couldn't help but be startled. A few minutes ago everything seemed so calm but now Sinclair was flustered with anger and Carter had a devious spark in his eye, an ulterior motive bubbling beneath the surface.

"What the hell's going on here?" Jack asked.

But Carter dismissed their presence. Their arrival was irrelevant compared to his demand for answers.

He cleared his throat. "Are you proud of your actions? The blood on your hands?"

Katrina's heart skipped a beat.

Oh shit – he's confronting him. Already?

A part of her expected that this was inevitable. But another part still couldn't believe it was happening; a situation where Carter took her line of enquiry and fashioned it into a weapon in order to compel the truth into existence.

It was her that had been driven by scepticism. It was her that had desired answers. Now they would finally fall into her possession as well as the opportunity to witness the horrifying resolve which was required in order to unearth them.

"What does this have to do with anything?" Sinclair said. There were shreds of guilt marked across his face. Each seemed like a gateway to another moment of redemption he so desperately sought.

"More than you think. Whatever you've done, it calls your entire character into question. That's why it concerns me."

"Well it shouldn't," Sinclair snapped.

"So you don't deny it then?"

Jack, Katrina and Elizabeth all watched in fear as Carter, his personality so deviant from what it once was, meticulously skewered Sinclair's psyche.

"Fine. I've made mistakes. Who hasn't? But whatever you've seen − I'll tell you right now, it's only half the story. Most of it's probably not even true. Lies. Fiction. Bullshit."

"I've read it in your file. It sounded pretty clear to me."

Sinclair felt as if the air had been yanked from his lungs.

"What else did you find out?"

"Look, everyone calm down," Jack said. "Let's just take it easy ok."

Jack had no intention of letting the situation get out of hand. An escalation of this magnitude wouldn't be ideal for anyone.

"It's not my job to uncover these things and then tell you," Carter said. He spoke as if Jack were a casual painting on the wall. "You need to start telling me the truth. From this point on."

"Why would I bring any of this up?"

"No, I mean what happened last night. All this stuff…it's on the periphery. It just tells me how compromised you are when it comes to investigating this issue."

"Carter, please" Jack implored.

"Jack, this doesn't involve you," Sinclair said. "Stay out of it." He turned to Carter. "You don't think I'm up to the task?"

Jack could see situation slipping out of his control.

"That's what I'd like to know. Whether you've got a handle on what the hell is happening."

"I'm getting sick of this fucking shit. Stop speaking in

circles. What do you fucking want from me?"

"I want the fucking truth. I want to know what made you who you are. What turned you into some unstable and unpredictable son of a bitch? I want to know if you can be trusted. I'm running it through my head and I know I'm still missing something."

Sinclair wasn't speaking and Carter needed a reaction. Fast. He needed to push harder.

"This all started when your wife passed away right?"

Sinclair began to tremble. *How could he know all of this?*

"I think that's when it happened. Right? Yeah. That's when you really changed for the worse."

Katrina struggled to fathom how Carter accumulated so much information in such a short period of time. Between now and her conversation with him he somehow learnt the most intimate pockets of Sinclair's history and read them back like a part-biography, part-expose.

Has he been looking into Sinclair this entire time? Even before I approached him.

It was the only explanation she could think of. And as a result, it meant Carter had far too much power in this confrontation; every ounce of which he was ready to wield in order to get answers.

"Choose your next words carefully Carter."

"Is it?"

Sinclair refused to reply. As each revelation came to light he could see himself falling further into darkness.

"If it were just one thing then maybe I wouldn't care," Carter continued. "But there's just so much. And then I found out you're former Zero Bridge. God only knows…"

Sinclair shook his head, his face teeming with fear.

"Even if you find Stafford…£250k won't pull you out of debt. So many expenses, so many liabilities. They really do stack up don't they? Addictions aren't cheap either. It's a real shame."

"I even started wondering...how much for the *soul* of Sebastian Sinclair...for him to sell out a client. You're not really carrying your weight on this matter, you haven't really done anything – I wonder...is it on purpose?"

Sinclair's face filled with repulsion.

"You think I've got something to do with it. You think I've been bought?"

Carter shrugged his shoulders. "A man of your character...I wouldn't put it past you."

Sinclair could see the subtle shift in confidence, the trust dissipating from the faces of Jack, Katrina and Elizabeth.

"Where do you get the right?"

"What right?" Carter asked, puzzled.

"The right to claim I'm a villain. To stand on your moral high horse and tell me that I'm wrong and I've done bad. Don't think for a fucking second I don't know the kind of guy you are. *Investor?* Not for a fucking second. Appearing at a time when these two fuckers go missing. Are you kidding me? I don't know who the fuck you are but you definitely got something else going on here. I fucking know you do. You tell us...what do you gain...what do you achieve when it's all over Mr Michael Carter?"

"This investment is important to me. Stafford's return cements it. But presently you're the single greatest obstacle to that outcome and I won't allow it. And judging from what I've heard so far, you need to get off this investigation...now.

"I'm not fucking doing anything. You can't prove a single thing you just said. I told you I left at 11. I didn't do half the things you think I did so I don't know what the fuck you're talking about. And I sure as hell wouldn't sell out Elizabeth!"

Carter examined Sinclair very closely. The way he breathed, the manner in which he spoke, the rattling of his bones. All of it in an effort to better understand the man who'd potentially deceived him.

More than most, Carter certainly knew about deception. He regularly stood from the trees and looked down on those that might attempt it again, spitting from the skies whenever someone presumed they could shroud his vision.

"Do you really think anyone here trusts you now," Carter asked. "The only thing I see is a track record of failure and betrayal. And what...because your wife is dead. Why can't you just tell me truth?"

"I...am...telling you the truth."

Sinclair was doing everything in his power to hold himself back.

"I told you, I've already seen your file. Enough people have died because of your actions. No one wants another. Save yourself the honour. Christ, do you even think your wife would respect you right now? A man who's *massacred hundreds*. A *coward* who'd be willing to betray the man he's been tasked to save..."

A whirlwind of anger overcame Sinclair.

"You fucking bastard!"

He launched himself at Carter but Jack leapt in between, desperate to keep them apart.

Jack struggled to keep Sinclair where he was. He gripped his arms and forced himself forwards but it wasn't enough.

"Sinclair, I'm sorry but you have to tell me now. Do you know where he is?"

"Enough of your shit!"

At this point his strength was far too much. Sinclair flung Jack into the edge of the door and stormed towards Carter.

Carter pivoted to the side and pushed Sinclair behind him and into Stafford's desk. Piles of papers dropped to the floor, and one of Stafford's trophies was catapulted into the wall as Sinclair collapsed across the desk.

Carter stepped backwards. "What aren't you telling us?"

"You don't get to speak about her. Or what I've lost. I've had enough of this."

Jack tried to approach him but Sinclair pushed him to the side. "Get the fuck off me."

Carter stared into the eyes of an uncontrollable force. One that he alone had unleashed. A man ruled by turmoil and anguish alone. He had initially wondered whether Jeff was wrong. It may have made things easier and yet his scepticism was so far from the truth; so far from anything he'd imagined even if he had believed him.

"You're going to pay for this," Sinclair said.

At that moment Sinclair did what Carter hoped might never happen. Carter always knew it was a possibility but he hoped he may have gotten an answer before it came to fruition.

Sinclair drew back his charcoal jacket and lifted his 9mm pistol out of his holster. Carter immediately went for his own but Sinclair had the advantage. He was immersed in rage and adrenaline. He was faster, more agile. He had far too much to prove and was unrivalled in what he might lose.

As Carter raised his gun Sinclair had already pointed his weapon in his direction.

Everyone stepped back in horror.

Events had collapsed around them and Carter instantly realised that it couldn't end now – not like this. He was far from finished. He couldn't die at Sinclair's hands.

In the seconds that followed, fate chose to align with his belief.

Sinclair pulled the trigger and fired. He pressed it over and over.

However, something happened. Something no one expected. Not a single bullet was fired.

Carter had drawn his weapon and was stood ready to shoot but stopped. He saw, like everyone else in the room, that there was no ammunition present in Sinclair's weapon. The sliding mechanism at the top of his gun had locked backwards.

Why would he carry a weapon with no ammo? Obviously you keep some in the pistol. Exactly for a situation like this I would guess.

Had the gun been loaded Carter would have been dead and yet he stood alive and well.

Sinclair was baffled. He couldn't figure out why it was empty. He always kept it loaded.

Carter took a deep breath, calming his nerves and lowering his weapon. Everyone else in the room took a sigh of relief.

"If you're as smart as I think you are," Carter said, "then that weapon would already be loaded."

Sinclair stood in silence, his empty weapon still pointed at Carter. He was still staring at the locked slider.

"Which means that in some way, shape or form," Carter continued, "you must've fired every bullet in that clip."

Carter thought for a moment.

He denies being at the Grayson Arms. Refuses to acknowledge half the things he's done. But Jeff said it, didn't he... loss of memory. And he doesn't remember firing the weapon...what if he's not lying...

If the latter fits the build of the former...

Carter's pulse began to accelerate aggressively.

"How many bullets are in that clip?"

Sinclair was still silent.

"Sinclair!"

Silence.

"Answer the fucking question!"

Carter's patience was wearing thin.

Sinclair turned his eyes up from the slider. "Eight."

"You don't remember firing eight bullets. You don't remember leaving the Grayson Arms at 1.30am. Just as you attacked those men. Just as you received a phone call from Elizabeth telling you that Stafford and Max were kidnapped. Not too far from where you were – that you'd receive £250k if you find them. The exact same time that two men, those who took Stafford and Max, were executed on the street, eight bullets across the two of them."

Sinclair dropped his gun on the ground and fell back against Stafford's desk.

"It was you…wasn't it? You killed them and you don't even remember. And you must've saw them too – Max and Stafford. But you don't remember any of it. Not a single thing."

Carter took a brief pause to collect his thoughts.

"Christ, I knew you were out of control but this is… And you know what, this wasn't even the alcohol was it? This…this was something else. Some kind of…sick, twisted addiction to violence."

Sinclair slid against the side of Stafford's desk and slowly fell to the floor. He sat upright, his knees bent against his chest. He clutched his head in his hands, as if in agony.

As Carter watched Sinclair's mind begin to unravel, deep down he knew that he still didn't know everything and that his work remained incomplete.

The dust settled, he readied a different kind of weapon and prepared to fire once more.

CHAPTER 20

Like an imposing, imperial tower, Carter loomed over Sinclair as he sat clutching his head. A dark cloud had cast itself over Sinclair and Carter could see faint wisps of perspiration on his shirt and a jitter in his hands which resembled someone who might also be shivering.

"I'm afraid we're not done here."

Carter clutched Sinclair by the collar of his shirt and lifted him up. Sinclair did little to resist, his legs numb and devoid of any feeling. As he lay in Carter's grip, he felt as if he was sailing through the air, the lower half of his body barely functioning.

Carter looked on in disgust as he saw a lifeless expression on his face. It was the mark of man with no purpose. It epitomised a man of nothing and a willingness to stand for nothing. Such was the antithesis of Carter's being.

Carter slammed him into the wall. "Don't bow out just yet," he whispered. "We're not finished."

There was a sinister undercurrent to his voice. It forced Sinclair to momentarily snap out of his self-pity and consider the severity of his situation.

Carter stepped closer, tightening his grip. "Do you remember what happened?"

"I-I."

"Answer me."

"Carter, you need to stop," Jack said trying to come between them. "We're not going to get answers this way. We need to calm him down. We need to get him at ease. Jesus, we don't even know what's happened."

Carter turned to him, keeping his hands enclosed around Sinclair's shirt. "Listen Jack. He forgot. I don't know if it was the alcohol. I don't know if it's years of drug abuse, mental anarchy or whatever fuck else he had wrong with him, but it means he has no recollection of beating the shit out of however many people he did at the Grayson Arms. It means he doesn't remember killing two men on the street. And he doesn't remember seeing Stafford and Max. The very people he's been told to find. Does he sound reliable to you? Are you telling me you really trust a man like that?"

"Yea-well. No. I get that. But you think he's going to unravel with you smashing him into walls."

"I need to do something Jack. And this is what I do best."

"Jack, just leave Carter to it," Katrina cut in.

Jack looked around to see her leaning against the wall. She had her arms folded, as if she were trying to tell him *I told you so*. It was also the picture of the young woman observing from afar while attempting to hide an uneasy desire to persevere.

That image was all Jack needed in order to suspect that Katrina may have had something to do with this. Clearly, expressing her concerns to him wasn't enough. Instead, she had decided to confide in someone she didn't completely trust and evidently, lacked the foresight to predict how they might respond.

All the while, Elizabeth stood between them both,

trying to rationalise the revelations which were coming to light. She had promised Sinclair as the man who would have answers; someone with deep experience and critical thinking who would generate the solution they so desperately sought. But this moment in time painted a very different picture. Carter had reduced him to liar and a shell of unbalanced temperament that lay in the centre of a predicament that no one could have envisioned.

"Give him a minute," Elizabeth said. A modicum of guilt rang in her voice. As if Sinclair was somehow her responsibility.

Carter loosened his grip. "No less."

He watched as Sinclair slowly regained his senses. Faint memories of his past meandered into sight and then quickly faded away. Each was wrapped in a fog of misinterpretation as he struggled to distinguish truth from falsehood.

The minute lapsed and Carter's muscles stiffened.

"Let's take this from the beginning." He let go of Sinclair's collar and stepped back. "What do you remember about the Grayson Arms? Do you remember attacking those men outside?"

Sinclair closed his eyes. "It – it had been a few hours. I had been drinking for a few hours. Maybe more. But I remember seeing some guys at the bar. I remember things escalated."

"Why?"

"I – I don't know. We went outside and then…I was just…"

"Ok, ok. I'm not going to ask you for details. I'm not interested in that. You attacked them. You hurt them. For whatever reason. None of my concern. That's fine. And then what?"

"I walked around. I was still in a haze. I can't remember how long for. I just sort of drifted from place to place."

"Why is he remembering this all now?" Elizabeth asked.

Carter took another step back. "It's possible the memory about Stafford and Max triggered something other related memories. If I had to guess."

"Where did you go next?" Carter asked, turning his attention back to Sinclair.

Sinclair opened his eyes. He stared at the ground, still trying to amalgamate his thoughts.

"Don't know. I kept walking. Then I stopped. I felt this vibration on my pocket. My phone. I picked it up and stared at it."

Elizabeth leaned forward in amazement. *Christ. He can't mean.*

"It…was Elizabeth. I thought why not take the call, so I answered. She told me about what happened to Stafford and Max. Said she needed help. But it wasn't my problem. I didn't want anything to do with it but then…"

"She offered you the money."

"I needed it. I couldn't afford not to. So I said yeah. And then it gets…"

"Gets what?"

"I – I don't know. I can't…"

Carter briefly turned away. One of Stafford's trophies lay by his feet. The edges were scuffed and the base had cracked. He was careful not to step on any documents but also felt too preoccupied to pick anything up either.

"You went after them. Right? Max and Stafford. As soon as that call was over. Why?"

"I can't remember. I just…" His eyes expanded with concentration and he searched his mind the way someone dug through an empty, endless sack. "I just felt like I needed to go and get them…there and then. I'm not –"

"If you don't remember then that's fine," Carter shrugged. "But I can probably fill in the blanks. I think I have enough."

Elizabeth gently scratched her nails against the fabric of her suit. It continued to glow exquisitely as it hugged her thin frame.

"So why did he go there then?" she asked.

"You," Carter replied.

"*Me?*"

Elizabeth purposely raised her eyebrows and made a show of her mystification.

"Yeah. You rang him. You rang a man who had just come off the back of one fierce assault and decided to propel him towards another. Someone who was not in his senses. Someone who has a history of violence, hell-bent on harm and has absolutely no problem dropping a body if it means being the hero. Jesus, he'd probably do it even if you didn't call him."

"You're saying this is my fault?" Elizabeth retorted.

"Of course not. You didn't shoot anyone. That's on him. But you definitely set him on his way. Probably hung up that phone and thought he had an opportunity to put some bodies in the ground and get paid for it. Given Sinclair's disposition, given who he is and what he's done...I'm not at all surprised he went to kill them."

There was no reason why Sinclair would disavow any of Carter's statements since he knew they were almost certainly true. But despite all of this, for his own sanity, Sinclair couldn't help but try and ignore what Carter was suggesting. His preference was that he could forget or at the very least hide his sins and transgressions. Yet, the more Carter spoke, the more they etched themselves into his mind and inflamed his guilt.

Carter tapped Stafford's trophy along the floor with the tip of his shoe and moved back to face Sinclair.

"So what do you remember then?" Carter said. "After the call."

Sinclair lifted his head.

"I know I headed for the Field. I knew where it was

and I knew they couldn't have gotten far. And I was right. I walked and I walked and then I saw it. Just like she described. Some old man, and a youngster, being carried away by these two men in the heart of night."

"What did you do?"

"I did exactly what someone like me *would* do. I drew my weapon and I walked towards them. One of them shouted. I don't remember which. He panicked and pushed Stafford behind him. I didn't hesitate. I fired three shots into his head. His body dropped like a bag of sand. The other tried to remove his weapon. I emptied my clip before he could do anything. His blood stained the pavement. Empty eyes looking back at me."

Sinclair's face was ingrained with concentration and a pulse of anger.

"What about Stafford and Max?"

"Terrified. Both of them. I got closer. But when I tried to speak I couldn't. They were scared. And so they ran. I wanted to follow them but...I fell. I collapsed. I couldn't move. Something just...my body just gave up by that point."

"Where did they go?"

"They ran down the street. I saw them go into some hotel. The Canal, I think it was."

Carter's attention fell on Jack, Katrina and Elizabeth. "Do either of you know it?"

"Yeah," Jack said. "It was probably the only place around here that was open at the time."

"So you're saying they're safe. Stafford and Max," Katrina said.

Sinclair shook his head. He took a deep breath. "A car pulled up behind them. I saw two men get out and follow them in. I tried to get up but I didn't have the will. They must've been with the two men who came to the Field."

"What do you remember after that?"

"I passed out. Everything went black. When I came to

I was home. I didn't remember anything."

"That's not true. You remember our call," Elizabeth remarked.

"I only remember it because I saw the message you sent me. It was enough to help me recall our chat, and nothing else."

"And then you came here," Carter said. "Under the guise of a man who knew nothing."

"It wasn't a guise. I really didn't know!"

"Keep your voice down," Carter warned.

"When I asked you," Katrina added, "about what happened last night – you acted as if everything was fine."

"I couldn't risk losing the opportunity. I needed the money. If I told you the truth – that I didn't remember anything that happened the previous night – would you have really let me continue?"

"Probably not," Katrina said.

Sinclair was breathing heavily. He leant forwards against Stafford's desk, continually running the sequence of events in his mind from start to finish. He sought to place the incident in his mind, as if he were inserting a deleted scene from a film, but found that he lacked the state of being that might accompany such an experience. Instead he felt like an observer who merely watched the memory from the outside.

"I guess you weren't lying when you said you'd kill the people who stood between us and our friends," Jack muttered. "I just didn't realise you'd already done it."

"Don't condescend to me," Sinclair snapped.

"It's merely an observation."

"Oh, how I wish I was more like you Jack!" His voice lifted an octave and squeaked uncomfortably. "Nobility above all else. Although others might call it something else in this circumstance."

"I'll take that over depravity."

Sinclair's temperament rattled his body, hinging

between anger and distaste.

"Enough. We're not done." Carter stepped forwards, breaking the line of sight between Sinclair and Jack. "What do you remember about the men? The ones who went into the Canal."

"I still don't remember anything. It's unclear. I –."

"Stop fucking around. I need more!"

Sinclair was overcome with anxiety. His breathing started to intensify.

Carter moved closer, his eyes searing with fire.

"Carter, I can't –"

"You just don't have it in you, do you?"

Carter slammed his palm on Stafford's desk and the shockwave rattled a jar of pens clumped together in a clay pot. His disappointment diffused throughout the room but Carter still found himself overwhelmed by frustration.

"You were obviously the wrong man for the job," Carter continued. "And you lied about your failures. You know, if you lived in my universe…you'd have died a long time ago. I'm even a little surprised you're still here. With your track record, maybe you should do the universe a favour…"

"That's enough!" Elizabeth shouted. "We have what we need. He's not going to tell us anything more. He doesn't *know* anything more."

"There's always more."

Sinclair's hands were like vices; clutching the table as he tried to maintain his composure. He was starting to tremble.

"We have our answers Carter. Stop with this ridiculous assault. He doesn't deserve this."

"Elizabeth, your friend is morally flawed in more ways than you can imagine. He's a straight killer. He purposely lied to us and he diverted us from the answers we needed. And he jeopardised this entire investigation for the sake of his own monetary gain. Let me be clear – he absolutely deserves this."

"You talk from a position of high ground?"

"What's that supposed to mean?"

"Just that I've met a great many men in my time, all of whom were very quick to dish out judgement as if it were their own right. So few ever got it right and so few were ever exempt by their own standards."

Carter chuckled. "Wisdom is an admirable quality Miss Jones. I just wish you were wise enough to have known that your man couldn't be trusted."

He glanced in Jack's direction and Jack saw in him a faint feeling of satisfaction. It seemed like a valve had been turned; a short burst of steam had erupted and Carter had finally calmed down.

"You can stay here and look after him," Carter said to Elizabeth. "I'm going to the Canal." He turned to Jack and Katrina. "You both coming? I think I might need directions."

They nodded. As quick as the circumstances may have changed, neither of them had a choice. The clock was counting down and they needed to make progress as quickly as they could. Following Carter was their best bet at this point.

Carter glanced at Sinclair. His expression rang out with disgust before he swiftly rushed out of the office, Jack and Katrina following behind him.

Katrina couldn't help but grapple with a sense of responsibility over the events that had taken place. Although she understood the necessity, the guilt for tearing into Sinclair's psyche was all too clear. She may not have delivered the outcome but her role as a messenger to the man who theorised a solution no one could have predicted was enough to find her culpable.

What she also realised, whether she liked it or not, was that her faith in finding Stafford and Max now sat squarely with Carter and Carter alone; a man that she struggled to understand but one who also had a resolve that unfortunately reminded her of someone else she knew.

CHAPTER 21

Once Ajay and Vijay had left the private dining area, an awkward silence permeated across the room. No one felt like speaking or eating. No one even wanted to move. The quiet had brought the mechanics of the room to a standstill.

Half-finished pieces of bread and sporadic glops of olive oil lay across a table with two empty chairs.

Jack was afraid to make eye contact with Max. He knew his error was anything but erroneous and contrary to what he'd been instructed and yet nevertheless, he did as he pleased, forcing his solutions upon the world.

Max finished his glass of wine. He placed it on the table and pushed it into the centre of the table.

"Happy?" Max unexpectedly blurted out.

Jack wasn't looking at Max but he could see his fiery gaze from the corner of his eye, beating down upon him like rays of sunshine in the Sahara.

"Listen, I wasn't –"

"Shut up!" Max fired. "You goddamn idiot. What the fuck were you thinking?"

Max had forgotten Marina was still sat around the

table. Her eye flared up as soon as Max started speaking.

"Max, that's no way to talk to him," she said.

"I think it's warranted. He just wrecked this entire fucking deal."

Jack continued to look away. "They deserve a solution. If there *is* one, they should *have* one."

"Fuck me, did you not hear a word they said. They are fucked. Both of them. Every 'solution' you think you have, has been presented and then wiped away like a bug on a fucking windscreen. There is no solution."

"Someone is missing-"

"No! You should've done as you were told. You knew it was a hot topic and you still went for it. Do you just get a fucking kick out of ignoring what people say? Do you honestly think you know better? That you know these guys better than I do – guys I've known for years."

"I thought I could help…I thought I could figure something out."

"You didn't help fucking no one. Not them, and definitely not me."

"He gets the point," Marina said. The soft sound of her voice brought the tension to a halt. "Cut him some slack."

"That's tough to do, partly because I know exactly where you're about to land on this whole matter."

Marina fell back in her chair and raised her eyes to the ceiling. "I told you from day 1 Max – I don't want to put up my end of the capital unless I've got a partner. An extra person gives you some more liquidity and makes the whole venture a lot safer for me. My board won't allow anything less."

"I know they won't. But you shouldn't feel bad. This situation isn't your doing."

Max refilled his glass. "I fucking hate this shit."

"But you're still drinking it?" Marina asked.

"Someone needs to."

"Well don't hog it all," Marina said. She took the

bottle from Max and topped up her glass. "Max, you've got to remember, Ajay and Vijay were on thin ice as it was. Anything could've set them off."

"Which is why I worked so hard to make sure that we avoided all those possibilities."

"You don't control fate Mr Mortimer." Marina spun her glass in her hand, and took a large gulp. She continued to spin the glass, watching drops of wine slide down along the edges. "You too Jack. No one man can solve every problem that comes their way just because they will it."

Jack was staring at the table. His heart was pounding. The realisation was dawning upon him now. There would be no investment. There would be nothing to trade with. And that would mean nothing that could generate a return for the company. The entire venture was about to come crashing into the ground because he'd been adamant to try and solve someone's problem for them; by virtue of believing that he had skills and knowledge to do so. Was it naïve? Yes. Was it foolish? Yes. Was it absurd to believe that it may have turned out any other way than it did and that there would be something other than the consequences that had been set forth upon reality? Absolutely, one hundred percent, yes.

And despite all of this, Jack still, without any remorse, in the back of his mind, could feel that something was still missing. Something that everyone was not considering. In the face of absolute failure and the collapse of everything he, Stafford, Max, Katrina and Elizabeth had worked towards, his belief in his own ability to find something that no one else saw, eclipsed everything.

Marina sighed. "It's a real shame about Ajay and Vijay. That deal, on paper, looked remarkable. It was a sure fire way to make money. And the company didn't just sell chemicals to Nigerian companies. They sold to the Nigerian government too. That's why I brought it up initially. When I was doing research into the region, I saw that only recently, ministers had passed a law which said all chemicals which are purchased by foreign embassies and military outposts in the region must purchase from the government and no one else. Apparently a part of some new law to help local companies. Ajay and Vijay's company was essentially a sub-contractor to the government so they could provide those chemicals to foreign governments. Those continual sales to the government would have netted them a fortune. Now there's talk that the government might take state ownership of it to fulfil their obligations which is just a terrible, terrible, state of affairs."

Jack's head shot up. "So the CEO had won government public sector contracts. He was an ex-minister wasn't he?"

"Yes," Marina said.

Jack still wasn't making eye contact. "The same CEO who went around paying bribes to private companies to win private contracts?"

"Yes."

"And these public sector contracts were for sales of chemicals to foreign governments."

"Yes."

"And now there's a possibility that the Nigerian Government will take the company and then, produce and sell the chemicals themselves."

"What are you saying here?" Max asked.

"I'm saying…that I was right to say that there's a solution here."

Jack erupted from his chair and ran towards the exit. He quickly turned around.

"Go outside, stop Vijay from getting into his taxi and bring him to the bar at all costs. I'll go get Ajay. And then…we close this deal."

CHAPTER 22

Carter hastily glided through the doors of the Field as Jack and Katrina rushed after him. The faint wisps of wind collided against the three of them. Carter's unbuttoned overcoat fluttered backwards into the distance while he waited for someone to direct him. Jack nudged his head to the right and Carter stormed down the street in a hurry.

"I can't believe we've finally got a lead," Jack said.

Jack's excitement seemed devoid of the circumstances that conceived it. So much was his dramatism that Katrina couldn't help but wonder whether Jack thought he was being filmed.

"I told you I'd get him back," Carter said.

"Yeah. I never thought it'd happen the way it did though. What we did to Sinclair I mean."

"I know what you meant. But what are you saying?" Carter's tone became sharp. "You feel sorry for him?"

"No, I get it. He's not who we thought he was. I just wonder whether it was all completely necessary – the way we went about it."

"I don't regret it Jack. I did exactly what was required. Any less meant that Sinclair would have found a way out of it and continue keeping the truth from us."

They took another right at the end of the street and spotted a homeless man wearing a large tan hat and resting against the wall. He briefly opened his eyes and then fell back into his mid-afternoon snooze the same way an elderly farmer might initially greet someone on their porch.

The Grayson Arms wasn't far from where they were and Katrina noticed pubs of a similar nature. Cheerful and merry pedestrians wandered by, stumbling from left to right. One tried to open a pack of cigarettes and dropped a bunch on the floor. A flock of old vans and lorries rumbled down the road and covered their view of the street with a dull blank canvas. The fumes engulfed the air and left a charcoal taste in their wake while a cyclist tore between them and raced down a side road.

"I guess we didn't really have much of a choice," Katrina said. "But I was just shocked at how much you knew about him. I thought I dug up a lot – but you knew way more than anything I could've gotten a hold of."

Carter eyes were fixed down the street.

"How did you find it all out?" she asked.

It was the obvious question. How a man, potentially under the appearance of an investor, was able to gather so much confidential information in such a short period of time. Notwithstanding his willingness to stare down the barrel of a gun to get the answers he needed, as well as extract an almost impossible truth from vague facts and recollections.

"I *am* an investor Katrina. Just not in the strict definition you're used to. What that caveat means is that I'm slightly more well-connected; enough to get what I need when I need it."

"Still doesn't tell us very much does it," Jack remarked.

"I liked riddles when I was a kid," Katrina said. "These

days, I find them…"

"The best way for me to be honest," Carter interrupted. "Appreciate the sentiment."

Katrina crossed her arms over her cardigan. *Another non-answer.*

After several minutes they found themselves at the front entrance of the Canal. Bathed in light blue paint with uniquely wide doors, the Canal was a hotel venue for loners or professionals rather than tourists. It encompassed a silent, depression era sensibility which never made it particularly appealing to the average holiday goer.

They all walked inside to what was a well decorated reception area and two staircases of equal size, one leading upwards and the other down. There were old fashioned lamps clung to the walls and some burnt out candles in various clusters around the room. As well as the lamps, there was a large chandelier which kept the room reasonably bright and vibrant.

There was a young man sat at the counter who, unless they approached his desk, didn't seem particularly engaging.

"You been here before," Katrina said, glancing at Jack.

"Yeah, once or twice. Still looks the same to be honest."

"Well which way then?" Carter asked.

"I think the rooms and the restaurants are upstairs. The restaurant is on the top floor and there's a small bar downstairs. Thing is, if Stafford came in here, unless he rang the bell at the desk and waited a few minutes, he wouldn't have been served here. He probably needed to find someone as quick as possible."

Katrina scratched her head. "So you think he went downstairs."

Carter spotted a small sign near the staircase. "It's pointing to the bar below. If Stafford and Max came here that might've been their best chance at finding someone."

"Makes sense," Jack said.

"To be honest what matters is whether there's any cameras," Carter said. "And for a venue like this, I'd expect they do."

They all proceeded downstairs, gripping the stair railing as they made their descent. The railing felt cold and its chrome metallic colour glimmered against the light of the lamps. Three pairs of footsteps, deeply meshed between one another, smacked against the marble staircase, over and over until they reached the bottom.

Immediately in front of them was a doorway leading to a large room. The floor was sticky and made a kissing sound each time someone moved. Inside a bar extended from the entrance right the way to the end of the room. The surface had a certain shine to it and seemed to have just been wiped down. Shelves of bottles sat behind it and were on display as if they were in a used bookstore. On the other side were tables situated around the room and surrounded by dark cushioned chairs. Tall and narrow menus were planted in the centre of each table like a flag poles and waved the names of cocktails to passers-by.

Fancy, Katrina thought.

There was a young man at the far side of the room who was sat on the bar and on the phone. He craned his head towards the entrance and watched as everyone entered. Swinging it back into place, he continued with his conversation while tapping away at a tablet computer on his lap.

Carter examined the room carefully looking for any sort of camera equipment. As he continued to peer across the walls Jack tapped him on the shoulder.

"Up there. Far left."

In the far left corner of the room there was a small black cone with a miniscule red light.

"Good," Carter said. "We just need to be sure Stafford

was in here now."

The man at the end of the room had finished his conversation and made his way towards them, his tablet clutched between his fingers.

"Afternoon," he said vibrantly. "My name's Marco. What can I help you with?"

He was young, plainly dressed in a white t-shirt and a pair of light blue jeans. His beard was faint although long enough that someone could notice it was slightly uneven.

"Are you the owner here?" Carter asked.

"Sort of. My dad is actually, but I take care of most stuff around here."

"Right, well, I was wondering if you were working here last night - between 1am and 3am?" Carter asked.

"Are you a police officer?" Marco's voice turned slightly tense.

"No. I just need some help with a few questions."

Marco's breathing slightly dropped in pace. "What questions exactly?"

"Well firstly the one that I just asked?"

Carter's tone was borderline sarcastic and Marco looked either too tired or too indifferent to even notice.

"I was…but by that time there's no one really here on the ground and bottom floors so all of the staff are sent upstairs to take care of admin and other things in preparation for tomorrow morning."

"So you're saying that if someone came down here, no one would have any idea," Jack said.

"Well…no," Marco muttered.

"I'm looking for two people," Carter said. "I need to know if they were here last night and I guess the only way to find out is by looking at the footage on that camera."

Carter pointed to the far left corner of the room. Marco spun around to get a look at the camera in question, a slight reservation creeping into his mind.

"You know I can't just show any random bloke our

CCTV footage," Marco said sharply. "Why should I let you see it?"

"They're in danger," Jack said.

"No offence mate, but you could easily be lying. I get enough of that as it is. Can't take any chances. Plus my dad would probably kill me."

"We only need it for a few rooms," Katrina said politely. "It'll hardly cause you a lot of trouble. I swear."

"Yeah…sorry – still not convinced."

"You don't get it," Jack said. He was starting to get agitated. "This is our only shot at helping our friends. There isn't another way."

"Mate – I really couldn't care less. You seem like a smart guy – I'm sure you'll figure something out."

Marco turned and headed for the staircase but Jack skidded to the right, blocking his path.

"No. You don't understand. This *is* the way."

"Move," Marco said.

"No. Not until I see the footage."

After so much confusion Jack wasn't about to let such a minor obstacle get in his way. He felt overwhelmed, not by fear or anger, but by an intense amount of determination.

Marco moved closer but Jack stayed where he was. "Mate this isn't happening. Don't make it a thing."

"I'm doing everything in my power not to so don't push me any further."

"Enough!" Carter snapped.

Carter took a sharp breath and pulled back the edge of his coat.

Marco felt his heart almost stop as he realised the conversation may have just taken a turn for the worse.

Yet, much to everyone's surprise Carter drew a thick, black leather wallet from his inner coat pocket. The surface was flat and there were virtually no scuffs or marks on the sides. It appeared brand new; possibly purchased that very day. Carter opened it and placed a large pile of bank notes on the bar counter.

Having emptied the contents of the wallet, the pile was significant and sufficient enough to keep Marco's pulse racing.

Carter watched as Marco's eyes were fixated on the bank notes. His neck craned forwards as he attempted to examine their authenticity.

"That's £1,000 right there. I'll pay it to you right now if you give me that footage."

"Are you...are you being serious?" Marco stuttered.

"What do *you* think?"

Jack could tell that this might not have been Carter's first bribe and seeing as he walked around armed with a 9mm pistol, falling shy of the Bribery Act was probably the least of his worries.

Marco took a quick look around the bar and then cast his hand over the pile of notes and spread a few over the surface. Each looked like the one before it and his eyes widened. He glanced up at Carter who didn't seem particularly fussed with what was going on. He grouped the notes back up as quickly as he could and slipped them into his back pocket.

Marco switched on his tablet. After tapping several icons he placed it on the bar. "The footage is on there. Controls are pretty obvious. Widgets at the top let you switch between the rooms."

He walked out of the room, trying not to make eye contact. "You got ten minutes."

Carter placed his wallet back into his pocket.

"That was easier than I thought."

CHAPTER 23

Carter picked up the tablet and began forwarding the footage to the correct date and time while Jack and Katrina huddled around him.

"What time should we start from?" Carter said.

"We got in touch with Sinclair around 2am," Katrina said. "That was just after Stafford was kidnapped. That might be a good place to start."

"Alright."

Carter focussed on a camera that was near the entrance and ran the footage at a quicker speed.

He hadn't noticed the camera on his arrival which made him suspect it was carefully hidden. It also meant that whoever pursued Stafford and Max wouldn't have noticed it either.

As the footage played everyone's sights were locked on the screen, analysing it for the first sign of anything unusual. At first all they could see was the entrance, faintly lit and empty. If it weren't for pieces of rubbish rustling outside the door, they may as well have been staring at a still image.

The minutes ticked away and Jack could hear the

methodical tapping of Carter's fingers against the back of the tablet growing faster. Jack sensed that if they hadn't been there beside him he may have started shaking the tablet in the hope it might spur some activity.

Could Sinclair have been wrong? Carter thought.

He obviously wasn't in a state where he'd remember anything. Maybe this is the wrong building.

They continued to wait.

C'mon! Where is he?

There and then an elderly man in a jumper unexpectedly burst through the entrance. Behind him was a young man, cloaked in a sharply tailored three-piece suit. Both their faces were horror struck and they moved so frantically that it seemed as if they weren't in control of their own bodies.

"Shit…they were actually here," Jack said.

Carter flicked between the different cameras as they made their way through the hotel.

They walked past an empty reception desk, briefly leaning over to see if there was anyone they could speak to. Realising there was no one around they rushed down the stairs and into the bar. They paced up and down and their heads swivelled from left to right like a pair of out of sync pendulums, desperate to find anyone that could help. The quality of the footage may have been poor but the distraught looks on their faces were as visible as they needed to be when it became apparent that there was nowhere to go from here.

As the footage continued, Carter spotted something on another camera. Two men. Both making their way inside and down the stairs.

"There they are," Carter said.

He was right. Sinclair was actually right.

"Who are they?" Katrina asked.

"I can't make them out," Carter replied.

One of the men was nothing short of a titan, almost

bursting out of the suit he was wearing. The other was tall, albeit still shorter than the other, and wore a dark grey buttoned up trench coat.

As they descended, the panicked reaction on Stafford and Max's face became all the more clear. Jack could imagine it; the ominous sounds of footsteps resonating through the bar, gradually moving closer and closer, echoing in their ears and calling for their surrender.

It was painful to watch. He couldn't fathom what they may have been feeling at that point; a raft of fear and uncertainty as two figures pursued them in the aftermath of an abduction and dual execution. The terror was no doubt unbearable and it continued to evolve across their faces moment by moment.

When the steps stopped, four men stood in the bar.

Stafford and Max stepped backwards but the man in the suit drew his weapon almost instantaneously. Stafford briefly spoke but it seemed to fall on deaf ears. After a few seconds Stafford and Max were marched outside and the two men followed from behind, monitoring them like prisoners. The transition to capture was so sudden and in those moments the colour drained from Stafford and Max's eyes and it was there that the helplessness of their circumstance became unmistakeable.

The cameras trailed their rise back to the surface but Carter quickly paused the footage and flicked to the camera which displayed the staircase. The frame on the tablet was the clearest image they'd seen of the kidnappers so far.

Carter removed his phone and took a photograph of the men on the tablet. Carter put his phone away and took a sharp breath.

"I wonder who they are," Jack said.

Katrina looked at Carter who was scrutinising the image. His face was riddled with focus.

"Do you know them?" Katrina asked suspiciously.

"I don't know."

"It's not a hard question."

Carter didn't reply. His phone buzzed. He had received a text.

Suit – Arthur Cassano. Security Consultant for Terrence Caulfield (lawyer).

Other – call me. Now!

"According to my associate, the man in the suit is someone called Arthur Cassano. Some kind of security consultant for a lawyer called Terrence Caulfield."

"What the hell would someone like that want with Stafford?"

Carter shook his head. "Not sure. But his day to day profession is probably distinct from whatever he's doing here. I assume he's just been hired to do a job."

"But we can find him," Jack said. "We know who we works for. We can track him down."

"Yeah."

There was an uneasiness to Carter as he spoke. It wasn't the man in the suit that had caught his attention.

Jack and Katrina found it hard not to notice. The expression was out of turn for someone who normally seemed so calm.

"Who's the man in the coat?" Katrina probed. "Your *associate* say anything about him?"

Carter didn't say anything. He was staring at the tablet again, shut off in his own little world, running scenarios and alternatives through his head, each more complex than the last.

"Carter!" Katrina said, trying to get his attention. "Who is he?"

"I'm not sure. Not yet."

Before Katrina could press further she noticed her own phone going off. It was Elizabeth.

"Shit. I promised I'd tell Elizabeth whether Sinclair's story checked out. Give me five minutes."

Katrina stepped outside while Carter continued staring at the screen.

"Carter?" Jack asked. "How would you even know this guy?"

Carter raised his head. "I'll know soon enough." He removed his phone. After tapping a few buttons he placed it against his ear, taking several steps away from Jack.

"Jeff. What is it?"

"Don't be stupid. You know why I told you to call me."

The way Jeff reacted sometimes reminded him of an overzealous American preacher. He lectured rather than spoke and the words dropped on the world with a large thud.

"I might've figured it out, yeah. If I'm honest I wasn't too sure initially."

"Oh, make no mistake. It's him all right."

Carter sighed. "Alright."

"Listen, this whole venture is getting to be a little more problematic than we first planned and that's not to say it wasn't problematic already. That guy is going to cause way more trouble than anything we were expecting. I mean seriously, who the fuck would get him involved? For this?"

"I don't know. But he's here. And I can deal with it."

"*Deal with it?* I don't fucking think so. Listen, I was reluctant initially but I want to send in some of my guys. They'll back you on this. Especially when things are getting a bit too dangerous for my liking."

"Absolutely not. As soon as anyone steps on the ground you'll blow everything. I don't need any protection."

"You're one man. And he will do something you won't expect. Take the reinforcement. I'm not letting you bare a risk like this."

Carter often studied a person's choice of words. They

provided a rare perspective into how one interpreted their surroundings and their influence or authority over others. He thought about Jeff's quite regularly.

"Anyone you send is going to cause me more issues than its worth. I'm better suited to handling this on my own. Plus, I've got the kid. Morse."

"The kid. The maths kid? Fuck off."

"Yeah, I mean it. He's good. He's sharp. And he's perfect for this. He's the right kind of mind. This situation doesn't require your lug-head team. You'll only make matters worse."

The statement caught Jack's attention. *When did I become a part of this?*

Jack could see something about the way that Carter spoke in that he expressed a unique form of confidence; one that was accompanied by the faintest form of deceit.

"Listen, if you think the boy's up to it. Sure – act at your own discretion. But don't forget why you're there – and what your objective is. A lot of people are depending on you Carter. Remember, I've given you a long leash but do *not* turn this into some one-man crusade. This is very much a controlled experiment. *Understand*."

Carter glanced at Jack, and then to the two men frozen on the tablet. "*Understood*."

"Keep me posted Carter. I don't want this to get out of hand."

"Yeah."

He hung up.

This isn't his battle. I'll handle it myself.

Jack could see the tension burrowing away into Carter. Something about the phone call had perturbed him.

"Carter, is everything ok?"

"No," he said exhaling. "Jack, we have a problem."

"What?"

"The man on the camera. The one in the coat. When you and Katrina asked me earlier, whether I knew him…the answer is yes. Not personally but I know of him."

"Who is he?"

"His name is David Kessler."

Carter walked to the tablet, analysing the image again, as if it might yield more details or answers previously unseen about a man he knew so little about.

"He's an operative…for hire. He's responsible for conducting all sorts of operations in various jurisdictions. He sets up small teams where necessary and he's normally paid very well for his services."

"Like a mercenary?"

"In a sense…yes. Kessler is a little different. He doesn't always fight wars per se. Not anymore anyway. But don't be surprised if he's the sort who's responsible for one."

"How would you even know about him?" There was a small quiver in Jack's words.

"I told you I was well-connected Jack. I cross a lot of people with a lot of problems and Kessler's a name that's appeared more than once. Repercussions aren't uncommon when he's a piece on the board."

"So he's dangerous?"

"Yeah."

"Well, what does that mean?"

"It means there's a large sphere of influence around Stafford's kidnapping. He must've been the man on the phone – the one on speaker – but ultimately working under the employment of someone more unstable – probably Reinhart if our guesses are correct."

"We still don't know that," Jack said. "It's only a hunch."

"It's the only one that makes any sense right now. I'm inclined to go with it until something better comes along."

Instincts were all Carter ever relied on anymore. They were his lifeline to judging a situation, gauging dishonesty and anticipating the future. He may not have known Stafford or the situation very well but something told him that the unexpected arrival of Reinhart was too precarious to ignore.

"Do you know anything about how this Kessler guy operates?" Jack probed.

"Not a lot. I hear he runs his jobs with serious precision. But with this one he probably wasn't expecting Sinclair to shoot down two of his men, which meant he had to get involved himself. He always was…adaptable."

Given the nature of who he was and what he did, there were types of individuals – those that were precursors to risk or danger – that Jack might never encounter. In fact, the same could have been said about almost anyone. But as of right now such people were continuing to infect Jack's universe at an alarming rate and it was as if someone was pulling back a curtain and revealing a world that he had never taken notice of.

"If this is the situation then why did you think that *I* can help?" Jack asked. "You said that on the phone didn't you?"

Carter had forgotten what guilt felt like. The turmoil was, up until now, a distant echo in his mind. So few moments in his life allowed for its emergence.

"Jack, I'd like to ask you something."

"Sure."

"What do you want out of all this?"

The simplicity of the question reminded Jack of something he had been entangled with in the past. The answer was obvious but in previous instances it had felt unknowable.

"Stafford and Max," he replied. "What else were you expecting?"

"I thought there may have been something else."

The damp smell of stained alcohol still roamed the bar. As Jack tried to generate a response he felt a momentous whiff suddenly stun his senses.

"As much as this situation is a curse," Carter continued, "I know that for you...deep down...it's a blessing too. Isn't it?"

"What the hell are you talking about? Are you suggesting I wanted this?"

"Of course not. No one ever asks for the trials. Sometimes they're just placed upon us."

"I still don't get what you're saying."

"Really? Huh. That's surprising. I thought you of all people would understand. The young, sharp crusader with the will to do anything and save everything."

"That's not me," Jack chuckled. "Seriously."

Carter took a step closer. His black shoes plunged into the squeaky wooden floor.

"You didn't ask for this. But at the same time you did. I bet you always wonder...what if it were to happen – could I. Could I do that which was necessary? Would I have the skills and the mind to *execute* on that which was necessary? Who, but me, has the knowledge and moral virtue to take the path of least destruction and maximum justice? Who...*if not you*?"

Carter watched as Jack's face filled with doubt and confusion. He didn't know what to make of anything he was hearing. Despite it all, underneath the discord, was a minute shard of hope, beckoning to the possibility that Carter saw what Jack saw and wanted what Jack wanted.

"I don't think I've done something like this before. This guy you're talking about is..."

"Dangerous," Carter added. "Almost certainly. Kessler isn't like ordinary people. That's why I can't do this on my own. I need someone there...someone who knows what to do. One that has the intelligence but also the will."

"But what if I don't?"

"People like you and me...we never really know. But

I can see it Jack. I saw it immediately. You have what I have. Deep down, you know the world has changed. It isn't what it once was. And that it deserves better."

Jack tried to avoid eye contact but he could still hear Carter speak and that was enough for him to see the valour in his expression.

"You'd choose me…over the people your associate wanted to send?"

"Yes. I would. They'll screw this up for us. They won't get Stafford and Max back. Trust me. They don't have what it takes. But this way…we can do it. We get them back and the story comes to a close."

"But not without risk."

"Jack, I won't lie to you. This could turn bad at the drop of a hat. But if this is to come to an end, if we're to finish this off, then we'll need to take this line of action. There's no other way here."

"I think that…" Jack was wavering. An uncertainty still lay in his voice.

"You don't think you're up to it do you? Is that what it is? Is that what you're afraid of?"

For a split second Jack remembered back to all the times he possessed the wisdom; all the moments he'd been scolded for acting on the basis of knowledge; all the events where he was the only one willing to act and secure certainty while others stood by. But this time…maybe it would be different. This time, he would be untethered in his capacity and fortitude. This time, nothing would stop him.

"No…I'm not afraid of anything. I can do it. Whatever it takes."

Carter pulled his jacket forwards and smiled. "I know you can."

He turned around and stared into the empty space that filled the bar. In the night it was probably filled with energy and charisma but there was none of that right now.

A bleak silence roared against the walls and provided nothing more than a remnant of what it was. It was as if the echoes were merely illusions of joy.

"You mind if I ask you…what is your relationship with Katrina exactly?"

"We're strictly friends," Jack replied, somewhat puzzled by the question.

"I see," Carter said. He continued to look away. "So I imagine you've probably lied to her a few times."

"Sort of. It's rare. But most of the time we're pretty honest with each other. No reason not to be."

Carter stopped and raised his head, as if the next words he selected held a great deal of importance to him.

"I hate to break it to you Jack but she wasn't exactly honest with you today." Carter turned back around just in time to witness the confusion on Jack's face. "You do realise she went to the Grayson Arms to look into Sinclair."

"What? How the hell do you know that?"

"She told me when she got back. She never went to see that friend of hers. She went to find out if Sinclair was telling the truth. The stuff she learnt gave her some cause for concern so she passed the information on to me and I used it to help me build a picture of who Sinclair was."

"What has this got to do with anything?"

Carter could see the dissonance exerting itself in Jack's question.

"There's something I need from you Jack. But before I ask, I wanted to put things into perspective. I need to know whether you're willing to lie to Katrina."

"Why are you asking me to do that?"

"After what I've told you, you must understand how dangerous this is. The more people that know, the greater the risk to all of us. It's for everyone's safety we keep this from as many people as possible. That includes Katrina."

"I don't think she's anyone we have to lie to. She's a

part of this. She deserves to know the truth. She's not a child."

Carter sensed the wavering he heard in Jack's voice earlier but this time he was visibly more agitated. Carter could even spot his eyes quivering slightly.

"People only know about Kessler at their own peril. You have to understand this Jack. It's far better if we keep it from her. I wouldn't say it if it wasn't important but it is. I also thought if I told you about her deception earlier on maybe it would be easier for you. Maybe it wouldn't feel so wrong."

"It doesn't matter. It still does."

"Ok. Say you tell her the truth. At what cost Jack? You willing to put her in danger? Just because she's your friend you think you owe her the truth. What you owe her, more than anything, is her safety and protection – by whatever means necessary. Even if that includes lying to her."

Carter moved closer, sensing the reluctance in Jack beginning to dwindle. "In the long run, it'll work out fine. We'll have Stafford back. She'll forgive you. But right now – I need your help, and your help alone."

"Christ. What the hell do I tell her when she asks what's going on?"

"It's simple. Just say we're seeing Cassano – and that's it. Nothing about Kessler. You act as if it's nothing.

"She won't accept it."

"Well you better pray she does. You do whatever it takes Jack. For everyone's safety."

Jack could sense the war in his conscience, the question of what was best eating away at him. He took a deep breath.

"Ok," Jack said nervously. "I don't like it…but if that's what it takes."

"It's the right call Jack. One day you'll thank me."

After what had come to light, Carter knew Katrina was

best left out of this. But for more reasons than he'd disclosed to Jack. He knew she would figure out what was to come; the consequences of crossing someone like Kessler. She may have even realised why Carter chose Jack, over a team of professionals, to bring back Stafford.

Hers was a type of intelligence that spoke to caution and reason rather than action and vengeance. Carter was of the latter, and he didn't need someone of the former at this point. More importantly, not someone who had the potential to pull Jack from the path they were about to embark upon; who might allow him to see the light of restraint and fear. Carter needed the Jack Morse of now, as he was, confident, bold and willing to do whatever it took, and somehow and in some way, still slightly unaware of what may lie along their descent.

CHAPTER 24

Katrina returned to the bar. Having been outside she realised how humid it was underground and her face turned flush. She unbuttoned her cardigan and her blouse shone through the dim fog.

"Elizabeth was happy to hear Sinclair's lead checked out. She said to keep her updated."

"Sure," Carter said.

"How's Sinclair?" Jack asked.

"He's doing ok. Better than before."

There was a brief moment of silence. Katrina noticed an uneasiness in Jack just as Carter picked up the tablet and headed for the exit. He moved quickly, shuffling past Katrina as if she were a stranger on a train carriage.

"Where are you going?" Katrina said.

The behaviour hadn't gone unnoticed.

"I'm going to hand this back to Marco. I think we have what we need."

"What about the other guy? Who was he?"

The gripping force of curiosity still glowed in her eyes.

"Jack can tell you. He said he wanted to speak to you about something else so I'll meet you outside."

He walked up the stairs and left them alone, continuing to look away.

"What's he talking about?" Katrina asked, looking puzzled.

"Me and Carter are going to see Cassano."

"The guy who took Stafford? That giant?"

"Yeah."

"Well I'm sure that'll go off without any trouble."

"It's the only lead we have to Stafford. We have to do it."

"At the cost of your own safety? Your own life?"

Jack shook his head in frustration. "Don't be so dramatic. It'll be fine."

"Fucking hell Jack!" The intensity of Katrina's voice bounced around the room. "Have you even stopped to look at what's going on? As soon as Stafford was taken we were out of our depth...*you* were out of your depth. But now...I don't even know what to think or what we're getting ourselves into. This is starting to get out of hand – in a way we couldn't have imagined. Please...just leave this to Carter. Let's end it here. Please."

"Carter can't do this on his own. He needs help."

"Then he can get it from someone else," Katrina snapped.

"No! He said he needs it from me."

"*From you?*"

"Yeah. He said it himself."

"Really?" Katrina said suspiciously. "No offence Jack...but why?"

"He needs someone with the intelligence...someone who'll do what's right...someone with the will."

"*With the will?* Get a grip Jack. Are you even listening to yourself? Self-belief alone won't save you. You're a mathematician and technologist. You write equations and programs. You might have big ideas and plans for the world but make no mistake – you are not a solider and you are *not* a hero."

"Maybe not. But I'll do whatever I have to in order to get Stafford and Max back in one piece."

"Oh yeah? How are you going to do that? What exactly do you think you bring to the table Jack? Got some secret skills or powers I don't know about? Anything else apart from that preconceived arrogance that you flaunt around with so much confidence? What the hell is underneath it all Jack? Where does it all come from?"

"Look, I can't describe it. But...he gets it. Carter understands. For the first time...someone..."

"Jack, you are nothing like Carter," Katrina interrupted. "Don't pretend like you understand each other. He comes from a completely different world."

"That's the thing...I don't think he does."

For a few minutes Katrina thought the possibility of making progress still existed but that certainty was slowly evaporating. Her growing frustration led to a gaze of such ferocity that, sensing the anger, Jack was forced to break eye contact. He kept his eyes on the ground, fiddling with the buttons on his blazer, as if his mind was preoccupied with the triviality of his appearance.

"What about the other?" Katrina asked after a brief period of quiet. "The one with Cassano. The one who made Carter stop dead in his tracks? Did he tell you who he was?"

"Katrina, I – I...can't tell you that."

Jack slowly raised his head but saw that Katrina wasn't looking at him anymore. She had turned around and was facing the empty space. Her head was in her hands, her face in disbelief.

"Look, I'm sorry," Jack continued. "Carter and I agreed it was too dangerous. We're going to go it alone. The less you know the better. It's safer this way."

"Jack, this is a fucking joke. The fucking *hypocrisy*!" She faced Jack again, her face glistening with anger.

"You've stood here acting like everything is fine and then at the same time you refuse to me tell the name of the man you're after. Someone who's so dangerous that if I knew even the slightest detail it could spell disaster."

"Katrina, please. You've got to understand. If Carter's right then I have to keep this from you. I'm doing it to protect you. I care about you."

"*Care about me!* Wow, how chivalrous. Although clearly not enough that you think I might deserve the truth."

"If we're talking about truth," Jack retorted. The abrupt switch from empathetic to hostile caught Katrina off guard. "Tell me, which friend did you go to see earlier? The one that works around here. Tell me more, please. I'm dying to know how that all went."

"Fuck sakes, he told you that didn't he? That fucking prick. He's so much smarter than he appears. Is that how he convinced you that this little plan was ok?"

"It doesn't change the fact it's true."

"This is completely different. Don't try and draw equivalences between my actions and yours. It isn't going to work."

"Katrina, you just have to trust us. If we do it right…we'll get them back. Look, for the first time I feel like…"

"Feel like what?" Katrina said abruptly. "You said it earlier. Finish the fucking sentence. Go on."

There was that feeling again. The one that Jack found so difficult to describe. He knew it only as the intersection of belief, pride, courage and nobility; the perpetual force that drove the motion of his being.

"Like there's some meaning…to what I'm doing," Jack said. "Doing what I ought to do…after so long."

Katrina's eyes flared up again.

"This was never about Stafford was it? To you, it was always about something else. The second you heard that voice on the phone it was a call to your crazy ideology."

"That's not true!" Jack fired. "What else brought me so far?"

"That's precisely what I'm saying Jack. This entire ordeal was an excuse for you to whisk yourself away without a care in the world, arming yourself with a man that you don't understand, who's just as unnerved by reality as you are."

"Every step of the way I've been in control. I know what I'm doing."

"No you *fucking* don't. You have *no idea* what you're doing. You always think you understand. You always think you get it. But you can't be so naïve…not this time. You're not a bad person Jack. You're not dark, you're not violent. But this is about to become a reality for you and no noble world view or moral wisdom or whatever you think you have is going to save you."

Katrina hadn't realised but she was trembling. Her body was shaking with anger.

Jack sighed. "I have it under control."

Katrina shook her head. "I care about you so much Jack. So, so much. But I just know that you're destined to suffer if you keep pursuing a life that doesn't exist. One that you so desperately want to be true."

She turned around and headed for the stairs.

"Katrina…" Jack stuttered. "I –"

She didn't turn around. Nor did she reply.

Jack stood still, unable to speak, unable to discern truth from uncertainty, fixed in his place as he watched her leave.

Katrina stepped outside. She glanced around the street and saw Carter leaning against the wall, his hands plugged into his pockets, calmly musing to himself. He noticed her immediately and spun his head in her direction.

She stared at him, her gaze filled with disdain and

distrust. It seared through him, marked with anger and not an ounce of forgiveness. Carter stared back, his eyes cold and emotionless. He knew what she was thinking. And she knew the same of him.

After a few seconds she looked away and proceeded down the street and back to the Field.

There was nothing more for her to do here.

CHAPTER 25

Jack and Carter were sat in the back of a taxi speeding into the City of London, the contents of the outside world one big blur from where they were sat.

Jeff had provided him with the address of Terrence Caulfield's offices. If Cassano were to be anywhere, the offices of his employer would be the most likely place. Carter wasn't surprised the offices were in the City. A person such as Caulfield probably had much to gain by being located amongst banks and businesses.

To what degree he was aligned with Cassano was still unclear. It was entirely possible Caulfield had no knowledge of Cassano's life outside of work and was completely innocent in the matter. Either way, Carter had an intention to find out.

Jack and Carter were both sat in silence. Something about Katrina's departure had shaken them up; Jack in particular. Keeping the truth from her wasn't something he was accustom to and he could feel the guilt etched into his character. In a way he welcomed the feeling since it served as a reminder of how difficult the choice had been while at the same time he also acknowledged that any essence of guilt would do nothing to change the reality of his relationship with Katrina. The damage had already been inflicted and he wondered if there was anything he could do to reverse it or at the very least, mitigate it.

The car pulled up to a small set of newly built offices. A handful of windows decorated the outside and sparkled in the sunlight.

Carter paid the driver and they made their way inside. They passed an empty reception desk and, when unable to find a lift, ascended two flights of stairs, past bays of empty offices on the ground and first floors. The staircase was dimly lit, the small bulbs at the top of the ceiling almost ready to extinguish at the first opportunity. Apart from the presence of Caulfield, the offices appeared almost abandoned.

At the peak of the stairs was a small brown coloured door. Carter pushed it open and was suddenly stood in a small, bright, white painted room.

In the centre of the room there was a young woman sitting by a wooden desk mindfully organising some documents across several folders. She immediately saw Jack and Carter and presented them with a warm smile.

"Good afternoon," she said. Her makeup had been applied immaculately and made her cheeks glow like the colour of strawberries. She wore a bright green short sleeved dress and one inch heels of the same colour. She had short, thin arms which hung over a wireless keyboard that she had been deftly typing on and her smile somehow made the room grow even brighter.

"Do you gentlemen have an appointment for today?"

Carter moved towards her desk. "No, unfortunately we don't," Carter said politely. "However this is quite an important matter so we were hoping that maybe Mr Caulfield could make just a little time to see us. He knows who we are."

"Hmm." The receptionist appeared slightly uneasy,

tapping her pen against her keyboard. "Let me just call him and check. He's a very busy person, as I'm sure you're aware."

"Oh, I'm very much aware," Carter said reassuringly.

His tone was so comforting that even Jack couldn't determine how he was going to proceed next.

The receptionist struck one of the buttons on her telephone and waited patiently.

"Hi Mr Caulfield, sorry to disturb you. There are two men here to see you. They said it's very urgent."

She stopped for a second and then looked up at Carter. "Could I ask for your name please?"

"Edward Stafford."

Jack felt like the air had been knocked out of him. *Oh shit.*

Carter was looking for a response, however unpredictable it might be.

There was a door just to the left of the receptionist which slowly creaked open. In the gap, a large man peeked his head outside. Upon spotting Carter he swung the door open and stepped outside.

Cassano, just as colossal as the camera footage had suggested, stood before them. His expression was fierce yet Carter could still spot an ounce of panic on his face. As he suspected, no one in this office was expecting a visit from Edward Stafford.

"Karen," Cassano bellowed. "Mr Caulfield said you're okay to finish for the day. We can see these gentlemen through ourselves. If you want to leave then go right ahead."

"Oh thank you," she said gleefully. "Let me just pack up my things."

Jack caught sight of Cassano, his miniscule, stone-like eyes screwed into his face like permanent fixtures. His huge frame rattled ever so slightly despite his wide stance and legs that were planted into the ground like steel bollards. The buttons of his suit were almost impossible to close since his chest stuck out so far, as if someone had inflated him with air, and the muscles on his neck were so thick that Jack couldn't seem to tell where his face ended and his neck began. He had a buzz cut which seemed like it was performed on a fixed fortnightly schedule although the brows on his face were thick and carelessly misshapen.

Jack quickly peered at Carter. His body was deadly still. He observed Cassano the way a scientist might watch a predator in the wild that was obviously ready to pounce.

Everyone patiently waited as Karen packed her bag, counting the seconds, sheltering cordial pleasantries. Unaware of what was happening she began to hum a catchy melody to herself. She pushed her keyboard across the desk and tapped her heels against the floor as she muttered lyrics to herself. She gently shook her hips and Jack thought she may as well have been on stage.

She took her bag and bolted for the exit, her hips continuing to drift from side to side. As the base of her heels hammered the floor, each of her steps across the room felt like an eternity and shouted into everyone's ears. They burned through the guise and the hole in everyone's smiles widened. They waited, but she never seemed to get there – as if time were playing a grand cruel trick on them.

Jack felt himself turning numb, unable to move.

"See you on Monday," she said, opening the door.

"And you Karen," Cassano replied.

Carter took a sharp breath, his black cloak rising into the air for just a second.

That's what you think.

The door shut and Cassano swung his titan like arm at Carter.

Carter's mind jolted into action. He evaded the strike, parrying it to one side and rushed forwards, viciously driving his fist into Cassano's exposed ribcage and then again into his nose.

He thrust the back of his foot into the side of Cassano's knee, his body collapsing downwards and instantly launched a fierce assault upon him.

Cassano attempted to fend Carter off, sending a blind jab into his face and pushing him back for a few seconds but Carter was undeterred, relentless in conviction. Before Cassano could even regain his senses and see through the specks of blood lodged in his eyes, Carter bolted forwards and slammed his fist into his throat.

Cassano let out a horrifying gasp for air. It stunk of pain and agony.

Carter proceeded forwards and continued his barrage of attacks, each as brutal as the next, slowly crushing Cassano's will to continue. He fell backwards to the floor, the thud booming across the building.

Jack glanced at Carter. His knuckles were stained with blood, the colour red scattered across the white walls while his blue eyes flashed with the wrath of devastation.

Is that what he was planning all along?

Jack hadn't bothered to ask Carter what his intentions with Cassano were. He assumed there may have been some sort of tense conversation and yet within moments, both Carter and Cassano, submerged in their embedded nature, had engaged in exactly the same style of confrontation.

Cassano was lying on the floor and using what little energy he had, quickly dragged his hand behind his jacket and removed a pistol. Carter, as if he were already aware and waiting for just the right moment, stomped his foot, crushing the bones in Cassano's wrist. He viciously twisted his heel until Cassano's palm opened up.

Carter used his other foot to kick the weapon backwards and then drew his own silenced firearm from behind his coat. Cassano watched in terror as Carter fired a shot into each of his knees, letting out a howl of pain as the bullets collided against his bones.

Jack was stunned. Cassano was a tower of strength and aggression, undoubtedly the nightmare of numerous men and yet Carter had incapacitated him in under twenty seconds with an unprecedented level of force.

Who the hell trained this guy? And what for?

Carter flicked his gaze upwards, his pistol clutched tightly in his hand. He saw the door of Caulfield's office wide open. Stood at the back, behind a great oak table, was a man dressed in a dark navy three piece suit. The suit was thinly pinstriped and only just revealing a pair of gold circular cufflinks set inside a crisp white shirt. He was wearing a thinly knotted dark blue tie and his hair was perfectly combed back. A panic-stricken look sat on his face, as he stood shaking, and in absolute fear of what was to come.

As Carter stormed into the room Caulfield was desperate for composure, his cufflinks drumming back and forth against his shirt.

Left with no choice, Caulfield lunged forwards and tried to attack Carter, who, merely sidestepping, struck his palm against Caulfield's face.

Caulfield fell back against his desk, his senses in complete disarray. Carter grabbed him by the throat and pushed him further into the table. His back seared in pain as his spine was slowly crushed against the table by the strength of Carter's antagonism.

Carter, with his pistol gripped in his other hand, placed it firmly on Caulfield's forehead. His finger was carefully curled around the trigger, steady and patient.

Caulfield's heart began to race. "Please…don't-"

"Shut up," Carter said.

Carter let the silence settle in Caulfield's mind for a second.

Caulfield's perfectly aligned tie was now jagged and

disproportionate. His neatly bound hair had strands flung in different directions and his solid white shirt was crumpled beneath his suit, drops of blood sprinkled across it.

"Start walking," Carter said slowly. "I have some questions."

Carter gripped Caulfield by the collar and led him out of the office and into the reception area keeping his gun sown to his head. Once they were outside he threw him against the reception table and turned back towards Cassano who was still trying to lift himself upright.

Carter pointed his pistol squarely at his head. From where he was sat, Cassano could only see the silencer and its dark barren hole. Everything else was blacked out, his gaze centred on the object of his potential demise.

"Where is Edward Stafford?" Carter asked menacingly.

"I've no idea what you're talking about," Cassano spluttered.

"Well then, where is David Kessler?"

What started as reservation was replaced with fear as Cassano came to realise the breadth of Carter's awareness.

"I told you…I don't –"

Carter fired another shot into Cassano's leg. Cassano expelled a terrifying shriek that visibly rattled everyone's psyche. The only exception was Carter, who continued to remain undisturbed.

There must've been other ways to find answers but Carter's first instinct was physical ferocity, shades of which ran parallel to his assault upon Sinclair. He deployed it as if it were nothing and Jack had never witnessed anything like it.

"Mr Cassano, right now, I know more than you can possibly imagine," Carter said. "I know you're an associate of David Kessler and I know that together you kidnapped Edward Stafford and Max Mortimer last night. Think carefully before you answer me."

Cassano was panting heavily. The three bullets that had pierced his legs were taking their toll, his body continuing to weaken. The bruising and battering he'd taken didn't help and the pain finally began to register as the adrenaline in his body dissipated. While Cassano waded through the agony it slowly dawned on him how much information Carter had accumulated. That information, however he may have attained it, had ultimately led him here and it seemed as if he wasn't going to stop until he left with what he came for.

Carter's attention moved to Caulfield. "Where are they?"

"My god, what are you talking about," Caulfield stuttered. "Those names don't mean anything to me."

Carter moved closer. "There were two men murdered last night. Two men who kidnapped Edward Stafford and Max Mortimer. Both were working with Arthur Cassano and David Kessler. After they were killed, Cassano and Kessler found Stafford and Max and took them away."

Cassano gripped his legs in pain, the extent of Carter's knowledge continuing to frighten him. *How does he know this all?*

"Terrence," Carter said. Under the surface his voice had a dark resonance which continued to escalate even as he stopped speaking. "I have little time for untruths. Although it may be the predicate of your profession, right now I need you to be completely honest with me. Do you understand?"

Caulfield nodded his head in a nervous jitter. "I am…but it's like I told you – I don't know who you're talking about."

"Enough of this," Carter snapped.

Carter viciously swung the top his pistol across Caulfield's face, the metal shockwave thundering through his bones. Caulfield fell back against the table, desperately clambering on to what he could so that he might stay upright.

"You've had enough time," Carter said to Cassano. "You ready to answer?"

"Can't answer what I don't know," he replied.

"Pity." Carter fired another bullet into Cassano's leg.

The sound of gunshots continued to jolt Jack. Despite the number of times he had heard it, it still felt unfamiliar. All he could hear was the desperation for truth. The boom of the shot was catastrophic, echoing through the room and casually passed Carter by.

Cassano yelled in agony. He kept his eyes glued to the ground, trying to avoid eye contact, anything to stop himself thinking about the pain.

Carter had seen it before. The preconditioned mind, set to protect allies no matter the cost. He needed to break down the architecture holding Cassano's allegiance to Kessler in place otherwise he'd fail to get the information he needed.

"You'd really die for him wouldn't you," Carter said. "Someone who just drops from the sky and hires you for a job." Carter edged closer to Cassano. "He'd kill you the first second he felt it necessary…you understand that don't you?"

"If I spoke a word to you right now then he would definitely kill me."

"Well then, what if I killed him first?"

"I highly doubt that," Cassano laughed, his face flinching in pain. "Have you met this man? I don't know who you are, but as dangerous as you might be, David Kessler is in a different league. He always will be."

There was a certain sublevel of fear in Cassano's voice which made Jack shudder. Even after suffering such cruelty, such pain, Cassano still wasn't ready to betray Kessler's trust.

"I don't care who he is. I'm here for Stafford, and if I need to kill David Kessler in order to find him then I will. Tell me…why were you trying to take him?"

"You're never going to see him again," Cassano mumbled. He started to laugh again. "Not Kessler, not Max, not Stafford. None of them. *Never*."

Carter knew his influence was deteriorating. Cassano wasn't going to give up Kessler without good reason.

There's no way this idiot is getting in my way. Not when I'm so close.

If Carter was going to get anywhere he needed to accelerate his resolve, no matter the consequences.

CHAPTER 26

"I guess it's going to come to this then," Carter said.

He glanced at Jack and drew a small knife from his jacket pocket. The blade was viciously straight with a tip sharp and precise enough to select an individual strand of hair. The handle was dark blue and had a slight curve on the end. It fit snugly under the base of Carter's hand and his body felt complete whenever he held it.

Jack eyes widened. "Carter, you can't kill him."

"This isn't to kill him Jack. But pretty soon he's going to wish I would."

Jack's inability to even consider such a possibility blatantly stuck out. His lip quivered as he tried to muster a response, his eyes wobbling, refusing to stay fixed on any given point.

In the corner of his eye Carter could see that Cassano was watching him. He had seen the glimpse of terror materialise on his face. Both of them knew what was going to happen next. He spun the blade in his hand, Cassano's eyes following it every direction it turned.

"Jack," Carter said. "Come over here."

Carter took a few steps away from Cassano, ushering

Jack over with his hand.

Jack slowly followed, unsure what was going on.

"What is it?"

"Jack, I hate to say it…but this isn't a one person job."

Carter lifted the knife up, the shine of the blade glimmering in front of Jack's eyes. "I'm going to need you to help me."

Jack leaned back. "I – I don't know. I don't think I can…"

"It's nothing serious," Carter said. There was a soothing tone to his voice, one which felt disarming. "You don't need to do anything bad. You just need to hold him down, probably for a few seconds at a time. That way I can do what I need to do."

"Jesus, I – I don't know anything about that sort of stuff. I –"

"You're a man that does what's necessary Jack. I know you are. I wouldn't have brought you this far if I didn't think you were up to the job."

"No, it's not – it's not that, I mean…" There was a slight stutter in Jack's speech. "You just shot him right? Four times. I think he would've talked by now. I don't think stabbing the hell out of him is going to do anything."

"No," Carter said shaking his head. He was still holding the knife in front of Jack. "This is going to be something very different. I know that, and he knows that. We'll get something. Trust me."

"You're acting like this is normal. How are you not worried?"

"Jack, when you know you're on the right side of the war, the possibility of anything else is too terrible to imagine. These aren't the decisions that worry me. It's the decisions I *don't* make. Not doing what I have to. That's what worries me."

"But there could be…"

"*Another way?* Another way of getting Stafford and

Max? You know one?"

Jack's face filled with concentration but he couldn't think of anything. Anything which might change Carter's mind.

"Think as hard as you can…there's no alternative here. We don't do this, we don't get them back. Cassano won't give up what he knows."

"How can we be so sure?"

"I've crossed men like this before Jack. He won't. And then Stafford and Max will belong to Kessler. And I swear to you, as soon as the situation presents itself, Kessler will kill them both."

The possibility had lurked in the back of Jack's mind but he always avoided saying it out loud. He was worried that if he said such words out in the open, he might accidentally invoke their realism or raise their probability.

"I need your help, or else Stafford and Max die. It's our last chance."

Carter spotted Cassano's pistol on the floor. He leant down and picked it up, holding it out in front of Jack as if it were some sort of archaic offering. "Take it just in case. And then follow my lead."

Jack stared at the weapon. There was something oddly alluring about an instrument of violence; particularly one capable of instant death. He placed out his hand and Carter put it in the centre of his palm. In that moment he was unsure what commanded the power; the weapon or the man that wielded it.

Jack closed his hand. His fingers gripped the pistol and there was a moment where he lacked the clarity of mind to draw judgement; judgement on the circumstances and judgement on himself. He didn't know whether he was ready. He didn't know what was about to happen. The uncertainty surrounded him. There was a remote possibility that maybe he wasn't prepared for what came next or that, in fact, whatever Carter deemed as wisdom was not his natural inclination, but artificial in both appearance and belief.

Clutching the weapon as tightly as he could, ambiguity paraded through Jack's eyes. He took a sharp breath and slowly placed it between his waist and jeans.

Carter spun the knife in his hand again. "You sure you're ready?"

"Yeah…I'm good. It's under control."

Carter nodded and walked back towards Cassano. He was still on the floor, panting heavily.

Carter flung both of his hands down towards Cassano and grabbed a hold of his shirt. Cassano tried to struggle but he barely had any energy to fight back. With all of his might Carter pulled him up from the ground and threw him against the reception table just as Caulfield jumped out of the way.

"You should've answered me when you had the chance," Carter said.

"Look, don't," Cassano pleaded.

Cassano was desperate to escape but the pain in his knees left him holding on to the desk for support. Just as he looked around, Carter struck him in the nose.

"Jack, clear the table!"

Jack ran over and swung his arm over the surface of the table like a wave crashing over the sand. Karen's keyboard along with a small PC monitor, folders, pens and pots smashed against the floor.

Carter pushed Cassano against the top of the table and using his right arm and the weight of his body tried to hold him in place.

"Jack, grab his hand. Put it down against the table."

"No!" Cassano screamed. He swung his arm around violently, almost hitting Jack several times.

"Stop resisting!" Carter fired as he smashed the side of his hand against Cassano's bicep.

The jolt of pain momentarily paralysed his arm and

provided just enough time for Jack to grab a hold of it and drop it on the desk.

"Keep it still," Carter said as he held the knife in his left hand.

He spun it around and quickly dropped its tip just above the centre of his palm.

"Where is Edward Stafford?!"

Cassano violently struggled but Carter's previous attacks had taken everything from him. He couldn't fight back.

"Where?!"

You're not getting in the way of this!

Carter slowly pressed the edge of the knife into the back of Cassano's hand. Within moments it cut into his skin and the blood began to seep out and Cassano and let out a horrifying scream. He continued to shake his body, doing his best to jolt Carter and his blade away but Carter had pressed his weight in exactly the right way to minimise his movement.

Jack was using all of his energy to keep Cassano's arm against the table. He could feel his pulse, almost like an internal tremor, vibrating against the skin and bouncing against the table. Every few seconds Jack would lose momentary control and then force his arm back down while Carter gradually drove the blade further into his tissue.

"Edward Stafford! Where is he? You took him and you know where he is. Tell me!"

Jack tried to look away from the blood but the only alternative were the tears beginning to materialise in the blood shot eyes of Cassano, his mouth agape and bellowing with torment as the knife was beginning to arrive closer and closer to the end of the table.

Is this really happening. Am I actually doing this?
What the hell is happening?!

Jack tried to shake himself out of his reality but it was

no use. Right now, him and Carter were torturing Cassano for information. They were causing untold pain in their quest to return Stafford. He felt Cassano's arm rigorously shaking but so much of it was coming from himself. His own body couldn't believe what he was doing; as if it were trying to rattle the darkness out of him.

We need to think of something else. We can't keep doing this.

"Stop! Please!"

"Not until you tell me where he is."

For a split second, Jack's grip weakened slightly and he nearly lost control of Cassano's arm.

"Keep him steady Jack!" Carter pushed the blade deeper. "Come on Arthur. Don't be a fool!"

There has to be another way to get Stafford and Max back. There has to be. Think. Think. Think!

It was at that juncture that Jack figured it out and saw the idea pop into his head. It felt hazy, fused together by various moving parts, all of which were still uncertain but nevertheless within his grasp.

"Carter – stop!" Jack exclaimed.

Carter held the blade where it was. He elevated his eyes, studying Jack's resolute focus. He tried to gauge how serious he was; whether it was possible that Jack had something worth pursuing or if the stress of the situation was becoming too much for him.

"Jack, we've been through this. We're not stopping. There isn't another way."

"No, I think there is. I think I've got something."

Cassano doesn't look like he's about to give anything up. It couldn't hurt to hear him out.

"What then?"

"Take the knife out and leave it to me."

"You better know what you're doing."

"I do…"

Just the thought of Carter easing his attack brought

solace to Cassano's mind.

"Fine. But if this doesn't work…" Carter dropped his eyes to Cassano's sullen face. "We do it my way."

The fear suddenly rushed back into Cassano's expression just as Carter lifted his knife and took a step back.

Cassano whimpered as the blade left his skin and splashes of blood stained the table.

"Your move."

He knows what we're willing to do. He might be more likely to cooperate this way.

Jack let go of Cassano's arm and moved to the front of the desk so that he had a clear view of Cassano. "I'd like you to tell me. Reinhart's the one who hired Kessler isn't he?"

Jack was indulging on speculation. He still had no evidence to confirm his suspicion of Reinhart's involvement. He was fishing with a hook that could crumble at any moment but he didn't have another option.

Jack carefully observed Cassano, the way a man might appreciate a work of art, attempting to spot whether his hook had sunk in.

Cassano didn't respond. The anxious look on his face suggested he wasn't going to confirm Jack's suspicions.

He gently sat up, raising his body with his left hand. He quickly gripped the hand that had been pierced by Carter's blade and tried to cover the wound. The blood was still pouring but less so than before.

"I don't need you to agree," Jack said. "But we can link you, Kessler, and *Reinhart* back to Stafford and Max. Reinhart – a guy who's not unknown – a guy who lives for his enterprise and reputation. He thought he could take them and get away with it, without anyone knowing…but he failed. And right now, we have enough leverage to destroy everything he has."

Where is he going with this? Carter thought.

There was a brief period of silence.

"So what?" Cassano said. "Why not just do it?"

Got him!

It may have been a hunch, but Cassano had finally confirmed Reinhart's involvement. Without it, Jack's plan may have collapsed before it began but now he was in a position to leverage the situation.

"We want Stafford and Max. So we're willing to negotiate."

"It sounds more like a threat."

"I don't care what it is. But it should be enough to bring him to the table. And if he doesn't come, we'll devastate him."

"You wouldn't. Not when Stafford's life is at risk."

"If we do nothing he's as good as dead," Carter said. "You're forcing our hand here."

Carter finally knew what Jack was up to. It was a masterstroke of manipulation and one he hadn't thought to consider.

"Call him," Jack said. "Present him with the ultimatum and see what he says."

"If I call, you realise Kessler will quite possibly decide to kill me."

Jack leant forwards. "If you don't tell them what we're planning, and then we go ahead and do it, Kessler will probably kill you for sure."

"Don't worry Jack. I don't mind taking another try to get what we need."

Cassano's eyes shrank at the thought of Carter's blade severing another piece of his body.

Caulfield was leaning against the wall, still bruised and battered. "Just do it," he mumbled. "They're not giving you much of a choice in the matter."

Cassano's heart was pounding. As he weighed up the problem he immediately knew that any misstep in his decision making would no doubt cost him his life;

decisions which were being imposed by two men, one of whom had a resolve that extended into near unlimited savagery.

Cassano exhaled. "Fine. I'll put you in touch with him."

Jack breathed a sigh of relief. Had he not agreed, he may have been forced into a very different option, the execution of which might have demanded something Jack was possibly incapable of providing.

Carter placed his knife back in to his jacket. He couldn't help but feel astonished. He'd believed that Cassano couldn't be reasoned with and that in such an impossible scenario, his approach was the only one that could be successfully deployed. Jack had evidently proved him wrong.

Carter's affinity for conflict may have distorted his ability to recognise a solution but it appeared that Jack didn't suffer from such a shortcoming. There was purity to his mind, not wrought with loss and rage, still bound by a pursuit of ends unattainable or not.

Carter could hardly recall those moments of his life anymore, where he thought those thoughts. They felt so distant, far removed from a life once lived, and replaced with a conscience that understood the implementation of one solution and one solution only.

He watched Jack draw his breath, wondering how long it would be until such a philosophy might finally cascade its way into his mind.

CHAPTER 27

"Do you have a way of contacting him?" Jack asked.

"Yeah." Cassano slowly removed a phone from his jacket pocket. He unlocked it and started typing a number.

"You don't have it saved?" Carter said.

"He told me to memorise it."

Cassano handed the phone to Carter. He tapped the number on screen and put it on speaker. Eventually the ringing stopped and someone answered.

"Yeah."

The voice was cold. Just as Jack remembered it.

"Kessler," Carter said.

There was a brief pause. "Who is this?"

"My name is Michael Carter. I'm on the phone with Jack Morse."

"Jack Morse? The same Jack Morse I spoke to last night. Isn't that a nice surprise?"

"I think there's a few things we need to discuss."

"Where's Cassano?" Kessler said abruptly.

"Cassano's fine. He's just next to me."

The faint sound of Kessler's breath fell over the speaker. It was monotonous, rhythmically cycling over and over.

"Okay Mr Carter, tell me…what made you go to so much trouble to incapacitate Arthur Cassano and then contact me?"

"Because…I'd like to make a proposition."

"I'm not in the notion of negotiating with a man who's out of his depth."

"Even when you and your party have everything to lose?"

"Are you attempting to threaten me Mr Carter? If you really want your friends back then you should just ask."

There was a momentary break, as if Kessler had taken a second to briefly smile to himself.

"So if I asked you for Edward Stafford and Max Mortimer would you give them up?" Carter said. He ushered in a wind of sarcasm.

"Unfortunately it's not for me to decide."

"Well I'd like to meet the person who does."

"And why's that? Because you think have leverage over me. That you have some sort of power."

"I'd like to think so."

Carter was trying to coerce Kessler into making a snap decision but he seemed too calm and controlled to make a mistake. His disposition was shielded from Carter's piercing inquisitiveness and it was supported by a layer of composure and fortitude that few may ever break.

"Do tell…how exactly do you intend to influence my decision?"

"You're working for Joseph Reinhart."

"I don't know who that is."

"I think you do," Jack added. "I met with him the other day. Right now, he's the only person who has a reason for taking Stafford. The only person crazy enough and stupid enough to even try something like this."

"Really?"

Something about the way Kessler spoke made Jack

shudder. His complete lack of disregard made Jack wonder what else he was hiding. The last time they spoke Kessler had outmanoeuvred him almost effortlessly. At that point Jack also had no idea who he was or what he was capable of. Last night he was a man of the unknown. Today, he was a man of unparalleled danger.

Jack composed himself before he replied. "Yeah. And given what we know, there's nothing to stop us from destroying his reputation, his enterprise. He wouldn't survive the fallout from something like this."

"Jack, last night you tried presenting me with some sort of ultimatum. I'm going to respond with the same exact answer. You do anything of the sort, and I'm going to kill Max Mortimer. Do not test my resolve."

"I thought about that…"

"Enough," Kessler interjected. "Don't pretend as if you don't care. You don't have the will to sacrifice Max. Just so you can go for Reinhart? I hardly think so."

Jack was struggling for a response. Kessler was right – leaving Max to die just to destroy Reinhart's reputation wasn't something he was willing to do. Kessler already knew. It wouldn't even result in Stafford's return. The plan was entirely theoretical and an aggressive way of trying to bring Reinhart to the negotiating table.

"They might come for you too," Carter said. "You really willing to take that risk?"

"What are *you* to this problem?"

The question caught Carter off guard. "Just a concerned party. It's a financial interest more than anything."

"Well, Mr Carter, concerned or not, you can send whoever you want. I've killed hundreds of men. If any authority want to send their men to their graves then so be it. I'm a living, breathing death warrant and every intelligence operative, soldier and mercenary on the planet knows that."

Jack and Carter could only help but watch as their leverage began to slip. If they didn't think of something quickly Kessler would have no reason to continue talking.

"Does Reinhart know about this?" Carter asked. "You might be willing to kill Max in return for destroying Reinhart's reputation but I don't think he is."

"But you won't sacrifice him."

"Jack won't. But I might."

"Then you lose the only man who can finish this little product of theirs."

"Well that's not true."

Carter hesitated for a split second and then continued. "We don't need Stafford. Jack can do it himself."

Kessler's perfectly synchronised breathing took a sharp deviation. "What do you mean?"

Carter gripped the phone tighter. His stratagem had clearly rifled Kessler. "He's Stafford's protégé. He knows everything already. Might take him a bit longer but it's not impossible."

Jack turned to Carter in bewilderment. *I don't think that's going to fucking happen.*

Stafford's understanding of the problem was far more advanced than his own. If anyone with the faintest idea of Stafford's work were to question Jack on its specificities, it would immediately become apparent that this was an area where Jack knew almost nothing.

"So, you still willing to take that risk?" Carter asked.

"Let's hear them out."

The voice that spoke wasn't Kessler's. It was more familiar. It had the same nuance of confidence and pretentiousness. The same voice that Jack heard a few days earlier.

Reinhart cleared his throat. "You're driving a hard bargain Mr Carter. This negotiation is much more interesting than the one I had with you Jack. You've up-scaled in your style. Nice job. You finally piqued my curiosity."

"It's not an empty threat," Carter pressed.

"No, probably not. I didn't realise that Jack knew what Stafford knew either. Never got the impression at our meeting."

"There was no reason to bring it up," Jack said. He was doing his best to avoid going into detail. The slightest misstep could cause their position to collapse.

"So what is it that Stafford knows which you can reengineer exactly?"

Shit.

Jack started running through all of his conversations with Stafford, every remark he'd heard which might've been related to his area of work, desperately trying to amalgamate them into some sort of coherent and half sensible narrative. His throat started to tremble, considering whether what he was about to say might provide even a vague representation of intelligence.

"Well, Stafford's work focussed primarily around sentiment analysis. So he designed the algorithms that scraped data sources and mined them for text related to investments which then gave him a score on how the market was feeling."

"I see. And you can do that too?"

"It's not impossible. NLP is something I have experience in so I can finish whatever Stafford started. That's not a concern."

"What's NLP?"

Carter saw Jack's expression switch from concern to confusion.

"NLP as in…"

Jack waited for a response, but the silence lingered far too long. "Natural language processing."

"Oh yes, of course. Sorry. Just a bit out of touch there. Been a long day…obviously. But it sounds like you understand Stafford's work. I won't deny that. It's impressive."

"Yeah."

None of this made any sense. Jack's answer was extremely vague. To any layman, it may have sounded wonderfully intelligent but in substance yielded almost no relevant information at all. He may as well have been a rookie technology journalist. Any investor in this type of technology would have known exactly what Jack was referring to and probed him further. Yet, Reinhart knew nothing of the sort. Something was amiss.

"Ok gentlemen," Reinhart said. "You've convinced me. Let's make this happen."

"I'm going to send you an address." Kessler was speaking again, his voice much sharper and precise than before. It's a house, owned by Reinhart, out in Belgravia. Be there in less than an hour. Don't come armed and don't bring anyone else. If you don't adhere to those rules or someone appears in the middle of our meeting, I will execute Edward Stafford and Max Mortimer without hesitation. Do you understand?"

"Yes," Jack said.

For his own sake he tried not to repeat the words back to himself.

"I look forward making your acquaintance…Jack."

The phone disconnected.

Jack turned to Carter who drew a breath of relief.

"I wasn't expecting that," Carter said.

"Nor was I. But it worked."

"Yeah. It's not over yet though."

For an instant Jack considered what may have happened if Cassano hadn't given up Kessler's number. If Carter took control of the scenario, where would it have led? Would the violence have continued? Would it have become more painful? What might have been expected from Jack? He'd found it unbearable for even the brief time they had engaged in it and all the while Carter seemed unhinged.

How was he so unfazed?

Carter was certainly ready to do whatever it took to get Stafford and Max back. If Jack's plan had gone awry, then they may have had no choice. Otherwise, Stafford and Max would have certainly died at the hands of Kessler.

Is that what it takes?

As Jack passed the phone back to Carter he felt a small vibration. A message with an address had appeared.

Carter glanced at it and then slipped the phone into his pocket.

"I'm going to hold on to this if you don't mind," Carter said, turning his sights towards Cassano.

"Do I have a choice?" he replied.

Carter ignored him and made his way to the exit. Jack followed behind him.

"You won't see me again Mr Carter," Cassano shouted. "He'll probably kill me. And he'll probably kill you too. You have no idea what you're about to do. No idea!"

Neither of them turned around. They continued walking, Cassano's words lingering in the back of both their minds.

CHAPTER 28

Ajay was sat by a small two-person table in the corner of the bar, his back against the entrance. The table was empty, apart from a small menu and a thick red candle. The smell of liquor soaked the air, drowning his senses and lulling him into a sense of tranquillity.

Every so often he turned around to watch as people entered and exited the restaurant. No one seemed to be entering the bar; as if no one felt like drinking this evening and that everyone in the world had suddenly found the solutions to their problems all by their lonesome.

The barman was wiping down the surface of the bar with a white rag. He seemed fixated on one particular spot, continually scrubbing with such determination and aggression that he hadn't even noticed that Ajay entered.

Ajay didn't seem to mind that he hadn't been served. He wasn't really in the mood to drink anyway, and the panting and exhaustion from the barman suggested that he was probably preoccupied. He wasn't quite sure why he'd decided to come to the bar other than the fact that it proved to be a convenient escape; a way of leaving the dinner and not having to stand outside the restaurant with his brother.

A conversation he couldn't bare to go through again.

As soon as Ajay heard them, he turned around. A rush of footsteps; someone had stormed into the bar. He thought it may have been someone else; someone with an equally dismal problem who had sought solace in the place where men came to disappear and to forget. But he was wrong. He recognised the man who had entered.

"I thought I made it clear that I didn't want any part of this deal, or that I didn't want to be disturbed Jack," Ajay said, shaking his head. "What don't you get about that?"

Once Jack entered the bar he almost broke into a small jog. His body was lit with excitement, as if some electric current had charged him on the way down the stairs. His eyes were sparkling and he could barely stand still as he tried to explain what he was doing here.

"Ajay, you've g-got to listen me. I think I know a way out."

"My god. You really don't know when to quit do you son. I asked you ten minutes ago whether you had any ideas and I think we came to the consensus that you don't –"

"I do!" Jack said confidently. "I have an idea. One that I think no one has thought of. One that'll put the ball back in yours and Vijay's court."

"You're saying you think you have a solution that neither our legal team nor our investigations team has spotted?"

"How big is your investigation team again? Two people if I recall."

"Yes."

Jack crouched down so he was level with Ajay. He placed his hand on the table. It started to tremble, bopping up and down against the table.

"Vijay said they're not expected to do much. They don't know what to look for. But I do…something I think we're missing."

Ajay pressed his finger against Jack's hand and stopped it in its place.

"I'll hear you out. But if this is another waste of time you're going to severely regret it."

"Max and Marina went to get Vijay and are bringing back him here. Once he arrives…I'll tell you what I've got in mind…"

After a few minutes, Max paced into the bar, Vijay and Marina just behind him. Marina's heels smacked the floor as she struggled to keep up with Max's almost supernatural speed.

Jack and Ajay were stood at the far end of the room, almost hidden by the gloom that surrounded them. Jack wandered up and down while Ajay stared at the candle that was still burning on his table, glowing brightly in a room that seemed to become murkier as time went on.

As Max slowed down, Vijay stepped ahead of him and pointed his finger at Jack.

"You better have a good reason for bringing me back here Jack. I'm a hard man to impress, even at the best of times."

Jack froze in his place and gathered his thoughts. "The investigation you've got going on…I don't think those people know what they're looking for and I don't think they have the scale or manpower to figure out what I think has happened."

Vijay adjusted his suit jacket. "What makes you think that?"

"Because…if you had this idea, I think your problems would have gone away by now."

"Bold words Mr Morse. The next ones better be worth my time."

Everyone was clustered together in a large circle, eyes all focussed upon Jack. Before he spoke he suddenly realised how important his next sentence might be. They were the words that would determine whether his company would survive; whether he could continue to look Stafford or Katrina in the eye. Max held him responsible for what happened and now it was his responsibility to fix it. Its future, and that of his friends, lay in his hands.

"The guy who ran your company. What's his name?"

"Anthony Okoro," Ajay replied.

"Ex-government, if I understand correctly," Jack said. Ajay nodded.

"This is a guy you know paid bribes and won private contracts to sell chemicals. We know he possibly overcharged for the chemicals and skimmed some money off the top to keep the whole arrangement in order. And, you were even lucky enough to sub-contract to the Nigerian Government. Right?"

"What's your point," Vijay said.

"Well, my thinking is...if Okoro already paid bribes to private companies, how do you know he didn't pay bribes to public officials too? If Okoro purposely overcharged private entities for his chemicals, how do you know he didn't overcharge the government too and collude with certain members of the government to do it?"

Ajay removed his glasses and rubbed his eyes. It was an evening that was beginning to wear him down and he could feel his energy whittling away.

"Jack, you're not really helping. You're only thinking of more things that Okoro did wrong. More things that are going to cause us a bigger liability."

"But is it really *your* liability? Think about it...people in the Nigerian government itself were complicit in purchasing overpriced chemicals from Okoro. But those same chemicals were sold to foreign embassies and military outposts. Let's take the UK for example. They couldn't buy those chemicals from anywhere else – the UK government had to purchase them from the Nigerian government, and indirectly, from Okoro. The costs of those chemicals were almost certainly inflated...and so if the Nigerian Government wanted to turn a profit, they would have sold them at inflated prices. A few members of the government would have known that, having worked with Okoro to do it, and would have knowingly defrauded the UK government, maybe even taking some of the excess where they could. If anything, they probably defrauded every foreign government in the country using Okoro and his company."

Ajay and Vijay looked at one another. A flicker of excitement sparked across their faces for the first time since this entire saga had emerged.

"I think members of the Nigerian government know what happened," Jack continued. "I think they're using you both as scapegoats to hide what they did. I think you should counter-sue, or threaten to tell the UK and US governments what really happened in return for getting your money back. I bet if you call those investigators right now, and tell them to dig around for emails or documents relating to Okoro's dealing with the Nigerian government...you'll have all the leverage you need."

"Shit," Marina exclaimed. Her soft Spanish accent pierced the tension in the room. "I think he's right."

Ajay put his glasses back on. "Let's make the call."

"Agreed," Vijay said.

The two of them returned to the private dining area, walking side-by-side, and muttering to one another.

"I haven't seen that sight in quite a while," Marina whispered to Max.

"No...I don't think anyone has."

Five minutes passed. Then ten, and then twenty. No one spoke to one another. Everyone wandered around the bar in silence, stepping in random directions. The barman had heard snippets of their earlier conversation and quickly realised that there was no point offering any of them a drink. Instead, he decided to clear up the tables, every once in a while catching a glimpse of panic stricken faces and jittering bodies.

After almost thirty minutes of unbearable waiting, the sound of two pairs of footsteps spiralled across the bar and caught the attention of everyone. Ajay and Vijay stormed inside with so much charisma, that the dark murk of the bar felt almost non-existent.

"They found it!" Ajay shouted. "They actually found it!"

"You're kidding," Max said as a surge of relief filled his body.

"We called our team in Lagos. Told them to start searching emails right this second and look for evidence of government bribes; some kind of conspiracy between Okoro and the government. And low and behold, they started catching leads. Tons of them. Hundreds of emails suggesting there was a plan to sell chemicals at inflated prices to foreign governments. We've told them to ramp up capacity and see what else they can find."

"God, that's amazing news," Marina said. "Who would've thought?"

"I truly can't believe it." Vijay said. "I can't believe no one realised this. No one, and I mean no one, saw this as a possibility. Not us, not the investigators out in Lagos, and definitely not the lawyers who are supposed to be advising us on the matter. No one except you…Mr Morse."

"I guess I was wrong to doubt you Jack," Ajay chuckled. "I suppose I should apologise for my hostility earlier."

"Don't worry about it," Jack said. "I get where you were coming from. I'm just glad I could help."

Ajay grabbed Jack by the shoulder and pulled him closer, as if he were an old school friend. "Jack, you did more than help. If we threaten to counter-sue with all the information we have, we'll bring those fools to the table with a settlement so large we'll have turned a bigger profit than if we just decided to sell the company the old fashioned way."

Vijay walked over and smacked Jack on the back. "You just made us a lot of money boy. And that's without the AI! God only knows what he could do *with* one, right?"

Max's pulse started to quicken. "So hang on…"

"Yes, yes, I'm very sorry Max," Ajay confessed. "I think we were both a bit too hasty before. I think you can count us in for your little plan."

Max did everything he could to hide the torrent of relief that surged on to his face. To no avail, a huge smile swept across his face. "You really mean that?" he asked excitedly.

"Of course," Ajay replied. "With a guy like Jack on board, I think we're in good hands. Count me in for £35 million."

"Same," Vijay said.

"Well, you boys are getting ahead of yourself," Marina quipped. "I can't back down from this now. Max, put me in for the same. I think there's enough liquidity now for me to really get my beak wet."

Max's face dropped.

£105 million!

He and Elizabeth had only targeted £50 million. The amount secured was over double that. He never imagined he would walk away from this dinner with that amount of capital. Even more shocking was that less than an hour ago, he thought he would be walking away with nothing; a venture lost to insolence and foolishness. He was dreading how he may have to tell Elizabeth and Stafford what happened. Now he was considering what might be the most interesting way to break the good news.

"Shall we finish dinner," Ajay said, pushing his

glasses against the bridge of his nose.

"I like that idea!" Marina said. "As long as we get more wine…"

Everyone scampered out of the bar and towards the restaurant but Max noticed that Jack was still stood by counter, pondering to himself, as if he wasn't even paying attention to the commotion.

"I'll meet you all up there," Max said. "Give me a few minutes."

"Sure, take your time," Vijay said.

Max paced towards Jack. "You deaf or something. We're heading to dinner. Come on."

Jack shook his head. "No. I'm not. I'm pretty sure of that because I heard £105 million just a second ago. Not £50 million. And not 0."

"Damn right," Max said. "Hell of a win. Not bad."

"Better than not bad," Jack said impatiently. "I'd say pretty fucking good. Actually, I'd even say…next time, you need to trust me and trust that I'm capable of doing more than just 'what I'm told'. Because whether you like it or not, or maybe you didn't realise up until now, I *do* know what I'm doing."

Max unbuttoned the top button of his shirt and loosened his tie. His suit suddenly looked more casual and relaxed and yet his face was anything but. His eyes flared with anger and his mouth started to quiver.

"Let's make one thing really clear Jack. This is a win. No doubt. But you got so, extremely fucking lucky, it is unprecedented. You got no idea Jack. That theory of yours, was a moon shot. The odds of them finding some email which proved it were a million to one. If they didn't, this entire deal would've burnt to the ground."

"But they did find it! And so I was right to raise it!"

"No! You raised those questions because you wanted to. You disobeyed me because you thought you knew best. It's only when Marina mentioned that thing about their government selling to foreign governments that you got the idea into your head. You didn't have an answer before that. Before that point, you risked everything because you're an arrogant son of a bitch who thinks he knows better."

Jack stepped closer to Max. "I *do* know better...and that's why we're leaving this place with far more money than you would've got."

Jack stormed out of the bar and headed upstairs.

Before Max joined him, he patiently waited another few minutes on his own. He wondered, over and over, how long it could last. How long, before it all came crashing down.

CHAPTER 29

Jack and Carter stood on a desolate street somewhere in Belgravia. Vast houses accompanied by pristine, well-kept gardens consumed their line of sight. Not a flower or ornament was out of place and Carter wondered whether anyone actually occupied any of the homes. Given there was no shortage of foreign investors who felt a need to diversify their investments, his best guess was probably not. From the outside the houses constantly felt clean and fresh. The wind would blow and there was nothing on the street that might move. He was reminded of a London that he only ever saw on old naïve television; prim, proper and upper-class.

At the very minimum, in front of every other home was a luxurious car parked by the pavement. Some of the more obscure models appeared as if they emerged from a mothballed Department of Defence project that had run out of money. Others were nothing different from what one might expect on the front page of a popular car magazine.

The taxi journey had been reasonably quick but long enough for Carter to plan his next move. He had arranged for a car to be placed near Reinhart's address which he would use to deposit their phones and weapons. If everything went as planned, they'd use the car to return to the Field although it very much depended upon the outcome of their discussion.

Carter's gaze wandered around the street until he spotted the most inexpensive car on the street.

That's it alright.

Carter walked towards it. For a second he thought its colour was maroon but there was enough dirt across the exterior to suggest that in a previous life it was possibly red. The numbers on the license plate were the sort he hadn't seen in many years and were fixed over chunky tyres didn't have as much as tread as he may have expected. There were some squashed insects on the windscreen and the colour of the wing mirrors was of a different shade compared to the rest of the body.

"Is that our car?" Jack asked.

"Yeah."

Carter slipped his hand under the metal body. He could feel drabs of oil seeping into his fingers. Jack watched carefully as he shuffled his hands across the underbelly of the vehicle until his hand eventually came to a stop. He stood up, holding a small key attached to a keyring in the shape of a metal cube.

"Under the car. Really? What if it was stolen?"

"On this street," Carter said sarcastically. "Take a look around. Any thief who came to this street to steal this car probably needs to re-evaluate his career."

"True," Jack said smiling.

Carter opened the passenger-side door and took a quick glance inside the glovebox.

He saw a small box of tissues, a windscreen scraper and another silenced 9mm pistol.

I forgot how resourceful Jeff could be sometimes.

Carter extended his hand out. "Jack pass me your

weapon."

Jack handed Cassano's pistol to Carter who placed it inside the glovebox. He had kept a hold of it all this time. Jack had only ever fired a pistol once when he was at a gun range several years ago. Apart from the basics, he knew very little about operating a firearm. If an actual gunfight broke out, after emptying the initial clip, he was confident he wouldn't be much use from that point onwards.

Carter took off his coat and threw it into the back of the car along with Cassano's phone. He removed his weapon and its holster and stowed it inside the glovebox.

Carter attempted to close the box but noticed the windscreen scraper was protruding forwards.

He dropped it on the floor, making just enough space for the box to close. The cache of weapons inside almost made it look like the contents of a military supply drop. He gave it a firm push and slammed it tightly shut.

Carter locked the door and placed the keys in his pocket.

"Not going to put those under the car then," Jack said smugly.

"I'll probably hold on to them this time," Carter said.

"Hey, before we go, there's one other thing I want to mention."

"What is it?"

Carter detected the caution in Jack's tone and it reminded him of when had spoken to Jeff earlier that day.

"It's about Reinhart. When I spoke with him on the phone, that is. There was something he said that didn't quite sit right with me."

"What did he say?"

Before he replied, Jack cast his eyes around the street. Nothing moved and all he could hear was the mild chirping of some birds. He felt like the world had stopped.

"Reinhart didn't know what NLP was?"

Carter's face was blank. "Why's that matter?"

"Whether *you* know what it is or not is irrelevant. But he's an investor in this sort of technology. He has a number of investments already. It's his job to know. And it's so elementary. I was worried that I'd get found out by saying something non-technical but nothing happened. He sounded…sort of incompetent."

"You sure? That's a big statement to make from just one short conversation."

Jack ran it through his head again. For a second he wasn't sure if he was jumping to conclusions.

"Think carefully Jack. Forget about Stafford, forget about Kessler or any of this nonsense. With no prior information, what would an independent observer say about your conversation?"

"They would say…what I said. He doesn't feel like who he's supposed to be."

"Ok. Well our initial thought was always that Reinhart was unstable. An investor who wanted Stafford's algorithm for himself when he realised he might be losing out. But you're saying that –"

"I think he doesn't know anything. There's no way he understands why Stafford's algorithm or product might be the best. He doesn't even know the name of main branch of his work. I just can't see why he wouldn't. I know it's a long shot, and maybe he was being forgetful, but I think there's something wrong here."

"What's even weirder is that he asked us, as if he were some sort of authority on the matter," Jack continued. "It seemed like he was trying to impress *us*. Convince *us*, that he really was an expert on the topic, you know."

"Yeah. So he pretended, so that we believe his intentions for taking Stafford were genuine?"

"Maybe. I don't know yet. I just think there's more to him."

"Possibly. Let's just stay observant. We'll take it as it

comes."

Carter collected his thoughts, letting them settle amongst the carnage of his other ideas.

Was there another motive for taking Stafford? Other than money?

All along Carter had suspected some sort of unbalanced and crazed individual at the heart of the problem but now it seemed as if there was something else. Another variable he wasn't considering.

Could it be related to…no. There's no way. It wouldn't make any sense.

Jack and Carter walked to the address they had been texted.

As Jack struggled to make sense of Reinhart's position he remembered what Cassano said as they left; that they had no idea what they were about to do. He wondered whether there was any truth to the statement. Did he know? Did Carter? Was there something behind Reinhart's position that they never thought to consider; a black swan in the Field.

Sometimes Jack felt as if no one really knew anything. Other times he felt as if he knew everything. The dichotomy had placed him at a crossroads many times before and his confidence always pushed him towards the latter. It was a position that had yet to fail him.

Nonetheless, revaluating the circumstances again, Jack certainly understood Carter's position that Cassano was the villain and so there was no reason for him to have taken Cassano's opinion seriously. It was designed first and foremost to deter them from their actions. He would've said anything at that point. Jack may not have known what was to come, but he wasn't willing to back down at this point. He had come too far to give up.

They both arrived at the house. From the outside its size felt overwhelming. Three floors were drenched in a white, glossy coat, the shine of which caught the final rays of sun as it begun its descent just before the afternoon came to a close.

Jack stared at the door and noticed something out of the ordinary.

"It's already open."

Carter exchanged a prudent glance with Jack and moved forwards. There was a small footpath and then the door, open ever so slightly. It was gently touching the frame and required only a small push to shut it completely.

Carter tapped the door and let it drift open. A quiet creaking noise spiralled down the corridor, its walls barren apart from a few coat pegs near the entrance. He slowly entered, vigilantly scanning the area while Jack followed behind him.

At the end of the corridor Carter saw an open doorway. There was a large wall ahead of it and to the left he could see the room potentially opening up.

Carter stepped through the doorway, holding his breath before he turned the corner. He edged around, slowly at first, and then stepped into the room. It was vast, and like the corridor, empty apart from a large wooden table with two seats on both sides and a small pile of blank papers in the centre. Ahead of the table, to the right, was a large door and another at the far end of the room.

The entire house felt like a makeshift warehouse rather than a home. Instead of living, it seemed that its primary purpose was to hold prisoners.

Jack and Carter's footsteps echoed against the walls, their feet knocking against the wooden flooring.

Jack placed his hand on the table, tapping his fingers against the cold, solid surface. The noise he made was miniscule although he soon heard something far louder.

The sound made Carter stop dead in his tracks.

Footsteps. One at a time. One person.

They were purposeful steps, in that they were

purposely loud. The noise was coming from the far end of the room and increased in volume.

The individual finally walked into the room. A pistol was anchored in his hand, directed towards both Jack and Carter.

His presence was immediate, looming over the both of them. He looked as he did in the CCTV footage, still enshrouded in a dark grey trench coat. The coat was open and underneath he wore a dark brown shirt, loosely tucked into a pair of black trousers.

He stepped closer, meticulously observing them both although he gave more attention to Carter than Jack. It seemed as if he knew who might be who and which one was of more interest to him having not ever seen either of them at that point. His look was one of both menace and inquisitiveness, his face static and motionless but his eyes glaring into every crevice of detail before he might finally have to speak.

As he took each step, his black boots bounced against the floor, the thud resonating around the room.

The thudding stopped, the movement stopped and David Kessler stood in his place, a weapon marked on Michael Carter, steady and calm, his expressionless demeanour morphing into a scrutinising gaze.

"Mr Carter…and you, Jack Morse. Thank you for both being so prompt."

CHAPTER 30

Kessler examined them both carefully, his eyes scouring beneath black, shadowlike hair.

"I'm sure you boys won't mind if I double check that you did as I instructed."

Kessler drifted his weapon from Carter to Jack. "Come over here."

Jack walked to Kessler who quickly searched him, checking for any weapons and then removed his phone. Having done the same with Carter, he watched as they both stood side by side again.

"Good," Kessler said softly, switching off the phones and placing them into his pocket. He turned his head back to the door from whence he came. "You're alright to come out now."

Jack and Carter followed Kessler's point of focus as if they were magnetised. Another pair of footsteps begun to vibrate through the room and their curiosity flared up.

A few moments later another man walked into the room. Jack remembered him well, the same scar of delight marked upon his face.

He was wearing another grey suit, clad against a light

blue shirt, and wore his expression with a sophistication that smartened his appearance in a way that few others could replicate.

Joseph Reinhart smiled at Jack. Where someone might expect warmth, Jack felt ravaging ice.

"Good to see you again Jack."

Next to Kessler, Reinhart appeared quite short, although such was the way that he carried himself that anybody would think Reinhart believed himself to be the most grandiose of individuals.

"So you're the one that took him," Carter said calmly.

Reinhart started to laugh. It sounded wheezy, as if most of the joy and humour in his body had dried up.

"I am."

"You ever stop to think this entire plan was a bit much?"

Reinhart's baggy suit floated above his shoulders, the sleeves encircling wrists that looked like a pieces of wire.

"It probably seems that way. But it makes a good degree of sense when you think it through carefully. I had been planning a similar venture for quite some time and was hoping no one beat me to it. That was until I found out dear Elizabeth Jones was out looking for funding for her own trading business. So I had to make a decision. Not an easy one I tell you but a necessary one. I decided to act. I met with them and then took a view on how I'd proceed."

"And your view was to kidnap Stafford and Max?"

"Well, initially just Stafford. Max was collateral damage. If I removed Stafford then the company would come to a halt and I'd regain a position of power...or so I thought."

Reinhart spun a passing glance at Jack who, on the face of it, seemed relatively calm.

"And you decided to kidnap him. Not kill him? I feel like that would've been an easier option."

"I'm not as vicious as you are Mr Carter," Reinhart remarked. "I wasn't ready to resort to cold blooded violence. This seemed like an amicable compromise."

"An extreme one nevertheless."

"It's just business."

"Either way, you understand why we're here don't you?"

"No. Afraid I don't."

Carter paused. "To negotiate Stafford's release."

Reinhart shook his head. "I'm afraid I have to tell you Mr Carter, there isn't going to be a negotiation. You see, I've done some thinking and...*I've changed my mind.*"

The aurora in the air changed and Carter suddenly found himself in one of those rare circumstances where he realised he may not have been as free as he might've liked.

"I don't think that's wise. I told you earlier, there's evidence you masterminded this whole charade...I can destroy everything you've built. Think twice before –"

"I'm stopping you right there," Reinhart said, placing out his hand. "I only asked you here because the both of you were a threat to my position. Now that we've isolated you, Stafford's business comes back to a halt."

"No. You've still got too much to lose."

"Not really. And I'm not concerned. I was worried you'd cause more trouble if I let you remain free so getting you here seemed like a much better option. And now I have you. It worked out very well actually."

Carter felt his pulse racing. Had Reinhart really brought them here solely to lock them away? Had their plan at leveraging his reputation been completely pointless?

"I have people on the outside...they'll make it happen."

"Then let them. But no one's getting Stafford. And no one is probably going to see either of you again."

"Don't fuck around," Carter said. The frustration was becoming evident in his voice. "We both know you're lying."

"But I'm really not Mr Carter."

"We'll see," Carter said. He stepped forwards. "Give him up…or else."

Jack had seen this exact scenario before. Reinhart's complete unwillingness to concede any ground or to provide any basis for his actions or decisions. He did as he pleased, disinterested in the concerns of the opposing party and arguably an impossible man to negotiate with.

"Or else…really?"

Something about Reinhart's flippant tone was enough to set Carter off. He continued forwards to Reinhart, his fists clenched but Kessler swung his gun towards him.

"Stay there or I'll shoot you where you stand. I won't ask a second time."

Carter stopped. He took a deep breath, slowly regaining his composure.

Kessler stepped backwards and opened one of the doors behind him. "Get inside."

Carter nodded.

"Do anything crazy and I won't hesitate. You're just lucky he likes having people alive."

Carter stepped into the room. Apart from a small chair and four walls of cream paint the room was completely empty.

Kessler closed the door from the outside and locked it.

"Finally. He was beginning to annoy me." Reinhart said. "Now that's dealt with, I think I'll attend to the other matter."

Reinhart walked back the way he came and fell out of sight.

Kessler glanced at Jack. "So why did *you* come here? Why not just leave it to Carter?" He ushered his head backwards.

"I promised I'd get Stafford back. At all costs."

"Promised who? Yourself?"

"Does it matter?"

"Of course it does. If you're promising yourself then there's no reason to see it through other than your pride. And trust me, men who follow their pride often follow a path to their demise."

"It's not pride," Jack said confidently.

"Call it whatever you want. I've seen it all before. Christ – let me ask you something. What do you make of me?"

Kessler moved closer. "Who do you think I am?"

"Carter told me who you were. Some mercenary. Killer for hire."

"But what does that even mean. Do you even understand what those words are?"

Kessler's words were cold, cutting through the air. Something about the way he spoke chilled Jack's nerves. He found himself struggling for a response.

"I kill people Jack. I kill a lot of people. I end their lives. Do you know *what* that means? Have you ever seen it? The end of the soul…"

"Do you have any idea what it would take to stop me? What you'd need to be capable of. If you were to ask the men that died they'd only tell you what's not enough. Shamefully, they too, didn't know the answer."

"These theatrics aren't going to deter me," Jack said.

"The way you hesitate when I put reality at your feet. The way you quivered when I told you that I'm taking Max. That I'd kill him if you cross me…you'll never be ready…not for a man like me."

"But you're still just a man. At your core, you're still like me."

Kessler grabbed Jack by the throat and slammed him against the wall. "Am I? *Jack Morse.*"

Jack tried to fight back, Kessler's relentless grip

slowly squeezing the life from him. Jack pushed forwards but Kessler slammed him back into the wall, the shock crashing against his skull. The force was sudden, as if from nowhere, its power derived from another realm. The oxygen from his body slowly began to dissipate, his muscles started to weaken. Jack's sight started to falter but the remorseless image of Kessler continued to pervade his vision.

"You have no idea what reality is Jack Morse," Kessler whispered. "*No idea.*"

Kessler removed his hand from Jack's throat and moved back. They could both hear footsteps.

"Looks like he's here."

Jack gasped for air, his throat searing in pain. Kessler had only held him for a few seconds but it felt as if it were an eternity, infinitely at the behest of a torturous soul.

As Jack looked to the end of the room, panting away as oxygen slowly refilled his lungs, he saw Reinhart re-emerge from the door. However, just behind him, came the man he'd so desperately sought. The one he'd been looking for this entire time. The man he'd find at all costs. Edward Stafford.

CHAPTER 31

Katrina had taken longer than normal to walk back to the Field. The extra time away from anyone she knew, anyone she recognised and anyone she cared about provided her with the opportunity to clear her mind and draw some sense from what had been happening. Even if there was just a scrap, she was desperate for some momentary relief from the chaos that was engulfing her life, and those around her. Much of it was a result of external forces which were out of her control. But there was also chaos that resulted from something internal. They were the subtle mechanisms of the soul; the thoughts that played in people's minds. They were the ideas that somehow found solace in the current circumstances and suddenly became realised in the physical.

Every time Katrina approached a path she knew would force her closer to her destination, she purposely searched for a side street which might extend her journey further. She walked as slow as she could, observing every crack and crevice on the ground, smiling at every shopkeeper or stall owner who crossed her way, and made every effort to watch the clouds go by. At certain points she would even come to a standstill, fixed with her thoughts. Passers-by carried befuddled looks as they tried to understand what she was doing, theorising whether she was either drunk, high or mentally unbalanced.

Eventually, Katrina realised she couldn't ignore her destination any longer and returned back to the Field. Upon entering the square, she saw Elizabeth sat upright in the corner, her head tilted back. Her phone lay on her lap; a pair of earphones protruding from the bottom and into her ears.

Katrina could see that she was on some sort of business call although she received a wave and acknowledgement as soon as she entered. Elizabeth gestured towards the corridor, and mouthed the word 'Sinclair'.

Katrina figured Sinclair was still in Stafford's office. She wasn't entirely keen on visiting him but also knew she couldn't ignore him and so made her way down the corridor and into the office.

The piles of papers and trophies that had previously been scattered on the floor were back in the correct place. Overall, the office was still a mess and yet if it were any different, then something would have felt out of place.

Sinclair was behind the table, leaning on his side against the back of the room and staring down at the street from the window. He watched as people plodded along and across the road, mostly on their own but on certain occasions as small conglomerates.

He hadn't said much since she left. He had spent his time in solitude, reflecting and considering what came next for him. The realisation that he murdered two men in cold blood was still a resonating force in his mind and seemed to result from an instability he appeared to have no control over. Such a realisation was hard to ignore and one he was trying to come to terms with.

Having been fixated on the flurry of individuals outside, it took several seconds for Sinclair to realise that he wasn't alone. He spun to the side and spotted Katrina in the doorway.

There was an awkward silence in the room as neither of them seemed to greet each other. Before it became unbearable, Sinclair pushed himself off the wall and stood up straight.

"Good to see you back," he said. "Where's everyone else?"

Katrina could sense that Sinclair was really asking about Carter. Despite whatever reluctance or fear she may have been feeling, there was a side of her that knew Carter's attack against him was anything but gentle. Whether he got the right answer, or whether he would ultimately bring Stafford back, Carter's willingness to attack and to manipulate scared her considerably more than anything Sinclair may have been capable of. To that end, their distrust of him was something they could both potentially agree on.

"Jack and Carter decided to continue," she replied bluntly. "They have a lead and they're running with it."

"Why didn't you go along?" Sinclair asked.

"Because it was apparently too dangerous and Jack didn't want me to get hurt."

"Dangerous? What the hell happened?"

Katrina turned away, her hair fluttering across her face.

Sinclair walked around the table and took one of the chairs which was awkwardly placed against the side of the wall and dragged it into the centre of the room.

"Sit down Katrina."

"I'm fine. I'll just stand." She continued to look away.

"Just take a seat. Please."

Katrina cast her hair to one side and sat down. Sinclair fell back against the table and folded his arms. He stared at her intently.

"What did you find at the Canal?"

Katrina slowly recalled what she saw on the CCTV footage; Stafford's panic-stricken face, the unknown man who came to take him away; the man in the coat; the man that made Carter's eyes freeze; the man whose identity she still didn't know.

"Why did you come back here...without knowing?" Sinclair probed.

"I had been outside, speaking to Elizabeth. But when I came back Carter left me in the room alone with Jack. That's when he told me that he and Carter were going it alone. He said it was safer if I stayed out of it."

Sinclair was beginning to hear traces of frustration in her voice and he knew its source was the same reason that the story had suddenly piqued his interest. It wasn't that the identity of the man on the CCTV footage remained a mystery but rather why she wasn't being told.

"Wait. Are you talking about this man's identity or continuing on with the investigation?"

"Look, I had no interest in following Carter on some merry chase through the city. I was done at that point. What I didn't get was first, why Jack wanted to go along on for the ride. And two, why he didn't want to tell me what was going on. The way he broke it to me, he made it out like it was so dangerous to even know the name of this mysterious kidnapper and yet, it was apparently fine for him to run off and take him down."

Katrina leant forwards in her chair. She dropped her head in her hands.

"I left him alone for five minutes...and he got him."

Sinclair's leg quivered slightly. "You mean Carter?"

She lifted her head and nodded. "I don't know what he said. But he got Jack on side. Convinced him that only the two of them together can bring Stafford back and that Carter can't do it without him. He's going to dive head first into something he doesn't understand...all because one guy knew exactly the right words to say."

All the while Sinclair wondered what the purpose of Carter's appearance was. What was driving his actions? What drove Carter to accumulate so much information on him and unravel his history? What possessed him to draw Jack further into this problem?

Sinclair knew better than to think Carter was operating upon a single dimension. Human beings such as him were far too complex to act in the name of selflessness or profit alone. Multiple variables were colliding against each other under the surface, and Sinclair could see that their collisions were clearly pervading through the lives of others.

As he watched someone, who for the most part had obviously disliked him, struggle to come to terms with the fog that fell over their life and that of their friends, he wondered whether the circumstances were fair. For everything that Sinclair had done, what was taking place now felt alien to him. Engaging in this behaviour was beyond him; he didn't understand it; he lacked the capacity to perform it. It required a quality that was unknown to him and he was beginning to see the misery it brought. The very fact that he knew so little about it meant that he could empathise with the confusion Katrina was feeling.

"Listen," Sinclair said. "My read on Jack is that he isn't stupid."

"It's not about that!" Katrina snapped. "It's the fact that he's so fucking foolish sometimes. So arrogant! He just thinks he'll be fine. He just thinks that he'll deal with whatever comes with his way, without any plan or any ideas. He thinks everything doesn't apply to him."

"We all have some of that. Our self-worth comes from our ability to recognise that our lives have some significance."

"This isn't about self-worth. This is something else...this is...not realising when to quit. Not realising when enough is enough."

"Even that," Sinclair said calmly. "We all do it."

"I-…"

Katrina paused. When she entered the room, she wasn't expecting that she'd pour out her anger over Jack's actions. Not least to Sinclair; someone who she'd initially held with an extremely high degree of scepticism. But for whatever reason, he seemed different to her at this point. As if within the last few hours of solitude, he had somehow composed his anger and inner resentment.

"Look…I'm not denying that. It's just that with Jack…it's more real to him than it is to other people. He really believes it. *Really believes.*"

Sinclair unfolded his arms and placed his hands against Stafford's desk. His fingers tightly curled around the edges while pressure slowly built up against the tips of his fingers as his nails dug into the wood.

"I guess you know him better than I do."

"Yeah. I do. But then again…" She shuffled around in her chair and tidied away the hair that had fallen in front of her face. "There's a lot of things I like about him too."

"Oh yeah," Sinclair chuckled. "Like what?"

Katrina sat back in her chair and stared up at the ceiling, as if she were watching the stars.

"Probably that sense of humour. Although it's pretty fucking annoying sometimes too."

Sinclair burst out laughing. "Well, no one was ever perfect."

"No. They aren't. I'm definitely not. I'm sure Jack looks at me sometimes and thinks what the hell is going on with her. What a weirdo. Why can't she keep her head screwed on straight? Why can't she take it easy for once? Why can't she just give people the benefit of the doubt? Why can't she…believe in something a little bigger in life? But guess what…I actually know those things are wrong. I'm aware of them. I have self-awareness! But

Jack…he doesn't. Not in the slightest bit. He's…blinded."

Sinclair observed her carefully. The jolt in her expression, the slight rise in the pitch of her voice.

"You don't agree?" she asked.

"Not entirely. You say that you're aware but…are you? We never know the things that blind us." Sinclair took a deep breath. For a second it was as if there was something stopping him from speaking. "I loved my wife…I loved her more than anything. I always had. It's hard to describe but it's how I drew purpose in life. Knowing that as I lived and as I acted, she was there too. In the same way, sometimes being blind to the wider world gives people the capacity for purpose too. It focusses the mind on one thing. And you see that's the thing; when you lose whatever gives you purpose in life, you're destined to be lost. So is it really that bad? Is it really that bad that someone like Jack has a bit of purpose in his life?"

"No. I just wonder if it's too blinding. I mean, even before this whole thing happened, Jack and Max had met with some of our investors. Jack almost screwed the whole thing up!"

"What?"

"Max gave him instructions not to talk about a certain thing that was sure to get them riled up, and he did it anyway. They got so angry they were ready to pull their funds. It would've wrecked the whole venture…all because Jack thought he knew better and felt the need to bring his opinion up. He was that arrogant, that he almost destroyed the company."

As Katrina's eyes drifted down from the ceiling and towards Sinclair she noticed that something else had captured his attention; something behind her.

Katrina swung her head backwards and saw that Elizabeth was stood in the doorway.

"Wrecked the whole venture you say?" Elizabeth asked curiously. She moved forwards into Stafford's office. "You're going to need to elaborate on what exactly you mean by that."

.

CHAPTER 32

Katrina froze in horror.

How long has she been there?!

"Well?" Elizabeth asked.

"Look, don't worry. It's not that important."

"Not that important. If what I heard is correct, Jack almost singlehandedly destroyed this business. I'd say that's pretty important."

Katrina knew there was no backpedalling at this point. Elizabeth had heard everything she needed in order to understand the extent of Jack's actions and there was nothing Katrina could say which would stop her from demanding answers.

"I only say that because Jack also fixed it. I just want you to bare that in mind."

"I am baring it mind. But I also couldn't care less. This is something that concerns my company – in a significant way – and I deserve to know about it. I knew something wasn't right as soon as Max made that funny remark about the dinner last night. I would've asked him myself later that night but I obviously didn't get that opportunity."

Katrina stood up so she could see Elizabeth clearly.

Sinclair was still sat against Stafford's desk watching as Katrina gathered her composure.

Elizabeth was naturally a towering figure but Katrina forgot how personified that trait became whenever her demeanour turned hostile. It was a talent she hadn't yet mastered; the skilful balance between pleasant and ruthless. It turned Elizabeth from close confidant and astute business associate to unrelenting, shrewd and determined at just the right moments and frequently enough that she was both admired and respected.

Elizabeth remained in the doorway, stood up straight and peering down at Katrina who began to explain what happened that evening.

As Katrina described the events she noticed that there was little change in Elizabeth's expression. She didn't seem to react nor did she interject; her face remained perfectly still throughout.

Once Katrina finished she stopped, almost desperate for sort of response.

Elizabeth took a small breath and gently took a step forwards. "I can't say I'm not surprised."

"You knew he'd do something like this?" Sinclair asked.

"Not this situation exactly. But it was always clear he'd act like this at one point. Max and I recognised his nature – the moment we met him. The sheer level of self-belief – it was shocking."

"Yeah…" Katrina said.

Katrina struggled to fight the reluctance cast over her face. She could do nothing but agree with Elizabeth.

"It's terrifying though isn't it? This whole venture might've died in an instant – and I never even knew."

"We would've told you –"

"I would fucking hope so," Elizabeth fired.

The spike in tone caught Katrina off guard who jolted back slightly.

Elizabeth moved towards one of the shelves in Stafford's office. Her eyes glossed over the various books and their titles, many of which were either covered in dust or contained words she couldn't begin to pronounce. She removed one of the books and flicked through the pages, curious whether she might understand what was going on. Inundated with equations and notation she quickly placed it back where she found it.

"But even you have to appreciate," Sinclair said, breaking the silence. "Jack got a better deal than anyone ever expected. And he only got it because he was willing to face the problem head on, rather than ignore it."

"Sinclair, you're giving him credit for something that happened entirely by luck."

"It's not luck! He found a solution. He figured it out."

"He only figured it out *after* the investors walked out. When he raised it, he didn't have a clue. At that moment in time, he disobeyed what Max told him and went with his gut – and put everything at risk…all because he felt like it. You don't understand…it's the principle. The inability to abide by it is inherent to who Jack Morse is."

Sinclair shook his head. "You know how many chaotic things I've done over the years? How many people I've disobeyed? You know how many of them worked out too?"

"And how did that all end for you?" Elizabeth noted. "Not well, I imagine. My point isn't about what Jack did today. It's about what he does tomorrow. It's about how long it can all last?"

Elizabeth tried to gauge an expression from Katrina but she seemed lost in the reality of Jack's predicament, unable to generate a coherent response. For the most part, she agreed with what Elizabeth was saying. There was nothing she could say which might prove to be an adequate defence of his actions.

"So what are you going to do?" Katrina asked.

Elizabeth sensed an element of fear in Katrina's question, as if she were eluding to something drastic.

"I'm probably not going to do anything. What can I do, apart from hope that everyone tries to keep him in check; tries to stop him doing anything seriously stupid. But really, there's nothing I can do. He'll do whatever he wants regardless. The only thing we can do is wait…wait until he learns it all for himself."

Elizabeth turned around and continued to browse through Stafford's bookcase, seemingly disinterested and as if she'd given up on the problem entirely.

Unsure how to respond, Katrina slumped back in her chair, trying to think of a better solution. After several minutes, she realised she couldn't.

CHAPTER 33

Stafford innocently stared at Jack, his eyes torn with angst.

"Jack, what are you doing here?" Stafford asked. "You shouldn't have come."

There was a wobble in his disposition which was synonymous with the mild shuddering of his body. He appeared still but the collars of his shirt seemed to jitter from side to side. As he turned to his captors, his words sailed off into silence while a menacing grin appeared on Reinhart's face.

"Come on…you too," Reinhart bellowed.

A moment later, just as dishevelled and equally as surprised at what was happening, Max also entered the room.

"Jesus, I can't believe it. You honestly came here to get us back?"

"He did, didn't he?" Kessler muttered. "Whether that was the right decision or not is…yet to be determined."

Max's ink coloured suit had lost its shine and there were more creases than Jack remembered. The brown Oxfords he normally wore were loosely tied and with very little effort while his hair lacked its regular tidiness as strands drooped over the sides of his ears and forehead.

"Why don't we all take a seat gentlemen," Reinhart said. "We have a lot to discuss."

He steered Max and Stafford to the table and they both sat down. Reinhart dragged one of the chairs from the opposite side and dumped it next to Stafford.

In the bleak silence, the scraping of the chair legs against the floor were like nails on a chalkboard. The sound rang unnaturally in everyone's ears and only Kessler appeared not to notice. He constantly seemed both aware and unaware of everything, actively choosing what might draw his attention.

"Sit down Jack," Reinhart said.

Jack did as he was told while Kessler's gun continuously pointed at him as he moved.

As Jack sat down, Kessler's attention turned to the door just besides them. The way he stared suggested it was calling out to him and it was becoming difficult for him to ignore. He flicked his eyes to Reinhart.

"I think I'd like to spend some time with Mr Carter," Kessler said. "You fine out here?"

Reinhart removed a small pistol from his inside pocket. "I'll be ok. I don't think anyone is going to cause a fuss out here. Just don't harm him."

"Fine."

Kessler opened the door to his right and entered the room, shutting it behind him.

"Just the four of us it seems," Reinhart said.

No one responded.

They were all looking at Reinhart. His thin frame gave the impression of a man that was mostly harmless but they sensed elements of unpredictability and the tendency towards volatility. The slight flick of his brow or the random surge in the tone of his voice made for a person that was accustom to acting as he pleased and knew no authority.

In the ensuing silence Reinhart scrutinised as many of Jack's qualities as he could; the way he dressed, the way he sat, the nature of his expression and even the style of his hair. All of them gave him some indication of who he was and why he was here but they weren't enough. Access to the inner sanctum of his mind still remained out of reach.

"There's one thing I have yet to figure out," Reinhart said.

No one had spoken for at least a minute and everyone realised that Reinhart had probably been conversing with himself.

"Be honest Jack," he continued. His face seemed warm and comforting. "Did you really believe I was going to give you a reasonable investment when we met earlier this week? I mean it was clear that I wasn't interested. I had my own venture. My own plans for a fund. I made the whole thing so obvious but you were quite adamant. Very adamant in fact."

What the hell is he getting at?

What Jack found the most peculiar was that he still didn't know the game that Reinhart was playing. He continued to maintain the façade; the one where he cared about the business and the industry. But from what he knew so far, it was anything but true.

Jack noticed the scepticism scuttle on to Max and Stafford's face. The same scepticism he was feeling. Just like him, they still couldn't figure out what was going on.

He wasn't in the mood to respond but he realised he didn't have much of a choice. If he was going to build any picture of what Reinhart was up to he needed to engage with him in at least some capacity.

"Yeah. Well, I thought there was scope to change your mind."

"No. Never. It was always the plan to push you away.

Elizabeth saw that. But you – and Stafford – both didn't catch on."

Reinhart watched as Stafford's body turned slightly outwards, attempting to avoid facing him.

"Did you know about this Max?" Reinhart asked. "The hopeless attempt by these two."

"Elizabeth might've mentioned it to me," Max said flatly. He seemed disinterested in Reinhart's question and let his focus drift towards the window. Anything, not least the outside world, was more appealing than his predicament right now.

How did it all come to this?

Max had grown accustom to gauging to what extent a situation was veering in his favour and correcting his course as necessary. The slight drooping in an individual's expression or the shuffling of a foot was enough to tell him something was amiss. He enjoyed navigating towards amicable understanding and excelled in the art of people.

But for the past few hours his knowledge of emotion had told him, over and over, that Reinhart's motivations for this matter almost certainly lay elsewhere; or with someone else.

"I get the feeling you would've noticed," Reinhart said. "I'm kind of glad you weren't there actually. Pragmatists can be such a pain. They stop others from being so reckless. Although, I bet you've already caught a glimpse of that."

Max still seemed indifferent but Reinhart could see that he knew what he was referring to.

"What's interesting is that it continues," Reinhart said. "Except this time you have an ally, a more experienced operator, from the world of bad decision making. *Michael Carter.*"

"Who's that?" Max asked.

"You think Jack found you both all on his own."

Reinhart's face lit up. "No. He had some assistance. How did he cross your path exactly?"

"He said he's an interested party," Jack replied. "And wants a cut in the investment."

"Oh. Well, he doesn't strike me as an investor if I'm completely honest with you. He seems a little more *roguish* if you ask me…don't you think? You must've been very desperate. I mean, to be fair, you can tell by someone's actions how desperate they are. You went so far as to partner with a man that you don't even know…or, in fact, understand."

Before Jack could respond someone entered the room. He had come from outside. The sound of his footsteps was almost non-existent. A young clean shaven man with combed blonde hair stood opposite Reinhart. His attire was plain; black trousers and a tightly zipped up jacket. There was little emotion on his face and he seemed wholly interested in Reinhart. It felt as if he hadn't noticed anyone else or that they didn't warrant his attention.

"Mr Reinhart," he said bluntly. "Where is he?"

He spoke with a deep flare, as direct as one could be yet maintaining a solid level of respect.

"He's in that room over there," Reinhart said, prodding his neck to the side. "What's your name son?"

"Benson."

"Okay Benson. I'm glad you made it here so promptly."

"Not a problem."

"Kessler is in the room too…so try to be careful when you enter. You don't want to alarm him. I'm sure you've heard what he's like."

Benson nodded and walked towards to the room.

"Events are accelerating gentlemen," Reinhart chuckled. "Accelerating indeed."

.

CHAPTER 34

Inside of a small square room, Carter was sat staring at the cream paint on the wall. The coat was fresh and covered the entire room. There weren't any windows or objects to catch his attention and so Carter increasingly found himself looking at the same patches of wall over and over again.

The lack of ventilation also meant that it took very little to recognise the humidity surrounding him. Carter licked his lips and tasted a hint of sweat and he could see portions of his shirt stuck to his forearms. The heat didn't make him feel uncomfortable but in combination with his circumstances and everything else, he sensed the onset of frustration.

He contemplated where he was going to go next. Reinhart had shot down his attempt at a negotiation, cast him into a silo and left him with no alternatives. Despite his familiarity with deception, something about being lied to often riled him up.

The truth surrounding his predicament was already dawning upon him. That without getting out of this room he stood no chance of finding Stafford and Max. And ultimately, would fail his primary objective, the goal that brought him to a most unexpected world, in the company of people so unattached to the universe he resided in.

Kessler was stood opposite him, both hands in the pockets of his coat, his focus shifting up and then back down.

"I will be honest Michael, I was a little surprised when I received your call."

"I expected as much."

"I know Cassano fairly well. He wouldn't have given up so easily. You must've done quite a number on him. What did you do to him? What did you do in order to get him to talk?"

Carter shrugged. "Not much."

"Bullshit."

Kessler examined the facetious expression on Carter's face. Something about it suggested little remorse for his actions.

"How much pain must you have inflicted? Must've been quite a poor sight." Kessler raised his head, his imagination running rampant for the briefest of seconds. "And poor Jack Morse."

Kessler tried to catch a shift in Carter's expression but it remained stable; as if he were holding it on purpose.

"He must've been mortified," Kessler continued. A small grin appeared on his face. "How far did you go until he got you to stop eh?"

"He suggested an alternative and I took it. Doesn't really matter though does it? Anything that got us here was a win."

"I don't deny that. I just want to know the specifics. Shots fired, bones broken…lives taken? How much of it went in – what people are capable of. Because I spoke to him…he doesn't look like a man who's learnt anything. Not from you anyway."

"I think you'd be surprised."

"Whether he's a different man or not, he's not like us."

"I'm nothing like you," Carter retorted.

Kessler found considerable enjoyment in Carter's distaste for him. His face resembled a young child during a summer afternoon, where the dry air tasted sublime and the future felt impossibly divine.

"The denial in your eyes is very sweet. It's like you actually believe what you're saying."

Carter leaned forwards in his chair. "*I do.*"

Kessler grasped the response with suspicion. All he heard was a scripted incantation and embedded in the words was an inherent frailty which served as a futile reminder of who Carter believed he was.

Carter could clearly see the cuts on the sides of Kessler's boots, as well as the wear and tear on his coat. A handful of light jagged marks were scattered across the back and along his sleeves. Together they told a disjointed story of lives that were certainly taken and painted a picture of resoluteness and discord. If he had to guess, the marks may have been accumulated over many years but served as discreet badges that could be worn proudly.

"So let me ask you then," Kessler said. "What do you want with Edward Stafford? Some mathematician turned entrepreneur. What's he to you?"

"He's an investment opportunity," Carter replied stiffly. "I saw it and given what's happened, I'm leveraging the situation."

"Don't give me that shit," Kessler warned. "No one does this – any of this – for an investment. No one goes to these lengths. No. You're something else. So don't treat me like a fool."

"Well, I'm sorry. I don't know what else to tell you."

"Where do you come from?"

"Nowhere interesting. I spent some time in the military."

The faded reply made Kessler consider whether his

questions were finally wearing Carter down. His shoulders slumped underneath his white shirt and Kessler noticed how Carter didn't bother to sweep away the strands of hair pressing against his forehead.

"I know a lot of people that carried a gun. But they don't carry themselves like you. What else happened to you? Who's responsible for bringing *this* version of Michael Carter into the world? The version I'm looking at."

"I wish I could tell you but that's mostly because we're the result of a lot of different things right?"

Kessler smiled. "Aren't we just."

"And you – who's your maker?" Carter probed.

"I don't have one. I'm just a product of the times. I guess you could say that I was made from the failures of men like you. Manifested to tie up loose ends and burn away the ideologies you brought into existence."

A dark current undercut his words. "You should be lucky I'm not the violent type," he added.

"I've read your profile...don't kid yourself," Carter said sharply.

"Truth has an interesting way of being distorted."

"It does, doesn't it? Just like when people claim to know something they definitely don't. Claiming to know theories and technologies they couldn't possibly understand. Fascinating when people do that, right?"

An unnatural silence fell upon the room. In such small surroundings it resonated aggressively.

Kessler had nothing to say but he was thinking, very carefully now.

"Who's Reinhart working for?" Carter asked.

"No one. This is the end of the line."

"And how can you be so sure?"

"Who else would bother doing this?"

Kessler quickly observed the variation in Carter's voice. With just an ounce of confidence he'd perked up and his eyes were shimmering.

"I'm going to let you in on a little secret…Reinhart is not interested in Stafford for the reason that he's told you."

"And how would you know that?"

"Jack," Carter said motioning to the door, "knows what he's talking about when it comes to this technology. And he can spot a pretender a mile off. When he spoke to Reinhart…he spoke to a pretender. He doesn't know a damn thing about their company or the technology. He's here to play a different game."

"Well, it's not my concern. I get paid either way."

"Quite right. As long as you're okay knowing it's not for the reason you thought it was."

"You're a serial liar Mr Carter. I've no reason to believe you."

"Maybe. But I think there's a good possibility you don't know who you're working with."

"Does Jack Morse know who he's working with?"

Carter sat up straight. "He knows what I'm willing to do."

"No, he doesn't…not yet."

There was a small noise, tearing Kessler from his thoughts. The door handle was creaking. Kessler drew his pistol and aimed it at the small gap slowly materialising between the door and the wall.

The door opened just a little, and the body of a young man appeared.

He slowly crept into the room, Kessler's weapon fixated upon him.

He turned his attention to Carter and then back to Kessler. "David Kessler…I've been sent to inform you that you're officially relieved of your duty here."

Kessler stayed as he was, digesting what he just heard.

"Your service to Mr Reinhart has been very much appreciated. You'll of course be compensated for your time and the matter with which you assisted."

Kessler stormed out of the room, pushing Benson to one side. Reinhart was sat at the table, his gaze lifting upwards.

"Something the matter," he asked.

"Who the hell's he?" Kessler fired.

"That is the man who will be taking over security arrangements. Your job here is done David and believe me when I tell you that I'm incredibly grateful for your help. It's just time to pass this work to someone else now. The hard part – your part – is done now."

Kessler didn't say anything. Jack had yet to see him angry or annoyed but there was a small tension floating beneath his words.

"So what happens to everyone here?"

"The less you know, the better David. I just need someone to guard Carter. That's all. I'd say that this, the logistics of bringing Stafford in, is over."

"This doesn't make any sense. Why this guy – for Carter? What else you got planned?"

"Nothing."

"It doesn't look like nothing Joseph. I'd like to know…because I don't like to be lied to."

Benson stepped back outside, his eyes glaring at Kessler.

"What are you hiding?"

"David, don't push me."

"I'll do whatever I like. What are you not telling me?!"

"Enough!" Reinhart said. He swiftly raised his hand into the air and viciously slammed it on to the table. "Stop asking me these questions. You did your job and you will be paid for it. What comes next does not concern you."

Reinhart was breathing heavily. The action was so unexpected that it caught everyone off guard. Jack could still even see the table rattling in its place.

"You should go," Benson said.

"Maybe I should," Kessler said calmly.

Kessler removed the phones from his pocket and threw them to Benson, one by one. "They belong to them."

He turned and headed for the exit, his eyes briefly catching Jack's.

"No hard feelings," he said. "Who knows…maybe we'll cross paths again."

Jack's mind flashed back to that first phone call – the man who would do what he must to ensure what he set out to do. Those words, the words he'd just heard, almost any of the words Kessler directed at him, felt as if they were the words of a man who believed himself grander than mortality – as if he circled somewhere beyond.

Kessler made his way outside, Carter's ideas still spiralling through his mind. As the thoughts grew something emerged. They turned from thoughts to curiosity, from curiosity to paranoia, from paranoia to suspicion, and from suspicion to vengeance in the name of nihilism.

CHAPTER 35

Benson walked back into the room and found Carter hunched forwards in his chair, trying to determine what was going on.

Benson stared at him, carefully scrutinising every detail he could, the way someone might analyse the photograph of an old friend.

Staring directly back, Carter was unable to match his level of intensity. He seemed engaged with facts and observations that Carter wasn't privy to as he looked for something else that lay under the surface.

Carter had possibly hoped to start some form of dialogue but Benson stood silently, his stance rigid and his face devoid of any emotion.

During the ensuing silence, he wondered about who he was, his connection to Reinhart, and why he, instead of Kessler was now guarding him. There was a mist gathering in his eyes; it had been accumulating since he first arrived and now for the first time he truly felt blind.

Benson eventually turned and swung the door the shut, the remainder of their time to be no different than the time that came before.

The door slammed shut and everyone watched as Reinhart's thin face momentarily sat idle. The longer he waited, the more it seemed that his skin hung on the edges of his nose and cheek bones. After a brief pause, his face suddenly animated to life, creaking and turning like a machine in an old factory.

"Before Benson arrived I was making a point…about Carter. The reason for his appearance."

Reinhart's eyes darted towards Jack, expecting a reaction but Jack's mind appeared to be elsewhere.

"Jack." He tried to get his attention. Jack gave him the satisfaction, briefly making eye contact. "You're not concerned by it are you? His sudden appearance."

"Not as much as you are apparently," Jack replied sharply.

Jack was trying to be evasive but he couldn't ignore the trace of reality that undercut Reinhart's question. He thought back to Katrina's constant, overarching scepticism of Carter; her violent frustration as he continued to deny the facts she so fiercely attempted to highlight to him.

I never said she was wrong. I should have at least told her that.

"You must realise it," Reinhart said. He tapped his pistol on the table to ensure he got everyone's attention this time. "That he has some plan or machination of his own."

Stafford adjusted his collar, seemingly agitated. "Joseph, why do we care? We're all sat here now. Does this Carter person really matter to any of us?"

"He certainly does. He represents Jack's inability to see deception. He represents the idea that wormed its way into his mind – the one that said he should come here – that he was smart enough and strong enough to play the game that he's never played."

Reinhart's words encompassed a sting. The type that was unexpected and all the more painful. They irked Jack; annoyed him; pushing him to do something he ordinarily would not.

"It's kind of ironic you say that," Jack said.

"Why?"

"Because I see it right now...the deception...staring me in the face."

Jack saw the displeasure flicker in Reinhart's eyes.

"I know you're not who you say you are," he continued. "I know you don't know anything about what our company does or the industry we operate in. I know that you're playing the part."

Reinhart's face filled with distaste. "Don't try to peddle this nonsense to me."

"We'd never even heard of you before you called," Jack snapped back instantly. "We were grateful for the call – that's the truth. But we knew you weren't a commodity. All the way before any of this – we knew we were scraping the bottom of the barrel."

With each passing second Stafford and Max watched as Jack dialled up the pressure. They could see the aggression flourishing in his eyes, emanating from a place unfamiliar to them but one that was slowly finding its roots.

"Come on..." Jack felt his body turn slightly tense. "Who are you working for?"

Reinhart's face dropped. "Excuse me?"

Everyone could see that the question had thrown Reinhart off balance. He was leaning forwards, his head tilted to one side but filled with equal parts anger and curiosity.

"I wish I could say you were the guiding mind for everything that's happened, but the more I think about it, the more I feel like there's someone else who's made the decisions."

A sour look filled Reinhart's expression. "You're making some very bold statements Jack. Especially from someone who knows so little about what's going on."

"Possibly. But whether you are, or you aren't, we always knew there was little substance to who you were."

Reinhart stomped his foot on the ground. "Are you trying to be funny! You – the boy who barely knows where he is – so unfamiliar or unaware of what's on the next page – so reluctant to even consider the possibility of what might lay ahead."

"Be honest...did you kidnap Stafford and Max for another reason...another person?"

Jack completely ignored Reinhart's comment. There was a small part of him that heard it and yet there was another part that pretended as if it were never said.

"I mean, if it's true," Jack continued, "it's funny that you're willing to lecture *me* about manipulation."

"I know a lot more than you think Jack. You just wait and see."

"But do you?" Jack sneered. He raised his eyes, wondering whether he'd elicited any sort of reaction. "If I were in the business of deception, I'd make sure I tell you half a story; half-truths and half-falsehoods – to make you feel like you were central to my plan, important to –"

"Don't act as if you know anything about importance," Reinhart shouted.

"As if you do," Jack chuckled. "Is *that* supposed to be funny?"

Reinhart was trying to compose himself but Jack persisted.

"To be important is for your actions to have some significance. Some meaning. Do you honestly think you've done that? Do you think it's true? Or are you like the rest of us? Delusional, and merely a footnote to history."

Reinhart clutched his gun, tighter and tighter, the

metal slowly sinking into his hand. He pushed it forwards, jolting it in Jack's direction.

There was a slight apprehension in Jack's disposition. For a split second it felt as if Reinhart's threat of violence may have quelled his hostility but then his body suddenly jolted back to life again, renewed with a new found sense of vitality.

Jack craned his head forwards. "No one ever enjoys that realisation do they?" he said openly.

Stafford turned to Jack, his eyes widening in horror. Neither Stafford nor Max recognised him.

What is he trying to accomplish? This is suicide!

Reinhart was breathing heavily. He was staring at Jack, ferocity searing through his eyes. His temper was beginning to boil, trickling through his body.

"Your arrogance is going to bring you a lot of pain Jack. Mark my words."

"I think it'll bring you far more pain than it will me."

"I promise you," Reinhart whispered. He stuttered slightly. "I will devastate you…"

Jack raised his eyebrow. "I don't fear threats from a pretender and a nobody."

Jack saw the violent surge in Reinhart's eyes. They sparked, a flash of light blinding Reinhart with rage, Stafford with fear and blessing Jack with opportunity.

Reinhart raised his hand up into the air, his gun gripped tightly. His hand was so high up, he hadn't even noticed. He had been so theatrical that he didn't see it.

As soon as the weapon lifted into the sky, out of their way and into the open, Jack quickly slipped his hands under the table. With all his force and valour, he launched the table upwards, flipping it in Reinhart's direction.

Reinhart only had one hand free to push the table back but it wasn't enough. The weight of the table was too much, and collapsed on to Reinhart, who, already off balance, stumbled off his chair and on to the wooden floor.

Jack had only seen it once; the uncontrollable rage that spun through Reinhart's mind, the unbalanced way in which he raised his fist in anger when Kessler had challenged him. A table, far flimsier than it appeared; one that could be used to incapacitate his opponent.

There, in its entirety, lay a circumstance that was in his favour – one that he had no choice but to recreate. Such a moment hinged upon whether Jack could bring Reinhart into that state of mind once again. Fundamentally, it relied upon whether Jack's instincts were correct – would Reinhart fall prey to an assault on his ego and self-imposed importance.

Even if he were right, a thousand things might've gone wrong. Reinhart could have fired his weapon at a whim. He may have swung his arm horizontally. He may not have even lost his temper. Jack had continued to remind himself of every possibility and yet ever present was the fact that there were no other options. No alternative to their situation unless he acted.

And such actions proved not be in vain.

The table slammed against the floor, booming across the room.

Jack leapt off the seat, ran towards Reinhart, and grabbed the hand that was holding the pistol.

He dragged the arm away from him and pounded his other hand into Reinhart's face. He struck him only a few times until his grip loosened and Jack could snatch the pistol from him.

He stood up, stepping away from Reinhart's beaten body. Turning around, his focus latched on to the room next to him.

Jack's heart turned to stone, mere seconds to react.

CHAPTER 36

Jack stepped back around the lopsided table.

The handle began to turn.

Stafford and Max were still sat in their chairs, both astonished and terrified at what they'd just seen. As Jack moved backwards he pulled them up from their seats and behind the door.

The handle swung downwards, the door burst out to the left and Benson stepped out, drifting his gun across the room. His eyes immediately caught sight of Reinhart, clutching his face in pain.

He aimed his pistol to the left and then back to the right, taking a quick scan of the room. As his pistol veered right he felt a sharp jab into the back of his head.

"Drop it," Jack said, emerging from behind the door.

Benson was silent.

"I said drop it."

There was still no response.

"I'm not messing around. Drop the weapon. Or I'll shoot."

"No…you won't."

"You want a fucking bet."

"You won't. I'm almost certain."

Jack could feel his hand shaking. He felt feverish, his heart pounding.

"Jack, just back off," Max pleaded. "Let's go."

"No. Not yet."

"My god," Stafford said. "He's not going to back down Jack. We have to leave. Please!"

"I told you – no!" Jack fired. "If we go, they'll kill him."

"You're talking about Carter?" Max said.

"Yeah!"

Max edged forwards. "Jack, I get you want to be the hero, but this isn't worth it. There's nothing we can do."

"I wouldn't be here if it wasn't for him. I owe him this much."

"You don't owe him your life."

"You two can go…but I'm not going anywhere. If he's smart he knows he needs to drop that gun. Otherwise I end this now."

Stafford was starting to lose his temper. "For god's sake…don't be so…"

"What?"

"Stubborn!"

"Reminds me of someone doesn't it," Jack remarked. "Stay out of it. I've got it under control."

Benson chuckled. "You should run while you can little man. You're not cut out for this."

"You better believe I'll pull this trigger. Drop the damn gun!"

"I hope you realise that once you do you'll have to live with the fact that you are not the same man you were. Do you think you can do it?"

More and more Jack saw a vision he couldn't turn away from. One where he may actually have to fire. He tried to make out its conclusion but it was blurred; distorted at the edges. He sought clarity, wading his hands through the noise but continued to be met with resistance.

"I meet so many who think they get it. They always die. But then more just seem to take their place. It's like natural selection doesn't apply here."

The heat continued to sear through Jack's body. Beads of sweat trickling down his head. The muscles in Jack's hands tightened. If he gripped the weapon any tighter he felt he might snap it in two. His finger straddled the trigger, scuttling backwards and forwards.

"Do what you want. When *he* finds you…you'll never know life the same as you know it now."

"Stop fucking around. Drop it!"

"Jack, just go!" Max said. "He won't give in."

"It's under control. Shut the fuck up and stay out of this. I'm getting Carter out of here. I'm not leaving him to die."

Benson spun around. He had seen an opportunity and struck. For him, it was the moment to finish off the man he believed to know nothing.

But Jack had struck first. At the first sight of movement he pulled the trigger. He hadn't even thought about it. Fear had taken over. The fear of death, failure and the unknown. He had come too far to let it end this way. Nothing would stop him – not even Benson, and not even the possibility of killing another man.

Jack was engaging with a new realm. One he was not familiar with. One which gave him new meaning, new fears and new possibilities. Here, actions weren't violent. Instead, they were necessary. Necessarily for the good and nothing else. What may have happened had he not done as he did.

Incumbents of this realm invariably knew what was right since they were the most moral of all. Surely violence and death weren't the way but maybe there were exceptions. Maybe sometimes Jack might allow himself to skirt the rules he prided himself on. If it was for an outcome that upheld the righteous, maybe he could take the briefest dance with darkness.

As brief as it was, and as he watched Benson fall to the floor, Jack's body pulsated with pain. The act of firing had done something, as if the action were a vice on his soul, squeezing the blood in his body. For all his rationalisation, there was a detail he couldn't reason away, a pain that refused to disappear. There was something calling out to him, as if it were being dragged away, warning against whatever was preparing to take its place.

Benson's gun slid across the floor and Jack looked up.

Carter stepped out of the room. His white shirt glistened in the final moments of sunlight as he took a sharp breath.

He surveyed the pain and the destruction, his expression fixed and indifferent. He turned to Jack.

"I never doubted you. Not for a second."

CHAPTER 37

Carter quickly assessed their position. Calculations and predictions passed through his mind in a matter of moments as he decided what to do next.

"Jack, take Max and Stafford back to the car and bring it outside."

Carter threw him the keys. "Once you're there just wait. I'll deal with these two myself."

"You sure you don't need any help," Jack said. "What about Benson? He's still –"

Carter shook his head. "It'll be fine Jack. Don't worry."

Jack glanced down and saw Benson sprawled across the floor. The bullet had pierced his abdomen but he was still breathing. The shot hadn't been fatal.

Jack sharply raised his head, scrubbing the image from his head.

It's fine. He's still alive. Carter is safe. Nothing to worry about.

"Alright. I'll bring it around."

"Thanks."

Jack, Max and Stafford left the house and headed back

down the street.

As soon as Max stepped outside he felt the cool wind hit his face, a feeling he hadn't experienced in hours.

Just as he came to his senses, he noticed that Jack had already paced ahead of him and Stafford. Max tried to catch him up but just as he approached him Jack seemed to accelerate forwards.

"Jesus, fuck Jack, slow down. Give us a second will ya."

Stafford was still lagging behind them.

Jack briefly turned around, glancing back through the corner of his eye. "Sorry." He lessened his pace although not by very much and continued to speed ahead.

Max stopped where he was. "Jack, that's enough."

Jack halted mid-step and turned around. "What's wrong?"

"Can you like…slow the fuck down? If you hadn't noticed, we've been held captive for over twelve hours. Try giving us a second."

Stafford finally caught up to the two of them. "Why have you stopped?" he asked, carefully hiding the sound of his panting.

"Jack's going a bit too fast for comfort."

Jack's legs were jittering and his eyes quickly shifted from side to side, as if his body were overcharged with energy. There was an uncomfortable expression on his face as the three of them stood still.

"Carter asked us to get the car so I'm trying to get to it without wasting any time."

"Oh yeah. This new friend of yours."

"Fuck off Max."

"No, no. I'm just curious. Same guy who you only recently met. Same guy who, in order to save, you were willing to shoot someone. That guy – Carter?"

Jack's legs stopped shaking. "If it wasn't for us…you'd still be there right now. You really going to lecture me on this?"

"No one is denying what you did Jack", Stafford said. The soothing manner in which Stafford spoke alleviated some of the tension in the air. "I speak for both of us when I say that you didn't have to do what you did. It was brave. But dangerous. Max and I are just…worried about you."

"What do you mean?"

"Up until yesterday, you were a mathematician. Today, you held a man at gunpoint and threatened to kill him. And then you actually shot him."

"You need to stop worrying. It's done."

"Yeah I know…but still. You were ready to risk your life – in order to save Carter. There was a chance to go and you didn't take it. That in itself says something."

"Well, I'm sorry I did the right thing and didn't leave him behind," Jack said. His voice had risen slightly. "I'm sorry I operate with some honour. I'm sorry that I do what I need to when it counts."

"Jack, I don't dispute the efficacy of your actions."

"Then why are you acting like it? We risked our lives to come here – Carter and I - and the two of you don't even seem to care. You're only safe and breathing the air of these streets because of what I did and what I was willing to do."

"Calm down," Stafford said.

"I am fucking calm. What I don't understand is how the two of you can be so ungrateful."

"We never said we were," Max said bluntly.

"Then act like it. No one else could have done what I did. No one else could have figured out who had taken you. I know you like to think that I'm just lucky all the time but maybe now you'll finally understand."

Stafford cleared his throat. "We just want to make sure you're ok. Whatever you did in order to save us…we *do* appreciate it. There's no question of that. But don't deny that it wasn't easy. These weren't simple actions."

"Yeah, yeah I know."

"Tell me something," Max said. He rubbed his hand against his trouser and tried to iron out some of the creases. "How did you find him?"

"Carter?"

"Yeah."

"He came to us. He offered to help find you and in return he wanted a stake in the investment."

"Wait. He just came to us – for an investment?" Max looked startled. "And then decided to get involved in investigating a kidnapping?"

"No other reason?" Stafford asked. "Just...the money."

"Possibly. He hasn't exactly said."

Jack examined the expressions on their faces. Without saying anything their scepticism was lain bare.

"Don't give me that fucking look," Jack snapped. "I get that it's odd. That's a fair assessment. But that doesn't mean that he didn't give a 100% to bring you back. "

Max shook his head. "No. I won't disagree. But I do wonder...what else was Mr Carter looking for?"

Jack spun around and headed towards the car. "I think we're done with this. What's the use if you're not even going to –"

"Oh give it a fucking rest," Max shouted. "Me, me, me, me, me! This isn't about you!"

Jack stopped. His back was still turned. As the adrenaline started to wear off, he could slowly sense the touch of wind against his skin.

"Aren't you even the slightest bit curious?" Max asked. "Not even a little?"

They could all hear the slight hum of nearby cars parading down the street as afternoon morphed into early evening.

"We should go," Jack said. "Otherwise we'll be late."

CHAPTER 38

Carter watched Jack, Max and Stafford leave the home. He heard the light patter of footsteps trailing on to the pavement and down the street as they made their way back to the car.

Carter walked around Benson and lifted his pistol up from the floor. He grabbed Benson and sat him up against the wall.

Jack had shot him in the abdomen and although he was severely injured he still appeared to be conscious.

Benson looked up, breathing heavily as Carter stared down at him, Reinhart's pistol pointed squarely between his eyes.

"Who are you working for?"

Benson didn't reply.

Reinhart was leaning against the toppled table. His once parted hair was scuffled and messy.

"Are *you* going to give me an answer to that question?" Carter directed to Reinhart.

"He works for me."

"And who do *you* work for?"

"I don't work for anyone."

Carter tapped the base of his pistol against the wall and watched as the echo rang across the room and injected dread into Reinhart's body.

"Joseph…don't lie to me."

Reinhart wanted to speak, to give himself a moment where he might justify himself but he couldn't draw out the words in time.

"You're not an investor. And you didn't take Stafford for the reason you said."

"Carter, please…"

"Shut up! I want a fucking answer."

Carter pointed his pistol back at Benson. "Anything to add?"

"I don't talk to fools."

"What did you say?"

Benson's cold tone and shrewd face did little to calm Carter's nerves. He remained silent, not a smile or a snigger. The expressionless image on his face in the heat of such adversity seemed like a talent.

Carter crouched down and pulled Benson by the collar. "Who told you I was a fool?"

Benson stared at him coldly.

After a few seconds Carter removed his hand from Benson's collar and struck the side of his hand against his throat.

Benson coughed violently, spluttering as he attempted to catch his breath. The jagged pain in his throat roared into his lungs.

Reinhart scrambled backwards in panic.

"Now you have a reason not to speak," Carter said, standing up. He turned his gaze to Reinhart.

"Don't speak to this man," Benson gasped.

He was still trying to get his breath back, his hand clutched around his throat. The air in his body felt tight, desperate for oxygen.

Carter crouched down again. "He'll say what he has to

in order to repent for the things he's done today."

"He'll do no such thing. Your time of reckoning is going to come soon enough."

Carter struck Benson in the face. Just as Benson's head flung backwards, Carter slammed the bottom of his weapon against the bottom of Benson's skull, knocking him unconscious.

Carter had encountered men like Benson before. He wasn't like Caulfield or Cassano. He was too disciplined and too loyal, which meant Carter wasn't going to get any information from him. The longer he stayed conscious the longer he'd have to convince Reinhart to stay quiet – to protect the man behind the curtain.

Reinhart was crawling backwards, the fabric of his suit scraping against the floor.

"Sit on the chair," Carter said.

Reinhart got to his feet. He spotted one of the chairs that hadn't been flipped over and sat down.

There was no table in front of him and Carter could tell that the exposure was making him feel uncomfortable. The vulnerability crept into his body language; closed off and afraid.

Carter walked to the chair and stood facing him. He kept his pistol by his side, swinging it back and forth, stirring the uncertainty in Reinhart's mind.

"Now…who made you kidnap Stafford?"

"No one! How many times have I got to tell you?"

"Tell me something about natural language processing?"

The question completely caught Reinhart off guard.

Carter leaned forwards, his eyes filled with vivacity. "Well…can you?"

"I mean, it's an area most engineers in Stafford's field would ordinarily –"

"Be specific."

"It – "

"Name another."

"Another what?"

"Another field. An algorithm. Anything"

"I can't just –"

"Yes you fucking can," Carter snapped. "This is your goddamn profession. There's no reason why you shouldn't!"

Reinhart was struck with panic.

"I know you don't know a damn thing. And I know you've been lying up until now. So, I'll ask you again…who…do you work for?"

There was a certain type of menace that looped itself around Carter's words and it raised the fear in Reinhart exponentially.

Reinhart heard it distinctly. The propensity for inflicting violence. There wouldn't have been a struggle or crisis of conscience for Carter. Its emergence in him would have been as natural as breathing.

"I made him a promise," Reinhart said. "That I'd never say."

"It's time to make a new promise."

Reinhart's mind was teetering. He began to take deep breaths.

"He wants you dead…more than any man I've ever seen him speak about."

Carter's heart started to race.

No. It can't be.

"Who?"

"We made a deal…him and I…for the greater good was what he told me."

"Who!"

"Soren…Soren Lancaster."

Carter stepped back in horror, eyes widening. If only for a brief second, a deep trace of fear and realisation momentarily revealed itself.

Before he knew it, he had composed himself, leaving

his mind to burden the terror alone and begin generating what had now become a desperate attempt for a solution in the face of something he had never expected.

Carter tried to take a hold of the fear but he felt it evaporate. As it lurked away into the ether, in its place he saw the founding principle that had brought him here in the first place. The tenet that drove his rage and had led him so far.

Reinhart barely noticed the deviation in Carter's psyche, his body stunned by his own act of betrayal.

"Does Kessler know about him?"

"No…only me, and any men he brought with him."

He glanced at Benson, his unconscious shell sprawled across the floor.

"Is he in London?"

"Yes."

"And he's here for me?"

"Yes."

Just as he started this journey Carter wondered over and over whether there was a possibility he had missed something. Had there been a facet of the problem he'd forgotten or was he secretly being outplayed. Had Soren done it once more?

"What was supposed to happen here…what were you planning?"

Reinhart didn't want to respond. He had already said too much. But the second he said that name he knew Carter wouldn't stop demanding answers.

"We needed you out in the open. He knew you'd come for Stafford. He knew you'd come if we took him. Then we'd make our move."

Stafford? How in the hell would he have known?

"Call him."

"What."

"Call him and tell him everything is still going as planned."

"I - I can't do that," Reinhart stammered.

"And why not?"

"I can't lie to him. He'll know."

"Ah but you see, he won't," Carter retorted. He lifted his pistol up, slowly turning it in his hand. "You've been doing it all day haven't you? I'm sure you're pretty good by this point. What's a few more minutes going to hurt?"

Carter's insistence was toxic, forcing Reinhart to slowly come to terms with what was about to happen. To refrain from doing as he was told would lead to his demise; to succumb to Carter's request would mean he'd have only been responsible for delaying it.

No one had ever crossed Soren and lived. Reinhart knew that he wouldn't be an exception to the rule. He was important but he wasn't that important.

All part of the plan. For the greater good.

Words that he had heard over and over again. Like clockwork, they went around in his head, convincing him to do what he was told, to act as he must and to play the part that he was given. Who, if anyone, could outsmart him or defeat him. Definitely not Michael Carter. Whatever plan he might've had, who's to say Soren had not already prepared, not already predicted, what was to come. That was his ability, his claim to the supernatural. It's what some men knew for a fact and what others believed. Reinhart suspected Carter would learn it soon enough.

Reinhart removed his phone and started dialling.

"Put it on speaker."

Reinhart made the call and after a few seconds someone answered.

"An update," Reinhart said. "Benson is here and is guarding Carter. Stafford, Max and Jack are here with me. Everything is going as planned."

"Good."

"An ETA?" Reinhart asked.

"I'd say a few hours. When the sun sets."

"Alright. Till then."

Reinhart hung up the phone.

Once Carter heard the voice on the other end of the line he knew Reinhart wasn't lying.

If it were anyone else, they would have heard the voice of an ordinary man; deep, calm and relaxed. However, there was something which few heard, and others did not. Felt only by those who knew who was speaking. Resonating with men who knew what he was capable of; who knew what pain he could wrought, what misery and suffering he could inflict and what little remorse he held.

Reinhart placed the phone back into his pocket. "Satisfied?"

"What did he mean...ETA until what?"

Reinhart smirked. "Until he comes for *you*."

CHAPTER 39

Carter was scrambling for clarity. He lay in freefall, struggling to find any kind of lifeline. The situation still wasn't adding up.

"How did he know?"

"Know what?"

"How did he know what was going to happen. Where I'd be?"

Reinhart laughed. "Because he's so much smarter than you are and so, so many more steps ahead."

"How!"

Carter was beginning to lose his patience.

"He knew what you were looking for. Not investments or wealth. Not what you told your dear friends. No. You wanted revenge…more than anything else…and he knew it. You'd gotten so close once before. He wasn't about to risk it happening again so he struck first."

A torch had suddenly been cast over the elements he had ignored. Carter saw it now. The gaping hole in his plan. The outcome he never predicted.

"We knew Stafford and Elizabeth were looking for an investment, and we knew they'd struggle. So Soren sent me in – to play the part of the obnoxious, unstable investor; one whose primary intention was to reject their idea. And then, in a moment of desperation…there would come a call from the offices of Mark Nalbanthian. But wait…you already know this part don't you?"

"How did you know I'd…?"

"You don't think Soren knew that you were on the hunt for him…that you'd call in the help of anyone to find him. Searching and digging for any trace of him or his aliases…one of which was…Mark Nalbanthian? You think he'd forgotten that you knew all about his previous business interests in technology. He knew you'd find him…and he knew you'd be there."

"But this whole charade…it was so that I could strike him first. I knew that he'd be here. It doesn't -"

"Doesn't add up?" Reinhart interrupted. "And then just when you think you have the perfect plan, your chance for revenge…the man of the hour goes missing. The only man who could make that company work. The most important of them all. As soon as Soren finds out, it's all over…he'd hear the news and leave…never to return. No meeting, no opportunity to strike, no nothing. That is…unless you found Stafford. Brought him back as if nothing ever happened."

"We thought we had been pretty good. I set myself up as the perfect suspect, building in a real motive, drawing as much realism as we could. But even then, we were confident you wouldn't find him. And then in the midst of confusion, when you least expected it and would be most vulnerable, we'd send Kessler to capture you. He didn't know about it at the time, but when you contacted *us*, that's when we had to…adjust. We decided to bring you here instead. It suddenly became far easier than we ever expected. Kessler was reluctant, but I knew it worked perfectly. We'd just lie, bring you here, and then imprison you. I contacted Soren while you were all speaking to

Kessler and he sent Benson to look after the situation until he arrived. Kessler was no longer needed and so we sent him away."

Carter wasn't normally a victim of surprise but whenever he was, it surged through him, not necessarily as aggressive as adrenaline but certainly just as unnerving. Outmanoeuvred on a scale he couldn't have imagined, there was little else he may have felt at this point.

"It's like I said. He knew it all along…that which you cherish so much but made you so weak and predictable. If he created the perfect situation, he knew you'd come running. And then he could finally put you to rest once and for all just as he should've done so long ago."

Reinhart's stance widened and he immediately seemed more presumptuous; to the extent that he had apparently forgotten the dilemma he was facing. Something about recounting his narrative to Carter had obviously bolstered his confidence.

"So what was *your* part?" Carter asked. "Just the scapegoat?"

"More or less. I was the intermediary. The one separating you from him. Why would you have ever suspected Soren when there was an unstable and aggressive investor willing to pull the strings? I mean, did you ever really think this could all be connected?"

There were only a few occasions where Carter considered the possibility of Soren's involvement but in each case, there wasn't a tangible link leading back to his previous actions or motive. The scenarios were so far disconnected that it would have been idiotic to suggest they were related.

"I suppose my doubts arose when we realised you didn't know what the hell you were talking about," Carter quipped.

Reinhart looked slightly displeased at the comment.

"So where is he now?"

"There's a suite of offices that Elizabeth, Stafford and Soren were set to meet at. He's there. Waiting."

"In the meeting room?"

"No. He's booked a suite at the top too. He wanted a place where he could wait and observe."

All Carter could imagine was a vast tower that loomed over city, where no movement or action was hidden and where there was enough information to foresee what came next. To have stood at its summit would have meant limitless knowledge and it was moments like these where Carter recalled that Soren had never been far off from such a feat.

"And it was him who hired Kessler?" Carter asked.

"Not quite. It was Soren's idea but the contract was through me. Soren wanted to keep some distance."

"Sounds unlike him."

"Kessler's crossed paths with a few of his associates before and it hasn't always ended well. Needless to say, he didn't trust him very much."

"So why not hire someone else."

"We needed someone who could execute our plan perfectly. Kessler was the only man in London at the time who could do it to our standards."

"And yet it still didn't go to plan."

"Well, we didn't expect some lunatic to burst on to the street and start shooting people," Reinhart scoffed.

"No…don't think anyone did."

Reinhart stretched out his arms. "How much more do you need to know Mr Carter? I don't think there's anything more I can really tell you."

"No. Probably not."

Carter observed Reinhart's disposition. There was an air of confidence to him. As if he took pride in the events that had followed, as if he enjoyed being a part of the plot that was designed to bring about Carter's end, as if, despite whatever the circumstances had become, to have been a central mechanism in Soren's scheme brought him some modicum of happiness.

Carter couldn't waste any more time. He knew the moment had come. He walked over to Benson, still motionless and sprawled across the floor. He lifted his pistol and aimed it at his head, pulling the trigger. The sound ravaged through the room, tearing apart the tranquillity.

Reinhart jumped back in his seat in dismay. "What on earth!"

Carter held the gun in its place. He looked down at Benson registering an odd sensation of unawareness. He was elsewhere, unable to see what others saw, lost in the corridors of satisfaction and retribution. His eyes glided towards Reinhart.

"No…" Reinhart pleaded.

He took a few steps in Reinhart's direction.

Reinhart tried to momentarily get up from his chair but Carter shook his head in defiance.

"I told you everything!"

"It doesn't matter. You're both too dangerous to be left alive."

Carter lifted the pistol and pointed it at Reinhart.

"I'm not a threat," Reinhart begged. "Lock me up, send me away. I'll pay you a fortune just please…"

"If you're associated with that man then you'll always be a threat to me."

Reinhart's body was beginning to tremble.

"You can't. He told me…told me that you're a man of principle."

"Yet you're in alliance with a man who's not."

Reinhart froze.

"So you see…this *is* a matter of principle."

Carter fired a round into Reinhart's head.

His body sunk back into the chair, sliding down and

collapsing against the floor.

Carter holstered his weapon and removed his phone. He started dialling.

"Jeff. Reinhart is dead. I've got Stafford back."

"Good."

"The situation is more complex than we thought. I interrogated Reinhart. He said that Soren orchestrated the kidnapping to lure me out, using himself as a scapegoat. Soren's plan was to use the kidnapping as a way to capture *me*. He already knew that we'd try and target the name Nalbanthian and planned around it."

"Fuck. You can't be serious."

"The whole thing was a setup...a farce. But I know where he is. I can put it to rest."

"To have planned that far ahead..."

Carter could sense the jolt in Jeff's disposition. The stutter in his words; the dismay at having been outsmarted.

"I just...I never expected anything like this," Carter said.

"No," Jeff said bluntly. "Not in the slightest. What now?"

"I need someone to get to this address and clean up what's happened. The bodies of Reinhart and his guard are here."

"I'll send someone. Kessler?"

"Gone. He was relieved of his duty. I don't really care for him right now. He's not important and not our primary focus. We've got bigger problems to deal with."

"Agreed. Don't forget what we're trying to do here. We need Soren alive – at all costs. That's the only reason I agreed to you doing this. Lives are at risk here Carter. A lot of lives. Don't forget that. We need to know what he knows about Haddad which means I need you to stay focussed."

"I've been focussed longer than you can possibly

imagine. I'll do whatever I have to. After what he did...he'll suffer."

"I know. Keep me posted."

Carter hung up and went outside. He saw Jack, Max and Stafford sat in the car, patiently waiting.

Before he got inside the thought came to him once more. Whether peace of mind awaited him at the end of his journey. Would he find what he was longing for? Soren had burnt so much of him away that sometimes he wondered whether the same man was pursuing him. Was it a shadow of his former self cascading through the world, searching for the opportunity to restore balance? Sometimes he felt sadness, other times he felt rage but more recently he had felt nothing. It was as if his body knew how to act without thinking; deriving an unconscious purpose in order to find the vengeance he desired.

He opened the backdoor and sat inside.

"I guess there's a meeting we need to get to," he said cheerfully.

Jack tapped the accelerator and the car began to growl as it sailed down the street.

Carter gazed out of the window and into the recesses of society, curious as to how many were willing to do as he'd done, and to do as he would.

CHAPTER 40

Earlier that day…

The streets in the City had grown unexpectedly quieter over the past few hours. The afternoon lull meant that a few professionals were groggily stumbling down the pavement in search of pick-me-up coffees but apart from that there was little to no activity. Even the congestion on the streets was barely noticeable. The occasional bus whirred by without stopping, fast enough that it was almost impossible to realise how few passengers were inside.

Down a small side street, which undoubtedly went unnoticed, an inconspicuous dark blue car had been perched between two small white vans. One of them was being unloaded by a stout elderly fellow who had already grown tired from the day's work. He wiped the sweat from his brow before carrying a small crate of water bottles into the shop adjacent to him and in the corner of his eye he saw the owner of the car, who had only parked it a brief moment ago, swiftly exit and glide down the street in a matter of seconds.

A short distance from the car, David Kessler had turned on to a main road, his coat hanging back as the wind blew against him. He slowly approached a set of offices and cautiously turned around from time to time despite the hollow commotion around him.

Vast, lofty buildings hovered in the sky and draped him in shadows but directly in front of him was a small, well-kept building. He entered unannounced and climbed the stairs one by one. The crooked lighting masked his presence but it couldn't hide the thumping of his boots so he treaded as silently as he could. After two flights he stepped into a large open room, bearing witness to exactly the two men he would have expected in the offices of Terrence Caulfield.

The moment Kessler had received a phone call from Michael Carter, he knew the only option was to burn his existing network. The fact that knowledge of Kessler's existence was a rarity meant that he could traverse the world in as unfettered a fashion as possible. But having succumb to Carter's successful interrogation, Cassano had turned himself into a liability, posing a risk to Kessler's very way of being.

Even Caulfield sensed the impending danger. After their encounter with Carter he was desperate to leave the country as quickly as possible and had no intention of sticking around for what came next.

In the back of his mind he wondered whether he should travel alone and leave Cassano to stir in the mess he'd created but then he also acknowledged that he wouldn't get far without him. Cassano had a network of foreign contacts that could assist in concealing his identity. It was the only thing that may have proved effective in fending off any pursuit from Kessler.

Naturally, it meant that before he could go anywhere, he needed to provide Cassano with urgent medical attention. The damage he suffered at the hands of Carter was considerably severe and so the best he could do was to call a doctor who could see to his injuries just enough that he might be ready for a short-haul flight.

Once they had gotten to safety Caulfield would have been in a better position to find better treatment. After the doctor had done his best and left, Caulfield quickly took to booking flights to wherever they could find.

It was as Kessler arrived that Caulfield was in the process of organising their escape.

Cassano was under the impression that they had more time. He believed that Kessler might not strike until Reinhart's plan was complete and therefore supposed they had enough time to make their escape.

Whatever hope they had left was shattered by Kessler's entrance.

The door swung open and Kessler said nothing. The second he pushed it open he had already removed his pistol and fired a bullet straight into Cassano's head.

Kessler swung his weapon in Caulfield's vicinity and fired again. Caulfield's body fell backwards, his head knocking against the table.

Kessler took a second to observe the room one last time. Only yesterday Cassano had been standing beside him, dragging Stafford away into the darkness.

He caught a glimpse of the assault Carter had laid upon them both and he continued to wonder.

Who was he?

Kessler had previously worked with Cassano on several occasions and knew what he was capable of. For something like this to have happened, for all of his ferocity, skills and training to have suddenly become useless, meant that there existed a vehement and near-limitless force underlying Carter's quest for answers.

Kessler walked back down the stairs and left the building. He assumed someone would eventually find Cassano and Caulfield and past experience had taught him that murders could never be pinned on ghosts; they were two deaths that would probably go unanswered.

He stepped outside and headed back to his car.

With each step he carefully reiterated his thoughts back to himself, meticulously and methodically, over and over.

Who else is there? Who haven't I considered?

There were no ideologies that mattered to Kessler, no values that he believed in. He merely exercised malevolence without question.

His aversion to a value system made him the perfect vehicle for countless ideologues. Despite their intentions, he remained an unbiased party in their affairs, having done as he was instructed and leaving the results of his actions to those that had commanded him.

Where such individuals hid their actions under the guise of grandiose beliefs, Kessler took full responsibility for the destruction he sowed. He was neutral, a champion of balance and the existence of nothing. But it was those that pursued misguided dogmas who challenged the balance he strived for. They were the threat. That's what he'd come to realise over the years.

Was he another? Michael Carter?

To have pursued Stafford so far, surely there was something driving him. Something transcendental. He must've found the link to Cassano somehow.

But who is he?

Who would know?

There was only one place that would provide him with answers.

Right now it was quiet. He knew the risk of detection was low.

But he needed to get there now.

Kessler raced to his car and sat inside. He closed his eyes, picturing his destination.

He imagined all those that had come before him.

Searching for knowledge, or for wealth or for some vision of the future.

However, Kessler searched for something else. He searched for something far more elusive.

He searched for closure.

And every day he would find it and every day he would search for it again.

.

CHAPTER 41

Sat outside his simple and quaint home, Ken Schaffer gazed into the heart of his village. He didn't have much in the way of electricity given the rolling blackouts they had been experiencing this week but he was fortunate enough to have put on a pot of coffee at the crack of dawn before there was another outage.

He had filled up two large ceramic cups as far as he could and left them on a wooden fold-out table in front of him. What appeared to be two second-hand dining room chairs were parked by the table, the bases of which were covered by worn-out cushions. Ken was sat on one and Michael Carter was sat on the other.

Ken's road was narrow, with barely enough space for one car to drive down. Opposite him were homes similar to his, each painted with vibrant colours and images. Outside, a young fair skinned woman was thrashing large blankets against the air and hanging them out to dry. Unlike her home, the blankets were mostly plain; beige coloured and torn around the edges. Despite the effort or the hour of day, she didn't seem exhausted which Ken seemed to admire.

Two stray dogs that wandered around the village every day were passing by the woman hoping she might offer some spare food. Both were scruffy, with small sullen eyes and thin bodies although the appearance of a weak frame didn't stop either of them from scampering down the pavement with excitement.

On one occasion, not too long ago, the woman had felt sorry for them and left out some of her family's leftover dinner and now the dogs saw her home as a natural checkpoint on the search for a meal. Clearly too preoccupied and ignoring them, she meticulously continued with her work while the dogs moped around before leaving to see what else they might find. One of them stopped to sniff the blanket that had just been put out to dry but the woman smacked the stand with the side of her heel and scared it off.

The early morning Colombian sun was beating down and Ken could hear the rumbling of delivery trucks on a nearby street making their way to the cities of Antioquia.

The humidity was creeping up but the heat hadn't got to the point where he felt tired or sluggish. Behind the village, in the distance, he could spot columns of trees and fresh vegetation looming over the horizon and providing some variety to the plain blue sky.

Ken leaned forwards and grasped his coffee cup. As he took a sip he felt his beard scratch the edges. He continued the hold the cup in one hand, the grey in his beard glinting in the morning sunlight.

His eyebrows were thick and bushy, under a shield of thin brown hair that sat flat over his head. The sleeves of his shirt were rolled up unevenly and he wore large baggy cargo trousers. Across his right forearm was a faded tattoo of a large, black sword pointed in the direction of his hand and across the left were several healed cuts and scars.

Carter was dressed in a similar fashion although his shirt was much less worn out and his trousers were slightly more fitted. His face held a small amount of stubble but he could feel the skin on his face drying out in the heat. Unlike Ken, he hadn't touched his coffee yet, preferring to speak first.

"It's certainly good to see you mate. It feels like it's been forever."

Ken stared forwards, watching as the woman dropped another blanket over the washing stand.

"Maybe for you. Life goes pretty quick here if you'd believe it."

Ken spoke with an affable American spring in his voice. He put people at ease whenever he met them. Had he liked, Carter was sure he would've excelled at international diplomacy.

"I can actually. But I'm happy to hear it. How have things been going out here?"

"Congress has been getting real worried these past few months."

Carter's eyes gleamed with curiosity. "Why's that?"

"They don't like what's happening to the Government's forces. They don't think they're up to the challenge."

"No?"

"Rooting out the militias isn't easy. They're all holed up in the jungle somewhere and it's not like anyone's had any success so far. My friends in the capital suggest Congress has taken an interest in what I have to offer."

Carter craned his head backwards to see if there was anyone else around. He gripped the side of his chair and leant across to Ken. "Do they know...the *extent* of our capabilities?"

"Yeah...they know. No one's turning us away."

Ken watched as a small smirk materialised on Carter's face. There was a vibrancy to his expression that Ken envied. Years must've gone by since his own face displayed that type of enthusiasm.

Carter lifted his cup from the table and fell back in his chair. He took a small sip. "Do you get to visit the cities much while you're here? I know there's some great stuff to see out there."

"Occasionally. I do most of my work here though. In fact, I don't really mind it here. It's peaceful. I like it."

Behind the woman drying clothes, a young boy stepped out from the doorway to her home. Lodged between his right arm and ribs was a football while his other free hand rubbed his eyes. He wore a thick blue vest and shorts, was slim and had bushy black hair that ran over his ears.

He briefly stood in the sun, slowly perking up the way a flower might bloom through spring. Fully stretched, he dropped the ball and slowly dribbled it down the road past Ken and Carter. Ken raised his hand to wave and the young boy waved back sheltering a colossal smile as he continued down the road.

"You know he walks past here every day, same time," Ken said. "He goes to this small patch of grass down the street and spends about four hours kicking the ball against the wall. Sometimes with friends if they're around."

Carter observed the boy from afar, stumbling side to side as he tried to keep the ball between his feet.

"After he's done, he comes back, helps his mom sweep the house and chop vegetables for the rest of the day," Ken continued. His eyes fell back to the woman. "You ever help your mom in the kitchen Michael?"

"Not really. She used to tell me off for dropping stuff so I stopped. Did you?"

"No. Probably should've though."

Ken placed his cup on the table and leant back in his chair. He glanced at Carter and saw the angling expression on his face. It was young and fresh and it meant that Ken could decipher it at a whim. Ken believed that for every ounce of mystique that a man possessed, he had almost certainly lost an equal amount of idealism. Charisma was the antithesis of the enigmatic.

"Is there something else you'd like to ask me Michael? I don't imagine you flew all this way just for a cup of coffee."

Carter clasped his hands together and placed them on his lap. "I was contacted by someone recently. A former financier who's turned his attention to global affairs. I think he might be what we've been looking for. He has the ability to expedite operations across all regions. Inject cash everywhere, scale things up faster than ever."

"Where did he get the funds from?"

"Closed down all of his old investment vehicles and taken out the profits."

"I see. What's this guy's name?"

"Soren. Soren Lancaster."

"Never heard of him."

Carter took a sharp breath. "Neither have I."

"And what…you want my thoughts? Is that it? Is that what you came here for?"

Carter stared at the ground, unwilling to reply, as if he were transfixed with his own ideas.

"I mean…" Ken continued after a short pause. "We don't actually need him do we. As far as I'm aware, we're doing just fine. We're doing what we're doing and there's nothing more to it."

Ken watched as Carter's gaze became ever more vehement.

"But what if there's more to do. What if it's not enough?" He closed his eyes. "Maybe this is what we need. Maybe this is how we finally do it."

"This was never going to happen in a day. Cash or no cash. That's not how it works."

Carter finally turned to face him. "But what if it could?"

"What if it could?" Ken repeated. He shrugged his

shoulders. "I honestly don't know Michael. I'm too *old* to know. I'm too *tired* to know. But I *do* know…that I trust you. And I know that you'll make the right decision. You always do."

Carter rested his forehead against his hands. His eyes were shut again and his breathing intensified. After a minute or so he sat up right and took a swig of his coffee.

"Did I tell you I met someone recently," Ken said.

"No," Carter said. His expression suddenly seemed normal. "Kept that one a secret didn't you?"

"Maybe. Met her last year while I was running a job in the city. She works for a charitable foundation."

"Wow. Noble line of work. Maybe she'll finally help you fix your degenerate ways."

"I hope so," Ken chuckled.

"I hope you're not going to abandon us for true love."

"Oh, I don't think I could do that. I enjoy our chats far too much Michael."

Carter smiled. "Do I get to come to the wedding then?"

"In addition to the three people in this village that I know, I don't see why not."

Ken waded his hand through his hair and pulled it neatly to one side. As the morning sun beamed into his eyes, he felt the thin, waning slivers slip through his fingers.

"I think she'd like it here," Ken continued. "I certainly do. Like I said…it's quiet here." He paused. "I enjoy watching the sun fall. I enjoy the silence. It reminds me of my thoughts. It reminds me of everything."

"What do you mean by everything?" Carter asked.

"I just…" Ken suddenly felt his mind empty as if overcome by a force unbeknownst to him. "I don't know. I don't know what I meant. I'm sorry."

Carter slowly nodded and they both sat back in their chairs, watching the early morning sun continue its ascent through the sky.

CHAPTER 42

The evening was starting to settle in. Everyone's eyes were fixed either on the continuous glow of taillights that accompanied them through a long queue of traffic or the constant view of the same street that never seemed to pass. Jack's hand was scrunched around the gearstick while the other sat loosely against the top of the steering wheel.

He glanced to his left and saw Stafford fixated on a queue slowly building outside of a post office. Max and Carter were in the back. Occasionally Jack peeked in his rear view mirror to see what they were doing although they both seemed lost in their own worlds.

As the car trudged onwards, Max and Stafford's heads were still filled with vivid images of two men traversing the city in order to recover them. Jack had spent the first leg of the journey recounting the details of their recovery; whether it was the complexities of dealing with Sinclair or the violence that ensued when they crossed Cassano and Caulfield. At times the narrative sounded too good to be true, peppered with moments of intelligence and countless instances of luck.

Jack briefly turned around to Carter. "Do you think we

should tell Elizabeth? About what's happened?"

"No," Carter replied. "We can tell her when we get back. I still don't know if there's someone else working with Reinhart. If we tell her and she contacts Nalbanthian, word could possibly get out. I'd rather we keep this to ourselves."

"Sure."

The last thing Carter needed was for Soren to realise that he was on to him. If Elizabeth decided to reconfirm her meeting it would suggest that they'd found Stafford, destroying any element of surprise Carter might have possessed and propel Soren into high alert.

"And Reinhart?" Max said.

"I locked him and Benson in the room I was held in and barricaded it. The two of them weren't really willing to tell me anything useful so I could see the whole thing was going nowhere. A contact of mine is on their way to take over while we see this through."

Max started fiddling with his seatbelt, pulling it forwards and watching it snap back against his chest. "What happens to them?"

"Don't know. We'll cross that bridge when we come to it."

The car continued to march down the street.

"Look, I'm sure you've been expecting this question for a while now," Max said glancing towards Carter.

"Go on."

"What was your play in this really? You're not an investor, let's be honest. I'm grateful and everything...don't get me wrong."

Carter folded his arms. "I'm sure."

"But I'd like to know why you got involved."

Jack tightened his grip around the steering wheel.

I guess that's one way of finding out, he thought.

Up until now, Carter had failed to provide an adequate response. Jack always sensed him sidestepping the question at every turn and dodging accountability wherever he could.

Carter leaned back in his seat. He stared up at the roof of the car and dropped his shoulders so that his arms slouched against the upholstery.

"I guess now's as good a time as any to explain."

His attention shifted to the street and he began to gaze out of the window. "My client is a private person so I don't think he'd appreciate me going into too much detail so I'll keep it brief. But let's just say that he and his department focus on certain kinds of unsavoury individuals and organisations."

"Government?" Max asked.

"I don't think it's for me to say. Either way, for the past few weeks, him and his colleagues had been focussing on two particular individuals. Both men were involved in previous matters of interest and they got word that they'd both be here in London working on a separate operation. Almost by accident, my client got a hold of a communication that suggested the timeline had scaled up and they were to set to execute imminently. The communication didn't say much but it eluded to two things. One – they were working for someone else – someone potentially quite important. And two – their operation involved someone called Edward Stafford. Of course, it's probably worth noting that these were the same two men that came to the Field last night and took the both of you away."

Carter paused momentarily, stroking his hand along the cheap plastic panel underneath the car window.

"My client didn't have anyone on the ground and so by the time they got the communication, they realised they might be too late. That's when I got the call to go in and handle it."

"What's your relationship to your client?" Max asked.

He watched as Carter continued to fiddle with the

plastic on the car. A small piece had snapped off and Carter was flicking it back and forth.

"These days I'm something of a contractor. But in the earlier days I regularly worked alongside my client and so we have something of a pre-existing relationship. Obviously, our areas of expertise overlap and I just happened to be here in London so that's why I got the call. It also helps that I don't have any affiliations with anybody which makes things less conspicuous. Unfortunately, by the time I arrived, both of you had already been taken."

"Did you know who they were working for?" Max asked. "The people that took us?"

"Not at the time. But right now it's pretty safe to say that they were working for Kessler."

Max was still recalling brief flashes from the previous night. He could still feel the bruises on his arms and shins as he was dragged out of the Field and forcibly bumped into doors and railings.

The sound of Sinclair emptying his clip echoed in his mind. It had reappeared again and again over the course of the day. The sound of violence propagating through the air and piercing the men who sought to take them away.

He recounted the way that the air turned dry and devoid of any energy when Kessler first stepped into the bar. His skin tingled with dread just thinking about it.

"There was an option to tell everyone this from the start surely," Max said. "Why wait this long?"

"Be realistic," Carter scoffed. "My client had no intention of telling anyone what they were doing. More importantly, I had no idea who I could trust – not at that point. The less everyone knew, the better. And whether you knew it or not, I don't think it was about to make a difference."

"Telling us the truth?"

Carter noticed an edginess to Max's tone.

"Yeah. What good would that have done exactly? It's not like Jack or Katrina or even Elizabeth had any experience dealing with these types of situations. The information didn't exactly sit well with their natural skillset."

"No. That's quite accurate."

Max raised his eyes to the rear view mirror, catching a brief glimpse of Jack. His attention was still on the road.

The car came to another halt and Jack quickly craned his head around the car headrest. "That guy you speak to – he's your client I presume?"

"Yes."

"And your objective," Max added. "What did your client want you to do exactly?"

"Find out who was behind the operation and neutralise them."

"*Neutralise?*" Max said, lowering his voice.

"*Stop*," Carter retorted.

"I see. Well, Kessler's disappeared now. Jack tells me one is severely injured and the other two are dead. Where's that leave you?"

"Realistically, Kessler will probably go underground. It's the best we'll get for the time being, I suppose. I don't think anyone expects him to be operating here anytime soon. What happens next is down to my client. Hopefully they can figure out what Reinhart was doing and close that loose end too."

"At first I thought he took us to get information out of us," Max said. "Maybe try and help his own fund or something. But he never even asked us any questions about the algorithm. Didn't really say anything."

"Yeah…" Carter said. "If one thing is clear now, he wasn't interested in the business. And was definitely involved with something or someone else. I guess me and Jack turning up probably threw up a slight variation in his plan."

"Well, for whatever reason you came here," Stafford said, "I'm still very grateful."

"Yeah," Jack said. "I wouldn't have been able to do it without you. And thanks for being honest. I get that it's difficult given the circumstances."

"Don't mention it. After what's happened, you all probably deserve the truth – to the extent I can deliver it."

"Yeah, I appreciate it," Max said. "It all sounds pretty intense."

Carter turned his head to Max and smiled. "Well, what can I tell you?"

There was a softness in his voice that was uniquely disarming, as if he could've been speaking to his grandson.

"No, no. It just um…sounds kind of…both vague and theatrical at the same time. You know?"

"You don't believe me?" Carter said. His tone turned slightly more defensive.

"I do…" A hint of scepticism rose to the surface of his reply. "But you could do a better job of convincing me."

"What do you want me to say Max? I can only tell you the truth."

"And that's all that I would expect. I'm sorry, maybe it's the fact that I'm not used to this kind of stuff, these kinds of stories…they're all –"

"Max, just leave it," Stafford cut in. "Honestly. At the end of the day, Carter risked a lot to help us. We didn't have anyone else. Whatever you might think, you owe him our thanks."

"Yeah, what the fuck Max," Jack added. "Have a bit of respect."

Stafford noticed the crimson shade of Jack's fingers as they clasped the wheel.

"Hang on. Don't think for a second I don't appreciate what he did. I *am* thankful for what's happened today. I'd say it a million times if I could. I just work in a business where it's important to understand how things work and I try to apply that to everything I do. If that comes across as rude, I'm sorry. I just…"

"Don't worry about it," Carter said. "I'd actually be a little worried if you believed me without asking at least one question!"

There was that tone again. Laughing in the face of absurdity.

For what Carter's words were supposed to be, Max didn't feel reassurance. Instead, he felt a shiver down his spine. He jiggled his shoulders trying to warm himself up but immediately realised that this had nothing to do with temperature. A different sort of disturbance existed in his surroundings; one that was responsible for his questions, his curiosity and an impending sense of dread.

When the car stops, I wonder if that's really journeys end.

"I bet they must really like you down at the office," Carter said.

"He's an acquired taste," Jack said. "And by the way…do you want this weapon back? I've still got it."

"Just hold on to it. We can deal with all this stuff later."

"Sure."

Reinhart's pistol was lodged between his jeans and waist. After a short while, Jack had grown accustom to it sitting there. He wondered whether he would ever fire it again. Given what Carter had just told him, it seemed unlikely but he also realised that Carter's own journey might be far from over.

I'm sure he needs it more than me.

For all that it was worth, Jack certainly wasn't wrong; just not for the reasons he had been told.

The traffic eventually diminished and Jack found himself making good speed. Everyone fell back in their seats as they sped up and swerved through the narrow streets. Rows of buildings continued to pass them and pedestrians continually tried to cut in and cross wherever they saw an opportunity.

Each time he changed gears, the car's engine rumbled awkwardly and then spluttered from behind. Jack's attention was fixed on the road but he could spot numerous specks of dirt and dust on the windscreen. As much as he may have liked to clean it, he was sceptical whether there was any water in the tank and so didn't bother.

Eventually they drifted into familiar territory and everyone breathed a small sense of relief. Within a few minutes they were outside the Field and Jack pulled up just across from the building.

Max and Stafford stepped out of the car and felt a hint of nostalgia as they stared up at the Field.

"As I walked out, coming back felt more and more unlikely with each step," Stafford said.

"Tell me about it," Max said.

Stafford glanced at Jack.

"Our meeting was scheduled for 6pm," Stafford said. "Given it's already past five, I think we should just head straight there. Jack, could you call Elizabeth and ask her to come outside. Then we can head straight there."

"Sure."

With the phone pressed against his ear, everyone couldn't help but notice an awkward stutter in Jack's voice while he attempted to explain that he, Carter, Max and Stafford were outside the Field and ready to leave for the meeting. He frequently stopped mid-sentence and on each occasion he turned flush.

"*Is that a joke?*"

"No…it's –"

"I'll be down in a second."

After a minute or so, Elizabeth stepped out of the Field, overflowing with scorn.

"Why did no one tell me about this sooner?" she said, storming down the street.

She stopped in front of Carter. Her eyes were drilling into him, demanding an explanation.

"Look, we thought it was safer this way," Carter said. "Just in case someone might find out that we got Stafford back and make another attempt against him."

She paused, edging away and staring into the street. Her face withdrew any expression of frustration and morphed into one that was significantly more pensive.

"I see. Guess that makes enough sense." In the corner of her eye she spotted Stafford and Max and swung her head in their direction. "Been a while hasn't it. It's good to see you both looking so well. You had me worried sick."

"Thanks," Max said. "It's good to see you too."

Elizabeth's appearance seemed to instil an awkward smile on Stafford's face; one of sincerity and a small attempt to express the satisfaction of returning to the place and people he considered home.

"It feels like forever since I've seen you," he said. "I mean, it really does. Sort of weird isn't it?"

"It is. Almost certainly. I think this is the only circumstance where I might have cared if you went missing."

"Glad this entire ordeal didn't cause you to lose your sense of humour."

"No. Although I'm curious how this all came to fruition."

Carter provided Elizabeth with a summary of the events up until now. As the story progressed, he could see Elizabeth's face becoming more and more baffled.

"Quite a story Mr Carter. Some of it almost as if it were the work of fiction." She caught Max briefly raising his head in earnest before quickly lowering it. "But it sounds like you put a lot at risk. I'm glad you were here to help."

"Don't mention it."

"And you…Jack," Elizabeth said, turning her head. "I suppose I expected nothing less."

A purposeful but sarcastic sense of warmth rallied outwards.

"Really?"

"Moments like this…it's probably what you always wanted isn't it?"

"The kidnapping of my boss?"

"Not quite. But I'm sure you catch my drift."

There was a part of Jack that could see where she was coming from and it was a position he didn't care much for.

Stafford innocently tapped Elizabeth on the shoulder. "I know it's all a bit rushed but we should probably get going don't you think?"

Stafford's touch burnt away the hostility winding its way through her body and her rigid posture loosened up.

"Agreed. We driving there?"

"Yeah," Carter said. "If it's ok with you, I'd like to tag along. Until this investment is secure I'd prefer to stay in the vicinity just to make sure there's no…unforeseen circumstances."

"Fine by me," Elizabeth said. "Max, Jack – you guys can head back up. Katrina and Sinclair are still there."

Jack suddenly froze. "Shit…I still haven't sent…"

"The results of the back testing?" Stafford said, his expression cast with panic. "God, of course. It completely slipped my mind."

Elizabeth rolled her eyes. "You have to be kidding me. Now, of all times, you decide to remember."

"Well, I was supposed to send it this morning but we were a little preoccupied if you hadn't noticed."

"You said last night that you have it on a USB?" Stafford said.

"Yeah. I can bolt home and email it to Elizabeth within the next ten minutes. I can probably get it to you on time if I leave now."

"Perfect. We'll head out now. Hopefully we get it by the time we turn up."

Jack started pacing down the street, while Carter, Stafford and Elizabeth hopped into the car.

The car sped off into the distance just as Max crossed the street and finally returned to the Field; as a man who was partially wiser but equally trying to forget.

CHAPTER 43

Elizabeth and Stafford were due to have their meeting at a suite of offices not too far from the Field. The journey had been quick, and the three of them were already making their way inside.

They entered a small reception and continued into a large foyer with various rooms encircling it. Some of the doors were still open. Stafford peered inside and could see men and women sat around large tables, notepads in front of them, frantically scribbling down points from someone at the head of the room. Others had people stood around large trays of food and drink, smiling and laughing.

There were two individuals in navy uniform on either side of the foyer, pacing up and down, regularly checking their phones, more concerned with appearing to be busy rather than actually attending to any of the guests.

The foyer itself was bright, lamps scattered across the ceiling and shining down from every direction. The floor was carpeted with deep red velvet. Each step felt soft, their shoes continually pressing through the ground as they moved forwards.

Past the final set of doors were a set of stairs, carpeted

in a similar fashion to the lobby. They were extremely wide, their edges wrapped with long silver rails.

Elizabeth eventually veered to the right. "This our room. 1.15."

Carter nodded. "I'm going to take a walk around just to make sure everything is fine. You guys should probably go ahead."

"Makes sense. If all goes well, I'll make sure there's still a place on the deal for you..."

"Well, I –"

"Not that you were ever interested were you," Elizabeth interjected. She smiled. "But if you change your mind, I might be able to work something out."

"I can see why you and Katrina get on," Carter chuckled.

"It helps in our line of work Mr Carter. You never know who you're going to cross."

"I'm sure. I'll be in touch."

He turned and headed up the stairs.

Elizabeth and Stafford stepped into the meeting room and closed the door behind them. Inside was a large round table surrounded by six chairs. Each chair had a notepad, a pen and a glass of water in front of it. Besides the table was a small wheeled stand with some more water and several plates of assorted biscuits.

There was a large monitor at the front of the room. As Elizabeth paced around the room, she caught her reflection in the screen. She didn't realise how much of a toll the day had taken on her. Her eyes were slightly bloodshot, and the slumped stature of her body emanated exhaustion.

Stafford poured himself a separate glass of water and bit into a biscuit.

"You know it's the weirdest story why Carter came here," Stafford said, finishing his biscuit.

"Is that right?"

Stafford took a sip of water. "Yeah. Really interesting fellow. He was employed by someone who was worried about the guys who took me – and who they were working for – although at the time Carter didn't know. His job was to basically find me, and stop them. Kessler, the guy who planned the whole thing – the one on the phone last night – got away but Carter dealt with most of the team so I think it's ok for the time being."

Elizabeth shook her head. "You actually believe him don't you?"

"He has no reason to lie anymore."

"He has every reason to lie Edward. Everything he told you was probably made up on the spot. You're just too narrow minded to see it."

"Christ. It's been all but half an hour and you're already back to what you do best – condescension at the most expert level."

"I'm just looking out for your best interest – both of ours in fact. You need to start thinking about what's possible, and with someone like Carter, a lot is possible. You just don't see it."

"I see more than you think. Don't be so quick to judge. It'll be your downfall if you're not careful."

"*Downfall*. Who the hell do you think you are Stafford? Speaking as if you ever even know what's going on. My judgement is the best thing we have going for us. And trust me - yours certainly isn't, I'll tell you that much."

"How so?"

"Jesus, when we met with Reinhart earlier this week. The way he continued to pummel us on that deal. You, and Jack, both couldn't see it. Absolutely oblivious. You just don't get it, the way that people work. Even Jack – you don't see it – how ridiculously confused that boy is. This stupid idealism that courses through his veins. The constant self-importance. The fact that you think it's ok –

for someone to be the way he is…it's terrifies me sometimes."

"Oh, don't be so dramatic."

"I bet you have no idea what happened at the dinner Jack and Max attended." Her voice was oddly filled with excitement. "The one with the investors for our fund."

"You mean apart from the fact that they secured £105 million of investor money."

Stafford took another biscuit from the tray and tossed it into his mouth.

"I'm being serious. You don't know what happened?"

He shook his head, his mouth still full.

"Max gave instructions to Jack to not mention the Hothi deal that went south. It's a sour topic for the brothers, and would've obviously led to friction at the table. We needed the funds and it made sense to keep things as professional as we could. But, lo and behold, the first opportunity he gets, Jack brings it up. Apparently, he couldn't help himself from giving his two cents and just as Max predicted, things got out of control and everyone left."

Stafford's body stiffened.

"Thankfully, by some miracle, Jack actually found a solution and got everyone back together. Everyone was so happy with the outcome that they all decided to go ahead with the deal. Good ol' Jack right!"

Stafford's eyes fell the floor. "Look, I didn't know this. But Jack's a man of solutions. I can…see why –"

"Really! You can see why he risked the very fabric of our business on a whim? You're a man of such foresight Edward. Where would I be without you?"

"That's funny. Make jokes. I'm just trying to help explain."

"You want to help? Smack that self-entitled fucking prick back to reality and tell him that he's not special and that he can't just do whatever he likes just because he thinks he knows what's best and unknowingly suffers from catastrophic delusions of grandeur."

The sudden surge in Elizabeth's voice echoed around the room, startling Stafford and catching him off guard. He wandered a few steps back, briefly making eye contact with one of the staff passing by who had opened the door and popped their head inside. The individual caught sight of Elizabeth's expression and then swiftly continued down the corridor.

"Jack's a person," Stafford said. He spoke plainly. "He should be free to do as he pleases. Just because he believes in something – something a little bigger than himself - you think that's wrong?"

Elizabeth leant against the wall. She tilted her head back, her eyes raised upwards. "Not all beliefs are made equal. And the two of you both need to get that. That boy needs guidance – and by not giving it – you've let him down more so than anyone else."

"Jack Morse is whatever Jack Morse may be." Stafford took another sip of water. "I respect the decisions he's made and I'll take no part in trying to change him. It's not for me to decide."

"No. I guess someone else will have to do it."

Above Stafford and Elizabeth there were several floors. The upper floors had a series of executive suites. They were more sophisticated than the other rooms. Each had some tables, several chairs and its own selection of drinks. Some even had vast windows that lay out magnificent views of the city. Around the windows were large soft curtains, tied around the edges, providing a flair which was peculiar yet at the same time suited to a room which itself didn't have much spontaneity.

The rooms were also spacious although not as well-lit as the rooms downstairs.

The man inside preferred the dimmer setting.

Something about bright rooms made him feel uncomfortable and despite any initial reservations, his associates grew accustom to the environment. It was one of many predilections that they came to understand and one of many predilections held by Soren Lancaster.

Seven floors above the meeting room, there he stood, staring out of the immense window. In his hand was a small glass of water. Every so often he would take a small sip and then place it back on a table beside him.

Although he had started the day with a three piece navy suit, as the hours passed he had done away with the jacket. The sleeves of his white shirt had been rolled up, his button undone, all masked by a finely tailored waistcoat and a somewhat loosened tie, the colour of which glowed mildly red in the faint darkness.

Soren stared closely at the window, trying to spot his reflection in the heart of the glass. He was almost clean shaven but if he looked closely enough he could see a very subtle indication of stubble beginning to appear.

He started to look closer, the years of stress and anger wearing down his face. The wars and all the rage that came with them was causing him to age quicker than he would've liked. There was a persistent battle torn look about him which forced many to rethink his experience and intelligence. His eyes were worn out, ready to collapse under fatigue and yet if examined in detail, they seemingly sheltered boundless oceans of knowledge, accumulated by lifetimes of victory, defeat and deceit.

He cast his hand through his hair, watching the strands of light brown hair sift between his fingers. He stopped and his hair sprung back into place, neatly swept against the side.

He took his concentration away from the reflection of himself and back outside. The sun was finally beginning to descend.

Soren turned around. There was a man standing near

the entrance to his room and two more towards the centre. All three were dressed in a similar fashion; suits, ties and shoes of varying colours and styles.

He stared at the two men in the centre until he caught their attention. The man near the door peered over in interest also.

"Gentlemen," Soren said curiously. "I do wonder. Has someone briefed you on exactly what's happening tonight?"

Soren's tone was cold, and at times even raspy. He spoke English with such unique eloquence that many often found it difficult to discern exactly how he was feeling at any given point in time or even what region he may have grown up in.

One of the men stepped forward. "No sir. We were instructed to protect you while we were here. I think another team will be escorting you once you're ready to leave."

"I see. Well I think it's important that someone tells you why we're here."

The man spoke with a very firm tone. "We can request a briefing after you've left if that's what you'd prefer."

"No, no," Soren said. "I'll tell you myself. I'll tell you the story. I pray that you remember it when you yourselves are in command one day. I pray that you remember it when the time comes that you'll need to vanquish an enemy unlike no other. One who was dead but somehow, no matter what you do or what you say or what you fire, just doesn't seem to die."

The men stood silent, observing the sudden spark of anger in their commander's eye.

"I'll start by telling you why I did what I did," Soren said slowly.

He paused for a second, looking back out of the window and then back towards his men, carefully observing their expressions.

"I did it because in years to come…I knew they would thank me. I knew they would hail me as a hero; for having the foresight that no one else did when it truly mattered. To do what had to be done."

"The foresight for what?" the man asked.

"The foresight…to kill those who had to die."

CHAPTER 44

Soren adjusted his tie, the deep red colour glistening in the dusky lighting.

"Let me tell you what it's like to see a man who doesn't die. One who should've died so long ago but returns with a vengeance the likes of which you might never see."

The guards were all staring at him, hooked on his words.

"Order and power are complicated things. But they often go hand in hand. Over the years I've done whatever I could to bring about order, in places that are all too fractured. If a region required power then that's exactly what I exercised. My last excursion was no different."

Soren paused. He closed his eyes ever so briefly and then reopened them.

"Just over a year ago I had taken a team to the Iraqi-Syrian border. We had set up a small military base and were conducting operations in the area. We had sought to stabilise the conflict but before we could establish a fully functioning presence, we came under attack."

"What did you do?" one of the guards asked.

"We fought back…but there was nothing we could do. There was something else behind the attack…something…unforeseeable."

The men were silent.

"I survived," Soren said. "And as a result, I learnt something that night. Something I probably shouldn't have, but something that has allowed me to finally strike back."

The sand crunched against Soren's boots as he briskly proceeded towards a small operational centre on the outskirts of his base. It was nightfall and colossal floodlights spread along the perimeter removed him from the darkness. Each one shone intensely and radiated an immense, hypnotic glow across the region he called his own.

He passed vast numbers of tents and structures scattered across the area. Many were for accommodation. Others, which were larger and more sophisticated, were for tactical and operational purposes. The structures were highly fortified, primarily holding vehicles and aircraft while some acted as storage for equipment and weapons. The steel that held them together was an amalgamation of silver and dust that encompassed the walls and thick roof sheets that sat over them.

Soren could taste the heat in the air, slowly eating away at his senses and stamina. Everyone in the base wore the same dark olive military fatigues, which did little to combat the stress from the heat. He saw groups of men occupying benches outside of their tents. Empty bottles of beer hung by their feet and destitute faces were stuck together by pensive thoughts. Their mumblings sounded like the whirr of a generator and whenever Soren nodded, they nodded back, eyes alert and respectful.

The operational centre looked more like a cabin than one of the other structures except that it didn't have any windows. Its oblong rectangular shape stuck out from everything else in its vicinity and as Soren approached the centre a stout guard quickly gave him a salute and then opened the door.

The room was bright and there wasn't much equipment inside, just as he'd requested. Pinned on the wall was a freshly printed map of neighbouring countries in the region along with several monitors that were all switched off. He saw a few fold-out plastic tables and chairs which looked rigid and uncomfortable and sat on one was an elderly, well-dressed gentleman.

He sported a thick rugged beard which consumed the edges of his face and what once seemed to be a full head of hair had diminished significantly leaving sparse, uneven patches littered over his skull. Stocky and overweight, his stomach spilt over his suit trousers like a wave crashing against the shore as he stood up to greet Soren. A flabby arm extended outwards and attached to the end was a thick, grubby paw that took Soren's hand and shook it vigorously. He pulled his arm back just before his jacket may have begun to tear and slumped back into his chair, seemingly out of breath but admittedly unwilling to show it.

"Mr Soren. It's a pleasure to meet you."

"Likewise."

Soren sat down and felt the fatigues instantly stick to his body.

"My name is Bilal Haddad. I was told you met one of our staffers recently, over in the city?"

Haddad's Middle East accent was thick but Soren caught the gist of whatever he was saying.

"That's right."

"He told me you were hoping to open some speech; with my government yes?"

Soren nodded.

"Well, I'm here now so anything you want to say, say

it to me. I have authority to speak for matters. Yes?"

"Yes."

Haddad closed his fists and placed them on the table. His fingers were tightly packed together like sausages and the circumference of his wrists was so great that wearing a watch may have been out of the question.

Soren detected abnormal bulges on Haddad's knuckles and scarlet etching that wasn't because of the heat. Tiny scars ran over and between them like rivers in a valley and Soren considered how common that may have been for a traditional government minister.

"Well, firstly thank you for meeting with me," Soren said. "I appreciate it's at short notice but I wanted to do this all sooner rather than later. I sense you have some understanding of what we're doing here."

"I get the impression you're fighting wars for someone. I don't really know who. I am only here to investigate and ask questions. Yes?"

"That's true. We've conducted some work not too far from here. But we're not really here on behalf of anyone. We're…independent. So, please tell me…what would you like to know?"

"I'd like to know why I shouldn't ask Moscow to blow you out of the sky!"

Haddad burst into a hearty chortle and Soren momentarily saw the mountainous width of his chest.

"Because." Soren paused and he stared at Haddad's hands again. "I'll bring something to the region that Moscow can't."

"Which is?"

"Stability."

"Stability," Haddad repeated. "Like peace."

"A step towards that. Yes."

"I hope you're not lying to me Mr Soren. Because right now this all sounds unbelievable."

Soren shook his head. "It shouldn't. My outfit is agile

enough to do what larger forces can't. We can infiltrate the villages that you'd normally overlook. We've got the knowledge and experience to take control, banish the militants and rebels that are fanning the flames of this war and then keep them out. You'd have a piece on this board that no one else could defend against. Everything would change in a matter of months."

Haddad was suddenly fixated on the map pinned against the wall. He pictured different regions and his imagination began to run rampant.

"As things calm down I'm well within my rights to start opening up dialogue with the West. I've heard a few nations might channel some aid over if things go in the right direction."

Haddad snapped out of his daydream. "You can start communications with United States?"

"It'll take some time but I'm confident I can make that happen."

"Mr Soren, that is not a bad offer. But do me and my countrymen really want more western intervention. Where does that ever get anyone in this part of the world?"

The sound of Haddad's excessive breathing filled up the room. The heaviness grew in intensity while Haddad angled around in his chair attempting to alleviate the tension in his chest.

"I told you, I'm independent. And I'm a harbinger of order. Only thing I want is stability. I don't intend to let anyone get in the way of that."

"That's comforting. It's also kind of funny. You want to hear something funny Mr Soren?"

"Sure."

"A long time ago I had a meeting just like this one. He said things like you and acted like you. Nice man. I liked him. American though. He said his name was Schaffer. I only met him once. He said he'd meet me again but I never heard from him after that. Shame. I was…disappointed. Now I wonder whether you'll do the same to me Mr Soren? Yes?"

"No."

"No?"

"No. I guess it's unfortunate he didn't finish what he set out to do. But then some men were always unreliable. They don't have the resolve."

Haddad nodded. "And so you do? Tell me something." Haddad leaned forwards and through the small gaps in his beard Soren could spot the chunky of layers of skin sitting underneath his chin. "We all have a purpose. I know my purpose. It's to protect my country. But what's your purpose Mr Soren? Why are you here?"

Soren placed his arms on the table and craned his neck so that his eyes met the tip of Haddad's nose.

"Sometimes I feel like…there's sheep that stray from the herd. You understand what that means? They're the ones that run from the pack and decide to do something else. Other sheep sometimes follow them. Or they ignore it. I do whatever I can, however I can, to keep the sheep together and towards their destination. That's the right thing to do. But make no mistake. I am both the shepherd *and* the executioner. I'll do either if I have to. That is my purpose and I've never known otherwise…yes?"

Haddad's breathing stopped and his face turned pale. "Yes."

Haddad eventually left and having secured his cooperation, Soren stared out into the sands, considering how many more alliances he may have to forge in order to fulfil his purpose, and as he'd done in the past, how many he'd potentially need to burn.

CHAPTER 45

Shortly after his meeting with Haddad, Soren returned to the camp and found two of his associates waiting for him. Both were stood patiently, having observed Soren for the entirety of his journey back. Their eyes had followed him the way a child fixated on a stray balloon.

The three of them wandered through the base and drifted in and out of visibility as they bounced between pockets of light and darkness. They passed a half-damaged garage filled with empty cargo trucks and a whiff of gasoline scampered past them.

Soren recounted the contents of his discussion and acknowledged that Haddad's true occupation wasn't exactly clear. Nevertheless, Soren was certain he'd convinced him of their value and would utilise their services.

The conversation progressed and Soren enquired about other operations in the region. Regularly recalling the most obscure details off the top of his head, associates found there was no such thing as an easy conversation with Soren.

Every so often he slowed his pace, mulling on his

thoughts as if for a brief period he were on his own, and then continued to ask questions. At a certain point he prepared for another moment of pontification and then everyone stopped.

Each of them was receiving a message from their own team. Soren felt a cold chill down his spine.

They all stared at each other in confusion. Soren spoke back into his headset.

"How many are there?"

"We can't be certain sir. There's five choppers incoming. There could be more on the way. Even some we haven't yet identified."

"Deploy a defensive squadron along the edge of the camp right –"

A violent explosion shook the ground, knocking the three men off balance.

Soren's associates turned to him. "They must be on the ground."

"Morris - go to the site, grab a team as fast as you can and hold a position there now!"

"Yes sir."

How do they know we're here?

Soren looked up into the distance, the sound of gunfire echoing into the night. He could hear the faint noise of a helicopter, slicing through the air. He turned his attention to the other commander who was shouting demands into his headset.

Soren tapped him on the arm. "Call in artillery teams now. Get them to start manning the turrets and unloading the vehicles we have locked in storage. Bring them out and send them in to co-ordinate with Morris. He'll need assistance as soon as possible."

"What about you sir?"

"I'll head back to the command centre and deal with this properly."

The two of them went their separate ways, screams and

gunfire beginning to tear across the base.

Soren continued to move, speaking into his headset and trying to gauge what was going on. Various channels across the base were unresponsive.

Have they knocked out our communications?

"Sir!" a voice shouted into Soren's ear.

"I'm heading to the central command," Soren fired. "Get everyone there now. Morris has gone to the breach site to hold the intruders off. I've sent Palmer to bring out artillery in case more troops come from the air."

"Sir, our radars are detecting imminent breaches in other areas around the base. Morris is covering the north, but we can see incoming choppers heading for the east."

"Contact Morris. Tell him this immed –"

Multiple explosions rang across the base now. Soren turned around. The north of the base was engulfed in flames. He could see more helicopters starting to fly in, slowly making their descent like a pack of hawks attacking their prey. In the air he could see the doors sliding open. Some were already open, men cloaked in black shooting at the ground.

"Sir, Morris's unit is down. We're sending back up now."

"Where the fuck is Palmer?! Get him there now."

Soren was running through the base now, the chaos of war showering through the night. He could hear the sharp sting of missiles, colliding against the roar of engines and smashing against the sands.

Soren finally made it into the command centre. There were a number of people sat at desks screaming into radios and headsets. Various screens were lit up, bright red dots edging inwards, converging on their location.

"What's the situation?"

One of the men walked towards Soren.

"Sir, it's not looking good. The attack is sophisticated. Excessive even."

"Is there anything we can do?"

"We're not at the stage where we can hold something like this off. We just don't have the resources. It seems like whoever's coordinating this assault either wants to kill us all or force us into a full scale retreat."

"Have we identified who's behind it?"

"Not yet. But given the execution, I've a feeling they've known what we've been doing out here for a while and want us out for good."

"That's what I was afraid of." The stern look on Soren's face remained as it was. "It sounds like we don't have the numbers. For god's sake, how did they even know we were here? We've only been here a few months. Has anyone figured that out yet?"

"No one knows for certain. As far as we're aware, we're meant to be ghosts in this region. So whoever's behind this, they had to have been gathering intel for a long time. There's no way else they could've known so much."

Soren's eyes turned to the screen next to him. He watched as the red dots continued to edge closer and closer to the centre. With each blip he felt his heart pound against his chest.

"Realistically, our capability to fight this off is unlikely," he said. "We need to get everyone out. Get as many of the aircraft and choppers out of here as well."

One of the men sat by the radar looked bewildered. "We can't just retreat. We'll lose the equipment, the aircraft. Everything we've built."

"Everything we've built will die in its entirety if we stay. This is too well coordinated."

"But Soren. If we –"

"They're not just here for weapons or blood. We don't have enough of that to justify an attack like this. They're probably here for our intelligence. And that's something I'm not ready to give up. A retreat will ensure that."

The man scratched his head. "Possibly. But what's to say it isn't something else?"

"It very well could be. But right now there's nothing to suggest that so I have to work with what's most likely."

The man, somewhat unconvinced, glanced back at the radar. His hair was thin and lay flat over the top of his head, concealing his forehead and the stress-induced wrinkles chiselled into his brow.

"I heard you met with Bilal Haddad earlier?"

The man was looking at Soren with great curiosity, almost unsure whether he'd even respond.

"That's correct. What's your point?"

"Timing is a bit suspicious isn't it? You meet with Haddad to discuss capabilities in the region and then as soon as he leaves we come under fire."

Columns of lamps which hung across the ceiling began to swing aggressively as another explosion shook the base and briefly obfuscated Soren's glaring expression.

"Haddad isn't our enemy. He's got everything to gain from this partnership and so wouldn't prepare a strike against us. Whoever's launching this attack is an enemy of ours and an enemy of his government. The attack was timed precisely for after he left so that Haddad would learn of our retreat and think twice about partnering with us or anyone else."

"So it's a message to Haddad too?"

"Possibly. But there must be something else. It can't just be that…"

"There are squads entering the base as we speak," a man operating the radio interrupted. "Firefights are breaking out on the northern regions of the base. Enemy troops are also making their way through the east. Cruisers and turrets are holding them at bay but we can assume they have heavy artillery. We had a report that RPGs burned a hole through some of our defensive choppers so our line can't hold on for long."

Explosions continued to resonate out from the distance as a cursed look fell across Soren's face.

"Tell them to hold the line and send reinforcements to assist in their defence. I need a heavily armed force to hold off the eastern attack while everyone makes their evacuation."

"Yes sir."

The man who initially approached Soren cleared his throat. "Sir, if our suspicions about their motives are true, then you need to evacuate as soon as possible. We've sent word to teams at the south to start preparing evac teams immediately. The south is the most heavily fortified area of the base and it's probably the safest right now. I suggest you head there immediately. We can handle everything from here."

Soren nodded. "Once I get south-side I'll reassume command so you have time to evac too. Make sure you all get yourselves out of here ASAP. They'll take this room soon enough. Be sure to burn it to the ground before they do."

"Of course. Thank you sir."

Soren turned around and swiftly proceeded outside, the bright spark of flames spiralling upwards. In the same direction, screams and explosions blew through the air. He watched as the flares from combat erupted into the night sky, almost indistinguishable from the stars, and started to run southwards.

CHAPTER 46

Soren couldn't recall the last time his pulse raced this way. Preparation was the cornerstone of his mind and for the longest time he had always been in control. But this was different. It reminded him of an earlier phase in his life which was engulfed with uncertainty, moments that caught him by surprise; the constant adaptation and the rush which flew through his body as the pressure built up inside of him. Such was its nature that it couldn't be recreated and yet at the time, he remembered that he often welcomed it too.

Nonetheless, Soren couldn't stop wondering who was behind this. Who might have been that relentless in order to gather so much intelligence, to muster so much firepower to blast away a small military presence in the Syrian region before it even started? There had to be something else driving this attack. He just knew it.

Soren continued to dash across the camp. He could see the helicopters flying overhead, glinting in the darkness as their blades caught the gleam of the floodlights. He turned a corner and could see a small squad of men in front of him heading in the same direction.

One of the men turned around and instantly recognised Soren.

"Sir. Are you heading south for an evac?"

"Yeah. What are your orders?"

"We were told to head south and await instructions."

"Alright. Let's keep moving."

Soren accompanied the men who led the way through the camp. There were about fifteen in total. They seemed calm and Soren could see from the way they breathed that none of them had yet lost their nerve. Four were stationed at the front, with three covering the flank. The remainder kept a strict formation in between the two ends. Each of them were carrying large assault rifles while Soren had a small submachine gun in his holster.

A steadfast expression occupied all of their faces but Soren could see the fear mounting in their eyes. This wasn't combat like they had experienced before. This time they were the ones that were under occupation and it was them who were at risk of losing their lives. The camaraderie clearly existed between them but each man wasn't willing to look at their comrade any longer than necessary lest they one day recall vivid memories of everyone they might lose today.

As they pressed forwards they suddenly heard a screeching sound pierce through their ears. Everyone raised their heads and saw multiple projectiles collide against two of the floodlights near the western wall. Both floodlights exploded, replaced by spires of flames.

"They're attacking the western gate!" Soren shouted into his headset. "I'm with a small squadron. We're proceeding to engage. Continue with the evac."

"Sir, you need to –"

"I need to ensure my base isn't overrun by enemy combatants. Coordinate the eastern defence. I'll handle this."

Soren's eyes instantly latched on to the leader of the

squadron. "Head in that direction. We need to hold them off until we have units that can manage a defensive line here."

The leader stuck his hand into the air and pointed in the direction of the burning spires.

They started to move, the sound of several helicopters buzzing in the distance. As they got closer the sounds got louder. In the embers of the shattered lights Soren could see them landing.

Soren tapped his headset. "I need preparations for a defensive perimeter towards the west ASAP!"

The squad rushed ahead, the sound of violent explosions blowing through the air mere metres from where they were.

They approached several small shipping containers, the explosions and spires just around the corner.

Soren tapped into his headset, switching his channel to match the squadron he was with. "They've breached the gate just around the corner. We can keep cover here. Hold your position."

They all waited in silence, against the containers, the noise of helicopter blades and flames fluttering through the night.

After several seconds, they heard the roar of an engine. The squad leader flicked his head past one of the containers and looked to his right. Instantly jumping backwards, two small desert coloured Humvees raced past him and towards the breach. He momentarily caught sight of the wide metal plates that were stuck along the outside and the colossal wheels which gritted against the sand. A mounted machine gun sat atop each of them, both manned by soldiers who were firing uncontrollably into the distance.

The cars whizzed past them and raged ahead until the team heard a series of thick hollow shots. The noises were distinct. They didn't sound like bullets.

After a second they heard concurrent explosions. The leader peeked out behind the container and saw five groups of men, clad in black moving in unison. Two soldiers at the front of each group were armed with grenade launchers, carefully moving forwards. In front of them, both Humvees were engulfed in flames. The leader slipped back behind cover.

"Sir, M32s. They've blown away the Humvees."

Soren took a sharp breath. "What's our firepower?"

"M4 rifles mainly. About half of us have grenades and M203s."

"Anyone who has an M203 attach it, and load up," Soren said. "Head up front. We need some sort of force or else we'll be annihilated before this thing even starts."

Several of the men scuttled to the front of the group slotting their attachments on to their rifles.

Soren tapped the squad leader on the shoulder.

"You and three of your men come out of cover and open fire in the next thirty seconds. Create enough suppression for us to get out and push ahead. There's two containers just near those Humvees. We'll head for those. The Humvees will provide additional cover if we need it."

"Got it."

Soren stepped backwards, drawing his weapon. He turned back and gave a small nod to the men behind him.

In patience and in the darkness, they all waited. The footsteps of their intruders grew louder. The squad leader gave a small nod. The three men next to him crouched down, all stood in one vertical line. He nodded once more and the four of them emerged from their cover and opened fire.

Two shots thundered through the air and collided against the intruders, lighting up the darkness with a flume of smoke and fire. In the passing seconds, the other two soldiers opened fire, the grenades exploding as they hit the ground.

In the chaos the intruders split off into separate packs, trying to dodge the incoming attack.

Soren led the men forwards and closer into cover just as the third set of grenades launched, spreading their soldiers between the containers and the flaming Humvees.

Realising what was happening the intruders opened fire, trying to hold Soren's advance.

Soren's men held their position and shot back. Grenades continued to launch across the air, the flames torching the desert ground.

Soren turned around and could see two more Humvees on their way. They burst on to the field and pulled up next to them and started to unload a flurry of bullets.

The intruders quickly fell into retreat, and dashed backwards.

Before Soren could proceed after them he gazed into the distance. He could see more choppers heading just south of where they were.

"They're trying to flank our position," Soren shouted. He pointed to the group standing by him at the container. "With me, now!"

Soren turned around and headed south towards the landing zone. One of the Humvees started to follow. They heard multiple explosions and gunshots as they started to move.

As they came closer they could see the choppers landing. There were several troops already firing at the chopper alongside a burning truck.

The doors to the helicopter slid open and more men started to jump out on to the ground and through the fences.

Soren ran forwards and started firing, maiming some of the first few men who made their descent.

How many men have they brought here?

The floodlights had fallen to the ground and were shattered. The only light in the area was from the flames of the burning vehicles. The intruders continued to land, their surrounding helicopters opening fire across the area.

Soren's men jumped for cover as the gunfire tore across the floor. Soren spotted the corpse of one of his men. He had been torn apart by the gunfire and was drenched in blood. His rifle lay on the floor just next to him, the M203 attachment still fixed. Soren picked it up and stared up into the sky.

He could see one chopper still in the air, preparing to open fire again while another was beginning its descent to the ground. Soren ran out of cover and fired a grenade at the airborne chopper. The grenade ricocheted against its blades and exploded in a burst of fury.

The chopper started to spin out of control and fell forwards. Some of the men started to leap out as its blades snapped off. It crashed into the ground, the collision of metal against the sand violently shattering across the base. Soren's men quickly opened fire at anyone still trying to exit the chopper, their bodies falling against its steel body.

Soren ran towards the enemies in the other helicopter that were beginning to land but the chopper he had downed suddenly exploded in front of him. He fell backwards, the smoke clouding what little sight he had left. He got to his feet and could hear gunfire. More men and vehicles were arriving behind him. The intruders ran forwards, viciously firing at Soren's men. Soren tried looking for his weapon, the heat of the wreckage searing against his face.

The smoke started to clear and he could see one more helicopter landing in the distance. The doors opened and out jumped a phantom from his past.

He dropped to the floor and looked Soren directly in the eye. Soren stepped back in horror as the man, as if he were under some sort of trance, raced towards him, his gun clutched tightly in his hands.

It can't be. He can't possibly be here.

He ran with such a ferocity and such an anger that Soren knew that it was indeed the same man; the same man he crossed so many years ago. One that should've died long ago and never returned.

And yet...in the heat of battle, Michael Carter had finally seen the core tenet of his vengeance.

The commander had landed and was now preparing to finish the assault once and for all. Mansoor had led the eastern attack and Carter had led from the west.

Just as he had promised, together, they would decimate Soren's insurgency before it even started.

CHAPTER 47

Soren was on his own. His men were scattered across the area. The intruders had already taken too much ground. His forces were in disarray. He turned and fell back towards two Humvees he could spot in the distance. They were both viciously shooting into the night, attempting to force back the oncoming assault.

Soren continued moving but a flurry of missiles raced past him and blasted his vehicles into the sky. The eruptions shook the entire base.

Soren quickly scanned the area. Amidst the flames he could see glimpses of his men falling back, desperately running for cover.

I need to get out of here...now.

Soren sprinted southwards, Carter still in pursuit.

Soren continued to run through the base, rushing past soldiers who were firing at the intruders, all of whom were breaching every part of the western wall.

Carter had left his squad and was in active pursuit of Soren. He was getting closer and closer, Soren's pace starting to weaken. The battle had tired him and Carter was gaining.

Carter killed every soldier that crossed his path. Each time he turned a corner he shot without a thought in mind, pushing their bullet ridden bodies aside like pawns on a chessboard.

As Soren ran he could hear the bodies dropping to the floor behind him. The gunshots felt so close. He knew Carter wanted him alive, even if it was just for a second. There was just as much revenge in his heart as there was curiosity.

Soren knew Carter would catch him soon enough. He drew his submachine gun and fired several shots behind him.

Carter saw Soren's hand slip downwards and slid behind a small container. He waited a few seconds and ran back out, continuing to chase him down, confident that Soren wouldn't be able to reload running at this speed.

The shots had put some distance between them but as Soren continued he could see two soldiers preparing to man a Humvee.

"Behind me!" Soren shouted. "Take him down."

One of them jumped upwards to man the turret but before he could get inside it burst into flames. Soren turned around and saw Carter holding an M32 in his hand, his rifle on the floor behind him.

Soren's heart started to race.

Carter fired again. This time at the vehicle, the explosion knocking Soren off his feet.

Carter dropped the weapon and ran towards Soren who rushed to get up but it was too late. Carter grabbed him by the throat and violently struck him in the face.

Carter tried to strike him again but Soren pushed his hand down and kicked him away.

"You should be a dead man," Soren panted.

Soren tried to back away but Carter ran forwards again, spearing Soren against a large storage container.

Soren spun him around and drove his knee into Carter's abdomen.

Carter retaliated and smashed his knuckle along the side of Soren's chin. The force of Carter's attack knocked Soren sideways.

"I'll die after I slit your fucking throat," Carter menaced.

As Carter stood up straight, one of Soren's men emerged from behind the vehicle and ran towards him. He lunged at Carter, a small knife in his hand. Carter shuffled to the side, pulling the man's arms away from him. Carter struck the side of his palm against his throat and twisted his hand, violently yanking it against its joints.

The man screamed in agony, falling to his knees and dropping the knife to the floor. Carter slammed his elbow against his nose. As the man fell back in complete disorientation, Carter leant down and picked up the knife. The man tried to strike back but Carter grabbed his arm and pulled him forwards, piercing the knife into his throat. He swiftly removed it, a stream of blood flowing down his neck.

Carter stepped back and spotted Soren sprinting for one of the rifles on the ground. Carter ran towards him just as he was leaning over and kicked him forwards. Soren fell to the floor and turned over just as Carter drove the blood stained knife towards his face. Soren rolled out of the way and kicked Carter in the chest.

Carter stumbled a few paces back, trying to catch his breath.

Soren leapt to his feet and continued for the weapon on the floor but Carter jumped forwards and pulled him back.

Soren turned around, attempting to strike Carter.

Before Soren could realise Carter sidestepped him and thrust the knife into the centre of his forearm.

Soren yelled in pain, and smashed his one free hand

into Carter's face. Carter scuttled backwards, spitting a speck blood on the floor.

Soren pulled the knife from his arm and gripped it tightly.

"I'm going to put you in the ground like I should've done all those years ago."

Soren leapt at Carter, wildly swinging the knife at him. Carter continually dodged the attacks, each one nearing closer and closer. Soren swung at Carter's chest but he jumped out of the way and grabbed a hold of his hand.

The two of them struggled over the knife, rocking it across the dark air, their hands gripped around one another, blood and sweat seeping in between their fingers.

The conflict continued and Soren felt his grip loosening. The pain in his wounded arm was becoming too much and he knew he wouldn't be able to continue any longer. He swung the knife towards the flaming Humvee, quickly letting it go. The knife spun through the air, and was immediately consumed by the fire.

The momentary surprise to Carter gave Soren enough time to retaliate. He catapulted his fist into Carter's ribs. Carter's body curved sideways, as if it were nearly torn in half.

Soren tried to back away but Carter persisted. He dove towards him and grabbed him by the throat and continued to attack him. No matter the pain that surged through Carter's body right now it was nothing compared to what he had been through at the hands of Soren. There was no composure or natural fluidity to his attacks. He struck and struck and struck, ensuring every hit were harder than the last.

Soren had made many enemies over the years but he had never faced an onslaught as relentless as this. Carter, the man who didn't die, a man with a passion for revenge that knew no bounds, would not stop. Soren wondered if there was *anything* that could stop him. He knocked back every strike Carter threw at him, and yet still, slowly and without realising, he could feel himself retreating across the sands, the sheer force of Carter's attacks enough to shake his arms and soul.

Carter slammed both of his hands down against Soren's arms, and flung his head into Soren's. The collision dazed Soren momentarily and Carter swung his arm across Soren's cheek with such ferocity that Soren fell to the floor.

Carter prepared to attack Soren again but before he could strike another soldier appeared from the shadows and attacked him.

The soldier tried to knock Carter to the floor but Carter deflected his attack, and threw him to the floor.

Carter looked up and saw Soren already on his feet fleeing the scene. He was shouting something into his headset.

"Don't you dare run from me!" Carter screamed.

The soldier on the floor swung his legs at Carter, trying to knock him over. Carter quickly raised his foot and stamped on the soldier's knee, snapping his bone as if it were just a wooden branch. He leant over and continuously drove his fist into his face. Over and over Carter attacked him until his hand started to shake uncontrollably and his knuckles blazed with a hot searing pain. He looked down and in the darkness he saw a pool of blood sat in the half mangled and shattered face of a solider on the wrong side of the war.

Carter continued to chase Soren. On the floor, he saw the rifle they were fighting for earlier. He quickly leant over and grabbed it.

Soren bolted around one of the corners and as Carter followed another soldier appeared. He tried to open fire but Carter smacked the butt of his rifle against his hands and then again into his face. The man, stunned, regained his senses only to see a flurry of bullets tear into his eyes.

Carter pushed him out of the way, edging around the corner and wiping the blood from his face. He saw Soren continue to drift away, his body burning with anger.

"Soren!" Carter raged.

Carter ran forwards, his rifle gripped tightly in his hands. Within seconds, before he could make up any distance, a convoy of three trucks suddenly drove in between them.

The trucks halted and out jumped squads of soldiers all heavily armed. The men all proceeded towards him, flumes of bullets ravaging through the air and in his direction. Carter desperately leapt for cover, the gunfire narrowly missing him.

He frantically searched for a way around the soldiers but there was nothing he could do. Every other passage he saw led to certain death.

Carter slipped out of cover momentarily, opening fire in a bid to push his enemies back, trying to search for anywhere else he might move to.

In those brief moments, as he scanned his surroundings, he caught hold of a distant sight. Between the trucks, he saw, for only a second, Soren. There he stood, his expression torn and his body broken, staring back, not with eyes of victory or relief but those of disarray and chaos. Other memories cycled along the periphery of that moment; from the periods before Carter became who he was now; when he could still rationalise the world, his allies and the meaning of truth.

The instance came to pass and Soren turned around, continuing his journey to the south of the base.

Carter surveyed the situation as best as he could but he knew he was out of options. His enemies continued to press forward, cutting off any other way to get to Soren. Waves of bullets continued to crash against his location, forcing him back into cover. With no other options Carter was left with no choice but to retreat.

He paced back and eventually returned to his team, finishing the assault he'd started. As the battle raged on, most of Soren's men continued to flee the base while those that remained didn't survive.

In the end, Carter and Mansoor took the base and everything in it for themselves. After the battle had concluded Carter walked the sands, surveying the destruction he had sown. Flames and fires continued to ravage across the area.

He eventually spotted Mansoor with a small group of soldiers. Next to them were five of Soren's men. They were on their knees, unarmed, shivering.

Carter came closer. "So it's done?"

"Yes. I have people unloading the containers. The shipments were just like you said."

"Good."

"Soren's?" Carter asked, glancing at the men on the ground.

"Prisoners of war." He turned to his men and nodded.

The men raised their rifles and opened fire. The shots echoed across the silence of the base and the bodies of Soren's men collapsed to the floor.

Carter's eyes remained fixed on Mansoor.

"So Mr Carter…did you get what you want? Did you find the revenge you seek?"

"No. I didn't."

"Well then, what do you do now?"

"I continue…until I get it."

That night Tarik, Mansoor and Faris had gotten what they desired. The base was theirs and they were free to operate in the region without the risk of a new enemy emerging. But Carter never quenched his thirst for vengeance. True enjoyment still eluded him and he wouldn't rest until he attained it.

After parting ways with Carter, Soren eventually made his way to the southern part of the base. He, along with

ASH SHARMA

many others, were able to evacuate the base safely. However, their presence in the region was lost. Shortly after the assault the local militia he had been working with was completely wiped out by Tarik's armies.

If there was one thing Soren knew for certain, it was that the battle had left him scarred. He had fought Carter and survived by just the skin of his teeth. Death could have come at any point that night and he knew that it would continue to do so unless he did something about it.

For hours to come he sat and thought. He thought about the resolve that Carter had employed in order to finally take his revenge. The planning, the precision, the financing was all so methodical because of a desire to see him dead.

Carter's greatest strength was his resourcefulness. His resolve was unparalleled. He was a man that refused to die and Soren would continue to be hunted until his last day unless he responded.

Before this ordeal he had known Carter better than almost anyone. He had known him to be calm and composed. There may have been moments of anger but even they were nothing but fragments within a man who was constantly under control.

But tonight had been different. He wasn't composed. He didn't speak with the elegant patience that he was so well known for. His words, his attacks, were fierce and chaotic. The unpredictability was new and Soren suddenly began to see...see that Carter was, at his core, blinded, with far too much anger and far too much power.

So Soren decided to utilise his greatest talent. He deceived. He would deceive until Carter suddenly saw the truth. And then he would kill him the way he should've done so many years ago and quash the foolish desire for vengeance that plagued the mind of man that so desperately had to die.

CHAPTER 48

Sent.

Jack was on his way back to the Field having just forwarded the back testing analysis to Elizabeth. Its primary purpose was to support the performance of their algorithm, highlighting its accuracy when tested against historical scenarios in the market. If the algorithm made money in the past, there was a very high chance it would make money in the future.

The results were stellar and arguably one of the best ways to convince an investor of the algorithm's success.

As Jack wandered down the street he knew there was nothing more to do except leave Elizabeth and Stafford to close the deal. His role in these affairs had come to a close.

Katrina was sat on one of the chairs in Stafford's office, quietly checking her phone while Sinclair was stood by the window again. Both of them had just watched as Elizabeth had bolted outside to meet with Stafford.

The happiness on her face was almost instantaneously replaced with anger when she realised she had been left in the dark longer than she should have. Having seen her storm outside, Katrina and Sinclair both felt an overarching sense of relief; that maybe the worst had finally passed.

They had briefly watched from the window as they saw Stafford and Max standing across the street speaking to Elizabeth. Next to them were Jack and Carter, both unharmed and well.

Everyone seems fine, Katrina thought. *It worked. They actually did it. Thank god.*

Even from this height Katrina could spot the sharp suspicion on Elizabeth's face. Whatever she was hearing, she wasn't completely convinced.

Within seconds, everyone went in separate directions. Katrina had expected Jack to accompany Max back inside but he'd gone in a different direction.

"Where's *he* going?" Sinclair asked.

"No idea. But I suppose the rest of them are off to that meeting though."

Sinclair suddenly remembered Stafford's significance in this entire matter. After everything that had happened, the trivialities of who did what had fallen by the wayside.

He was the brains behind this company wasn't he?

"If Elizabeth and Stafford get this deal closed, does that mean the business becomes a serious venture?"

"Yeah. It does. Sounds weird saying out loud but the plan is to hire more staff, buy better technology, a bunch of stuff. It'll be pretty exciting."

There was a hollow sound to her words which gave Sinclair the impression that her mind was engaged with something else.

"I'm sure it will. Despite everything I said, you all seem like smart people. I'm sure you're going to do just fine."

Katrina smiled. "That's quite a compliment. I appreciate it."

"Bet you wish I was this nice in the morning."

"It wouldn't have hurt," Katrina chuckled.

After not too long Katrina heard the sound of footsteps spiral through the corridor. She perked up and faced the door just as Max walked inside.

"Well, well, well, look who it is!" Max shouted.

Katrina leapt up from her seat and gave Max a hug.

"God, I never thought I'd be so happy to see you."

"Yeah, this response feels sort of weird. Not sure if I like it."

Max felt the dust from Stafford's bookshelves lodge itself into his nose and for the first time all day he felt like he had returned to some semblance of normality. He instantly sensed that his suit was dishevelled and patted his hands over it and tried to remove the creases that had embedded themselves into the fabric.

"I'm glad you're safe Max," Katrina said. "This whole thing has been…"

Max stopped patting his suit and quickly recognised the strain in Katrina's voice; the dull sense of fatigue in her eyes.

"Yeah…" He dropped his head. "I know."

Katrina grabbed Max's phone from a nearby table. It was the same phone that his kidnappers had searched him for the previous night.

"Might want this back," Katrina said, passing the phone back to him.

"Yeah. Thanks. God only knows the state of my inbox."

Before that instant Max hadn't caught sight of Sinclair; composed, observant and slowly making his way around the table. After what Jack told him, and the small glimpses he had seen himself, he was unlike anything he was expecting.

Where's the raging madman I heard so much about?

Max recalled the images from the previous night. The way in which he appeared from the darkness and shot down his kidnappers without any remorse. The bloodlust on Sinclair's face had been so visible and terrifying that he and Stafford were almost certain that staying where they were was not an option.

Neither of them ever predicted that the same man might have just spoken to Elizabeth or would've provided the vital clues required in order to find them.

Katrina glanced at Sinclair. "Sorry – I should probably introduce you both. Sinclair, this is Max."

They both shook hands.

"I think we're already somewhat acquainted," Sinclair mumbled.

"It's good to meet you under more…regular circumstances" Max said. "I heard you helped get me back. I appreciate it."

"Yeah…I'm sorry about what happened." Sinclair was struggling to look Max in the eye. "It was a testing time for me personally."

The tranquil nature of his voice contrasted with what he'd heard the previous night or the way Jack described his behaviour earlier that day. Instead there lay an entrenched longing for forgiveness which was still coming to terms with itself.

"It's alright. If you never did what you did, I don't think we'd be back here. So, thanks."

"I didn't do that much to be honest. I wouldn't worry about it."

Katrina smacked Max on the arm. "So what the hell happened? Elizabeth ran downstairs without telling us anything."

Katrina edged forwards. Max could see that what might appear as playful curiosity was a relenting desire to know the truth. The way her grip tightened around the back of the chair, the impatient tapping of her foot.

"It's a weird story if I'm honest," Max said. "I guess I'll start from the last moment you saw me."

Max began to recount the various steps of his journey; from the kidnapping to being held captive by Reinhart. Katrina's surprise at Reinhart's involvement was the same as his own when he first realised what had happened.

"An investor…behind a kidnapping? That sounds ridiculous."

"I don't write reality Katrina. It is what it is."

"Come on. Why did he take you?"

"We don't know. At first we thought he might've done it to get information out of Stafford and I, but it looks like there might've been some other reason. He didn't give anything up though. One of Carter's friends is going to deal with it apparently."

"Great."

Katrina thought that Max might probe her scepticism but she could see the exhaustion on his face. His eyes drooped slightly and his arms lay by his side, devoid of any vitality. She noticed the way he skipped over minor details as he explained events, as if he were rushing to end so that he could be done with it.

"But they got you out in the end?" Sinclair asked. "Jack and Carter?"

"Yeah. Stafford and I couldn't believe it when they turned up, not that they had a great plan. Eventually Carter got locked in a room with some guard and the rest of us were outside with Reinhart who kept us at gunpoint."

"Seriously?"

"Yeah. It was fine though. Good ol' Jack turned the tables…quite literally. Got the gun from Reinhart and then shot the guy guarding Carter."

Katrina's jaw dropped.

"What?! He *shot* him?"

"Yeah…"

"Are you trying to be funny?"

"I'm being serious. He shot him. Didn't kill him

but…"

"Jesus Christ." Katrina's face filled with disbelief. "Why?"

"Once he saved me and Stafford he said he needed to save Carter. Said he wasn't about to leave him. We tried getting him to leave but you know what he's like. The guard wasn't about to give up and then he fired."

At the time Max didn't realise how loud the gunshot was. Only now did its deafening blast appear in his mind and ring through his ears. Oddly, it wasn't the weapon that had stood out to him; it was Jack and the small tremors in his hand, the early tears in his veil of confidence.

"God, I can't believe it," Katrina said. "How is he?"

"The guy who got shot?"

"No. Jack!"

"Apparently he's fine. That's what he says anyway. We tried to probe him but he got defensive. Accused me and Stafford of not being grateful. Seems we don't appreciate his skillset."

The nonchalant way in which Max described the events made Katrina wonder whether he even cared. His words were empty, like he was reading measurements in a lab.

"What happened after he shot him?"

"Carter got out. He locked up Reinhart and Benson and that was it. We came here."

"So the job was a success," Sinclair said. "Carter did it."

Max didn't dispute whether Sinclair was happy with the outcome. But he wondered if Sinclair might have been more content if he had dealt with the problem himself when he had the chance. He spotted a glimpse of remorse for failing to act, and a remote element of jealousy for Carter; the mysterious wanderer that swooped in and made Sinclair to be the fool while emerging as the hero.

It was then that Max felt compassion for Sinclair. Here

was another that defined themselves by the hero's ideology and would live up to everything less, no matter the cost.

"Did Carter finally tell you why he's here then?" Sinclair asked.

"Yeah. He confessed he wasn't an investor. Apparently he's here on behalf of a client who intercepted a communication between the two men who came here last night. Carter's job was to figure out was going on. All he knew was that the two men were interested in Stafford."

"Do you believe him?" Katrina asked.

Max fell silent as he lifted his head in contemplation. "I'm split 80:20 on this."

"Eighty you believe him?"

"Eighty I don't."

"Well you wouldn't be the first to distrust Carter's motivations."

Max often recognised the difference between when Katrina was being playfully funny and when she was agitated. Something told him she'd been sceptical of Carter's motivations for a long time.

"That's fair enough," Max said. "But he got us back. There's no denying that. But if I'm honest, he's not what concerns me."

"I think he very well should," Katrina retorted. "I don't know what he's done but he's obviously gotten into Jack's head."

"*Has he?*"

"Of course! Why else would he be doing what he's doing?"

Katrina's voice had risen and her body became rigid.

"Oh I don't know…maybe because he's Jack Morse and he thinks he can do whatever the fuck he wants."

"No, no, no. This is different – he's –"

"Don't be ridiculous," Max snapped. "He's always

been like this. He was just looking for the opportunity. But I bet that underneath all that bravado, he's just like anyone else. Nothing special. Just another soul on the street."

"Max don't be an asshole. I know he's done some stupid stuff but…I'm sure it wasn't easy to do what he did."

"Ahhh look at you," Max said. He lifted his arms as if he were in celebration and his voice was blanketed with enthusiasm. "You remind me of Stafford. Trying to defend that idiot. That's just what we need."

"I'm not defending him!" Katrina fired.

"It definitely sounds like it. Do us a favour, and keep the empathetic bullshit to a minimum. Last thing I want is for that fucker to start getting more ideas."

"Oh fuck off Max. We're just not all selfish bastards like you are.

"Both of you calm down," Sinclair said. The authoritative bellow in his voice quickly brought them both to silence. "Jack did what he did. Chances are, these circumstances aren't going to repeat themselves, so stop getting worked up over nothing. Move on! I think we'd all benefit from that."

"Whatever you say," Max said. "If you need me, I'll be in the Square. I have some emails I probably need to catch up with."

Max walked back into the Square. Katrina looked on, somehow unsurprised at Max's reaction.

Some things never change.

Max sat down. He pulled out his phone and started flicking through unread emails.

He tapped in and out of his inbox, scanning whichever caught his fancy.

Max continued to scroll downwards until a familiar sight crossed the periphery of his vision.

He didn't realise how long it had been there. Seconds, or perhaps minutes?

The dark shade of a trench coat, worn by a man that had no business in a jurisdiction of peace.

CHAPTER 49

Max stood up, his mind suddenly stricken with shock. Before he could move the man had already closed the gap between them.

He tried to speak but the man clutched his throat and struck him in the side of his chest. The pain blasted across his ribs and ricocheted around his body, casting him into agony.

Max fell to one side while the man's cold grip continued to squeeze the air from his throat like a crushed balloon. He felt dizzy; his surroundings were in disarray and ghastly images passed in and out of his mind.

The man lifted him up and with his other hand launched Max back towards the entrance. His body crashed into one of the stone columns and landed on the ground.

Max screamed out in pain as the man glided towards him. The man he knew. The man that had held him captive.

Max continued to watch as David Kessler walked across the Square, his eyes fixed upon him.

Max used what little energy he had left to shout as loud

as he could. "He's here! Get out!"

Max realised he had never explicitly mentioned Kessler's name to Katrina or Sinclair. His explanation had been vague and left out a lot of details. As far as they were aware, Kessler would have been nothing more than the unknown man who took him and Stafford.

Sinclair heard Max scream and immediately stood up. *Who's he talking about?*

He turned to Katrina, her face immersed in panic. "Stay here. Don't move."

Sinclair pulled his jacket back and drew his pistol. He took a clip from his inside pocket and loaded his weapon. He racked the slider and held the pistol up, peering down the sight as he slowly moved out of Stafford's office and down the corridor.

Max was still on the floor, his face engulfed by terror as David Kessler stood before him.

"What are you…"

Kessler picked him up and slammed him against the column, punching him in the nose. Max's blood cut across the room and splattered against the white stone which encased the column.

Max tried to come to his senses but Kessler drove his knee into his abdomen.

He pivoted around the column dragging Max along with him.

Kessler pushed him against the pillar and leant downwards. "How did you get out Max?" he whispered. "Who set you free?"

Kessler already knew the answer. He knew Carter had something to do with this. There was someone in this building who knew exactly why he was here and Kessler would do whatever he had to in order to get answers.

Max's face was pressed against the stone, the weight of Kessler's strength slowly crushing his jaw. He could barely make out what was being said. What movement his face had left was nothing more than a shiver.

Kessler quickly removed his pistol. He waited patiently, the beat of his heart more composed than ever.

Sinclair burst into the room. His sight immediately fell on Kessler who emerged from his cover and fired two shots at him.

Sinclair leapt behind a column just next to him, narrowly evading the attack.

"Alright," Kessler said slipping back into cover. "Maybe this will be more entertaining than I thought."

"What do you want?" Sinclair said.

Kessler smacked his pistol against the back of Max's head who yelled out in distress.

The scream carried a panic and desperate cry for help; one that Sinclair wasn't willing to ignore.

"You don't need to harm him!"

"Oh, but I do…I suspect it'll make things a bit more interesting."

Max could barely stand. The only thing keeping him on his feet was Kessler clawing at the top of his jacket. His energy was completely drained, his eyes filled with water and blood. Despite it being so close, he couldn't even see the white stone in front of him.

For a second Kessler's hand lifted from his jacket and Max had a chance to catch his breath but before he knew it Kessler had already wrapped his forearm around Max's throat and stood him upright.

The grip was like a vice, cutting off almost every ounce of oxygen Max had.

Kessler held Max directly in front of him, his weapon drilled against his temple. He stepped out from behind the pillar, slowly edging out into the open the way a predator ventured into the wild.

Sinclair peered from behind his cover and saw a shadowy figure behind Max. A Max who was beaten and bloody, unable to stand, his body devoid of any being and ready to die at any second if Sinclair didn't do anything.

Sinclair raised his weapon and walked into the centre of the room. He tried focussing his aim on the man holding Max but he couldn't get a clear shot.

Kessler tightened his grip. His body was almost glued to Max's, not an inch between them.

Kessler approached Sinclair, sporadically drifting from side to side, varying his speed at a whim. The sheer randomness of his movements kept Sinclair desperately scouring for an opening, any moment where he could fire and not injure Max in the process.

"You really going to risk it?" Kessler said. He took another step forwards, strafing slightly to the right. "Kill me and you'll undoubtedly kill poor Max. Even if you fire, and by some miracle don't kill him, I swear by my last breath that I'll do it myself."

Sinclair didn't respond. As Kessler stepped forwards he could spot the twisted smile on his face. He saw Max more clearly, his eyes barely open and the blood from his face oozing on to the floor.

Sinclair's hand started to shake. He desperately tried to keep it still. His knee began to rattle, the movement spreading across his body. He was on the verge of shivering, shaking with a trepidation that he hadn't felt since his days at war.

Kessler watched him, realising he had seen it before. He had seen it many times. The fear of unpredictability.

His eyes were like glaciers and they sparkled with a charisma which was induced by nothing more than malevolence.

Max felt a light tug on his throat, and then a cataclysm of force against his back.

Kessler had lifted his leg and blasted his boot against Max's back. The impact sent him hurtling across the room and into the hands of Sinclair.

Sinclair was instantly taken by surprise and jumped

forwards, swinging his arm as quickly as he could and desperately trying to move Max out of the line of fire.

He flung Max out of the way and on to the floor but before he could even attempt to point his pistol in the right direction Kessler had already made his move.

Kessler let go of Max and dashed sideways, raising his weapon. As soon as Sinclair appeared from behind Max's falling body Kessler fired several rounds directly into Sinclair's abdomen.

Sinclair collapsed against the column behind him, his pistol dropping to the floor. He was gasping heavily, the faint, slow and broken sound haunting Max who was on his knees in total disbelief.

Max raised his head only to see Kessler towering over him. Kessler smashed his boot against his chest and knocked him backwards against the floor.

He steadied his weapon and fired a shot into his stomach and another in his leg.

The pain howled inside of Max. It took a hold of him, tightening itself around him in every possible way. He lay on the floor, unable to move.

Sinclair tried to speak, his head shaking back and forth as he attempted to sit up.

Kessler walked over to him in silence.

"Who…" Sinclair wheezed. "Who are you?"

Kessler bent down. "Men today just aren't prepared for what lurks in the darkness. I'm the very reality that comes knocking at their door."

CHAPTER 50

Kessler stood up straight and looked around the room. His eyes shuffled across the Square until they stopped at the corridor Sinclair had emerged from.

Kessler glanced back at Sinclair. "Something tells me you weren't sitting down there on your own."

Sinclair remained silent. He refused to make any eye contact and yet could still feel his body beginning to shake.

"There's an easy way to check this."

Kessler walked towards the corridor and stopped.

"I don't know who you are," he shouted, "but if you don't walk down this corridor in the next five seconds I will not hesitate to kill one of these bastards."

"What if there really isn't anyone there?" Sinclair coughed.

"I'm a man of my word," Kessler said, his gaze still fixed down the corridor. "One way or another."

Kessler waited in anticipation. He began to count. "Five…four…three…"

Before he could count to two, Katrina emerged from Stafford's office. She stood still for several seconds, staring down the corridor in a way that she had never done so before. It looked different and felt different, while at the same time had a resemblance to one she'd seen before, not unlike a dream.

Making her way down the corridor, the distance she traversed was vast. Her shoulders started jittering. The sounds of screams and gunshots raced around her mind, and now, an unknown voice with an unclear purpose was beckoning to her.

She moved forwards and could make out a tall man in the doorway. He stood with his arms by his side but as she approached him he stepped backwards, cordially inviting her into the room.

Katrina walked into the Square and the horror she lay witness to almost caused her to run back. She tried to look away, holding back the urge to retch but the first sight of Sinclair's body, affixed against the red stained pillar and Max a few metres away, eyes open and warped in suffering followed her wherever she turned.

Kessler lifted his pistol and pointed it at her. "Stand over there." He motioned it towards the centre of the Square.

She approached the centre of the room and faced Kessler.

"Who are you?" Kessler asked.

She didn't reply. Her concentration was latched on to Sinclair. She could see the blood soaked stains on his chest. His hand were clutched around his wounds, blood seeping through them. His shirt was a deep scarlet, its colour so vivid and, as if in some twisted form of irony, filled with life.

"Answer the question!"

Kessler stormed towards Sinclair and struck him over the head with the base of his weapon. Sinclair fell forwards, lacking the energy to even shout out in pain.

The sudden act of menace knocked Katrina into her

senses. "It's Katrina…Katrina Miller," she stuttered.

"Alright. That wasn't so hard. And who's he?"

Kessler pointed his weapon at Sinclair.

"His name is Sinclair."

"What's he doing here?"

"He's an investigator. We thought he could help with what happened."

"Help with what?"

Katrina could only watch as Kessler's aggression continued to escalate. His questions were direct and forceful, purposely drawing out the full extent of her knowledge and at the same time reminding her that he was not to be underestimated.

"We needed help to find Max and Stafford. Sinclair was here to get them back."

"I see. And do you know who I am?"

"You were the one on the phone…the one who took them."

"Yeah. But what else do you know?"

Kessler's eyes flooded with curiosity. He leant closer.

Katrina shook her head. "I don't…I –"

"Nothing then. That's good. Well, the only thing you need to know right now is that you're going to need to answer my questions."

Katrina tried to look him in the eye but she couldn't bear to do so. There was something about his eyes which frightened her. The lack of remorse or empathy had manifested itself somehow, and it stared back at her, a frightening signal, somehow indicative of what he was capable of.

Kessler started to pace around the Square. "Do you work here?"

"I…I – I work with…" She hesitated. "I work here with Max."

"And so you also work with Jack and Stafford?"

"Yes."

Kessler raised his head slightly.

"Alright fine. Well, can someone then tell me...who *exactly* is Michael Carter?"

No one spoke.

"One of you must know...surely?"

"We don't know," Katrina said. "He just came here and offered to help find Stafford. We weren't getting anywhere and we had no reason to say no."

"Why was he interested?"

"I'm not sure. He said he wanted an investment but I –"

"I already know that part Miss Miller! And it's obviously a load of shit. You'd have been a fool to believe it and yet, for some reason, you all did. So, I'm going to ask you again – why was he here?"

Katrina felt the sweat building up on the palm of her hands. She wanted to wipe it against her skirt but found herself struggling to move; the way someone's body might freeze in the midst of a nightmare.

"Afterwards he apparently changed his story," Katrina muttered. "Max said that he was here for a client. They intercepted a communication between the two kidnappers you sent here and Carter was trying to figure out what was going on. That's why he came here."

"And you believe that?"

Katrina shrugged her shoulders and for a second Kessler identified a spark of intelligence that he may not have initially appreciated.

"Of course you don't!" Kessler added. "It's all nonsense. Every last bit of it. I just wish you might've pressed him a little more for answers."

"We weren't ready to start questioning him...we just needed his help."

Kessler gazed around the room. "Well, it looks like he was successful. Max is right here...so he, Jack and Stafford must've all escaped too. You realise what that means don't you?"

Katrina could see that Kessler's eyes were awash with deviance.

"It means I have no choice but to hunt them down and finish what I started. To put an end to this tragic, tragic story. But it could turn out far worse if I felt you were keeping secrets from me Miss Miller."

"I don't know anything about him," Katrina implored. "I swear to you."

Kessler examined her face very carefully. Her mouth was quivering, her composure beginning to crack. He stopped pacing and walked towards her.

Katrina slowly moved backwards but Kessler's swift movement closed the gap between them.

"Please don't deceive me Katrina. I do *not* want to harm you."

Kessler was standing directly in front of her, so close that he could smell the light touch of her hair. A small wisp of perfume caught his senses, circling its way through his lungs.

He spoke so calmly but also with so much authority that Katrina didn't know how to react. His nature overwhelmed her, drowning her in confusion.

"Please," he whispered. "Don't…"

Kessler suddenly turned around and swung his pistol across the room, as if he were a swordsman, and fired two shots towards the ground. He took a deep breath, and then exhaled in an eerily calm fashion.

Katrina jolted back in horror trying to comprehend what had just happened and then she came to realise.

Max lay extremely still. Two bullets had just pierced his skull. His hand stretched halfway to a pistol that was on the floor next to him.

No one had even noticed; noticed Max crawling across the room and attempting to reach for Sinclair's fallen pistol; noticed Max's last ditch effort to take the weapon and eventually fire a bullet straight into Kessler's head. No one apart from Kessler.

The moment Max started moving, Kessler knew what was happening. Nevertheless he decided to give him a sliver of hope. To provide him with the belief that he could succeed, so that he had the opportunity to take it away in one foul swoop.

Sinclair stared at Kessler, his expression enraged. "You - ...How the fuck could you!?"

"What? Took action? Defended myself?"

"You –" Sinclair began to cough again, drops of blood hitting his shirt collar.

"Don't feel bad," Kessler interrupted. "He knew the risks."

Sinclair stopped coughing. "I swear...you're going to pay."

"There's a long list of dead men that have made that very same promise to me."

Katrina was leaning against the wall. She could barely move, her arms violently shaking. She couldn't think straight. The moment continued to replay itself in her head, each time filling her mind with a deluge of Max-related memories. She never realised how much she remembered about him, how many details and stories she had stored away. The recollections were already beginning to haunt her and there was nothing she could do to remove them from her mind.

Kessler turned to Katrina. "Stand up. We're far from done here."

Katrina stood up straight. She tried to avoid looking at Kessler but he somehow caught her gaze. She couldn't shake the lack of regret on his face. It was as if nothing had happened.

"What about you detective? What do you know about Michael Carter?"

"I don't know anything. He's a ghost as far as I'm

aware."

"Why is he here?"

"We told you…we don't know. He's lied to us about everything."

Kessler started thinking but Sinclair broke his line of thought.

"Are you afraid of him?" he inquired.

Kessler gave Sinclair a sharp look of dissatisfaction. "No…but I am curious about him. What he stands for? What he has to gain?"

"What does that even mean?" Katrina asked. A degree of anger was starting to materialise in her. "He never told us any of that. Why do you even care?"

"Men like him are unique. I've seen it before Miss Miller. They're like viruses…they have the ability to corrupt and to destroy."

"And you?" Sinclair cut in. "I know a virus when I see it."

"I'm not a virus detective. I'm the fire. I'm the last stage in the cycle."

Katrina shook her head. "You're not any of those things."

"You better believe I am. I don't cloud my actions with ideology. The people who act out dreams, they're the ones that cause the most destruction. But I do whatever I have to Miss Miller. I bring balance."

"No you don't! You don't need to be here! You didn't need to do any of this!"

"Oh, but I did. I'm here to end this foolish saga. I'm here to end everything Miss Miller."

"Don't give me that bullshit," Katrina snapped. "Believing in nothing is no excuse to kill people at a whim."

"It is when you need to do away with the remnants of some ideologue. When it comes to that I will do *whatever* I have to. You're all just pieces in Carter's game, whether you know it or not, and I won't allow it to continue."

"Do you even hear yourself? You sound like the very people you despise. Obsessed with some stupid idea about balance."

Kessler took a step towards Katrina. "Don't you compare me to *them*."

"How could I not? You're a gun for hire…how many of them have you fought for? You're a catalyst for the very problem you despise. You're a hypocrite."

"I never sided with their cause."

"It doesn't matter. Whether you like it or not, you still took a side didn't you?"

Kessler paused. He felt a subtle yet unusual chill through his body. Could she have been right? His actions over the years had probably done little to vanquish the very men he derided. If anything, he had probably empowered them; elevated them. Maybe being neutral wasn't enough. Maybe he needed to do something more.

Of all people, Kessler might never have imagined someone such as Katrina Miller forcing him to question his purpose. Here he stood, with absolute power and authority and despite it all, he had been challenged by a woman who had no leverage or influence. Someone who knew so little of his world, and in some ways, knew so much about what drove him.

"There aren't a lot of people who stand and challenge me Miss Miller. It takes courage to do that. There might very well be some truth to your words, and so maybe it's time I take a stand."

"Against who?"

"Against all of the misguided idealists of our time."

"Jesus. Take a stand? Are they really the source of pain and misery…compared to you…who's *so* much, more, worse than any of them. Far, far worse."

"Listen and listen closely," Kessler fired. "The only thing that distinguishes me from every other hero on this godforsaken planet is that I accept the malevolence that was handed to me. Deep down…they're just like me. This world is filled with a type of evil that you couldn't possibly understand."

Katrina's confidence started to falter. She was unsure how to respond but Kessler pressed on.

"You sit in your little office, with your dreams and your ambitions and your pursuit for some sort of happiness and tiny bit of wealth. But you don't see what I see."

"What do you see then?" Sinclair murmured.

He turned to Sinclair, the fierceness of his gaze intensifying.

"I see reality detective. I see how many people are truly like me…and it's frightening."

Katrina had never encountered a being like Kessler. His very presence shook her to the core. The capacity for violence, the scale and darkness of his philosophy. He was a reminder of the very world she sometimes imagined, the one she tried to forget, and the one that she locked away. Today, it stood before her, having wrought the destruction and carnage she wished might never have befallen her. What luck was it that they, of all people in the world, would suffer at his hands and experience the malice that countless individuals were so quick and eager to forget?

"I came here to find Michael Carter." Kessler lifted his weapon up. He analysed it for a second and then placed it back down by his side. "But if either of you really don't know anything."

Sinclair suddenly sat up, his heart racing with what little energy it had left. "Please…"

"How could you have thought that it would end any differently?"

Katrina was trying to understand what was going on. She was struggling to see what had made Sinclair react with so much fear. Then it hit her.

Kessler approached her again. He moved so close that his body was almost touching hers.

Katrina could feel the darkness in his breath. It was infectious. She could feel the hate and anger. She wanted to move away but she was frozen. His eyes stared into hers, burning away whatever hope she had left as she slowly realised what was about to happen.

"Thank you Katrina," he whispered. "I've truly enjoyed this. It's been a learning experience for the both of us. You've made me a wiser man."

He moved backwards and raised his weapon.

"Don't!" Sinclair said. He continued to cough, each more violent than the last.

"This is the way it has to be," Kessler said.

"It doesn't," Katrina said, shaking her head.

"Yes it does."

"Why?!" she exclaimed.

"Because you have nothing that I need. And you know far too much."

Katrina found it difficult to see. Her eyes began to well up.

"I don't know anything," Katrina pleaded.

Kessler stood very still, his arm still raised.

"For god's sake!" Sinclair said. "Don't! She doesn't deserve this!"

Sinclair started to breathe heavily. He tried to speak but he couldn't find the energy. His sight became fogged, his head extremely light. He tasted the blood trailing in his mouth. His heart started beating overwhelmingly.

Kessler turned around and saw him shaking his head again, his expression torn with anguish. He desperately tried to get his attention but his muscles began to fail. His movements started to slow and his eyes lost the ability to stay open, his final memories starting to come to fruition.

Kessler flicked his attention back to Katrina who had tears rolling down her face.

They felt cold as she tried to open her mouth. "I'm not a threat to you. You obviously know that. So why?!"

Kessler didn't speak. He just held his pistol while his thumb stroked the back of the handle.

Katrina wiped away the tears from her face, her body trembling uncontrollably.

"Think…just think. There is nothing that we can possibly do to you – no way that we can harm you. You don't have to kill anyone else – you don't have to – please! I don't even know a single thing about you. I – I…I don't even know your *name*!"

There was a moment of silence.

"It's David Kessler."

He opened fire. Three bullets cut through Katrina's stomach and she fell to the floor.

She started to bleed out, the blood tearing its way through her cardigan, its brightness ever lost.

The elevator door swung open and Jack Morse stepped outside.

That was the day where ideals died. That was the day he would never forget, and one that he would never forgive.

CHAPTER 51

Jack only had a second to respond. No one heard the elevator doors open giving him enough time to slip into a small corridor adjacent to the entrance of the Square. Kessler was hovering in the centre of the room and hadn't caught sight of him.

Had Jack made any attempt to sneak up on him, he'd be spotted almost immediately. He knew it wasn't worth the risk but he needed to get Kessler out of the Square. Katrina was on the verge of dying and right now there was nothing he could do about it.

Jack's mind was in complete disarray as he tried to devise a solution. He was trembling, his body shaking as he clambered for answers.

How can I get rid of him? What would make him leave?

Jack was desperate. He needed to do something.

For fuck sakes - she's going to die if I don't figure something out!

Jack's mind lit up. His idea was risky but he didn't have any alternatives. Right now, this was his best and only shot. He took out his phone and browsed through his contacts. He stopped at Katrina's name and pressed the call button.

This has to work...

After a second, he heard a small buzzing sound.

Take the bait...

Kessler walked over to Katrina's bleeding body. Her heart was pounding as he leant over and removed a phone from her sweater pocket. He stared at the screen.

"*Jack Morse?*"

Katrina's eyes widened.

Before Kessler could respond Jack quickly hung up.

Kessler held the phone in his hand for a few more seconds. It vibrated again. A message appeared.

Won't be back at the Square. Carter and I are planning to stick around at the meeting until it's over.

Kessler smiled. It felt as if the opportunity he was waiting for might finally have appeared. He knew the window was short but he had to act swiftly if he was to have any chance of finding Carter. He needed to get to the meeting immediately.

Kessler threw the phone on the floor and headed towards the corridor Katrina emerged from and towards the other elevator at the back of the building.

Before he left he took one final glance at Katrina. Her eyes were still filled with tears and she was starting to breathe erratically. He knew her death was imminent, her final minutes upon her. There was nothing more for him to say or do now.

He placed his gun inside a small holster and pulled his coat forwards, making his way down the corridor.

Stafford had told him earlier that day where the meeting was going to be. Once he was there he could finally bring this problem to a close.

He proceeded towards the lifts, fuelled by a wind of curiosity he hadn't felt in years.

As soon as Jack heard the distant chime of the elevator he ran into the Square and rushed towards Katrina. He dropped to his knees and pulled her on to his lap, quickly applying pressure against her blood stained sweater.

Jack's appearance was the last thing that she expected at that point and the sight of his panic-stricken face momentarily breathed life into her sunken expression.

"Katrina," Jack whispered. "Keep it together. I'm going to call an ambulance."

"Jack? What are –"

"Just hold on."

"No," she muttered. "You'll draw too much attention."

"What are you talking about?"

"He's left...to find Carter. To kill him, and to kill anyone that gets in his way. He'll know something is wrong. He'll know he's been tricked and come back."

"I don't care! I can't just leave you to die."

"Look at me!" Katrina's voice was already weakening and yet the desperation in her eyes was as strong as ever. "I'm not surviving this. There's nothing more you can do."

"Don't fucking say that!"

Jack couldn't comprehend what was happening. He looked around and saw Sinclair's corpse, propped up against one of the columns. Max's bruised body lay near him, echoing the terror he'd clearly witnessed before he was killed.

"So what do you want me to do then?" Jack asked. His voice started to crack. "Just watch you die? It doesn't make any –"

"For once in your life," Katrina wheezed, "could you just accept...that you don't get to win."

Jack's skin started to turn cold. Katrina's head lay on his lap and it frightened him unlike anything he'd ever experienced. It was the powerlessness...it was so alien and he didn't understand what it truly felt like until now.

It felt like a fog which had been encircling him all his life, rising through the air and gradually slipping into his body without him ever realising.

"Okay…okay," Jack said. You win."

There was a misplaced yet haunting expression of serenity on Katrina's face.

"I'm sorry Jack."

"Sorry for what," Jack said, looking bewildered. "I'm the one that should be sorry. I should've realised sooner…what would happen. I never thought that…"

"Jack, it doesn't matter." Katrina flinched in pain. "You don't need to…"

"Please stop speaking," Jack pleaded. "You have to let me help you. I have to do something."

"No."

"But I –"

"I'm sorry for what I said. I didn't mean it…I –"

"It doesn't matter."

"I'm sorry," she repeated.

"Stop speaking. Please."

"It's true – I – It –"

"I said stop!"

Jack was shaking. "You shouldn't be sorry for anything. You were right. You were always right. About everything. I just never knew what'd happen. I thought it'd all be ok. And now you're here…dying…not coming back. And it's all my fault. I let you down. I failed."

Jack could barely keep his composure. He could see the blood pouring out of her. With each second he knew her life was slipping away and there was nothing he could do. He gazed at her, desperate for some sort of response, an acceptance of his confession, and wishing for anything that might make the moment last longer than it should.

Katrina started to smile. "You're the last of the free men Jack."

She started coughing violently. She tried tilting her

head up but she continued to cough, specks of blood pouring on to her lips.

"Y - You...don't get to fail," she whispered.

The raw innocence in Katrina's eyes started to dwindle. With each breath, its touch became fainter, over and over and until Jack could feel nothing; it's warmth fading away. Her eyes sat as they were, devoid of any sparkle or glimmer that they once had. What remained was a dull stare of sorrow.

Jack carefully placed her head on the ground.

He was sat on the floor, his back against the chair, unable to move.

He sat for a few minutes, staring at the floor. He couldn't bring himself to look anywhere else. He didn't look but he couldn't stop seeing it. Katrina, Max, Sinclair; all of them had died because of him.

He felt as if he were in the centre of a battlefield. The first few images that caught his eye the moment he walked into the Square were resonating through his mind. The bodies, the blood, the chaos; Jack saw the struggle, so visceral and desperate. It made him shudder, imagining what it must have felt like to know that death was inevitable; that this was the moment their lives had culminated to and that there would be nothing more.

Jack tried to see the logic or rationale but all he could see were his own mistakes, and the conspiracy that fate had plotted against him. And what a conspiracy it was. It had taken one of Jack's only true friends; flung her down a path to her demise and left untold destruction. When he looked at it again he began to question why he ever thought they'd come out unscathed? Why did he ever believe they might survive? Could such foolishness ever really be forgiven?

But time and again he believed he knew. He believed he knew what was best. He believed that the world was different. Yet no amount of knowledge or intelligence or belief could have prepared him for this kind of future. The real future wasn't designed for people who wanted to smile. The real future encompassed desolation. The real future found enjoyment when its inhabitants suffered.

And here he was, in such a future that he once thought was better, not as dark, and not as corruptible. One which didn't hide the men of lies, the men of power or the men of malevolence. And yet, all along, they were hidden in plain sight. They were the men of reality; the ones he had never dared to consider.

Jack stood up and scanned the room, the rampant carnage and bloodshed scattered everywhere he looked. Jack could see the despair immersed into Sinclair's face, ever present and sown into his final moments. He caught sight of Max in the corner of his eye. His motionless body lay on the ground. A large pool of blood was spread underneath his head, slowly soaking into the carpet.

Jack couldn't think clearly. He didn't know what to do. He closed his eyes, trying to think of answers and then he heard something. A small vibration noise.

He immediately opened his eyes. As he edged closer he saw it. It was Katrina's phone. He ran over and picked it up.

Unknown caller?

Jack answered it.

"Good afternoon. Is that Katrina speaking?"

Jack froze.

A young woman spoke on the other end. Her tone was soft while equally professional. A certain element of warmth emanated from her voice.

"No…" Jack stuttered. "She's…unable to speak right now."

Jack paused and took a sharp breath. "I can take a message if you like."

"Perfect. Well, my name is Lea Stone. I'm calling on behalf of Nikhita Morris?"

Why does that name sound familiar? It's...wait.

"I'm not sure if Katrina mentioned it to you but Nikhita had a discussion with her recently. It was one regarding a partnership position in her firm. It specialises in, among other things, venture capital."

"Right, yeah...of c-course," Jack stuttered. "She did mention it."

"Well, Nikhita's thought it over and she'd like to make her a formal offer. I'm sorry it took so long. I know it's taken a bit of time but we were trying to finalise all of the details. I think now, we're dead set on the idea. We're certain she'd make a fantastic addition here."

Jack cleared his throat, trying to speak, but a flood of emotion was stopping him, his words cutting off before he could say anything.

"Sorry, are you alright there?" Lea asked.

"Yeah..." Jack said, finally able to respond. "It's great news. I'm just...not sure how I'm going to tell her."

Lea started to laugh. "I'm sure she'll be thrilled to hear it. Could you please pass on the message and then ask her to call us as soon as possible."

"Sure. Thanks for letting me know."

"Okay great," Lea said. "Thank you so much. Goodbye!"

Jack paused.

"Bye Lea."

Jack hung up. He could fell his grip beginning to tighten. Within moments he flung the phone across the Square, smashing it into the wall and shattering it to pieces.

Jack didn't feel sadness or anguish anymore. It was rage, it was anger. It felt so real and visceral, uncontrollable yet malleable. It was the sudden realisation that there was nothing he could do, nothing that would change anything.

He searched deep within, desperate for something to

seal the flood of vengeance that was beginning to materialise but there was nothing. It was the only thing he felt now. Cold in nature and raw in execution.

Jack left the Square, not before taking something he knew he would need.

He'd return soon enough but there was something else. Something which took priority.

He left the Square and like so many others that evening, made his way to the location of a meeting, the purpose of which he couldn't begin to realise.

CHAPTER 52

Months after his retreat, Soren was walking through the darkness once again. The searing heat he was once familiar with had been replaced by a cold, overwhelming chill that engulfed the night and cascaded between patches of ice, silence and rows of aging gravestones.

The shadows of long splintered branches sprawled across the ground while he moved in the faint moonlight. The cold air had dampened the grass and the smell was making Soren's eyes water. Before the tears may have formed, the harsh wind blew them from his skin and he felt a roughness against his cheeks as they turned flush.

Walking past the gravestones Soren glanced at the names and inscriptions, finding enjoyment as he guessed which ones may have been lies. He imagined final days which were abundant with false weeping and stories that had never been.

In the distance Soren glimpsed an elderly man making his way towards him. He seemed scared, constantly turning his head at every noise and rustle that came his way. Eventually he caught sight of Soren and his fear subsided.

Soren approached him, wading through the wind the way one might pass through a crowd. The man's appearance came into focus. His grey hair stood out in the darkness, combed and tidy, joint to a precisely trimmed beard which left little room for variance.

Reinhart looked at him and smiled.

"Joseph," Soren said extending his hand out. "Thanks for meeting me at such short notice."

"No problem. It's good to see you Soren."

They shook hands, both of which protruded from the enormous dark overcoats that concealed their nicely fitted suits. All that was visible in the darkness were a pair of starchy white shirt collars that stuck out over the top of the coats and the bright cherry colour which was painting itself over their cheeks.

Reinhart attempted to recall the last time he may have met Soren. It had probably been years and as he stood silently in the darkness, he studied Soren the way he'd study an old painting at a gallery. He saw someone that appeared more grizzled than before, as if age and stress were catching up with him, housing snake-like eyes which were red and dogged.

"God, how have you been Joseph? It's been too long."

"I've been alright thank you. Investment business has been shaky these past few years but I'm trudging along. You?"

"Same as I've always been," Soren said calmly. "Just trying to live out my days with whatever purpose I can find."

"I would expect nothing less."

They walked through the graveyard, admiring the shine of the moonlight as it rained across the fields.

"So what did you need?" Reinhart asked. "You said you needed to chat urgently."

"That's right. Look, I'll be honest…there's something I need your help with."

Reinhart scratched his head. "Soren that's going to be difficult. My businesses are haemorrhaging cash right now. Everyone in the game knows my returns aren't what they used to be. I can't help you with anything like –"

"Joseph!" Soren cut in. "I'm not asking you for money. I know you don't have it. In fact, I'm actually aware that you need it. That's sort of why I'm here. If you're able to help me...I have a feeling I can make most of those problems go away."

"How?"

"Help me and I'll pay you more than enough to pull you out of your mess."

"In return for what?"

Reinhart's face was awash with curiosity and as he leant in closer Soren knew that he had his attention. For the longest time Reinhart's financial suffering hadn't been a secret and that made him the perfect individual to tempt into his plan.

Soren stopped, his shoes scratching against the frost. He turned, closely examining Reinhart, his eyes vehemently staring into his.

"As we speak, there's a man...who wants me dead. And I need your help to capture him."

"I – I'm not a soldier," Reinhart stuttered nervously. "I – I can't do anything about that. What am *I* going to do?"

"You don't need to worry. I already have a plan. You just do *exactly* as I say and everything will fall into place."

Soren's voice could be unusually soft at times. His words exuded an inherent tranquillity which often comforted people in such a way that they might not ever realise what he was eluding to. It was as if unconsciously, people allowed him to exert influence in whatever way he felt necessary.

"Soren, you realise I'm not a killer."

"Obviously. I'm well aware of that. But I'm not asking you to kill anyone. I would never ask you to do that. I'm asking that you do something else."

"And what's that exactly?"

Soren smiled. "I need you to be…an investor…interested in a certain company…run by a certain individual."

"A *company*?"

"Yes. One that admittedly a few people are interested in."

"Including this man…the one who wants you dead?"

"Well, he's not interested yet. But he will. Once he knows that *I'm* interested."

Reinhart's face turned blank. "I don't follow."

"I'd like you to actively pursue this company. Make contact, initially suggest that you're willing to deal with them and that you'd like to take a stake in their venture. Then at the last minute have a change of heart and dismiss the whole idea. It's certainly harsh but these things happen in real life all the time. Shortly after, a company affiliated with me will decide to propose an investment and arrange a meeting. And then he'll come…"

"What? You can't be serious." For a second Reinhart wasn't sure if he heard Soren correctly. He mumbled the explanation back to himself, reassuring himself of the accuracy of what he heard. "That is far too risky. You can't account for all of those steps going how you say they will. And not least, at any of those points, he could plan *anything*. You'd be in too much danger."

"No…he won't know what I know. That I'm aware of his plan, aware of what he's plotting. Joseph, the truth is that he won't even make it to the meeting."

Soren started to laugh. "We side track the entire thing. Create a frenzied situation that forces his involvement; one which diverts his attention and clouds his vision."

"But how can you know?"

"Because it's exactly what he'd do. We'll leave him no choice. And he'll never even know I'm involved. He'll be too busy and then when the situation arises, we take him."

Reinhart looked around the graveyard. The low temperature was drying out his eyes, blurring his vision. He gripped his coat tightly, his fingers numbed from the cold, as if they'd been struck by a hammer.

"So how are you going to *side track* this meeting?"

"Simple enough. We kidnap the man in charge of the company. A mathematics professor."

Reinhart did little to hide the bewilderment on his face.

"Well," Soren added. "*You're* going to kidnap him actually."

"My god. So that's what you need me for is it?"

"Precisely. I can't do it. Our man has to think I'm unaware of his existence. I need to give him that impression. If someone else takes him, he'll be desperate to bring him back so I don't become complacent and pull out of the investment, and then leave. Amidst the pandemonium, we create a situation to capture him."

"How?"

"I can't know for certain. But with something like this, opportunities will continue to present themselves. We just need to prepare for them."

"Soren you can't possibly know how this will turn out. Anything could happen. A situation might never arise."

"This is my job Joseph. I assess and then I formulate. There *will* be a situation. We just have to help steer it along. Trust me on this."

"Jesus Christ. How would this man even know the professor was kidnapped? He's coming to the meeting to look for you. He'd have no idea he was even taken."

A look of delight fell on Soren's face. "You underestimate how well I know this man. He won't enter that room without a plan. He'll want to know everything. He'll make sure there's no complications before the meeting. He might even go and visit. Maybe even tell him the truth, who knows – but it's all so he can get to me."

"And then…when the professor's gone, and my enemy realises that he has no information, that his plan is on the brink of collapse, and that I could leave at any second and jeopardise everything he's worked towards…then, he'll have no choice. He'll *have to* search for him. He'll *have to* bring him back and ensure everything goes exactly as it was supposed to. All so that I might be none the wiser."

Soren examined Reinhart carefully, noting the element of uneasiness on his face.

"You look a little confused," Soren said, his face flickering with concern. "Is there something wrong?"

"Soren, this is all well and good but…I don't know anything about kidnapping."

"Don't worry about that. We'll hire someone to do it…a professional."

Reinhart noticed how undeterred Soren seemed by the thought. The mode of conversation seemed remarkably casual to him.

"Is this professional going to help capture your enemy too?"

"If it comes to it, then possibly. But more generally, no. I'd prefer some distance. The person I have in mind is highly skilled, but a bit unpredictable. That's what people who work with him say. And that's the last thing I need."

"So I contact him instead?"

"Yeah. He'll take the lead on the job and set the events in motion."

"But I still don't understand. What's my motive? Why would I go so far as to kidnap a professor?"

"It's multifaceted I'd say" Soren rubbed his hands together, the way a magician might prepare for a magic trick. "I think we go with the fact that you're interested in starting a similar company. The reason you meet with the team is to get a feel for where they were and then blow them off. I already know they're having a tough time getting an investment so they'll be happy to meet you. But play the unstable, obnoxious executive and send them on their way. Waste their time, tear up their dreams and give them a reason to think you're a suspect; that you're not a man that operates wisely. Then, you take the professor since that's the best (and slightly foolish) way to get a hold of their technology and extract the information you need. You probably don't even need to ask the professor any questions when you have him. As long as that's the impression that emerges then that's the story which will fall into place. We'll even feed it from our end. My financial contact is going to inquire about the investment after your meeting. We'll make sure to pepper the story with some anecdotes about how erratic you've been in recent years; especially due to your financial constraints and that you weren't particularly pleased about the deal. If they're smart...suspicion should fall on you pretty quickly."

"Right. So I set the whole kidnapping up to draw your man out...to have him focus on me...and not you."

"Exactly. There's a strong possibility that my enemy could suspect I have something to do with this. But, if we make this motive strong enough, he'll suspect *you* instead."

"He'd never see it coming would he?"

Soren nodded. "And in return...you'll be paid a fortune worthy of your efforts. Those troubles that plague you...we'll make them distant memories. I'm offering you the chance to start over Joseph. But that's only if you help me."

"Soren, I'm not much of an actor," Reinhart said hesitantly. "Someone will see through it. What if someone figures it out?"

"Don't worry. By the time anyone realises who you are it'll be too late. All you need to do is keep lying."

Soren patted him on the shoulder and smiled. "It's easy. *Trust me*."

They started to walk again, away from the gravestones and into the open. Up until now the gravestones were guarding them from the wind but as their protection diminished, the plummeting temperature seemed to knock against them unopposed and with ever greater force.

Soren watched as Reinhart ran the proposal through his head. He tried to peer into his mind, attempting to uncover the questions that were rattling between his thoughts. The more he knew, the more he could say to put him at ease. He, like many others, knew that Reinhart was partially unstable but he was also one of the few men he had enough leverage over; enough to draw him on to the board and play Soren's game for him.

"I st-still…" Reinhart stammered.

"Joseph," Soren said softly. "I need your help on this. If you don't, he'll eventually find me. I don't know when but he will. And he'll kill me."

"But I don't – it's just that…you've amassed so much power over the years. How could he possibly harm you?"

"Because he's powerful too." Soren masked his face with a cloud of anxiety and he dropped his voice. "I wouldn't ask if it wasn't necessary."

Soren could spot the distress on Reinhart's face. He still hadn't pushed him over the edge.

"Speak to me Joseph, come on. What's bothering you about this?"

"It's dangerous Soren. I don't know if it's worth the risk."

"You can't have reward without risk. And the reward here is freedom. Freedom from everything that's troubled you these past few years. Freedom to do as you finally please. I'm offering it to you…it's yours…but only if you're willing to take the *risk*."

As Soren recounted his plan Reinhart knew he

shouldn't have been surprised. Soren had accounted for every variable, analysing each one to its extreme. The entire thing was a colossal jigsaw, constructed with seemingly random moments and events, together yielding a solution that would devour his enemy. He was the definitive strategist, and it was unheard of that someone might try to cross him. It was what made the situation all the more peculiar. But no matter the danger, whatever Reinhart would gain in return for his assistance would fundamentally change his situation. Despite the disconcerting premonition that lurked in the back of his mind, he knew it was an opportunity he couldn't turn away, not only for his own gain, but to aid a friend; one of immense power and one that had assisted him countless times in the past.

"Okay…" Reinhart said reluctantly. "Only because I trust you Soren. You've never let me down before."

"No. Never. I knew I could depend on you. You're a true ally Joseph. Never forget that."

They continued to walk, the crunch of frozen leaves constantly breaking the silence in the air. Reinhart eventually stopped, his arms still shivering. Soren looked at him curiously.

"Soren, before this continues…I need to know something."

"What is it?"

"This man…your enemy. What are you going to do with him…once you have him?"

Soren paused. "I want to speak to him. Find out how he returned from the dead. And then I'm going to kill him."

"But what does that even mean - *return from the dead?*"

"It means that he should be dead…but he isn't. It means that he should've died…but he didn't. And now his existence threatens mine."

There was a short silence. They had stopped walking now, their feet starting to sink into the ice clad grass. As Reinhart stood still and continued to think he could feel himself plunging into the ground. It was soft and moist and he could feel the mud clinging on to his soles.

"There's one thing you haven't told me Soren," Reinhart said. He was looking at the ground, his head shuddering slightly. He wasn't sure if it was because he was nervous or because of the cold.

"Why does this man want you dead?"

Soren was staring into the furthest reaches of the darkness, away from the gravestones and into a blank point of abyss, unable to see anything yet somehow feel more than he'd felt in months.

"What…did you to do to him Soren?"

He continued to look into nothingness, his eyes completely devoid of emotion. "I killed him. I killed him and his friends; his allies. I killed them all before they became a threat."

"But he's still alive."

"Exactly!" Soren snapped. "He survived. I don't know how but he did."

"Why did you try to kill him? What made him such a threat?"

"Joseph, you have no idea how many years I have fought for. How many years I've tried to maintain order. I've killed countless people. Destroyed countless societies. I fought, and I fought, all to build a power structure capable of maintaining order. I fought to destroy chaos, and nothing else. The world needed order Joseph. It still does. But I've gone a long way to making it more than it was. And why not…if not because it was my duty. And I don't care who stands in my way. The side of any government is irrelevant. I do *whatever* I must. I'm a power structure in my own right, and I have done more for this world than any other."

"But many years ago, something happened. Something I never really predicted. Far away, some young man had an idea. Him and a few others decided they'd had enough. They were tired of the wars, tired of the pointless bureaucracy and tired of the mechanics that governed our system. They strived for something more. They believed…"

Soren paused, overwhelmed with momentary nostalgia as his mind descended upon the past. "They believed…something had to be done."

"Who were they?" Reinhart asked.

"Nothing more than misguided idealists," he spat. "Fools that didn't, and never would, understand why things were the way they were. But these men weren't ordinary. They were men of privilege, men of power, men of raw and undeniable intelligence. They were dangerous and they were the truest threat that we, as a collective, may have ever faced. Who were they even? To think they could dictate to us, to the world, about what came next, to change everything. They knew nothing. Absolutely nothing. They were willing to disrupt and alter the very order I had spent years building. They would've spawned nothing but unprecedented anarchy. They were willing to disrupt a system that could not be allowed to die. I had fought too hard to see it end that way. And so…I knew, without question, that these men…these idealists…they had to die. No matter the cost and no matter the consequences."

"These things don't happen silently. Others must've saw this coming?"

"No. Not a soul. People never realised. They dismissed them. Quietly muttering to themselves inside the structures that I alone protected. They didn't understand what was about to happen. So I alone acted…because it was my duty…my duty to the good."

"How did you do it?"

Soren leant forwards.

"*Deception*," he whispered.

Reinhart stepped back slightly, watching as a sinister look manifested itself on to Soren's face.

"I found him," Soren said. "My undying enemy. I told him I would help his cause. That I would be there by his side. Fund his endeavours. Fight his wars. And I did. Make no mistake Joseph, I certainly did."

"I gained his trust," he continued. "Him, his allies. Everyone. They all believed in me. That I'd give my life and soul for these ideals...ideals so misplaced and misconstrued. Time passed, and it felt as if we were all of a unified vision. I saw it come to being, manifested through our perseverance against the odds...and then I destroyed it."

Soren's voice turned sharp. "Eventually I sent them all across the African coast. I told them I had set up a series of meetings to source arms and supplies. Some were in groups, others went on their own but it didn't really matter in the end. The meetings were entirely fictitious. As they all probably came to realise, I had, in fact, financed a small team to assassinate them all simultaneously."

"And it worked?"

Soren nodded. "I gave my men free license to do whatever they needed to. Some were shot, others poisoned. I can't remember how many bombs went off that night. In every instance I got listings of the fatalities to be sure."

"After that," Soren continued, "the organisation disintegrated. I took the resources, the capital and whatever men lacked a conscience. Few knew what actually happened. Others had their suspicions. The rest were mercenaries who had little interest in asking questions. But then...after so many years...he came back."

Soren's eyes focussed on the darkness again, almost as

if in its heart, he could see the events unfolding before him again.

"He came for revenge. He came out of the fire and the darkness; armed, wealthy, powerful and relentless."

"Where?"

"On the battlefield. He returned with an army of his own and tried to destroy me. I never foresaw it. I never foresaw that any of them would survive and come back. I was so sure that my work was done."

"How could he have survived?"

"I have no idea. It haunts me every waking moment and it's what I intend to find out."

"So that's why you want him."

"Yes. And I know what I need to do. That's why I'm here. That's why I need your help Joseph. I need to finish what I started…for the greater good…or else this man…*he'll devastate everything*."

The cold wind continued its assault against the two of them.

"Alright," Reinhart said, his body shivering. "Anything you need Soren. You have it."

Soren smiled. He wasn't shivering. He just stood still, the cogs in his mind spinning and turning, placing all of the pieces on the board and watching as they all began to move, one by one.

Now it was his turn.

CHAPTER 53

Many, many years ago, there was an evening where the thoughts of the present plagued neither Carter nor Soren.

Carter was stood in the living room of his apartment. Specks of light from distant, towering buildings stood out in the darkness and flickered in his window. Far below, rows of cars paraded down avenues like gusts of wind. The sheer amount of light emanating from the city blocked out any view of the stars and with each glance at the sky, it was easy to feel isolated from the rest of the universe.

The room was vast, with high ceilings and swathes of open space. A square table and two chairs sat in the centre. A thin television, presently switched off, hung against the wall alongside an empty red plastic remote holder. In front of the television was a light brown sofa. The seats were plump and the arm rests were rigid enough that you could bounce a coin off of them.

The perimeter was marked with three thick wooden bookshelves separated by small cabinets filled with drinks, old photographs and large patches of artwork.

Carter was stood by a small cabinet, pouring himself a

whiskey. He turned around to the man sat by his table who seemed to be staring at the blank television.

"Soren, you want one?"

Soren smiled. "Sure Michael, why not?"

Carter took another glass from his cabinet and poured several fingers. The fiery smell of oak wafted through the room as he brought the two glasses to his table.

He sat down opposite Soren and noticed that his focus had shifted from the television to a painting on the wall which he was meticulously examining. The painting was of various protagonists across comic books, television, film and Japanese manga, assembled together against a dark backdrop.

"I didn't know you watch any of this stuff Michael?"

"More so when I was kid. Have a little less time these days…unsurprisingly."

"Yeah." Soren stared at one of the individuals in the corner of the picture; a war torn solider gripping an assault rifle. His bearded face was scarred and grizzled, focussing upon something far in the distance. "If I'm honest I never quite saw the appeal. The theatrics, the personalities, the impossible feats…these people aren't really a reflection of real life. You know that right?"

"What!" Carter began shaking his head. Strands of his vibrant black hair whipped back and forth. "I think you've missed the point. It's not about how realistic it is. It's about the lives they led and the decisions they made…in order to win…*at all costs*. They wanted to be heroic, and so often they weren't. They were people. Sometimes they were even villains themselves. And truthfully, that sounds a lot like real life to me."

"*Villains*. I wish they were so easy to spot." Soren picked up his drink and took a small sip. "Hiding away in the shadows. In the shows they're always so obvious. Ominous music, dark robes, surrounded by henchmen."

"Sometimes…" Carter's voice rang off. "Sometimes

they're not. Allies can become villains. Villains can become allies. Or heroes just self-destruct under the weight of delusion. My favourite villains were the ones which weren't even self-aware."

"That's all well and good. But let's not kid ourselves. You and I both know that the villains in real life…are *much worse* than the ones in fiction."

Carter studied the painting. For a second he recalled each of the stories that lay underneath, the journeys and struggles that made them who they were, the tragedies that had befallen them and the sinister antagonists that ravaged their lives and engulfed them in turmoil. He remembered the moments of desperation and the decisions that they couldn't take back. He remembered the parallels with his own life.

"Yeah…I don't think I'd disagree."

Carter had some of his drink. He let it sit in his mouth for a few seconds so that he could taste the spice fluttering on his tongue. "What do you think of the whiskey?"

"I like it. Really like it, actually. It's got a real kick to it. Better than that jet fuel we were drinking back around Christmas."

"Fuck yeah, in Montreal" Carter said, his eyes lighting up. "That stuff was horrible. I don't know where they found it and why that bar was stocking it."

"But it was the only thing they were serving that night!" Soren laughed. "I was honestly shocked. We must've cleared six or seven bottles without thinking."

"And then Schaffer. Jesus, he got absolutely wrecked on that stuff. The guy fell over like a hundred times…just to shake my hand."

"Oh yeah, the continuous handshakes. I almost thought we were at a fucking business meeting. That idiot."

"Ever since he's gotten married, Ken just cannot hold his drink anymore," Carter remarked. "Madly in love and officially a gentlemen."

"He's a far cry from his old self isn't he?"

Carter thumped his hand on the table. "And then that same night – Victor!"

"Victor fucking Morano. That's one bastard that doesn't know when to quit. He walks up to that girl, after getting rejected by like seven others, and she just *flat out* destroys him and tells him he's a prick."

"And then…" Carter said. He took a gulp of his drink. "Morano, as if he's suddenly a lawyer, says: 'okay Miss, prove that I'm a prick.' Of course, we're all stood there thinking you're out of your fucking mind."

"Then her husband turns up!" Soren exclaimed. "That giant seven foot fucking monolith who swears he'll tear him open like a Christmas present – whatever the hell that means. Then we all run over, pull Victor away while you…"

"While I," Carter cut in, "had to convince this behemoth that despite everything he just saw, we're actually really nice people and just want to have a drink and not cause any trouble and not flirt with the idea of adultery."

"We shouldn't have survived that one," Soren chuckled. "Of all the things we've seen over the years, that's one of the closest shaves that comes to mind."

"I think you might be right about that. What a way for it all to end huh? Some dive bar in Montreal."

Soren finished his drink and pressed his lips together as the lingering taste in his mouth slowly disappeared. His face turned slightly flush and a small bead of sweat materialised at the edge of his forehead.

"God, this was pretty good Michael." Falling into a momentary sense of pontification, he leant back in his chair. "Any chance I can play you for a bottle?"

"Depends on the game I'd imagine."

Soren snapped his fingers as if that were his process

for generating ideas. "Oh, I've got a game for you. I think you'll like it…"

"Really?" Carter said rolling his eyes. "Ok. You win and I'll give you the bottle. I win and you buy me another."

"Deal! Now go grab two pieces of paper and a pen. One piece for you and the other for me."

"Alright." Carter walked over to another of his cabinets and opened one of the drawers. He tore two sheets of A5 paper from a notebook and removed the pen he usually kept in its spine.

Returning to the table, he saw Soren smiling gleefully, like a child waiting for a slice of cake. Carter slid the pen and one of the sheets of paper across the table.

Soren took the pen and covered the paper with his arm as he wrote something down. He then folded the paper in half and then once more.

"Now…I've just written down a number between one and ten. I want you to do the same, and then fold the paper up. Then we try and guess each other's number. Whoever gets the closest wins."

"Pacman is a game. I wouldn't exactly call *this* a game."

"Well, Michael, you don't really have much here apart from books, a television without a remote and an immense legion of whiskeys so you're not giving me much to work with are you?"

"Fine. Whatever you say." Soren passed him back the pen and Carter scribbled down a number and folded up his answer. "So do I try and guess now?"

Soren nodded. "Your move Mr Carter."

"I guess nine," Carter said. He pointed the pen at Soren. Staring along its narrow surface, he could make out Soren's shrewd face just above its tip. "And you?"

"Seven."

Carter flung his pen against the table. It bounced off

the surface and on to the floor. The trajectory reminded Soren of a ballistic missile.

"Fuck sake. Are you being serious?"

"I certainly am."

"What was yours?" Carter asked.

"One."

"Gimme the paper. I don't believe you."

Soren folded his answer two more times and lobbed it over the table to Carter who hurriedly opened it up the same way he might unwrap a birthday gift. He stared at the answer and slammed it on the table.

"Don't fuck around. You cheated didn't you?"

"*Cheat!* How would I cheat Michael? It's not like I read minds and didn't tell you."

"No. You did something…"

Strangely, Carter could see that Soren didn't take any offense from the allegation. Lurking somewhere was a plan; a devious stratagem masked by whimsical good nature and an acute instinct for the future.

"How many bottles did we finish in Montreal again Soren?"

Soren was staring at the blank television screen again. Carter could spot a miniscule smirk in the dark reflection of his face.

"I'm even surprised you remember how many girls Victor spoke to. Or that marginally apt description of our aggressor…"

Soren turned back to face him; convivial as always. "You always get there in the end don't you Michael. That's why you always impress me…" His eyes flared up. "But a deal is a deal, and you still owe me that bottle."

Carter nodded intently. "Oh absolutely. You certainly win. You've technically followed all of the rules and so I must oblige. How could I not?" A quick flash of delight appeared on Carter's face as he flicked his head in the direction of his cabinet. "The bottle is yours. Grab it whenever you leave."

"Thanks."

"There's a recycling bin just outside the garage if you're looking for a place to get rid of it too."

Soren's glowing satisfaction swiftly went away. "Why would I recycle it?"

"Well we bet for that bottle. And the last two drinks made their way to this table not that long ago. What's left in my cabinet is an empty bottle with a nice label..."

"*An empty bottle?*"

Carter revelled in Soren's agitation, sloping forwards to get a better view while he tried to suppress his laughter.

"Never satisfied with following the rules are you Michael," Soren mumbled. "Always *unhappy* with the system. Always ready to *cheat* the system."

"If the system was rigged to begin with then maybe it's not such a bad idea..."

Soren rolled his eyes and crossed his arms. "You owe me a *real* bottle Carter. And you better make due on your promise. Can't just sack off responsibilities." He wagged his finger the way he would discipline a small child.

"It's a bottle of whiskey...not a loan from the IMF," Carter chuckled. "I'll get you one next time we meet. I know how you get about these things..."

"I'm just a fool for principle Michael..." His voice wandered off.

"That's not a bad thing I suppose."

"No..."

Conviction for principle was what brought Carter and Soren together. If not a desire for the ascent of their own ideologies, Carter struggled to imagine what may have aligned their paths to begin with.

Out of the blue he came, impassionate and willing to do whatever he must, however he must. Loyal yet ruthless, honest but deceptive, hell bound and vengeful. One saw the other in themselves, like for like, and it was the only moral indemnity either of them had.

Carter sighed. "After all these years, principle might be the only thing left of me. Everything else just…faded away. Got replaced with…" He stopped, his gaze latched on to a piece of nothingness. "I'm grateful. For everything you've done. Things would be different if you hadn't been around."

Soren witnessed the softness in Carter's eye. It wasn't the same frosty blue he had seen in war, or during times of violence. It was a calmer blue; like a lake, tranquil and undisturbed by the emotions that would so often plague him; that would keep him awake at night, and strike terror through nightmares that were resounding of the things he had seen, and of those that were yet to come.

"Please Michael, you don't need to thank me," Soren said, trying to hide his embarrassment. "I've done very little compared to you."

Soren's eyes drifted towards the painting again. A small team of superheroes were huddled together at the bottom, staring up at the rest of canvas. An expression of distaste fell upon his face. He glanced back at Carter. "You know Michael, I've always wondered what made you do it."

"What? You mean all this?"

"Yeah. Everything. Why did you do it?"

Carter shrugged. His voice turned extremely stiff. "It just…it has to be done. *Something* has to be done."

"And you truly believe that?"

"Yeah. More than anything."

Soren hesitated. "Well then, you'll always have my assistance. *Always*."

CHAPTER 54

The initial expectation was that Carter would hold the element of surprise. He had intended to arrive at Soren's meeting and finally bring this chapter to a close.

Instead, he was gliding through corridors in the upper echelons of that same building and trying to circumvent a plan that had been made in anticipation of his expectations. Such a plan could have only ever been executed by someone like Soren. It reminded him of many moments in their shared history but there was one that stood out in particular.

Even at the most arbitrary moments his mind would often flicker back to what happened all those years ago.

Sitting in a small hotel bar somewhere in Mombasa, awaiting a man he had never met. Someone from afar, someone he never saw, watching his every move.

The man in the shadows stood up and left as Carter sat alone with his thoughts.

His phone buzzed and despite not recognising the number he answered it.

He never realised that he'd one day be able to recall every word of that conversation. He could remember every pause, every breath and every shred of humanity. He'd replay it to himself over and over, torturing himself, merely as a reminder of what needed to be done.

"Carter…you need to get the fuck out. Now!"

"Schaffer?!"

Schaffer began to cough violently and Carter could hear the pounding of his chest over the speaker.

"What the hell are you talking about?" Carter fired. "Are you alright?"

"This is a-all a farce. Soren's set us up."

"What?"

"The meetings are a trap. They're shams."

"No. It –"

"He's killing us off. All of us."

"Don't –"

"He lured us away. Split us up. Picked us off."

"That can't be true. He wouldn't…"

"Don't be fucking stupid. He's the only one Michael. The only one who knows who was on the other side of these deals. It can't be anyone else."

"But why – why would he do it?"

Schaffer was panting heavily. "I don't know. But we were wrong. He's not with us Michael. He's against us. He's been against us from the start."

Carter couldn't understand what was happening. None of it made any sense. "He can't h-have –"

"He orchestrated it all…it's all a fucking lie."

Carter immediately stood up and ran out into the lobby. He slid in between various guests, the humidity wrapping itself around his skin.

"Where are you now? I'll come and get you."

Carter quickly spun his head around the lobby. His body started to shake. He desperately searched for someone out of the ordinary, any exit he might be able to use.

"We were at the port but no one was showing. Then a

group of guys in masks appeared. They shot up the place. Victor and Keller are dead."

"What?! But…"

"I can't get through to anyone else Michael. He must've got them all. He must've killed them already."

Carter was lost for words. He could his feel the world crashing down around him. He could barely stand. His mind still hadn't comprehended what he was hearing.

"Where are you? You need to get somewhere safe."

"I made it to a small warehouse, next to the port. But they've already entered. I can hear them kicking down the doors."

"You need to –"

"Enough. Get the fuck out of the hotel now. I need you to stay alive."

"But –"

"You only have one job now. And that's to kill him. Kill Soren."

They were words that resonated with Carter for years to come. Even amidst the chaos and fear of the moment, it was that command which stood out in his mind above all else.

"I need to – I need to get rid of this phone," Schaffer stuttered. Carter could hear the pain tightening in his chest as he spoke. "They can't know I spoke to you. He needs to think we're all dead."

"There has to be something you can do. Anything."

"No. Not now. My time's up."

"He can't get away with this. He just can't." Carter could sense the anger surging through him. "We trusted him. And now he's taken everything. He's destroyed it all."

Schaffer continued to gasp for air. "Not you Michael…not you. You can still take our revenge. Finish him, no matter the cost."

Schaffer hung up the phone and it was there, for the

first time that Carter recognised the feeling of vengeance.

What struck him was the sudden lack of anger. He had expected to be enraged but there and then his feelings were replaced by a cold desire for closure. It was as if from that point on the only way he could bring balance to his mind was to pursue such closure so that he might peacefully continue with the remainder of his life.

Carter's heart was racing. He had to get out. He turned his head and saw an exit at the back of the lobby. He ran, his body beginning to build just a small amount of speed until a colossal force blasted against him from behind, knocking everyone to the ground.

He remembered the heat searing against his back. His bones rattling, his body shaking as he tried to stand. Further on he could see swathes of people on the floor, injured or dead. Flames had consumed the lobby. The bar had been completely eradicated. His arms and legs were bruised by the sheer force that had propelled him to the floor. He saw blood dripping from his shirt and faint burns scattered across his flesh. As he came to his senses he tried to find some clarity in the carnage around him.

Carter recalled grabbing a hooded jacket from the corpse of a man not too far from him. He quickly ran outside through the back of the hotel and watched who fled the scene, noting every car that left amidst the anarchy; anyone that didn't seem phased by what had just happened.

After patiently waiting for the authorities he promised he could help find who was behind the attack. In return he asked for his name to be added to the list of the deceased and a copy of his medical records to go along with it.

In time Carter ultimately did as he had promised. He tracked down the men that tried to kill him and brought them to the police officer he bargained with. He then asked the officer in charge for one final favour; to ensure that the men behind the attack would never see the next sunrise. He left a small envelope on the officer's table and left Mombasa, not ever returning to the city where his life had imploded in just a matter of seconds.

But, after all this time, after years of planning, he would finally fulfil the promise that he made. He had failed once, but not again. Not this time.

Carter continued to walk down the corridor until he stopped. He was receiving a call.

Jeff

He answered it.

"Carter. What's your position?"

"You don't need to worry. I've got it under control."

"That's not what I asked you."

"I'm ready to engage. I'm about to handle this once and for all."

"*Once and for all.* Carter, that's exactly why I'm calling you. I know your history with Soren is complex to say the least, but we have a deal – remember?"

"Yeah."

"You remember the terms of this deal?"

There was a brief pause.

"Yeah."

"We need him alive. I don't care what he did to you. Who he harmed. Do *not* kill Soren Lancaster. Do you understand?"

"If it comes to it, and I have no choice…then I may have to break the terms of our deal."

"If, and only if, it comes to it – but you're *more* than capable of bringing him in alive. Don't try and tell me anything different."

"I wouldn't dare."

Jeff slammed his fist on the table. Carter heard the colossal thumping sound through the phone.

"This isn't funny Carter. Lives depend on you bringing Soren in alive. I told you from the very start what he was planning. Or have you already forgotten? Oh wait…maybe it's something else. Maybe you've chosen to forget?"

But Carter hadn't forgotten. He remembered exactly how this situation had come to be. Desperate for revenge and still remorseful for his failure at the border, he had continued to plot his next move. He scoured the world for any intelligence he could find on Soren; anything that might give him an edge on where he might appear next. But it was only when Jeff appeared that his fortunes changed. He had returned to the United States to see what else he could find and it was there that a former contact of his put him in touch with Jeff Mason; Jeff, who had a lead on the infamous Soren Lancaster, and was prepared to do anything to bring him in.

Carter knew he was affiliated with some branch of government but he didn't ask any questions. He only saw an opportunity to get what he wanted and he would partner with whoever he had to in order to do so.

The thundering voice and gruff, resolute persona reminded him of the archetypal military man. Broad shoulders rested under a thick square jaw and a clean shaven face that resembled a salt plain. Jeff's hair was short and jagged and he spoke with a directness that Carter found refreshing.

It was together that they uncovered Soren's next move and it was here that Carter finally understood Jeff's intentions.

"Bilal Haddad," Jeff said frankly. His shrewd eyes beamed at Carter like lasers. "You know him?"

"Soren reached out to him just before we struck him at the border. Other than that, not really."

"Haddad is a senior member of Syrian intelligence. He's been in the region for a long time. Got a direct line into the government and handles a lot of their military strategy. It's been a while but him and Soren are working together again."

"In what way?"

"He's not on the ground. But Soren is providing him with support and financing to clear out rebel groups that still pose a threat to the government. Whether that's your friend Tariq or anyone else, but Haddad has no problem massacring them all. And it's clear to us that a lot of people are going to die in the crossfire. That's one thing we're certain of. In fact, it's already happening."

Carter hadn't known Jeff for very long but this was the first time he visibly saw discomfort on his face. His jaw quivered as he spoke and his breathing intensified.

"Why are you telling me this?"

"Because whatever differences you have with Soren don't matter. I don't care who he killed or what he did to you. Your job is to bring him in alive. That's why I've asked you here. We need to know what's in his head so that we can manage whatever Haddad is planning. We still don't know exactly what he has planned but whatever it is, it's a hell of a lot worse than the plans they had on the border. It's already beginning to take on a life of its own and we do *not* like the look of it. If we get to Soren then we can figure out what's happening and put a stop to it."

"So you want me to bring Soren in?"

"Yeah. Go to London and intercept Edward Stafford. He's got a business meeting scheduled with Mark Nalbanthian, known alias of Soren. Then you take it from there. We'll fill you in on the details later but like I said, from the beginning we'll get you all the support you need. I'll be in constant communication whenever you need it. And once we get him, we can get the intelligence we need to stop the whole region going to shit. You just to have to keep your emotions in check alright. You going to be fine with that?"

Carter nodded.

"Don't lie to me. I'm telling you point blank right now.

When the time comes, you bring him in alive. Understand?"

"Yeah…I get it."

"Good. Like I said. People are going to die if we don't get this right. More than I care to think about."

Unlike Jeff, Carter refused to think about it. Even now, as his voice blared down the phone, Carter resisted pulling back the curtain and peering at the reality which faced them. The temptation to peek had grown with each passing day and now he was faced with the moment where he would have no choice but to make his decision.

"Lives depend on you bringing in Soren alive," Jeff continued. "His plans have to come to an end. I told you, right before this started, the amount of destruction he'll cause is unheard of. But we can't do a thing if we can't find out what he knows. If he dies – any chance of ending this will fail. Too many people are at risk. You have an obligation – to these people – innocent people – who don't deserve to die. Don't let your own desire for revenge get in the way. Do the right thing."

Flashes of a tranquil village in Colombia materialised in Carter's mind. He recalled the sun glaring down on him as an old friend reached over to hand him a coffee and recounted the joys and the woes that permeated his life; the way in which he had fallen in love and knew he would never be the same again. And then Carter recalled the vacant, painful emptiness and the void that continued to eat away at him.

"Jeff, I'll do whatever I have to. That's the only way this is going to play out."

"Carter, I will hunt you down if you dare go back on our arrangement. I swear to you. Do this, and you're no different from men like Soren."

"I understand."

There was a dark undercurrent to Carter's responses.

"You don't get it do you? If Soren dies, you won't just

have me to answer to, but your own conscience. Thousands. No, thousands upon thousands who *don't deserve to die!*"

"Goodbye Jeff."

He hung up the phone.

Carter walked towards his future, unsure of what he might have to do. He had come so far. If not for his revenge, may he have succeeded? May he have come this far? And if he did pursue his quest to the end, what might the cost be – not only to others – but to himself.

Soren stared out of the window and into the sunset.

The room had been silent for some time until a phone on the table started beeping.

Soren's eyes darted towards it. "Answer it."

One of the men rushed over and picked up the receiver. "Yes." He paused. "Excuse me. Are you sure? Yes, I'll let him know. Thank you."

"Who was it?" Soren asked.

"Reception. They just said that two people are sitting in room 1.15. They know we booked it but we had told them earlier that no one would probably turn up so they just wanted to double check."

"*1.15?* Are you sure?"

"Positive."

"That's where our *proposed* meeting was going to be. The only people who would be there are…"

Could it be…?

Soren's eyes suddenly surged with anger. There was only one way that the two people he was thinking of might be there. And if that were true, then it eluded to something else. Something far more sinister.

So he's here…

CHAPTER 55

Within minutes, one of Soren's guards was racing up a flight of stairs. His steps were heavy as he stomped on the ground with remarkable force and upon reaching the seventh floor he stopped to inhale a flume of dry air. It tasted patchy and stale, like it had been left out in the sun too long and carelessly brought inside without any thought.

The man turned his head to see if there was anyone else behind him, his paranoia beginning to get the better of him. He kept his hand tightly pressed against the small pistol hidden behind his jacket while his eyes scoured for any signs of disturbance.

As he stared down the bottom of the staircase he heard a small creak, a high pitched pop and then nothing.

The man fell to the floor, the blood from his head piercing the staircase and walls. Had it not been for the dim lighting, the damage to his surroundings may have been more obvious.

Adjacent to the stairs was a small room and from its shadow Carter emerged having been patiently tucked away in the darkness. He had already searched the other floors and realised Soren must've been on this one and so it was only a matter of time until someone of interest would eventually cross his path.

But in this stage of the game, there was no honour. Carter needed as many people removed from the picture as he could possibly muster and he wouldn't hesitate to do that in whatever way he saw fit.

Carter dragged the man into the small room that he had been hiding in. It was a small store cupboard, conveniently filled with cleaning supplies and the smell of which was strong enough to hide anything which might otherwise disperse out into the corridor.

Carter shuffled along the main passageway, making his way towards the series of executive suites.

He clutched his pistol tightly in his hand as he peeked into each suite, careful not to disrupt the long silence that hung through the corridor. One suite after the next was empty and Carter could feel the tension in his muscles beginning to rise as he came to realise what might await him.

As he approached the end of the corridor it was clear that there was only one room left. He pressed his back against the wall and carefully moved towards it. Sliding his head around the corner, he peered inside.

As he scanned the area, immediately in front of him, against the backdrop of a vast falling sun, stood a man, enclosed by a navy waistcoat. His back was turned as he stared out into an ocean of impending darkness.

Carter moved forwards, his feet lightly pressing against the wooden floor. Just as he was about to raise his gun he felt a tap against his spine.

"Drop it," a deep voice whispered into his ear.

Carter continued to look forwards. The man in front of him was still staring out of the window.

The warm breath of the man behind him slowly settled on to the back of his neck. The moisture fell on to his skin and poured into his body.

Carter raised his head slightly and opened his hand. The gun fell to the floor, and in that split second, as the man watched the weapon in freefall, Carter whirled around to face his aggressor.

Carter pulled the man's arm forwards, diverting his weapon's line of sight, and struck the two joints of his finger into the man's right eye. Closing his fist completely, he thrust his fist into his nose, the tears from his eyes already falling against his hand.

Carter twisted his arm and took the pistol from him. He threw the man behind him, his body flailing into the room.

Carter bolted back towards the entrance. He stopped, raised the pistol and sidestepped out into the corridor. As soon as he stepped out he spotted another guard, sprinting towards him. Carter opened fire and the man's bullet riddled body crashed against the side of the wall and slid across the floor.

Before Carter could turn around he was slammed against the doorframe, the side of his skull bouncing back as if it were a cricket ball. He felt a surging force drive itself against his hand, once, twice and then a third time. The pistol he was holding fell to the floor.

The man then grabbed his head and smashed it against the frame yet again. The jolt initially dazed him until he felt a meteoric fist propelled into the back of his head.

The man continued to pummel the back of Carter's head erratically and without any distinct pattern, like a defective jackhammer.

Before the pain became too much to bare Carter swung his elbow backwards into the man's face and then struck him again, his knuckles whittling away against the skin and bones of his attacker.

The man fell back a few paces but composed himself, standing upright and drawing a small knife from behind his jacket. He swung it around defensively and haphazardly forming a small yet distorted arc.

He stepped forwards, trying to force it into Carter's chest but Carter pivoted sideways, yanking his arm forwards and colliding his knee into the man's ribs.

The man lurched forwards, his arm still in Carter's grip. Carter violently bent his wrist, taking the knife from him with his other hand and impaling it into the side of the man's neck.

The man yelled in pain, shaking and staggering backwards until Carter removed the knife. The blood instantly poured outwards, the man slowly losing his balance.

Carter kicked the man forwards to the floor. The man's hands were tightly clasped against his neck, soaking up whatever blood they could whilst the remainder dripped between his fingers.

Carter was breathing heavily. His head was rocking from the attacks he had suffered. He tried maintain his balance, holding himself up against the wall. He clutched the knife in his hands. The dried blood was sticking to his fingers and the handle, as if it were impossible to let go at this point.

The man's shaking began to lessen in intensity. Carter watched as his hands slowly loosened from around his neck and slipped down his skin, landing against the floor besides a pair of lifeless eyes and a motionless corpse.

Carter turned back towards the room and saw nothing but the city skyline. The man in the waistcoat had disappeared.

But then, in the corner of his eye, he saw him. He was leaning against the side of the wall, Carter's pistol snugly held in his hand.

"Put it down Michael. It's not worth it."

Carter didn't speak. He just turned and stared at him for a few minutes, the silence slowly waning on the two of them. After all of the experiences they'd shared, it was difficult for either one of them to recognise what was happening. The entire moment felt surreal; the culmination of years of anger boiled down into a singular point.

The silence lingered for a few more seconds until Carter finally threw his knife to the floor.

"It's been a long time hasn't it?" Soren said.

Carter stiffly nodded. His movements seemed tense and rigid.

"Last time must've been over at the border if I'm not mistaken? God, now I remember it. The heat, the intensity, the excitement. I remember you. The way you jumped out of that helicopter with complete and utter ferocity; the way a young man with nothing to lose might. In all my years I'd never seen anything like it. I remember it to this day."

Carter firmly clenched his fists, the tips of his knuckles beginning to turn bright red.

"What would possess a man to come all that way, go to so much trouble, kill so many people?"

"Why don't you tell me?" Carter snarled.

Soren stepped backwards, agape. "Of course. How could I forget?"

"Stop fucking around!"

The anger and the echo from Carter's voice bounced around the suite and it was there that Soren remembered the fierceness in his eyes that night; the same night where he realised he was not as omniscient as he had once thought.

"Michael, at that point in my life I honestly thought I was done with your charade. I killed them all. Every last one of them. I was certain it was over. And then suddenly, you appear, like some nightmarish spectre. How is it that you survived where everyone else was lost?

"Why does it matter?"

"It matters because from that point on the sole focus of your existence was to find me and kill me. I think I deserve to know how that came about."

"You don't deserve anything."

Soren slowly raised his head and the expression on his face was one that Carter immediately recalled. It reflected the darkest side of Soren's personality; one that was capable of things Carter often turned a blind eye to. Looking back, he knew they were the things he should have never overlooked. Such qualities were indicative of an individual who was much more than he appeared.

"Michael, I could kill you right this second and I would walk out that door as if nothing ever happened. But I'm giving you a moment to explain your actions. That's an honour I wouldn't bestow on just anyone. I'm bestowing it on you because contrary to what you think, I did enjoy the time we spent working together. But don't you dare test my patience."

"Someone warned me..." Carter said abruptly.

Soren relaxed, dropping his head and taking a short breath.

"Just before your man had a chance to attack."

"Who?"

"Ken Schaffer. He survived just long enough to contact me."

"Schaffer! That's a name I never thought I'd hear again. The truest operative of them all. He always was astute wasn't he? Never quite trusted me though. Rightly so, I suppose."

"I guess that means he spent his final moments trying to save you," Soren continued. "Is that why you're here Michael? Here to avenge him? Here to avenge all the others that died following you down a rabbit hole?"

Soren could see a slight flicker of rage which had erupted inside of Carter. He was refusing to respond.

"You'd never believe me if I told you that it was all

necessary…what I did that day."

Carter despised that quality in Soren. It was the self-entitlement to power, as if to do as he pleased ran in parallel to what the world required. Amidst everything that had happened, amongst all of the carnage, Soren always appeared spotless. He was always pristine, always free of turmoil and pain. It made Carter wonder, again and again, how he could always rise unharmed from the ashes of any situation.

"How could it have been necessary?" Carter asked. "Killing all of them?"

Soren didn't reply. He was staring at the floor in a moment of deep contemplation.

"You owe me an answer. We trusted you. We brought you in. And after everything that you did, the lies, the betrayal, the pain, the bloodshed; if you're going to kill me then you owe me a goddamn answer!"

Carter took a step forward in anger but Soren's focus instantly ignited, immediately swinging the gun towards him.

Soren closed his eyes for a brief second and then reopened them. "As soon as I met you I knew I was right. As soon as I saw that…superiority; that misguided and misplaced idealism…I knew I was right to burn you all to the ground. Not a single one of you had the wisdom or the foresight to understand what you were doing."

"It didn't take any wisdom to understand that whatever system you were protecting had failed. And that we deserved far better."

"Don't be so naive!" Soren snapped. "You don't deserve a thing. I spent decades building and protecting these systems. And what? You thought you had the right tear them down? I admit they weren't perfect, but you better I believe I used them to wield whatever power I needed in order to maintain peace. And if you think I was about to allow some foolish, pathetic and misguided army of self-proclaimed heroes destroy all of it then you had another thing coming."

"You really believe that do you?"

"If I didn't believe it, would I have honestly travelled so far, shook the hands of your allies, stared you in the eye, tell you that I'm the man to bring your vision into reality, and then deceive as I had never done before. And then to kill, to burn, to destroy with nothing but the most noble and wisest of intentions. Do you think I enjoyed this excursion? Do you think I enjoy the betrayal? You don't think I believed...I believed that when this was all over, they, wherever *they* may be, whatever position they may occupy, would thank me...for doing what no one else could, for years to come."

"*You*...a harbinger of death. A financier of bloodshed?"

"Oh that's rich," Soren exclaimed. "The man who funded a battalion of Middle Eastern rogue rebels to come and attack *my* compound. You have any idea what they're doing now? They're waging war. They're waging war left, right and centre across the region with the funds and equipment you provided them with, just so you could come and seek your own crazed vengeance. You feel good about that? All the death and violence? Remember, I was trying to stop that if you'd ever believe it. At least until you showed up."

Soren started to laugh and underneath it there was a maniacal twist which relished and blared across the room.

"Don't try to take a moral stand with me Michael. Whether you like it or not, you and I are cut from the same cloth. You're no better than me."

Soren watched Carter closely, attempting to gauge how much anger might have built up in him by this point. He could see it pouring from his eyes and out into the open.

"How does it feel?" Soren asked. "How does it feel to

know that you've failed to gain the revenge that you so desperately sought *yet again?* Mustn't that be *so* frustrating?"

Carter continued to stare at him, his gaze wrought with malice. He knew Soren was right. He was helpless. There was nothing he could do.

How could I have let this happen? After everything that I've been through. It can't end this way.

"Whatever you might think, I won't find satisfaction in executing you. Not as much as I once believed. The only thing I know for sure, the only thing that'll emerge from your death…is its necessity."

Soren swung his pistol upwards.

"Goodbye Michael. It's been…insightful."

Carter could taste the certainty of death in his mouth. He began to tremble, not out of fear, but as a result of his defeat. After all of his struggles, he had still failed to execute on the one directive that Schaffer had given him. It was now that he slowly came to the realisation that someone such as himself would be relegated to a forgotten pocket of history while men like Soren would inevitably persist. He could see the devilish glow of satisfaction in Soren's eyes as he finally comprehended that the long road to victory might finally be his.

Soren was a heartbeat from pulling the trigger. And then he heard a small knock against the floor. He turned and spotted someone near the doorway. A man, as if some sort of phantom, had appeared without anyone noticing.

"No…you can't kill him yet," the man said coldly, shaking his head. "Not before I've spoken to him."

He glided into the centre of the room, his trench coat falling back and his pistol sat in his hand, fixed in Soren's direction.

A cruel smile hung itself across David Kessler's face.

"Soren Lancaster…as I live and breathe. This definitely makes things a little more interesting."

CHAPTER 56

"*He's* the reason you're here," Kessler said, examining Carter.

Kessler's face lit up, as if he had just completed a small puzzle.

"Downstairs, you have Ed Stafford ready for the meeting of a lifetime," he continued, "but after you made such a point of telling me you had no other motive…here you are, with a gun to your head by one of the most dangerous military commanders and financiers of our time."

"The fact that you're stood here and not somewhere in Belgravia probably means Reinhart is dead. And yet, I feel like this situation is so much more important."

"Why?" Soren asked.

"Because I finally have the chance to put an end to this charade you've all been playing."

"I think you need to leave," Soren said calmly.

"I don't think so. I want to know what's going on here."

"Still don't have all the pieces then, do you?" Carter quipped.

Kessler's inquisitiveness began to heighten.

"Soren's your employer. He hired Reinhart...to hire you."

"What for?"

"To get to me."

"Well then," Kessler remarked. "Soren Lancaster...a client of mine." He steadied his gun, shuffling slightly it in his hands. "You want to tell me why I'm finding this out now?"

"It's because he didn't trust you."

Kessler glanced at Soren. "Is that right?"

Soren was scrutinising Kessler as best he could. His face was brazen, the confidence enough to illuminate the darkness settling in the room and the unpredictability of his character disturbing what was once a field of mass certainty.

"Well...is it?"

"It is," Soren replied. "Don't take it personally."

"Oh, I won't. There aren't many people that do. Maybe you were wise to do so. But what about him..." Kessler's attention drifted back to Carter. "Tell me...who is he? *Really?*"

"Let's just say he's an enemy of the cause."

"*The cause.*" Kessler shook his head. He detested words like that. "What does that even mean?"

"I don't think you'd understand."

"Oh, of course not. I imagine it's one of those self-entitled, grand schemes that people like you take upon themselves to change the world for the better. Why am I not surprised? And then what? Carter being a thorn in your side was he? Had to teach him a lesson?"

Soren noticed his hand wavering slightly and steadied his weapon.

"For a long time I had operated mostly unchallenged. But there came a point where Carter, among others, emerged as something of a threat. I instantly knew the situation was too significant to ignore so I infiltrated his organisation and had him and his team eliminated. It just so happened that I wasn't as thorough as I should have been. Before my men could get to Carter, he was tipped off by one of his associates and managed to stay alive. Years later, he came back…and I just about escaped with my life."

Soren seemed to recount the story with a plain disposition. There was a startling clarity in the way in which he spoke; purely factual and almost no emotional resonance.

The tone wasn't lost on Carter who was instantly reminded of the remorse he had lived with ever since he failed to kill Soren that night on the border. As time went on, similar to the vengeance which lay within him, it had only metastasised and morphed into something cold, haunting him in his sleep and never allowing him any sanity.

"And that's why you're here," Soren continued. "You, along with Reinhart, and countless others, were part of a scheme to draw Carter out of hiding. That way I could finish the job I started."

"I guess those stories aren't half as untrue as I might've thought," Kessler said, arguably fascinated by the way in which Soren recounted his story but also finally understanding some of the mechanisms which had driven both Carter and Soren to this point. It was as if a light had been cast over the very fundamentals of their being and Kessler could see them for who they were.

Soren kept his eyes on Kessler. He wasn't concerned about his opinion on the war with Carter. He was more concerned about Kessler's intentions. At this moment, there was no discernible strategy to hand, and as a consequence, he was still trying to calculate a response to a man who had proven to be more unpredictable than Carter himself.

"Tell me something," Kessler said. "Give me one good reason why I shouldn't kill the both of you right now."

Soren gripped his pistol tighter. "We're at an impasse David. I don't think either of us would walk out of that situation alive."

Soren looked at Kessler very carefully, his sight somewhat blocked by the pistol he was aiming at his skull. He examined the nature of his eyes, trying to determine whether there was scope to edge the situation towards certainty.

"This isn't worth it," Soren said softly. "There's no reason to upset the balance."

Kessler's eyes flared. "Don't you dare talk to me about balance. Men like you, the both of you – you've done nothing but destroy it."

Soren was puzzled at his response. "*Destroy?*"

"It's all you've ever done – people like you. I've spent years fighting for men in your realm…men that see the world in their image; engaging in endless conflict for…beliefs that never mattered. And never will."

"Don't pretend like you know who I am. I've fought harder than you can possibly imagine. All of it to bring about balance."

"Liar." Kessler stepped forwards. "You fought for power and nothing else, all under the guise of heroics and freedom. But mark my words…you are not the champion of balance – not in the slightest." Kessler stopped, his eyes briefly circling the room. "But me – I fight for nothing but the end. The collapse of men like you. It's only then…that I know it'll be over. Until then, you're nothing but a threat to my existence."

"Enough of the theatrics. I don't have time for this. What do you want from us? Why did you come here?"

Kessler's eyes shuffled between the two of them.

"I see the way you look at me. The both of you. With disgust. As if I'm not like you; as if I'm not good enough;

that I don't believe in anything; that I don't fight for anything; that I don't serve a higher purpose. But you're nothing but a killer, a warmonger. And yet you have a *belief*, some naïve view of the world, and that makes it ok. But now...now I know. Take it away, strip out the lies you keep telling yourself, and then...you realise that you're no different from *me*. And I bet it scares you."

"Enough," Soren snapped. "You've made your point. We understand. Now leave."

"And what if I don't..."

Soren's pulse quickened. With each passing minute it had grown in pace and fervour, desperately trying to tell him that he stood on the precipice of danger.

"This matter doesn't concern you."

"By virtue of who you are, and what you stand for, it definitely does. Your threats don't scare me. I don't care who either of you are. I'll do the world a favour and kill you both right now without hesitation."

"I suggest you watch what you say," Soren said. "I don't think you've ever had a *real* enemy before. And I don't think you actually know what one's capable of."

Soren glanced in Carter's direction. "Ask him...I'm sure he'd be happy to tell you."

"He's still alive," Kessler said.

"It won't be the case for much longer. I assure you."

"Shoot me, and I doubt you'll last a second," Carter said. "Kessler will fire a bullet into your head the first second he gets."

"Maybe...but whatever happens, I know your fate is sealed. There's no options here. It's only going to end one way for you Michael."

As much as he didn't want to admit it, Carter knew Soren was right. Even if Kessler realised the opportunity to kill Soren, there's no doubt in his mind that Kessler would immediately turn the gun on him next. According to Kessler, he was just as idealistic, and therefore just as bad as Soren. Killing him would only be the next logical step.

He had no options. Both of them were too far away for him to leap over and disarm them. They were professionals – they'd kill him at the first sight of trouble. He was a fixed constant in a two-person showdown and there was nothing he could do.

Carter wondered; how did he come to be here. Events from so long ago, surrounded by men of a common purpose, all with honest motivations that later turned sinister. The inevitable conflict, the wars and the deaths that followed sometimes forced Carter to consider how far from Soren's description they might've straddled. An onlooker might suggest they were one in the same, opposite sides of a crusade which lost its meaning a long time ago.

Whatever purpose Carter had held his allegiance to was dead, replaced with aspirations for retribution; hopes that were burnt long ago and from their ashes born a hatred that had festered for so many years that in a simpler time, Carter might never have imagined it possible.

After all this time he could see the realisation towering in front of him; the realisation that, as he stared, powerless and weak, into the abyss which was Soren's grand and majestic plan, his desire might never be satisfied.

"Your move Michael," Soren said. "What are you going to do?"

Carter's hands were clenched and his breathing intensifying. An immense pressure surrounded his chest and he could feel himself losing control.

"There it is," Kessler whispered softly. "That rage, hidden beneath the calm, composed exterior; locked away and swapped with lies and deceit. Your existence…it's such a façade, do you know that? We're so alike…down to our very core."

Kessler took a deep breath, his coat gently rising for a

second and falling against his shoulders, like the descent of a feather.

"We don't need any more pretenders. I will kill you without a shred of remorse."

A current of unease flew through Soren. His finger drifted ever closer to the trigger of his weapon.

"And then…" Kessler continued. "I'll kill you…Soren Lancaster. Then, my duty here will be done."

Kessler peered down the sight of his weapon with extreme meticulousness, the red glow of Soren's tie catching the tip of his vision.

"I've had countless people repeat those words to me David. I'll take pleasure in knowing you were one of them."

A blanket of silence fell upon the room, ushering in a crescendo of tension that had been burning through the room ever since Kessler walked in. It had engulfed them all, binding them together, and forcing them to confront what was to come, demonstrating that quite possibly, maybe, they were fallible and that they could be destroyed.

It was that final moment, where everything changed.

Carter saw it. It happened so slowly, the impossible event, hurtling through the air, tearing apart any concept of fatalism that he may have come to accept in those final few minutes.

It came from the doorway, like a grenade yet more archaic in its appearance, spewing a thin stream of smoke. By the time it passed Kessler's face, it was gushing out dark grey flumes of mist into the air, the thick texture blinding his sights and his thoughts.

Kessler pivoted away from the smoke, unloading his pistol into the doorway. Before he could register anything he felt two bullets pierce his chest, his mind lapsing into a sudden realisation of what just happened.

Soren spotted the projectile gliding through the air and

within a heartbeat knew how to react. Kessler's back was turned and would inevitably suffer the damage from the smoke first. It gave Soren just enough time to shuffle out of harm's way and open fire.

It was there, in what appeared as an instance of opportunity for Soren, that hidden in shadow of the fog, Carter took the only chance he had.

He swooped down, lifting the knife he had dropped earlier, and rushed towards Soren, taking a hold of his forearm and viciously stabbing it, the gun dropping to the floor as Soren screamed in a fit of agony.

Carter flung his elbow across Soren's mouth and withdrew the knife. The blood erupted outwards as he threw it across the room.

Carter grabbed Soren by the neck and threw him to the floor, his body crashing against the wall.

The smoke started to rise up into the air and everything became visible again. The right side of Soren's shirt was stained in blood. He tried to stand but the pain was sending shockwaves across his body, forcing him to stay on his knees. He gasped for air as he held his hand around his wound.

He looked up and saw Carter standing a few paces back, his own pistol pointed towards him.

Soren desperately scanned the floor but he couldn't see any other weapons. The nearest pistol was just in front of Kessler who had fallen against the wall and was still breathing.

Soren had fired several bullets into the smoke and hoped that they were enough to kill him but it seemed they didn't perform the job completely.

Kessler was attempting to lean forwards and grab his weapon but then something happened.

A young man slowly walked into the room. Soren had never seen him before. But there was a look on his face, one that he'd definitely seen in the past. He'd seen the same one on Carter's face back on the Iraqi-Syrian border. One of hate; one of suffering.

He stepped forwards, pointing a silenced pistol at Kessler. He kicked Kessler's weapon backwards and attempted to keep his gun steady but it continued to shake violently in his hands.

Kessler sat up in earnest, his face lighting up with excitement.

"*Jack Morse,*" he spluttered. "You are a bold one."

Jack stood silently, breathing heavily.

Carter turned to him in complete disbelief. "*Jack!* What the fuck are you doing here?"

Jack didn't respond. He didn't even look at Carter. He continued to stare at Kessler, his eyes overwhelmed by something Carter couldn't comprehend.

"Jack!"

"Answer me!"

He didn't respond. He didn't acknowledge Carter. He didn't acknowledge Soren or the situation. He only acknowledged Kessler at this point. The mere essence of his existence eating away at his own, and the only solution to his turmoil, enclosed in his hands.

CHAPTER 57

Only a short moment ago, Carter had been on the cusp of death; a stone's throw away from imminent failure. But since then the situation had changed. It had been upended in its entirety and paved the way for a new outcome.

Carter turned to the doorway and saw a very small metal box on the floor and upon closer inspection, realised that it resembled a lighter. He tried to recall if the lighter was there before, or whether he had ever seen Jack smoke but nothing came to mind.

Jack was panting heavily, attempting to maintain a fraction of composure. The feeling was alien to him. The hate tore through him, accelerating as soon as he saw Kessler, forcing him into a state of mind where he could sense himself losing control.

Despite whatever he felt, Jack still hadn't fired his weapon. An internal conflict was raging, leaving him on the edge of one of most important decisions he might ever make.

"Jack," Carter said calmly. "You need to tell me what's going on here. Why are you here?"

Jack kept his sights locked on to Kessler.

"I'm here because of *him*."

Carter still wasn't following. He turned his gun and pointed it at Kessler.

"What did you do?" he fired.

Kessler smiled. "I brought balance."

Carter was suddenly overcome with panic. He couldn't bring himself to believe what he was thinking but the truth slowly sank in. What else could have possibly brought Jack Morse here, armed such ferocious anger.

"He killed them. He executed everyone. Everyone back at the Field. Max, Sinclair and…"

Carter stepped back. His hand started to shake.

"A-And Katrina…they're all dead."

"Jack…" Carter said, his eyes widening in horror. He wanted to apologise, offer some sort of condolence but he couldn't bring himself to speak. Something was holding him back. He couldn't figure out whether it was the shock, or the faint recollection of memories quickly invading his mind.

Carter watched as Kessler's face remained static. It lacked any shred of remorse, existing merely as an emotionally devoid perpetuity.

"How did you find them?" Carter fired.

Carter was struggling to keep calm, his throat quivering as he spoke.

"Are you honestly asking me that?" Kessler began to cough. A smile slowly creeped on to his face. "It was so obvious. I was searching for a connection to you, Michael. The only link that existed…the only place where there would've been a hint of who you were, was the Field. Surely you knew I'd go there eventually. What did you think would happen when this was all over?"

A terrifying realisation began to dawn on Carter. Something he had overlooked. Something which he never considered.

"I was a little surprised you didn't realise," Kessler

said. There was a wheezing noise roaming behind his voice, like a struggling motor.

Carter couldn't figure it out. How could he not have realised? *Why* didn't he realise? Was it really possible that his obsession with Soren became so fanatical, so consuming, that he had unwittingly ignored or even forgotten the harm that Kessler might've planned to inflict?

A grave error was rising to the surface of Carter's conscience and the more he thought about it, the more he understood the devastating consequences of his actions. In the corner of his eye, Carter could see Jack staring at him.

Does he know? Has he put the pieces together?

Kessler sat unfazed, his smile torturing Carter as he watched him.

Carter still had his pistol pointed towards him. He gripped it tightly. "I'm going to take pleasure in putting you out of your misery. You're going to pay for this. I swear."

He readied his weapon but Kessler began to laugh.

"Don't you want to know...Jack?" Kessler turned to him. "Why they brought me here. What made all of this possible?"

"He doesn't care!"

"Hang on," Jack interrupted. "What's he talking about?"

Carter shook his head. "Jack, it doesn't matter. It –"

"So he doesn't even know," Soren cut in. The excitement in his eyes was radiating across the room. "How interesting."

Jack hadn't taken much notice of Soren up until now. Before then, he was sat on the floor, very still, observing the situation as it unfolded before him.

"Carter, who is this guy?"

Soren's face was enshrouded with a horrifying glow.

Even in such an impossible situation, where his death was potentially imminent, somehow Soren had found a way to grasp the upper hand.

"Tell him Michael," Soren said, as he slowly got to his feet. "You're embarrassing me."

The pain in Soren's arm had subsided enough for him to finally stand up, his gaze directed at Carter and sparkling with deviance.

Carter looked at Jack. "Just say the word and I'll put an end to this."

"Jack..." Kessler said. "This entire situation only *exists* because of Michael Carter."

Jack's face turned pale, his body completely petrified. "What?"

"It was orchestrated by him," Kessler said, pointing to Soren. "Soren Lancaster. He planned everything...all to find and kill the most violent and vengeful person imaginable; the person who decided to come to London and do whatever it took to get...an investment in a technology company?"

"Stop this now!"

Carter stormed towards Kessler but Jack motioned to stop him.

"He doesn't have a reason to lie," Jack said. "I want to hear what he has to say."

"Just let me end this," Carter said calmly.

"No," Jack snapped. "What are you trying to hide?"

Jack was beginning to lose his patience. The anger which was nested inside of him was slowly trickling out into the open.

"I'm not trying to hide anything Jack. I just know it's not going to help."

"It'll help me understand what's going on here. It might tell me why this all happened. It might tell me who the hell you are!"

"Calm down."

"No!"

Jack turned his weapon to Carter. It shook uncontrollably in his hands, as if it were ready to fly out into the sky by its own will.

"Put the gun down Jack," Carter said gently. "Please."

"No. Not yet. I need the truth. And I don't think I'm going to get it from you."

"Oh you'll get it," Soren said. "I promise you."

Carter was in a nightmare. His heart was racing, slowly watching as the situation slipped through his fingertips like sand.

"I can see it from the expression on your face that you don't have a clue what's going on here," Soren said. "Let me explain Jack. Michael Carter came here – not to find Edward Stafford – but to find *me*."

"I don't get it. If he's here for you then what does any of this have to do with Stafford?"

"Jack – do you know who Mark Nalbanthian is?"

"He's…the person investing our company. Mine and Stafford's."

"Ever met him?"

Jack shook his head.

"Well, you're meeting him now. He's an alias of *mine*. One that Michael, and his friends, are all too aware of."

"But why would Carter care?"

"I harmed Carter a few years ago, and he's been hunting me ever since, fuelled by revenge."

"Don't distort the fucking situation," Carter said. "Jack, he did more than harm, I swear."

"Don't you think you've lied enough," Kessler cut in. "He deserves the truth."

"The truth! He killed everyone I cared about. Jack don't listen to him he –"

"I won't lie to you," Soren interrupted. "The only way to get to a position where I could stop Carter was to create a situation; one where he'd come after me. That meant while being an investor in Stafford, I had to secretly kidnap him too, knowing that Carter would come and find him, desperate to get him back so that I wouldn't disappear. But I assure you – I never intended to hurt Stafford. I was only ever interested in Carter."

"So he only came here for you? Find Stafford, so that he could kill you?"

"Yes. The truth is that your friends died…not because of the actions of Kessler, but because of the *inaction* of Michael Carter. I know *exactly* what he's like. He must've known Kessler would go and find them and yet he ignored it completely. He ignored it in order to come and find *me*, because deep down that's what he wanted, regardless of whatever happened to you or anyone else Jack."

Carter couldn't believe the sheer ridiculousness of what he was hearing. Every ounce of his spirit was telling him to kill Soren and Kessler and then be done with them and yet he couldn't. Right now, there was no way of predicting how Jack might react. Carter could still see him reeling from the death of someone he cared about. His instability was far too apparent, and unnerving to the point that Carter knew his own death might not be in the realms of the impossible. Right now, Jack was severely unbalanced, and slowly coming to terms with revelations that were revolutionising Carter, not as an ally, but as a master of deceit.

"Let me tell you," Soren pleaded. "Reinhart had explicit orders. I told him, he wasn't to hurt anyone. He was never going to harm anyone."

"But you hired someone who did," Jack replied sharply. "Surely you're to blame then?"

"Maybe you're right Jack. I accept my responsibility for my part in this. But I just want you to realise that the world is not as clear cut as you think, and that there were more forces at work then just mine." His concentration shuffled to Carter. "That everyone has an equal share in the tragedies we've seen today."

"Jack, you don't understand," Carter said. His voice was teeming with desperation. "Everyone I ever cared about is dead because of him. He killed them all. He lied to us, betrayed us, destroyed what we'd built. I had to stop him, no matter the cost."

"Even if it meant accepting the death of everyone around you. Did *they* not mean anything?"

"Jack you need to believe me – I didn't realise this would happen."

"And then you lied...again and again and again. Would this all have happened if you just told me from the beginning? You don't think I would've helped you."

"Jack...you couldn't begin to believe who this guy is, what he's capable of. To tell you what was really happening would've drawn you into something I couldn't protect you from."

"But it didn't matter did it? You still couldn't protect any of us. Your lies helped no one but yourself."

"It's so ironic," Soren said. "In your quest to avenge your former allies, those people that were here to assist you were summarily executed at the hands of someone that you alone, had the power to stop."

Carter could see the gap between him and Jack widening. The space was an ever increasing void of animosity and anger, and one that Carter was struggling to bridge. As much as he tried to reduce the distance, Soren worked that much harder to push them apart.

Jack's gun was still pointed at Carter, but his eyes fell upon Kessler again. Blood was pouring out on to his shirt. In some ways he didn't even appear injured, almost as if the desire to see Jack's confidence in Carter slowly rupture was enough to rejuvenate him.

"You need to tell me," Jack said. "Why?"

"What," Kessler coughed. "...why I killed your friends?"

Jack nodded.

"Because Jack…I had to. In order to bring this to a close…anyone that knew anything had to go. It's the only way things truly come to an end."

"But what the hell did they even know?" Jack demanded. "They couldn't have known anything!"

"Oh, they knew something." Kessler paused. "Well…then again, I don't think I'm being entirely fair. I don't think Katrina really knew anything about me actually."

Jack's eyes widened in horror.

"When I showed up she probably had no idea who I was. Only thing I could do at that point was…"

Kessler's voice fizzled off into silence as he mused to himself for a moment.

Jack's muscles stiffened. "Was what?"

"I told her who I was…"

Jack and Carter froze.

"And once she knew…I *definitely* didn't have a choice then."

Kessler started to laugh quietly to himself. The faint sound of his mania reverberated through the room and crushed Jack's soul as if it were nothing.

CHAPTER 58

Jack turned his gun away from Carter and towards Kessler. He took a step forward, his anger viciously escalating.

"I'm going to make sure you die for this. I swear it."

"And I welcome it Jack. I just wonder whether you've got the will to pull that trigger."

Jack's finger began to quiver. It was a hairline from the trigger, only the slightest movement enough to conclude what he might describe as a resounding nightmare.

"Jack," Carter said. "Nothing you say or do is going to force him to repent, or instil any fear. You can't reason with these sorts of people."

"He's right about that," Kessler said. "You also wouldn't be reasoning with me had I never needed to come here in the first place. If only someone had the foresight to stop me…"

"Enough!" Carter shouted. "Jack, stop torturing yourself. Just let me finish this, please."

Soren rolled his eyes. "There you go again Michael. Always trying to tell people how they should act out their lives. You have no concept of autonomy – no concept of the fact that Jack's his own man."

"Shut up!" Carter flared.

"No!" Soren replied vehemently. "I'm not done here! Not until I show you how ridiculous you sound, telling this boy not to kill David Kessler – you the same violent son of a bitch who's killed more men than I can care to count. You took lives without a second thought and here you are, parading yourself as some noble warrior. The sheer nerve."

"I-I," Carter stuttered. He tried to continue but he couldn't think.

"What?" Soren interrupted. "You sound like someone lost for words Michael."

"It's alright," Kessler chuckled. "I won't mind as long as it's what you want. I'll die in peace knowing my final act…was to bring balance to the soul of Jack Morse."

A darkness crept up inside Jack. He felt it climbing up through his body, into his hands, and scouring through his mind. It watched Soren and Kessler as if they were acquaintances, pushing Jack towards their acceptance. There was something that tried to resist but it continued to lose. Pounded down, again and again under the sheer weight and force of something that never used to be so strong; something that had new found power and infused with a belief that never used to exist.

"I won't allow this to continue," Carter said.

Carter swung his pistol at Soren who did nothing but let out a dismissive snigger.

"No." A peculiar look appeared in Soren's eyes. "You're hesitating. It wasn't there last time…but this time it's different. Something's holding you back isn't it?"

Carter froze. *Does he…*

"Maybe it's not revenge you're here for…maybe..." Soren smiled. "Jeff Mason?"

The sudden horror on Carter's face was enough for

Soren to be certain.

"Jesus Christ!" Soren burst into laughter. "He's the one helping you isn't he? Should've guessed. He really hasn't got a clue what's going on in that region right now. He's been trying to get a handle on it for years. There was a time where I used to respect the man but Mason must've been truly desperate if he was willing to get help from you."

"Stop fucking around."

"Oh, Michael. What did you agree with Jeff exactly? I'm dying to know. He gives you the support to finally find me and in return, what?"

Carter could see the cogs turning in Soren's mind. It took him no time at all to put the pieces together and Carter knew what was coming next.

"It's Haddad isn't it? Jeff and his people want to know what he's planning don't they? Why else would they come for me? Not like I know anything else they care about."

"There's no point protecting him now," Carter said. "He can't –"

"Wait a second," Soren cut in. "If you're here to deliver me to Jeff then that means…you're not here to kill me are you? You need to know what I know. And so you've agreed to bring me in alive…"

Up until now Soren thought he had sight of every piece on the board but this final revelation restored clarity to his vision. He finally understood the conflict that raged within Carter.

"All of this," Soren said softly. "All of it means that after everything that you've suffered through, everything that I did, you still can't kill me can you?"

There was a way in which Soren worded his question so that it begged for an answer. One that both of them knew the answer to but one that Carter couldn't bring himself to address.

"Well, I suppose you could…" Soren continued. "But that's all contingent upon whether you care about the thousands of people that might die at Haddad's hands if Jeff doesn't get the information he needs. But you would never do something like that would you Michael?"

"Don't do this. Just tell us what he's planning."

"This situation is out of my hands Michael. The fate of those people isn't up to me. I'm not doing anything here. *You're* the one who's at risk of doing something. Their lives are resting on *your* shoulders. But only if you have the perseverance to holster your weapon and allow me the opportunity to tell you how you might save them."

Carter's eyes seared with rage.

"That is…" Soren continued, "if you're willing to give up on your revenge? That very thing you've wanted for so many years, fought so hard for?"

"Why are you doing this?" Carter snapped. "They don't need to die!"

Soren laughed manically. "Just keep going Michael. Keep asking…I'll only tell you when I'm finished convincing Jack Morse of who you really are. I'll tell you when you realise that you will never be able to kill me. No matter how hard you try, no matter all the hardship, that everything you've done was worth nothing. You need me, Michael Carter, and there is nothing that you can do about it. Not unless you have the will to do what I think you might?"

"No…" Soren continued. "Surely not Michael? You wouldn't risk all those lives would you? Just to kill me? Not again – sacrifice innocent people to exact your vengeance?" He flicked his head at Jack. "What do you think Jack? Think he'll do it again?"

Jack watched as the sickening smile on Soren's face widened. "I don't know…I…"

"No," Soren cut in. "I don't think any of us do. You can't trust him in the slightest can you?"

"Do you see it now Jack?" Kessler asked. "The lies you told yourself. The things you ignored. Do you see it? Do you see the false dream that Carter tried to sell you? And the price he never thought to mention. Or what you'd lose if you decided to keep going."

"Shame on you Michael," Soren remarked. "Constantly lying – what kind of person are you?"

Soren's fingers were still tightly clasped around his stab wound. Blotches of dried blood were scoured across his arm and a trickle of blood was flowing between his fingers, slowly dripping to the floor.

"You're not doing this again," Carter said. "You've played with people's lives for far too long."

"And you don't," Soren said, looking sceptical. "What about Stafford or Jack? You used them as pieces in your own selfish game. Stafford, who you heroically tried to save, only so you could lure me out of hiding. Or Jack, the young idealist, who you tricked into thinking you were there for the greater good. Or even Katrina…"

Jack's eye started to twitch. His hand began to shake again.

"The woman that you just…sacrificed. Without a care in the world, so that you could come and find me."

"Do you think he's that stupid?" Carter probed. "That he actually believes what you're saying?"

"Whether he does or doesn't is irrelevant," Soren said glancing at Jack. "But there's no doubt in my mind that he will think twice about *ever* trusting you again."

Soren spoke with such a disregard for Carter's statements, as if his words were meaningless, that his command over the room was unrivalled. There was nothing Carter could do to regain control.

"Is that what you want Jack?" Kessler asked. "To be an ally to the man who killed the only true friend you've ever had. I remember seeing the sparkle in her eye when I mentioned your name and it was…*heart breaking.*"

Jack was ready to pull the trigger. Avoiding the urge to do so was unbearable and he could feel his judgement disengaging from his body. He visualised the moment over and over and it brought him a momentary pleasure that stopped him from executing the action in reality. But its effects were beginning to wane and Carter could see the ruthless torment bubbling in Jack's eyes.

"It seems that the harbinger of justice is not a just man at all," Soren whispered.

Jack glanced at Carter and saw the face of man which was horribly dishevelled, bruised with regret and scarred with anguish. Even now he struggled to understand where he came from or what he stood for.

"The last thing this world needs," Soren said, "is another misguided idealist. Don't believe in his lies Jack. Maybe, before I die…I can stop one more person falling into his chasm of deception."

Carter was plagued by desperation at this point. As the situation continued to unravel, Soren and Kessler had continued to corrupt Jack's mind, turning Carter into a villain and building up to a reaction that he wouldn't be able to predict. He needed to put a stop to it, regardless of the consequences and regardless of whatever regret he may come to face.

"Jack…" Carter's focus latched on to Soren. "I want you to take a step back."

"Don't listen to this fiend," Soren said. "I can see it in your eyes Jack…if you want to kill Kessler then do it. Don't let Carter take the only thing you have left…the only scrap of vengeance you might salvage from this endless abyss."

Jack stared at Kessler.

"Take your best shot," Kessler rasped.

"Jack, look at me," Carter said. "This has gone on long enough."

"You're right," Jack said. "It has."

"Are you going to give me the gun then?"

"No…I'm going to kill him myself."

"Shut the fuck up and put the gun down!"

The surge in Carter's voice echoed around the suite. Whatever patience he had left was all but gone.

"I –"

"No!" Carter said bluntly. "I don't give a fuck what you have to say anymore. I'm taking it from here. You are out of your depth."

"I've been fine so far."

"You are the opposite of fine! You don't have a goddamn clue what's going on here."

"Enough with the lecturing! I know exactly what's about to happen here. And I don't need your help to do it."

"Jack you better leave the killing to someone who knows what they're doing. You aren't cut out for this."

"Fuck you Carter! I've had enough of people telling me what I can and can't do!"

He swung his gun back towards Carter, his hand much more stable than before.

"Are you really going to shoot me Jack?"

"After everything that you've done…you bet I would."

"*Bullshit!*"

"You don't think I'd do it?"

"No. I don't think I see my death in your eyes. And I don't think you want to see anymore death than you already have."

"Jesus, enough of your shit! Why the fuck should I believe anything you say. You can't be trusted!"

"You think I'm a liar – that I ignored Kessler to come here – that I killed Katrina? Then pull the fucking trigger Jack and put me and my dishonesty out of my misery."

Jack could feel a stutter in his voice.

"What are you waiting for?" Carter snapped. "Go

ahead."

"Just kill him Jack," Soren hissed. "Do the world a favour."

"I –"

Before Jack's breath was even over Carter yanked his weapon forward and struck Jack's throat with the side of his hand. Carter twisted the pistol out of his hand, and kicked him back towards the door.

Carter stood, pistols sat in both of his hands as he took a sharp breath. "Stay the fuck back."

Jack was panting for air, his wrist stinging with pain. "No!" he gasped.

Jack ran for Carter but Carter quickly sidestepped him. He slammed his foot into the back of Jack's knee and flung him across the room.

Jack fell face first against the wall, near Kessler who still lay on the floor and unable to move. He was breathing aggressively and there was a tremendous amount of blood continuing to flood into the open.

Kessler gazed up at Jack, his face filled with a psychotic expression of satisfaction.

"You know what your failure means?" Kessler muttered.

Jack froze.

"It means…*that I will haunt you forever.*"

A gaping hole of terror filled Jack's eye, the last remnants of his innocence slowly draining away.

The sound after came so fast that Jack didn't even register it. A single bullet pierced Kessler's head, the blood splattering against the wall and down his face.

Jack jumped back in shock, Kessler's words, even beyond death, still continuing to resonate through his mind and conscience. His body lay, bloody and torn, yet more potent than ever. Ever living in the mind of the only one who would continue to suffer at the hands of his actions.

Jack glanced at Carter who stood where he was, emotionless, his pistol still aimed at Kessler.

Carter turned his weapon to Soren, his face unnerved.

Soren stood up straight, and despite the pain in his arm, carefully adjusted his tie.

"There's nothing else I can really tell you Michael. Nothing more I can say."

"I don't care about any of that," Carter said.

"Oh yes you do. You care if your revenge meant something. If your vengeance was truly worth what you sacrificed…what you *will* sacrifice…"

"Stop speaking."

"Was it worth Jack finally seeing the depths of your villainy and deception?"

"I said stop!"

"And the truth…is that more people had to die so you'd get it. And so many more to come. Innocent, innocent lives. How can you bare it?!"

Soren spun his head in Jack's direction, engraved with a sinister smile.

"Tell me Jack – was Carter's revenge worth having to see Katrina die in your arms?"

Carter pulled the trigger, and then again. Soren's body fell to the floor, the thud echoing through the room. The blood from his head started to pour out and spread across the floor, settling itself on the surface like oil resting on the sea.

Carter watched Soren very closely, staring into the soulless eyes that were left floating in scarlet water. He looked to see if there was any remorse left, any feeling of regret or sorrow but there was nothing.

There had been something in his eye the day that Carter met him. Even with all of his dishonesty, when Soren first approached him, there was something hiding it, sheltering it; a rage and will that rivalled his own. So vehement, that it had to have been what pushed him to the lengths he had gone; that which made him an adversary unlike any other; relentless, vicious and unforgiving in his torment, no matter the situation or the hand that had been dealt.

Carter wanted to tell himself that he was finally complete. That the day had come where he had found resolution. That on an existential level he could find some certainty; certainty that vengeance was his and that it was what he deserved after all this time, after so much sorrow, cascading itself without end and driving him to insanity.

And yet, Carter could feel it lacking. It grew in emptiness with each passing second. The longer he stared into Soren's eyes; Soren the strategist; Soren the calculated; Soren the feared; Soren the man who made armies hide and governments fall; Soren, who, even upon facing death, still had the power to devastate Carter's being one last time.

The longer he stared into Soren's eyes, the more and more Carter realised, that for everything he had sacrificed, for everything that he had become, he had been deceived; deceived into thinking that vengeance might bring him closure when in reality, it had only brought more death, more suffering, more hate, and the subjective, intangible balance of justice, measured on a scale determined by one and only one.

CHAPTER 59

Carter threw one of the pistols on the floor. Its metal casing made a blunt clunking noise against the wood. He holstered his other weapon and looked around the room. For the first time he had a chance to observe its subtleties; the stylish decor, the colossal view of the city and as of right now, a scene of exceptional bloodshed.

Jack pushed himself off the wall. He turned around, stepping away from Kessler's body. The small bruise on the back of his knee began to pound against his skin.

"Jack," Carter said.

Jack glanced over to Carter. There was a texture of fragility riddled into his face which Jack hadn't observed.

"I was never going to hurt you," Carter said. "I just...wanted to stop you from making a terrible decision."

"It wasn't your decision to make."

"Maybe not – but regardless of who he was – I knew you'd come to regret it."

"Fucking hell. How can you possibly know that?"

"Jack, take it from me. Killing a man in cold blood would have changed you forever. It's unlike anything else you've experienced. The feeling sinks inside of you, stealing everything good you might have left, turning you into a remnant of the man that you were yesterday. And right now, with all that's happened, with all that I've seen, more of those men, more vengeance, is the last thing that we need."

"I don't care about that!" Jack fired. "You got your revenge. But what about me. Don't I deserve mine?"

"This isn't about what *you* deserve. Don't tell yourself that killing Kessler would've made everything go away – that your life would be complete once you pulled that trigger because it wouldn't. That's not how this works."

"So it's okay for you then is it?" Jack scoffed.

Carter sighed. "Look, I'm a different sort of case."

"You fucking hypocrite! You wanted to kill Soren from the very beginning. You were never even going to take him alive were you? You'd already made up your mind. You've let all those people die, the ones he was talking about, just so you could get your revenge. Do you think that's a fair trade? Did their lives not matter Carter?"

"Jack, you don't understand the situation."

"Fuck you Carter! Stop treating me like I'm an idiot or a child that doesn't know any better. You had every opportunity to do as Jeff asked, to take Soren alive and save those people, whoever they might've been. But you didn't care about any of that. There's no denying it. You're a fucking killer; of unimaginable proportions. But you always think you know best, that you can do no wrong, by virtue of being *you*. With Soren dead there's probably no one to remind you of that is there?"

"I know that you're in pain Jack, but don't talk about men you don't understand."

Jack's face flickered with a spark of rage.

"Of course I'm in pain!" Jack snapped. "Surely you all of people would get that. He killed her Carter! He fucking killed them *all*, without any remorse. I'm never going to see her again…I'm never going to speak to her again. I'm never going to know how some plucky young girl is going to go off and change the world for the better. And not in some naïve idealistic way like you or me – I mean *really* change it. I mean she…Jesus Christ, she was something more. She was better than the both of us…and he fucking killed her! How could I not be in pain!"

Amongst the silence of so many fallen souls, Carter finally heard the distress in Jack's voice. It cried out with agony, consumed with suffering and so reminiscent of his own past. The man he'd met this morning had vanished, replaced with one whose soul was shattered and painfully reassembled with nothing more than hate.

"Jack, I understand how you're feeling. I wouldn't deny it for a second."

"Why didn't you just tell us the truth? We could've helped, done something, anything. Then maybe everyone would still be alive."

"We don't know that. Even if I told you the truth about Soren that never would've stopped Kessler from doing what he did."

"And yet, how could you not have known that?" Jack inquired. "What made you think that when he left, that was the end of it?"

"I just…I didn't realise. I never thought he would…"

"*Really?*" Jack's face bore a deep shade of scepticism. "Never thought? After the way you described him. How dangerous he was, what he had done…you thought everything would be fine?"

"I –"

"You were selfish! You were too preoccupied with Soren, too preoccupied with whatever revenge you wanted, that you didn't think for a second that we were at risk, that we'd die at his hands. It just passed you by like nothing."

"What do you want me to say Jack? That I fucked up.

That my obsession with Soren – the man who massacred everything I ever cared about – clouded my judgement for just a second!"

"That's exactly what I want to hear. That in the end, people died, because you lied to us and because the only thing you ever cared about, was yourself."

"I didn't do it for myself. Don't you ever tell me that."

"Of course you did! If you didn't, maybe you would've thought twice about the lives that'll be lost because you couldn't keep yourself from killing Soren. Maybe you would've thought twice about lying to us, or manipulating some young kid into thinking that he could save Stafford, that he was sharp enough, bold enough, that you needed him, that everything would be fine in the end."

Jack stepped forward. His leg was still in pain.

"And for what?" Jack continued. "Nothing but violence, and absolute devastation."

"Whether you think I'm a villain or not," Carter said, "I only ever became the man I did because I had to."

"Maybe...but we tell ourselves things all the time in order to make ourselves feel better."

Jack continued to stare at Carter, trying to determine if there was any truth left to extract. Even now, after everything that had happened, he still remained an enigma. There was little Carter could say to change his mind. The only thing Jack could see were eyes coated in ambiguity and deceit, continually fuelling the animosity between them.

"Again and again, you lied and deceived," Jack said. "But it's only brought death and misery."

"Fucking hell, don't let someone like Soren get into your head. This is *exactly* what he wanted."

"I don't care! He was right – regardless of whatever he did – he was right. You can't be trusted. You don't care about anyone, anyone that dies because of your actions."

"I – I…" Carter stammered. "I'm sorry Jack. I never wanted to see it happen this way. I swear to you."

"Don't come back here."

Fear began to encircle Carter's mind.

"Don't ever come back here. Leave…and don't return. We're better off. Better off…without any of this."

"Jack, don't do this. Please!"

"Hell, maybe even the world might be better off."

Jack made his way towards the door. His leg ached with each step. There was a weakness which started to permeate through his body.

"Jack!"

Jack slowly turned around. "We're done here…and I don't ever want to see you again."

Carter's eyes flared up. He started to laugh. It sounded irregular and twisted, as if he were confused and drowning in his own mania.

"What are you going to do!" Carter shouted, his eyes quivering in anger. "I know you so, *so* well Jack. More than you might realise. You really think you'll *change the world* if you go back. You honestly think so? Walk down those stairs – back to your papers, your equations, whatever purpose you think you're going to find – and you will change *nothing*!"

There was a short pause, a momentary ember of silence.

"Goodbye Michael."

Jack turned around, pressing forwards until he finally left the suite.

Somehow Soren and Kessler knew what Carter wanted and both spent their final moments, faced with impending death, to ensure that he would never get it.

Carter backed away from the bodies of Soren and Kessler and hovered towards the vast window at the back of the room. He walked closer, staring through the immense glass and out into the city skyline, cloaked in darkness and gloom.

The moment Jack had walked into the suite everything had changed. Kessler didn't care that Soren had shot him. They didn't care that they were enemies. At that point they saw a mutual opportunity – an opportunity to ravage Carter's future one last time and destroy Jack's faith in the world – to extinguish his beliefs with such maliciousness that someone like Jack would never dare to try and change the world.

And they might never have done it without Carter's help. Together, the three of them had burnt everything he had ever have believed in.

Now, only Michael Carter stood in the twilight; exactly how long for, he never remembered, but he stood, alone, silent, for hours on end, as the desecrator of ideals.

ABOUT THE AUTHOR

Ash Sharma was born in 1992 and grew up in Slough. He studied Mathematics at University College London and shortly after worked as a forensic accountant in the City of London. During this period, he was involved in a number of financial investigations across Europe and Africa while also writing in his free time. He currently resides in London.

Printed in Great Britain
by Amazon